"A fabulous debut filled with danger, imperfect but fierce found family, and the love story of two stubborn protectors, *A Lady's Formula for Love* is everything a romance reader who likes to ponder as well as cheer could want."

—Felicia Grossman, author of the Truitts series

"Elizabeth Everett's writing absolutely dazzles. Fiercely feminist, deliciously sexy, and bursting with intoxicating enemies-to-lovers goodness, *A Perfect Equation* is an instant historical romance classic and Everett an auto-buy author."

—Mazey Eddings, author of *A Brush with Love*

"Poignantly feminist and perfectly feisty! Letty and Grey's romance is a delicious journey from sharp-tongued disdain to smoldering desire."

—Chloe Liese, author of the Bergman Brothers series, on *A Perfect Equation*

"A sparkling debut full of humor, heart, and sizzling romance."

—Jeanine Englert, award-winning author of *Lovely Digits*, on *A Lady's Formula for Love*

"When a spirited mathematician and the straitlaced nobleman she loathes are thrust together to protect Athena's Retreat, witty one-liners, corsets, and sparks fly. A brilliant balance of comedy, sensuous romance, and smashing the patriarchy, the second installment of the Secret Scientists of London is a triumph!"

—Libby Hubscher, author of *If You Ask Me*

"With its engaging plot, memorable characters, spicy love scenes, and a bromance for the ages, *A Love by Design* is one book no romance lover should miss. Highly recommended."

—Historical Novel Society

THE
LOVE
REMEDY

Elizabeth Everett

BERKLEY ROMANCE
NEW YORK

BERKLEY ROMANCE
Published by Berkley
An imprint of Penguin Random House LLC
penguinrandomhouse.com

Library of Congress Cataloging-in-Publication Data

Names: Everett, Elizabeth, author.
Title: The love remedy / Elizabeth Everett.
Description: First edition. | New York : Berkley Romance, 2024.
Identifiers: LCCN 2023028932 (print) | LCCN 2023028933 (ebook) |
ISBN 9780593550465 (trade paperback) | ISBN 9780593550472 (ebook)
Subjects: LCGFT: Romance fiction. | Detective and mystery fiction. | Novels.
Classification: LCC PS3605.V435 L75 2023 (print) | LCC PS3605.V435
(ebook) | DDC 813/.6—dc23/eng/20230626
LC record available at https://lccn.loc.gov/2023028932
LC ebook record available at https://lccn.loc.gov/2023028933

First Edition: March 2024

Printed in the United States of America
1st Printing

Book design by George Towne

Dedicated to my husband, a real-life romantic hero

Dear Reader,

Like all my books, *The Love Remedy* is a historical romance with a hefty dose of humor. However, like all my books, it centers the experiences of women in a historical context with an eye toward current sociopolitical events.

The book includes elements that might not be suitable for some readers. There is an off-page sexual assault of a secondary character and an off-page induction of menstruation following the assault. Readers who may be sensitive to these topics, please take note.

With all my love,
Elizabeth Everett

1

~⫷⫷⫷⬥⫸⫸⫸~

London, 1843

"'OW MUCH FOR PULLING A TOOF?"

Any other day, Lucinda Peterson's answer would have been however much the man standing before her could afford.

Since its founding, Peterson's Apothecary held a reputation for charging fair prices for real cures. If a customer had no money, Lucy and her siblings would often accept goods or services in trade.

Today, however, was not any other day.

Today was officially the worst day of Lucy's life.

Yes, there had been other worst days, but that was before today. Today was *absolutely* the worst.

"Half shilling," Lucy said, steel in her voice as she crossed her arms, exuding determination. She would hold strong today. She would think of the money the shop desperately needed and the bills piling up and the fact that she truly, really, absolutely needed new undergarments.

"'Alf shilling?" the man wailed. "'Ow'm I supposed to buy food for me we'uns?"

With a dramatic sigh, he slumped against the large wooden counter that ran the length of the apothecary. The counter, a mammoth construction made of imported walnut, was the dividing line between Lucy's two worlds.

Until she was seven, Lucy existed with everyone else on the public side. Over there, the shop was crowded with customers who spoke in myriad accents and dialects as they waited in line for a consultation held in hushed voices at the end of the counter. Not all patients were concerned with privacy, however, and lively discussions went on between folks in line on the severity of their symptoms, the veracity of the diagnosis, and the general merits of cures suggested.

Laughter, tears, and the occasional spontaneous bout of poetry happened on the public side of the counter. Seven-year-old Lucy would sweep the floor and dust the shelves as the voices flowed over and around her, waiting for the day when she could cross the dividing line and begin her apprenticeship on the other side.

All four walls of the apothecary were lined with the tools of her trade. Some shelves held rows of glass jars containing medicinal roots such as ginger and turmeric. Other shelves held tin canisters full of ground powders, tiny tin scoops tied to the handles with coarse black yarn. A series of drawers covered the back half of the shop, each of them labeled in a painstaking round running hand by Lucy's grandfather. There hadn't been any dried crocodile dung in stock for eighty years or so, but the label remained, a source of amusement and conjecture for those waiting in line.

The shop had stood since the beginning of the last century, and even on this, her absolute worst day, Lucy gave in. She wasn't going to be the Peterson that broke tradition and turned a patient away.

Even though today was Lucy's worst day ever, that didn't mean it should be terrible for everyone.

"For anyone else a tooth is thruppence," Lucy said as she pulled on her brown linen treatment coat. "So I'm not accused of taking food from the mouths of your we'uns." She paused to pull a jar of eucalyptus oil out from a drawer and set it on the counter. "I suppose I can charge you tuppence and throw in a boiled sweet for each of them."

Satisfied with the bargain, the man climbed into her treatment chair in the back room, holding on to the padded armrests and squeezing his eyes shut in anticipation. Lucy spilled a few drops of the oil on a handkerchief and tied it over her nose.

While the scent of eucalyptus was strong enough to bring tears to her eyes, the smell from the man's rotted tooth was even stronger. She numbed his gums with oil of clove as she examined the rotting tooth and explained to him what she was going to do.

His discomfort was so great, the man waved away her warnings, and so, with a practiced grip, Lucy used her pincers to pull out the offending tooth.

Both wept, him from the pain, she from the stench, as Lucy explained how to best keep the rest of his teeth from suffering the same fate.

"You're an angel, miss," the man exclaimed. At least, Lucy hoped he said *angel*. His cheek was beginning to swell.

She sent him off with the promised sweets as well as a tin of tooth powder and, seeing there were no customers in the shop, she locked the front door and closed the green curtains over the street-facing windows to indicate the shop was closed.

Lucy's younger sister, Juliet, was out seeing those patients who were not well enough to visit the shop, and her brother,

David, could be anywhere in the capital city. Some days he was up with the sun, dusting the shelves and charming the clientele into doubling or even tripling their purchases. Other days, he was nowhere to be found. Days like today.

Worst days.

Lucy sighed a long-drawn-out sigh that she was embarrassed to hear exuded a low note of self-pity along with despair. Exhaustion weighed down her legs and pulled at her elbows while she cleaned the treatment chair and wrote the details of the man's procedure in her record book. She'd not slept well last night. Nor the night before. In fact, Lucy hadn't had an uninterrupted night's sleep for nine years.

Standing with a quill in her hand, she gazed at the etching hanging on the far wall of the back room, sandwiched between a tall, thin chest of drawers and a coatrack covered in bonnets and caps left behind by forgetful patients. Made in exchange for a treatment long forgotten, the artist had captured her mother and father posed side by side in a rare moment of rest.

Constantly moving, and yet always with time for a smile for whoever was in pain or in need of a sympathetic ear, her mother had been a woman of great faith in God and even greater faith in her husband.

"We work all day so we can make merry afterward," her father would tell Lucy when she complained about the long hours. Indeed, evenings in the Peterson household were redolent with the sound of music and comradery, her father loving nothing more than an impromptu concert with his children, no matter their mistakes on the instruments he'd chosen for them.

The etching was an amateurish work, yet it managed to convey the genuine delight on her father's face when he found himself in company of his wife.

It had been nine years since her parents died of cholera, a

loathsome disease most likely brought home by British soldiers serving with the East India Company. When the first few patients came to the apothecary with symptoms, the Petersons had sent their children to stay with a cousin in the countryside to wait out the disease. Lucy and Juliet had protested, both having trained for such scenarios, but their father held firm.

Her parents' deaths had come as less of a shock to Lucy than her father's will. Everything was left to her; the apothecary and the building in which it stood, as well as the proprietary formulas of her father and her grandfather's tonics and salves.

She had been eighteen years old.

"What were you thinking back then, Da?" she asked the etching now, the smell of vinegar and eucalyptus stinging the back of her throat. "Why would you put this on my shoulders?"

Her father stared out from the picture with his round cheeks and patchy whiskers, eyes crinkled in such a way that Lucy fancied he heard her laments and would give her words of advice if he could speak.

What would they be?

A yawn so large it cracked her jaw made Lucy break off her musings and remove her apron.

Exhaustion had played a huge role in her string of bad decisions the past four months. Ultimately, however, the fault lay with her. Lucy's guilt had been squeezing the breath from her lungs for weeks.

On the counter, slightly dented from having been crushed in her fist, then thrown to the ground and stepped on, then heaved against the wall, sat a grimy little tin. Affixed to the top was a label with the all-too-familiar initials RSA. Rider and Son Apothecary.

Rider and *Son*. The latter being the primary reason for this very worst of days.

The longer she stared at the tin, the less Lucy felt the strain of responsibility for running Peterson's Apothecary and keeping her siblings housed and fed. Beneath the initials were printed the words *Rider's Lozenges*. The ever-present exhaustion that had weighed her down moments ago began to dissipate at the sight of the smaller print beneath, which read "exclusive." The more she stared, the more her guilt subsided beneath a wave of anger that coursed through her blood. "Exclusive patented formula for the relief of putrid throats."

Exclusive patented formula.

The anger simmered and simmered the longer she stared until it reached a boil and turned to rage.

Grabbing her paletot from the coatrack and a random bonnet that may or may not have matched, Lucy stormed out of the shop, slamming the door behind her with a vengeance that was less impressive when she had to turn around the next second to lock it.

Exclusive patent.

The words burned in her brain, and she clenched her hands into fists.

One warm summer afternoon four months ago, Lucy had been so tired, she'd stopped to sit on a park bench and had closed her eyes. Only for a minute or two, but long enough for a young gentleman passing by to notice and be concerned enough for her safety to inquire as to her well-being.

While the brief rest had been involuntary, remaining on the bench and striking up a conversation with the handsome stranger was her choice, and a terrible one at that. Lucy had allowed Duncan Rider to walk her home; not questioning the coincidence that the son of her father's rival had been the one to find her vulnerable and offer his protection was down to her own stupidity.

Now, as Lucy barreled down the rotting walkways of Cal-
thorpe Street, she barely registered the admiring glances from
the gentlemen walking in the opposite direction or the sudden
appearance of the wan November sun as it poked through the
gray clouds of autumn.

Instead, her head was filled with memories so excruciating
they jabbed at her chest like heated needles, rousing feelings of
shame alongside her resentment.

Such as the next time she'd seen Duncan, when he appeared
during a busy day at the apothecary with a pretty nosegay of
violets. He'd smelled like barley water and soap, a combination
so simple and appealing it had scrambled her brains and left her
giddy as a goose.

Or the memory of how their kisses had unfolded in the back
rooms of the apothecary, turning from delightfully sweet to
something much more carnal. How kisses had proceeded to
touches, and from there even more, and how she'd believed it a
harbinger of what would come once they married.

A shout ripped Lucy's attention back to the present, and she
jerked back from the road, missing the broad side of a carriage
by inches. The driver called out curses at her over his shoulder,
but they bounced off her and scattered across the muddied street
as Lucy turned the corner onto Gray's Inn Road.

Halfway through a row of weathered stone buildings, almost
invisible unless one knew what to look for, a discreet brass plaque
to the left of a blackened oak door read:

TIERNEY & CO., BOOKKEEPING SERVICES

Lucy took a deep breath, pulling the dirty brown beginnings
of a London fog into her lungs and expelling it along with the
remorse and shame that accompanied her memory of Duncan

holding her handwritten formula for a new kind of throat lozenge she'd worked two years to perfect.

"I'll just test it out for you, shall I?" he'd said, eyes roaming the page. Duncan and his father had long searched for a throat lozenge remedy that tasted as good as it worked. Might Duncan be tempted to impress his father with her lozenge? His lips curled up on one side as he read, and Lucy recalled the slight shadow of foreboding moving across the candlelight in the back storeroom where they carried out their affair.

"I don't know," she'd hedged.

Too late. He'd folded the formula and distracted her with kisses.

"I've more space and materials at my disposal. I know you think this is ready to sell, but isn't it better that we take the time to make sure?"

It might have been exhaustion that weakened Lucy just enough that she took advantage of an offer to help shoulder some of her burdens. However, the decision to let Duncan Rider walk out of Peterson's Apothecary with a formula that was worth a fortune was due not to her sleepless nights, but to a weakness in her character that allowed her to believe a man when he told her he loved her.

Now, four months later, somehow Duncan had again betrayed her.

Having already lost the lozenge formula to Duncan's avaricious grasp, Lucy had been horrified to find a second formula missing. She'd come up with a salve for treating babies' croup, a remedy even more profitable than the lozenges. What parent wouldn't pay through the nose to calm a croupy baby?

Lucy was certain that Duncan must have found out about her work and stolen both the formula and the ingredient list for the salve.

This time, Lucy would not dissolve into tears and swear never to love again. This time, she was going eviscerate her rival and get her formula back.

Then she would swear never to love again.

"AND THAT IS WHY I WOULD LIKE YOU TO KILL HIM. OR, perhaps not so drastic. Maybe torture him first. At the very least, leave him in great discomfort. I have plenty of ideas how you might do this and am happy to present them in writing along with anatomically correct diagrams."

Jonathan Thorne blinked at the incongruity of the blood-thirsty demand and the composed nature of the woman who issued it.

He almost blinked again at the sight of her face when she leaned forward and into the light but stopped himself at the last second.

None of that now.

Never again.

He'd been in the back room when he heard her come in off the street, asking for Henry Winthram, the tenor of her husky voice sounding sadly familiar.

The sound of a woman almost drained of hope.

"Miss Peterson, I appreciate your, erm, enthusiasm?" Winthram said now.

Henry Winthram was the newest and youngest agent at Tierney's and, with his raw talents, he'd also brought along a decade's worth of experience handling a mind-boggling array of poisons, explosives, insecticides, and *scientists*.

Winthram brought the woman into the small receiving room.

"Tierney and Company are in the business of helping clients solve burdensome problems," Winthram explained.

"It would relieve me of a great burden if you would take care of Duncan Rider," the woman said quickly.

"I'm not a gun for hire, miss," Winthram informed her, sounding offended.

"Of course you're not. I'm sorry, Winthram. I don't want him murdered," the woman apologized. "I do tend toward hyperbole when I'm angry."

"You don't say." Winthram's head turned when the floorboards squeaked as Thorne came into the room from the hall where he'd been lurking.

"Allow me to introduce you to one of the senior agents," the young man said without bothering to hide his relief. "Mr. Jonathan Thorne, I'm pleased to present to you to Miss Peterson, the owner of Peterson's Apothecary."

For close to thirty years, the brass plaque affixed beside the front door of Tierney & Co. had advertised a bookkeeping service, but in fact, the five agents working here, Thorne and Winthram among them, did little to no accounting.

The books they balanced were more metaphorical.

Whenever the government had a domestic situation that could not be resolved through official channels and might lead to some embarrassment of the extended royal family or members of the government, Tierney's received a visit from a bland, middle-aged functionary who pushed an envelope across the desk and then disappeared. Shortly thereafter, a certain dignitary might find himself transferred back home after his superiors received information about said dignitary's unsavory predilections. A palace servant might suddenly leave their post the day after a cache of love letters were returned to one of the queen's ladies-in-waiting.

On occasion, Tierney's would agree to take on discreet

services for an ordinary citizen who had been wronged. A
widow would suddenly receive her late husband's back wages,
or a poor family's home be spared a tax rise.

The request by an apothecary owner for the assassination of
a rival apothecary was certainly out of the ordinary, but the
fact that the apothecary owner was a woman—an almost pre-
ternaturally beautiful woman—might have made the request
the most unusual in Tierney's history. Except, since Henry Winthram began working here, extraordinary women had been
showing up in droves.

Thorne nodded at Winthram and steeled himself to impas-
siveness before he walked to the ladder-back chair where Miss
Peterson had just risen to her feet and presented her hand in
greeting.

There were some ladies of the most elite circles of British
society who used to come and watch Thorne when he was a
famous prizefighter. They would scream for blood and shout
for pain alongside the common rabble from behind the safety
of long cloaks and heavy veils. Afterward they would remove
their veils and ogle him as though regarding an animal let loose
from a menagerie. Thorne hadn't cared. When he was drinking, he hadn't accounted himself much better than an animal.

Over time, the tally of his fights wrote themselves on his
face: ears that puffed to the side like lopsided mushrooms, a
poorly sewn cut high on his left cheek that left him with a per-
manent sneer, a bent nose. All these conspired to change his
appearance so much that his own mother had difficulty recog-
nizing him and the ladies no longer simpered at him. Instead,
they would hold their gaze in such a way that took in the whole
of him without having to examine his face too closely.

A technique Thorne employed now as he bowed over Miss

Peterson's hand, his eyes taking in her plain day dress of a faded India cotton print with a shawl collar up to her neck, her sturdy but well-worn boots, serviceable gloves, and ten-years-out-of-date straw bonnet, none of which could have provided much warmth on such a windy day.

What he didn't do was stare directly at her face. Beauty like Miss Peterson's elicited a reaction.

Thorne preferred to remain impassive.

She would be accustomed to some response, what with her perfectly round eyes and irises so dark blue they resembled the Mediterranean on the morning of a storm, full lips the color of a bruised rose petal, and cream-colored skin pulled taut over high cheekbones.

Fascinating how each person's face contained the exact same elements, but in one person, Miss Peterson for example, they were arranged so as to make a man stammer and blush, shuffle his feet, and work to wet his suddenly dry mouth.

Fascinating and dangerous.

Miss Peterson took her seat, and Thorne rang the bell for a servant to build up the fire and fetch another pot of hot water. When he judged Miss Peterson's bloodlust to have calmed, Thorne took a chair from against the wall and set it and himself in between Winthram and Miss Peterson.

"You must know Winthram from his days as the doorman at Athena's Retreat," Thorne said.

Miss Peterson sat straighter in her chair, clasping the strings of her reticule tight in her hands as she shot a worried glance at Winthram, who held up a hand to ward off her concern.

"The agents at Tierney's already knew about the club before I came to work here," Winthram assured her. "They've worked with Lord Greycliff and Mr. Kneland before."

That would be the Viscount Greycliff. His stepmother, the former Lady Greycliff, had used the money left to her by Greycliff's late father and converted a series of outbuildings behind her town house into a club. Most of London believed it to be a ladies' social club where women with an interest in the natural sciences would gather for tea and listen to lectures on subjects as varied as the proper means of cultivating orchids or how to use botanicals for better housekeeping.

Behind closed doors, however, women scientists used three floors of hidden laboratories to further their work in fields as varied as organic chemistry, ornithology, and experimental physics. When Lady Greycliff had come under threat last year, a former counter-assassin, Arthur Kneland, had been hired to protect her.

Much to Thorne's amusement, the intimidating man not only had gone and gotten himself shot for the umpteenth time, but had also fallen in love with the lady and now tried desperately to keep the scientists from wreaking havoc on the club and one another. On occasion, Kneland would help Winthram with small missions both to keep himself sharp and to pass on some of his skills to the younger man.

Having poached Winthram from the duties of doorman to serve as one of its employees, Tierney's had not entirely reckoned with the fact that the women scientists who had relied on Winthram to help them with their experiments now came to him for help with other quandaries.

Women scientists lived highly eventful lives.

"I use the laboratories of the Retreat since our space at the apothecary is taken up by our supplies and treatment room," Miss Peterson said now. "For *years* I worked to create the formula for a throat lozenge that reduces the swelling of a putrid throat as well as soothes the pain. I planned on patenting the formula, but—"

Despite his best effort, Thorne let his gaze rest on Miss Peterson's face, perhaps assuming the anguish contained in her voice would diminish the luminosity of her beauty. In fact, it added to it, and Thorne redirected his eyes to her clenched hands and listened to her tremulous voice and any clues it might provide.

"Before I could bring the formula to market myself," Miss Peterson continued, "I showed it to Duncan Rider. The son in Rider and Son Apothecary."

Unexpectedly, she launched from her chair and began pacing the room. Accustomed to the demure responses of the occasional gentlewoman or the humility of the domestic servants who sought Tierney's services, Thorne was taken aback by the ferocity in her manner.

Winthram showed no sign of surprise, and Thorne presumed this behavior was common among women scientists.

"Once I realized what that fungus-sucking tumor of a man had done to me"—Thorne swallowed a laugh and nearly choked while Winthram nodded his head in appreciation of the insult—"patenting *my* formula, I pleaded with him to do the right thing and either put my name on the patent or fulfill his promise to marry me. He did neither. I was tempted then to do him bodily harm, but I refrained."

"Most likely for the best," Winthram offered.

Miss Peterson stopped midstride, pointed a finger at the poor boy's head, and leveled a ferocious glare at him.

"Do you think so, Winthram?" Her voice rose now, and she advanced on Winthram, who sensibly leaned back in his chair, realizing it would have been better to keep his mouth shut until the end.

"Do you think so? Let me tell you, as bad as it is that that thieving pustule now makes a fortune from my hard work, today I learned something even worse. He has somehow come into my home and once *again* stolen my work. My formula for a new croup salve has disappeared."

2

---◄◄◄◆►►►---

"OH, SOMEONE IS GOING TO DIE, BUT IT WON'T BE DUN-can Rider. Read me the note again."

An apology sat on the tip of his tongue when Winthram flinched at his words, but Thorne swallowed it.

Thorne's first purse fights were held far from the tumult and notoriety of the London auditoriums of his later career. His second-ever bout took place in a muddy field halfway between Leicester and Peterborough. He'd ended the match being beaten bloody by a giant of a man named Dubbers. First or last name, Thorne never learned, but Dubbers was a creative bas-tard. After toying with him for the last few minutes of the fight, he'd gotten Thorne in a brutal hold and jabbed his elbow di-rectly into Thorne's throat.

Since then, Thorne's voice could be described as rasping on a good day. When he was irritated, it sounded like two pieces of rusted iron rubbed against each other.

Right now, Thorne was irritated.

A sheaf of auburn hair flopping over his forehead, Win-thram glanced at the note that had been delivered to the office a half hour earlier. With a hairless chin, wide blue eyes, and pale skin that stained red with every strong emotion, he appeared much more youthful than his twenty years. Having been born female, he would never grow a beard and was fated to appear forever young.

Not always a bad thing when it came to being a private agent.

"*Dear Winthram,*" the young man read. "*I appreciate your advice yesterday to check with the patent office before making accusations about Mr. Rider.*"

Winthram continued. "*I am in dire need of funds, however, and cannot wait to bring my formula to market. If I do not bring you proof of his theft by tomorrow morning, it means I was wrong, or I was caught. If the latter, please bring my sister Juliet to Newgate with money for bribes. And some cake, as I will no doubt be hungry by then. With fondest regards—*"

"What was she thinking?" Thorne interjected.

Winthram shrugged as he set down the note. "Miss Peterson does enjoy a nice piece of cake—oh." His cheeks flushed at Thorne's scowl. "Well, she weren't too pleased that we said to wait. I suppose she's thinking to take matters into her own hands."

Thorne suppressed a wince as he rose from his chair. The damp, chilly autumn air ravaged his old injuries. Each year the onset of winter brought a rediscovery of wounds he'd have barely noticed twenty years ago. He walked to the window of the same room in which Miss Peterson had sat yesterday, expressionless, as Thorne explained that Tierney's agents most certainly did not engage in assassinations and could accept cases only where the life or livelihood of the person was at stake.

Miss Peterson's lips had thinned to the point where they'd nearly disappeared, and the delicate wings of her brows pulled together to meet at a deep wrinkle at the bridge of her nose.

She hadn't argued, however, simply bid them both a good day and left without another word.

Thorne, like a fool, had brushed aside Winthram's worries, confident that a woman smart enough to run a business would take his advice and be practical.

Obviously, these women scientists were cut from a different cloth.

"Take matters into her own hands," Thorne echoed. "Meaning . . . ?"

"Well, if she's worried about being taken to Newgate, she must be considering sneaking into Rider's office and getting back her—"

Thorne had grabbed his hat and was out the door before Winthram could finish his sentence.

The impulse made less and less sense as a fine drizzle of cold rain crept beneath the collar of Thorne's greatcoat and ran in tiny rivulets from the cupped brim of his wool top hat as he trudged through the murky dusk, as there were no hacks to be found in this kind of weather. The kind of weather that seeps in through a man's boot soles and causes a throbbing ache in his misused joints.

How much worse would he feel if he hadn't quit drinking and fighting at the tender age of eight and twenty?

As he turned a corner into a narrow alley, the unhappy conjecture slid from his brain to be replaced with bewilderment. Bewilderment and a hefty dose of exasperation.

"They do not allow gifts of cake for prisoners at Newgate," Thorne informed Miss Peterson. Or rather, he informed her arse, which stuck out of a second-floor window above his head.

Miss Peterson's legs stopped kicking, and she hung there, limp, half her body wedged in the window, the other half growing wetter by the second. There was a small hole in one of her boots, and the sight struck Thorne in that soft place in his chest that most days he could ignore. Today was not one of those days.

"Of course, you can't be sent to Newgate if you haven't committed a crime," Thorne continued.

For a moment there was no reaction, then Miss Peterson's left ankle turned in a circle as if to say, *Go on*.

"From the crates overturned right here, I would guess that you made a tower and climbed up to get to that window, found yourself stuck, and accidentally knocked over your means of escape."

Miss Peterson's left foot tapped the side of the building twice.

Aha.

"If I were to stack the crates again beneath you, would you please climb down here so that we can speak face-to-face?" he asked.

Miss Peterson's left foot hung motionless for a moment, then slowly moved side to side.

"Is it the speaking face-to-face you wish to decline?" he asked.

The foot moved side to side again.

"You're well stuck, aren't you?"

Miss Peterson's left foot tapped the building in a grumpy manner, if a foot could be said to be grumpy.

She smelled like eucalyptus and chamomile.

The combination struck Thorne as both comforting and odd as it filled his nose once he'd rebuilt a tower of barrels and crates and stood behind her rounded arse.

"I'm going to put my hands around your waist," he said to the back of her. "When I pull, suck in your stomach and push with your arms against the wall in there if you can."

Miss Peterson's foot tapped in agreement, and Thorne bent

over her. She'd worn a dull gray pelisse for her crime spree, and the odor of damp wool competed with the eucalyptus as he wrapped his arms around her waist.

He'd not touched a woman in seven years.

Miss Peterson's beauty had nothing to do with the pang of longing that clawed at his gut, it was simply the soft curve of her warm body beneath him.

How he missed holding a woman.

Thorne left off his foolish pining and braced himself against the bricks as Miss Peterson's ankle spun in rapid circles.

"On the count of three, I will pull," he warned her. "One, two, three—ungh. For the love of God, how did you get yourself so stuck?"

Miss Peterson's feet scrambled for the walls, and Thorne helped her find purchase. After a terrifying moment where he considered having to push her into the room, he heard a quiet squeal, and he felt some give.

"That's it," he coaxed. Reaching under her, Thorne prayed he wouldn't grab her bosom by accident as he eased her torso out, careful not to squeeze too hard. With scarcely any room on the crate beneath him, there was no place for her bottom to go but right up against the front of him, and Thorne scrabbled for the mild outrage he'd felt upon seeing her sticking out the side of the building. When the back of her head finally emerged from the window, he breathed a sigh of relief.

"There now," he crooned. "We'll just get you down from here and—"

Oblivious to their precarious perch, Miss Peterson whirled about and threw her arms around Thorne's chest, her head coming only to his chin, the carpetbag in her hand smacking him in the back and nearly knocking them both two stories down to the ground.

"I knew someone would come," she said. Leaning back from her surprise embrace, she peered up at Thorne with a radiant smile.

The rain, his aches, the ridiculousness of him standing on top of a pile of crates to pull this strange woman out of a window—any combination of these would have put him in the foulest of moods. If he were honest, however, Thorne would later admit it had been her smile that gave him the most pause.

Her smile revealed two top teeth overlapping ever so slightly, a flaw that turned her remote, ethereal beauty into something more. Something human and attainable. Glowing with a combination of relief and gratitude, she gave off a warmth that made him want to set his hands to her face.

Thorne tried to convince himself he didn't want to touch Miss Peterson in particular. He simply wanted to touch someone else, anyone else, and find in that moment of flesh against flesh a place of recompense, a promise of forgiveness, a warmth that eluded him in the coldest part of the night. It took him far too long to break her hold.

After tonight, Thorne wanted nothing more to do with women scientists, Miss Peterson in particular.

LUCY HAD DAYDREAMS OF BEING RESCUED. NOT BY A knight in shining armor from a dragon, of course. That would be silly.

She dreamed of being rescued by a clerk. Or a carpenter. Someone who was trustworthy and organized and had no taste for fame or fortune. That was the stuff that dreams were made of. A bookkeeper would have been ideal, but this particular bookkeeper seemed as though he wanted to shove her back through the window he'd just pulled her from.

"I must apologize for my forward embrace," she said, yanking her arms back to her side, trying to appear penitent, the carpetbag pulling her too far back so that she swayed like a drunkard. "I was overcome with the greatest relief. Thank you so much, Mr. Thorne, for coming to my rescue."

For whatever reason, this was the wrong thing to say. Thorne's scowl deepened. The dim light of the alleyway painted black and gray every scar and groove on his weathered white skin.

"I did not rescue you," he growled. "I stopped you from making the worst mistake of your life. Do you know what they do to women accused of murder?"

Lucy gasped. "Murder?" Had the man fallen on his head? "I'm not here to murder anyone."

Slapping one great hand over his forehead and pulling it down over his face as though to wash away her surprise, Thorne held the hand over his mouth for a long moment while his eyes searched hers.

Finally, he spoke. "Miss Peterson. You came to our offices asking us to assassinate a man—"

"Thieving pustule," she interjected.

"Then you attempt to break into his home," Thorne continued. "And you are carrying a bag full of something suspicious. What am I supposed to think?"

A slight rustle came from a corner of the alley, and Lucy shivered. Dusk had passed, and the only light in the alleyway came from the windows of the building next door to Rider's apothecary. Lucy was far from home, her backside was wet, and an angry man now loomed over her.

Was it possible to have two worst days in a row? Did that make this the worst week ever?

"I don't suppose you came here in a hack?" she asked, knowing even as she spoke that if this were indeed her worst week ever, the answer would be no. When Thorne confirmed her fears, Lucy sighed.

"About the murder, Miss Peterson," Thorne began.

"This." Lucy held up the bag and again nearly toppled backward. Thorne reached out and encircled her waist with his arm, holding her away from him as though she smelled foul. Lucy quashed the urge to sniff herself and shook the bag instead so it rattled.

"This is full of medical instruments. I was . . . stopping in to see a customer too ill to come to the shop."

"Hmmm." Thorne communicated his disbelief with a growl.

"I wasn't going to murder Duncan," she insisted. "I was just going to . . . Never mind."

Thorne waited for her to finish, but she shook her head. What was the use? When he realized that she wasn't going to speak, he nodded brusquely.

"This won't take but a moment," he said, and, without further ado, picked Lucy up and swung her over his shoulder, then took a careful step down off the top crate. The rain continued to fall, and the stink of whatever lived in the corner of the alley wafted by on a cruel breeze. True, Lucy could object to being hauled about like a sack of flour, but it was the worst week ever. What did she expect?

Her bottom was even with his head, and every time he navigated another barrel, her hips bumped his ear. Lucy let go a long sigh, too tired at this point to have the energy to be humiliated.

When Thorne bent and set her on the ground, Lucy held the bag in front of her and stared up at his grim face.

"My brother, David, oversees our accounts, and he assures me that all is well, but I know he is lying. If I can't get that formula back, my business is going to close, and more than just my family's livelihood is at stake." Lucy took a deep breath and continued, pushing her words out before he could speak and tell her again about her foolishness.

"I cannot pay much, but what I have in savings is yours. There are rooms over ours that I can let you for free. I can give you medicine, I can . . ."

Lucy stopped at the expression on Thorne's face, for as she spoke, his glare grew fiercer and his scowl more fearsome. What else could he want?

"I do not want your money," he said. His voice was dry and crumbled as he bit out the words with an incongruously upper-class diction. "I want you to tell me the truth. What did you plan to do to Duncan Rider?"

Lucy twisted the handle of her bag in both hands. Her stomach hurt where she'd been stuck in the sill. Some splinters had found their way past the wool of her skirt and thin petticoats, and the cold was making her nose run.

"I was going to find my notes and prove Duncan stole them. Then, once I found them . . ." She peered up through the rain at the man before her. There was no one on the street outside the alley, and she could barely make out the lines of his face in the murk. Despite her vulnerability, Lucy wasn't frightened to be here alone with him. Something in the set of his shoulders and the way his gaze traveled the alley gave the impression that he hadn't finished rescuing her, so she kept going forward.

The only way she knew to go.

"I confess, I did bring along a tin of calomel to mix with his tea."

Thorne blew a long breath out between pursed lips. "And you thought to poison him with them?"

"If by poison you mean give him the trots, then yes," she confessed.

"Give him what?"

"Easy enough to slip in with the sugar since it has no taste, and he takes four spoonfuls for every cup." Lucy perked up as she imagined his discomfort. "It wears off after two days and is less than he deserves, but if I had succeeded, he would have lived in the privy for those two days."

"That was your plan?"

Her enthusiasm cooled at the disbelief and scorn in Thorne's voice.

"I'm an apothecary, not a master criminal," she said.

"True," he said, shaking his head. "You are not even a mediocre criminal."

Stupid to feel offended, but Lucy bristled nonetheless.

"It was a good enough plan," she said.

Thorne's head jerked back in disbelief. "Where was it good enough? The part where you got stuck in the window, or the part where you toppled over your means of escape?"

"Please," she said. "Just get it back for me, or if it wasn't him, find out who took it."

All the resentment she might expect to feel standing in front of a stranger who had the power to change the direction of her life, much like Duncan had done, was absent while Lucy waited for Thorne to make his decision.

In its place was the strange sensation that it was Lucy who had a hand on the scale and Thorne who weighed whether he was worthy.

3

~~-≪≪•≫≫-~~

"SHE IS A NICE LADY, MISS PETERSON. QUITE SENSIBLE. You will enjoy living in her building."

One thing Thorne learned early on in fatherhood was that lying to your child was the key to domestic harmony.

Carrots were what dwarves ate to give them the ability to see in dark mines, and if you ate yours before they cooled, you, too, might be able to spot gemstones in the dark. Baths were necessary because they washed away any leftover bad dreams from the night before. If you didn't go to sleep, you wouldn't grow big enough to ride a unicorn. Unicorns lived in Cheshire and only let little girls who ate their vegetables ride them.

Thorne had no idea what would happen when his daughter, Sadie, grew old enough to see through his lies and he would have to rely on reasoned arguments.

At nine, Sadie must have known the bit about the unicorns was a lie, but she humored him in a way Thorne found both endearing and disconcerting.

"We like living here," Sadie pointed out now. They sat at the table in the common room of their fourth-floor flat, having just finished a meal of cold chicken and bread.

A pile of peas sat shriveled on her plate.

"It's too bad you couldn't marry Mrs. Merkle," Sadie continued. "It would've made everything easier, wouldn't it? Did you get on one knee?"

Sighing, Thorne rubbed a hand over his eyes. To lie or not to lie?

Mrs. Merkle owned the building where they lived now, and Thorne paid her a small sum on top of the rent each week to watch Sadie when he worked long hours. A fellow member of his church, the widow had fit the definition of what Thorne believed was an ideal wife. She was plain of face, thrifty, and honest—to a fault.

"You're not much to look on, and you never married the child's mother," Mrs. Merkle had said when Thorne paid her a call. Mrs. Merkle's own flat wasn't much larger than his, although it boasted a settee covered in a dun-colored paisley print and numerous samplers stretched and framed on the wall, all of which had proverbs cross-stitched on them.

She'd continued in an offhand manner as if she hadn't just called him ugly and his daughter a bastard. "You're a hard worker, but I don't know how much bookkeeping will be in demand in a small town up north. You could take up a trade, I suppose."

A trade.

Thorne had forced himself to nod slowly as if considering the suggestion.

He'd taken a perilous fall from grace since leaving his family's home for a life of drinking and fighting.

This little widow's dismal assessment gave him an appreciation of just how far down he'd fallen.

Setting aside the notion of a trade, Thorne had cleared his throat. "I will admit when I came to see you with intention of asking you to marry me, I had no idea your cousin had passed away and left you such a generous bequest."

His proposal of marriage had been met with unexpected ambivalence. Mrs. Merkle had just received the news that her cousin in Scotland had passed away and left her a small house by the sea. It turned out that the practical Mrs. Merkle had a romantic streak in her and wished to return to the Scottish coast where she spent her childhood summers. A pale, thin woman with a sharp nose and a slight overbite, she favored dark colors and large shawls, always complaining of a chill.

"I've sold the building already and plan on leaving in a week's time. Of course, you can stay on," she had said. "The man who bought the building wants to cut the flats in half, though. I don't know as he'd let you keep yours without raising the rent." With a small sigh that might have held a note of regret, Mrs. Merkle patted her hair, tucked up in a heavy braid that she wound in a bun at the base of her neck. "Yes, a trade certainly would've come in handy."

What might Mrs. Merkle's reaction have been if Thorne had told her the truth? That he'd graduated with honors from Oxford, made and spent a fortune, and if he would only send his daughter away to a boarding school, his family would take him back and he could resume a life of privilege and power.

Thorne had said nothing in the end, taking his leave since the widow had much to prepare before her move. He'd searched the newspapers for rooms for let, but, not wanting to worry Sadie, he'd said nothing until he'd come home from his encounter with Miss Peterson, the opposite of his colorless landlady in every way.

"No," he said to his daughter now. "I didn't propose on

bended knee. I assumed Mrs. Merkle would think such a gesture the height of foolishness."

His daughter pushed her lower lip out, exhibiting an uncanny resemblance to his mother—slightly tilted teak-colored eyes, a tiny bump in the center of her otherwise straight nose, and flared cheekbones that gave her the look of a kitten. From her own mother, Sadie inherited the heart-shaped mole beneath her left ear, her copper skin, and her glorious black curls, which they were always wrestling into two plaits.

Thorne never searched for himself in her face.

"Miss Peterson and her sister are apothecaries," he told her. "They live with their brother over the shop, and we are to take the apartment above them."

"What has Miss Peterson done that you must go and fix her?"

Thorne had considered lying to Sadie about what he did—it worked so well with vegetables. Though his ego had shrunk considerably from his time as the toast of the gentlemen's clubs in London, it hadn't disappeared altogether. He gave his daughter the truth in small bits, bits he hoped made sense to her nine-year-old brain, for it had occurred to him on one of his first missions that someday he might not make it home.

He wanted to be someone his daughter could admire and dreaded the thought that he might die and she'd hear only about his former life as a prizefighter—a wasteland of alcohol and violence. His attempt to forget that period was thwarted by the aches in his joints that kept him awake well into the night, the long hours spent reviewing his choices and resolving to live a better life going forward.

In the end, Thorne told Sadie that he worked as a bookkeeper but was occasionally called upon to right a particular wrong.

Thorne considered how he would explain Miss Peterson and how her hyperbole nearly had him convinced she was a murderer while the two of them cleared the remains of their supper and tidied the dishes.

"Miss Peterson suspects a certain person has taken her work without permission. I will be working as a bookkeeper while at the same time asking questions to see if her suspicions are correct."

It had come as an unwelcome surprise how readily Thorne had caved and agreed to undertake the assignment for Miss Peterson. He still wasn't certain how she'd persuaded him to accept lodgings in her building along with a paltry sum in exchange for both accounting and investigative services.

Perhaps old age had softened his brain?

Sadie yawned, and Thorne fetched their latest book from the low shelf beneath the street-facing window. While he swept the floor and put away the last of the crockery, Sadie prepared for bed. After their prayers, they ended their day as they did most nights when he was home to take dinner with her, immersed in the great world beyond the confines of their quiet home.

Tonight, they roamed the streets of Saffron Hill with poor Oliver Twist, marveling at the casual cruelties that people will inflict upon one another and secure in the knowledge that while they had each other, such hardship would never touch them.

"YOU SAY HE *KEEPS* BOOKS?" DAVID WHISPERED IN LUCY'S ear. "Are you sure he doesn't hit them? With his face?"

"Shut up, Squeaky," Lucy whispered back, deliberately using her brother's hated nickname.

Luckily, Mr. Thorne appeared not to have heard that observation. He and his daughter were distracted by the task of opening every small drawer behind the counter and examining the contents. Their trunks and boxes stood forgotten by the back set of stairs while Lucy and David watched from the doorway of the treatment room, waiting to show them up to the flat.

Lucy's younger sister, Juliet, had questioned the choice to hire a bookkeeper at first, but her trust in Lucy's decisions about the business was absolute. The unwritten rule was that Lucy ran the shop and mixed the cures, freeing Juliet to diagnose the customers and work at her charitable clinic for women in the East End. Juliet had never once reproached Lucy about the loss of the formula—or even the affair itself—and for that, Lucy was eternally grateful.

David hadn't been as sanguine as Juliet about Lucy's affair with Duncan. Not so much because Lucy had an affair; mostly because he loathed Duncan. He hadn't blamed Lucy for the loss of income, either. A man who often let his heart lead him, David understood Lucy's naive trust in their rival.

Caring brother that he was, he'd thrown himself into searching out business opportunities to make up for their loss. Unfortunately, the first two "opportunities" included investing in a shipping company that didn't exist and buying a farm that turned out to be in the middle of the Sahara.

Since then, David had kept mum about his activities, frustrated at his own gullibility and inexperience. More and more, his nature was as changeable as the direction of the winds, sweet and affable one day, brooding and brittle the next. Lucy had not bothered to upbraid him for neglecting the one duty he had at the shop, the accounting, for David was not meant to live in a back office going over figures. That hadn't stopped him from grumpily questioning whether the expense of a bookkeeper could be justified.

If he weren't her brother, Lucy might have described his attractiveness as disconcerting. With delicate bones beneath his skin and wide dark blue eyes, he resembled a knight from a Crivelli painting who'd traded his armor and sword for a waistcoat and topper. He loved children and stray dogs and hated hypocrites and vinegar.

Thankfully, he seemed to be in a good mood as Lucy had shown Thorne and his daughter round the apothecary. When Sadie had read the label on one of the drawers, gasping in wonder, Lucy had encouraged her to open the drawer to reveal its contents.

Just as Lucy expected, finding an entire drawerful of glass eyeballs never lost its thrill.

Sadie's excitement had only increased with the exploration of other drawers, containing the likes of preserved earthworms and hunks of unpolished quartz.

"Crocodile poo," Sadie squealed now. The hair escaping her plaits looked like puffy clouds, and she grimaced sweetly when her father reached over to tuck it back into the braids.

None of the Peterson siblings had married, and there hadn't been a child in the apothecary since they were young. Even when Lucy was in the deepest part of her infatuation with Duncan, she'd never considered the possibility of children. The three of them had seen so many succumb to diseases endemic in the poorer districts of London, she doubted any of them had wanted to watch a child of their own suffer such a fate.

Lucy shuddered, the sudden weight of worry for this girl now attaching itself to her, and she resolved not to spend too much time with Sadie.

Sadie's giggles had the opposite effect on David, for his expression lightened.

"Alas. The last of the crocodile poo was ground into a salve over eighty years ago," David said.

Lucy held her breath, hoping he would have the sense not to follow up with the explanation that hundreds of years ago it was used as a pregnancy preventative.

Luckily, David still had some sense left in him.

He crouched next to Sadie. "Now, if you've the constitution for it . . ." He paused and peered at her in an exaggerated manner. "And I think you do . . . I will show you the more exotic ingredients we use in our work."

Holding up a finger, he leaned forward an inch and lowered his voice. "You must promise not to breathe word of their existence to another soul, however. The contents of our cures remain a secret."

Sadie's eyes widened, then narrowed in understanding, and she nodded her agreement. David rose and took down one of the jars containing the gnarled root of the ginseng plant. The ends had split halfway like two limbs, and the way the tuber twisted on itself resembled a dancing man.

The shop took up one half of the ground floor, the other half divided into an office, a treatment room, and the workroom. Attached to the back of the building was a storeroom where they kept their barrels of herbs and enormous jars of oils and astringents.

While David began an embellished tale of where they'd procured the root and its medicinal effects, Thorne wandered over to examine the treatment room, and Lucy joined him, leaving the door open so they could hear David and Sadie chatter.

"He won't tell her anything too frightening," she assured him.

"They're the same tales our grandfather told us when we were small."

Though Thorne was tall and wide of shoulder and chest, his movements were fluid. Through his woolen trousers Lucy made out the long line of his quadriceps, the muscles flexing when he knelt to examine the base of her treatment chair, running his gloved hands along the side of it. He'd worn gloves the other day as well, the mark of a gentleman. Or a man who wished to hide the skin covering misshapen knuckles, the outline of which could be seen even through the thick Woodstock leather.

David was correct that Thorne had suffered more than a few blows. She wondered idly how a bookkeeper would ever explain such injuries.

While Thorne scrutinized the mechanism that lowered and raised the chair, Lucy let herself stare, noting the simplicity of his frock coat couldn't hide its fit, which spoke of excellent tailoring. His curling brown hair was recently cut, and the skin on the back of his neck was clean where the collar pulled away as he bent. Yesterday, she'd been too distracted to question how a man with a history of violence written across his face had acquired such refined speech and polished manners. Given the quality of the wool making up Sadie's dress and her real leather boots, he spent money on the people he loved.

Thorne's manner toward his daughter was gentle, but he watched every move she made with those inscrutable eyes of his, and Lucy envied that little girl's certainty that her father kept watch. While he was not as handy as a carpenter, she felt strongly this man was a protector.

"You don't need to worry," he said.

Lucy pulled as much air as she could through her tight throat and forced her fingers to uncurl, smoothing the soft cotton of her skirts in a pathetic attempt to make herself appear unconcerned as she opened her mouth to assure Thorne that she was not worried, but he continued to speak.

"Sadie has devoured her share of frightening stories." He stepped away from the chair and walked back to the doorway, pride evident in his face as he watched his daughter. "I'm afraid her taste in literature leans more toward Charles Dickens than Sarah Fielding."

Lucy's cheeks burned with embarrassment that she'd thought his concern directed at her. Why should Thorne care if she worried? If she was veritably *drowning* in worry? Lucy's fears were not his concern. He was being paid to investigate a theft and hopefully collect enough evidence to bring charges against Duncan to the magistrate. That was all. Most likely, she and Thorne would have little contact while he was there.

That thought rattled round in her head like an abandoned wooden top as Thorne returned to his daughter's side. David had helped Sadie up on the ladder, and he and Thorne stood, faces upturned and glowing as if blessed in a shower of the little girl's laughter.

That night Lucy didn't even try to go to bed. Instead, when the dishes were cleared and the floor swept, she pulled off her petticoats and corset, changed into a ragged old day dress, and went to the workroom. As the rest of London settled in to sleep, Lucy let the scent of fresh thyme fill her nose as she distilled it down to an oil for a tincture. Hours passed, and the sounds from the street were muted to the occasional splash of a horse's hooves in a dirty puddle and the quiet tapping of the wind.

Two floors above, she fancied she could hear the heavy tread of a big man move about until even he fell silent, and Lucy carried out her work alone.

4

❖

"I MIGHT AGREE TO KILL THIS DUNCAN EVEN IF HE hasn't stolen your formulas. If he is responsible for *this*, death is the least he deserves."

Lucy would have laughed at Thorne's attempt at humor if she weren't so embarrassed when she lit the sinumbra lamp on a side table to reveal a mountain of books and papers.

She'd met Thorne at the threshold of the apothecary's cramped office this morning. The room was off the shop, had but one narrow window, a set of shelves built into the wall, and two ladder-back chairs as well as the desk. At least she assumed the desk was there. All she could see was parchment-covered chaos.

"While I blame Duncan for my distraction these past weeks," Lucy said, setting her hands to her cheeks to hide a flush of humiliation, "this mess is not solely a result of my inattention."

"No," he agreed. "I believe you said your brother, David, was in charge of your accounts."

A tiny hammer pounded at the spot between her eyebrows, and she pressed a thumb there to silence the noise.

"He's been busy with another business venture."

That was what David had told her and Juliet with controlled excitement a month ago. While he wouldn't disclose the details until he'd finalized them, this business venture was certain to change their fortunes. He swore it was legitimate and he'd found a trustworthy partner. He simply needed capital and some time.

Time Lucy didn't have.

"It would help if you could show me some evidence of other formulas in your hand or, better yet, early notes you took before completing the formula," Thorne said.

Lucy sucked her bottom lip into her mouth and stared at the mountain. "I've looked through for my notebook, but as for early notes . . . they could be in there. In the middle of the bottom part of the stack on the left . . . oh, goodness. It will take us days to find evidence and weeks to put this mess in order."

Thorne shook his head before she finished her sentence, then walked toward the chair nearest the desk. As he passed by, he reached out and patted her shoulder in reassurance before taking a seat.

"Do you doubt, Miss Peterson, that I can do both?" With a sigh of contentment, Thorne sifted through the first layer of papers. "Some of the agents pose as housekeepers. Some as butlers. We are adept at our chosen roles, and I am quite capable of organizing your books. An accounting audit is as seductive a pleasure as the collection of evidence. Much the same process, really."

Lucy said nothing. Partly because she found it inconceivable that a private agent—any person in their right mind, actually—would find enjoyment in *accounting*. Partly because she was frozen with apprehension from the sensations in the wake of his touch.

What terrible weakness lay within her that a brief, thoughtless contact felt so good?

When Lucy confronted Duncan at the theft of her lozenge formula, she'd accused him of seducing her. He, in turn, accused her of possessing unnatural carnal appetites that had unbalanced her brain, quoting an article from the *Gentlemen's Monthly Magazine* to prove his point.

The publication was a voice for the Guardians of Domesticity, a group that blamed the scarcity of jobs on women taking employment outside of the home rather than the devastating effect mills and machinery had on the craft workers and tenant farmers of rural England. These men, who had been replaced by structures made of metal, now streamed into London looking for work—and for answers, perhaps, as to why their way of life was gone. The farther afield they traveled for work, the less their wives were able to venture from the home, and they became confined both physically and mentally.

Lucy and her siblings had made fun of the Guardians at first, but those men then turned their attention to the women of Athena's Retreat. Recently some of them had been looking in her direction. The Guardians did not countenance a woman apothecary.

Their magazine, *The Gentlemen's Monthly Magazine*, printed articles full of hatred toward women of science and listed imaginary ailments of the brain and body of women with unnatural desires for freedom. The articles were cleverly worded so while the intent was clear, the actual text could be explained away as pious concern for the women's health and safety.

Thorne asked her a question, his attention still on the papers, but Lucy couldn't answer. Could Duncan have been telling the truth? Was it a sign of a mental disease that caused her to crave the feeling of being enveloped in another person's warmth and regard?

"What do you think?" Thorne asked. "Miss Peterson?"

He held a stack of papers out, one thick black brow raised in question.

"I don't know," she said aloud. In answer to his question or to her own, it was all the same. "I don't know where anything is, I don't know what I am to pay or what is to be paid to me. I am—"

Something like sympathy crossed his face, or perhaps it was pity and the scar smoothed away the worst of it.

"It is a good thing you have help," he said, ever so gently, as if he thought a harsh word might break her.

Perhaps it would.

Help. Everything she wanted and nothing she could ask for.

Lucy reached for the papers and forced herself to read the top line of the first page.

"Forgive me," she said to the invoice in front of her. "I don't—didn't—sleep well last night."

David or Juliet had opened the shop. Sounds of people treading heavily on the old floorboards, the scratch of tin against wood as the canisters were pulled from the shelves, and the murmur of impatient voices filtered under the door. Lucy's tension eased at the reminder that soon she would be in the workroom mixing cures—the one place where she was in control.

"Why would your formulas be mixed in with your financial papers?" Thorne asked as he pulled a pair of spectacles from his waistcoat pocket and set them upon the bridge of his nose, where they tilted slightly. He must be older than she'd guessed, unless whatever injuries he'd sustained to his face had affected his eyesight.

"There was a small explosion in the laboratory below my workroom at Athena's Retreat last month," Lucy said.

"A small *explosion*?" he asked, peering over the rims.

Lucy waved away his concern. "Tiny, really. We only had to

evacuate for a few hours, and no one was concussed. The floor-boards of the workroom had to be replaced, so I took my work home until the repairs were finished."

"So, your work has been sitting out on this desk for a month," Thorne said now, flipping slowly through a ledger. "During that time, how many people could have come in this office?"

Lucy had no idea. She sucked at her lower lip in thought.

"Just David and I."

Thorne's eyes narrowed. "Are you sure? That would certainly help implicate Rider."

"Oh, I'm sure," Lucy promised. Who else would be so cruel? "David is the only other one."

"Good morning, Miss Peterson."

A tall woman dressed in a beautifully tailored blue wool paletot and a distinguished velvet bonnet opened the door without knocking, a covered basket over one arm. The gold rims of her glasses glinted in the lamplight as a smile lit her long, thin face.

"Good morning, Mrs. Parekh," Lucy greeted her, hands rubbing together in anticipation. "What have you brought for me?"

"My husband's cousin's wife's aunt arrived yesterday from Junagadh, right on time," Mrs. Parekh said as she searched for a space to set her basket. Lucy dragged over the other chair, and Mrs. Parekh pulled back the cloth, exposing her treasure.

"Many of the pots broke in the voyage, but enough made it intact so I've some to share with you. We have two karira plants here, and I've included directions for how to grow. In addition, she brought a neem sapling..."

Twenty minutes later, Mrs. Parekh had left with Lucy's profuse thanks and the promise that the precious plants would survive the harsh London winter.

"Now be sure to tell David to pack you up a bottle of rosehip oil and bring another to your relative as a token of our thanks." Lucy waved goodbye, then turned back to the office. Her smile faded at the sight of Thorne balanced on the two back feet of his chair, hands over his chest and the expression of someone aching to point out the obvious on his face.

"The only people who come into this office are you, David, and Duncan Rider," he said.

"Yes," Lucy said. "And Mrs. Parekh, but only when she has plants for me. And Katie Quinlavin, the shopgirl, but she's worked here for two years now and never would do anything untoward. Otherwise, absolutely no one—"

"Hallo. Who have we here?"

Lucy winced at Thorne's raised eyebrows and turned on her heel to greet a man with thinning red hair and watery blue eyes who had entered the office without knocking. Dressed in a black wool coat and brown trousers too large for his lanky frame, he held his charcoal-colored felted cap in his long fingers and bowed quickly in Lucy's direction.

"G'day, mum," he said brusquely.

"Good day, Mr. Gentry," Lucy said. "How unexpected to see you in the office."

Gentry snorted as though she'd made a joke, and ventured farther into the room, leaning over to sniff at the neem sapling.

"Been thinking. Might not be anemia. Consid'ring the aches and sharp pains along with the exhaustion, might be an imbalance in my humors," he said. He cocked his head and stared at Thorne, then asked, "What do you reckon?"

Thorne set his chair back on the floor with a heavy thud. "I beg your pardon?"

"Are you not an apothecary?" Gentry asked.

"I'm not," Thorne said.

"What're you doing in the apothecary office if you're not an apothecary?" Gentry set his hands on his hips, lower lip pushed out and eyes squinting as if sizing Thorne up for a fight.

"This is our new bookkeeper," Lucy said quickly. "Mr. Thorne, this is Mr. Gentry. He never comes into the office—"

"Not 'less I've something to say to Miss Peterson the rest of those know-it-alls out front don't need to hear. I do some readin' of my own." Mr. Gentry tapped the side of his head with a skinny finger. "Miss Peterson and I have proper medical discussions 'bout my ailments."

Thorne nodded and scratched his chin. "You have many ailments, do you?"

Behind Mr. Gentry, Lucy shook her head wildly and put a finger to her lips, but it was too late.

"Well," said Mr. Gentry, "it started back in thirty-eight. Woke to a sore throat and tender nipples."

It took another ten minutes for Lucy to persuade Mr. Gentry to leave off his recitation of five years' worth of ailments and meet her in the treatment room for a "consultation" after lunch. During that time, Katie came in to fetch a box of lucifers, and Mrs. Patterson popped her head in to ask when her tincture would be ready.

Finally, Lucy shut the door behind her and leaned her body against it.

"I don't know that I can ever unhear Mr. Gentry's description of how to apply an onion poultice to one's nether regions," Thorne said slowly, his skin slightly ashen.

Lucy smiled sympathetically. "If it helps—"

Thorne held up a hand. "Nothing will help. Nothing. By God, the man has a gift for detail." He rubbed his face and then shook his head quickly like a dog trying to dislodge a flea.

"Miss Peterson," he said with the air of a man exhibiting great patience. "Do you care to revise your statement about who exactly can enter this office?"

Lucy opened her mouth to reply, when the door behind her opened, pushing her forward into the desk, dislodging an avalanche of black-and-white pages everywhere.

"Miss Peterson, Miss Juliet says you are to come—"

"Miss Peterson, I've left you the herbs you asked—"

"A thruppence to pull a tooth? Highway robbery!"

Lucy examined the wreckage at her feet, then glanced at the mayhem in the shop beyond the door before turning to face Thorne.

"There is a possibility . . ." she began, surprised her ears weren't literally aflame with chagrin.

"However slight it may be," Thorne supplied dryly.

"Yes, exactly. A slight possibility someone might have ventured into the office other than me, David, and Duncan."

"I see." The resignation in his tone made Lucy wince.

"These people are my family's customers. I've known them all my life," Lucy said. She tried to keep her voice level and calm, as Duncan's accusations of hysteria were still fresh in her memory. "They would never wish harm on me. Our apothecary is the only one that serves the East End of London with real cures instead of gin and opium. We never turn away a person in pain, whether they can pay or not."

Stepping around the drifts of paper, Lucy clasped her hands together, pushing them into her skirts to keep from reaching toward him as if he were a raft and she was treading water in the ocean.

"Once you sort through this mess, you will see how close to ruin we are because of this. If I cannot sell my formula, I've lost everything my father left to me."

LONDON WAS A CITY OF TWO EXTREMES. DURING THE day, commerce and the accumulation of wealth were the fuel that sent folks streaming down its streets at breakneck pace, humming with the energy necessary to claw a living from a tightfisted metropolis.

At night, the populace turned to pleasure.

The dimly lit streets of the nation's capital held temptations for everyone, whether they found relief in a tin mug of gin, the joyous cacophony of the theater, or between the satin sheets of expensive brothels.

In his younger years, Thorne had sampled almost all that the city had to offer. The rhythm of life after midnight was more familiar to him than the day, no matter how early he woke and how hard he rode himself. On this night, the laughter in the street below grew louder as the public houses closed their doors and revelers made their way home, hurrying to end their stories and say their last goodbyes.

The aches and pains of poorly healed broken bones and torn ligaments from a youth of excess kept him from his bed until the early morning hours, so he was still awake and dressed when he heard the Peterson siblings come home from an evening out. Thorne first checked his daughter's room and assured himself of her deep, uninterrupted slumber, then left their rooms and stood on the landing listening to the quiet merriment below.

From the slight slur of Miss Peterson's command that her younger brother stop his fooling about and open the door, Thorne knew she'd been drinking. The disappointment that welled up was unfair. Simply because he'd become a teetotaler did not mean the rest of humanity must follow suit. Who was he, of all people, to begrudge a woman who worked as hard as Miss Peterson to have a glass of ale in the local pub with her family?

A high, light giggle floated upward—that would be Miss Juliet, whom he hadn't met yet—and the Petersons finally closed the door behind them.

Waiting until all was quiet, Thorne made his way down the stairs, past the Petersons' set of rooms and into the apothecary. A light burned in the back room, and Thorne carried it with him into the office.

He was still of two minds whether Miss Peterson was correct that someone had stolen her formula for the salve—that catastrophe in her office meant the formula could be sitting right there amid the copious scientific papers, recipes for cures on parchment from the last century, six-page epic poems dedicated to Miss Juliet, unpaid bills, and a myriad of invoices for goods like myrrh, lemons, camphor, and linen.

That was just the first layer of papers.

He tilted his head up as though he could see through the ceiling into the apartment above. For a long, dark moment, he imagined what she might be like—Miss Peterson . . . Lucy—after she'd had a drink or two. More cheerful, certainly, than the woman he'd spoken with this morning who seemed as though she held her life together with jagged stitches of tenacity and terror.

Drink will do that.

The memory of the weightlessness that came at the bottom of a beer settled behind his forehead, and he sat in the office, unseeing, until the oil in the lamp burned out.

The next morning, Thorne was up with the dawn, brushing out his clothes and polishing his boots. When he was done, he and Sadie breakfasted, then bundled themselves warmly. It took an hour to walk her to school, and they discussed finding a different school nearby as they nodded to the coffee sellers and walked round the newsboys. Truth be told, Sadie had outgrown the lessons in the tiny set of rooms where a former governess lectured a handful of merchants' daughters on the basics of arithmetic and the structure of grammar.

As he waved goodbye, Thorne set the worry aside. He needed a clear head to begin the transformation this next step required. As he walked, his stride lengthened and slowed, shoulders back and chin up. The people around him morphed from individuals into indistinct figures deserving of acknowledgment only if they wore the right clothes or spoke with the correct dialect. The familiar sensation of privilege puffed up his chest. By the time Thorne reached the doors of Rider and Son, he'd regressed in empathy and increased his ego to reach the size needed for a proper aristocratic bearing.

That he'd succeeded was apparent the moment he entered the apothecary with the immediate deference shown by the shop boy in leaving a customer midtransaction and hurrying to his side.

"Good morning, sir," the boy said. "How can I help you?"

The inside of Rider and Son was a far sight quieter than Peterson's Apothecary. A few well-dressed women examined the contents of glass-topped cabinets and meticulously organized shelves. No sound could be heard issuing from behind the oak door at the side of the shop with a "consultations" sign hanging on it. Sunlight filtered through the windows onto newly swept floors.

At the center of the shop stood a large display. Atop a table covered in white linen were stacks of tin boxes lined before a sign that read "Rider's Lozenges" in red letters and beneath it the boast "Exclusive Patented Lozenges for the Relief of Putrid Throat."

"Have you heard of our famous lozenges, sir?"

The shop boy retreated to the counter to finish up with his customer and was replaced by a blandly handsome young man with clear blue eyes and a ready smile. The young man's blond hair was parted on the side, and he sported a set of fashionable muttonchop whiskers along his jaw that served to emphasize rather than hide a weak chin.

Thorne inclined his head in such a way that conveyed a tepid interest in something other than himself.

Obviously used to the affectations of the gentry, the man beamed.

"Allow me to introduce myself. I am Duncan Rider, the inventor of Rider's Lozenges." He paused as if waiting for applause to settle. "I am the first to discover how to cure a putrid throat in a lozenge. Why, Windsor Castle's housekeeper has ordered some specially made just the other day, and we count the Earl of Westwood as one of our most valued customers. He says his household will never be without a tin of Rider's Lozenges."

Duncan appeared so obviously pleased with himself, with the lozenges, with the world in general that Thorne instantly took him in dislike.

There was no reason to be that cheerful.

Ever.

"I'm impressed. Tell me," Thorne said slowly as he walked to the display and peered at the dozens of tins with their red and white labels. "What is the formula that gives the lozenges their potency?"

A blank look crossed the man's face for a moment before he caught himself and displayed that smile again.

"That formula is a secret, sir."

Thorne adjusted his top hat as he took in the rest of the shop. Like Peterson's, there were shelves of canisters and jars with contents both familiar and more exotic, but more room here was given over to dried goods and attractive displays of cosmetics and toilet water.

"If it's patented, it's not a secret," Thorne said when his gaze returned to Rider.

Again, the lines of the man's face smoothed except for a small furrow that bisected his brow.

Interesting.

Duncan Rider was an *idiot*.

This made Thorne's job a good deal easier, but it also made him wonder how someone as bright as Miss Peterson could stand to be in company with such a fool.

"Well, it's exclusive," Duncan said slowly, as if turning over the meaning of the word in his head. "That means no one else can make them. Only us."

Thorne did not want to confuse the poor boy any further, so he nodded in agreement.

"Friendly with Westwood, did you say?" Thorne asked.

That Thorne was familiar with the earl put Duncan right back on firmer footing. "Great friends, as a matter of fact," the young man said.

Westwood was a few years Thorne's junior and had not been an earl when they were at Oxford. Westwood hadn't been stupid, but neither was he especially bright, nor had he ever shown more than a nodding familiarity with morals or principles. He was also a gambler.

Just the type of man Thorne had allied himself with back then.

"You must tell him that Jonathan Thornwood sends his regards."

Duncan shook his hand like a man pumping water but showed no sign of familiarity with Thorne's family name, nor did he seem to make a connection between Jonathan Thorn-wood and Jon Thorne, the Gentleman Fighter.

Notoriety was a fleeting thing in London.

"I have a friend," Thorne said, picking up a tin and examining it. "His baby is suffering a terrible case of croup. Do you have any special cure for that?"

Duncan's brows rose. "No. Not that I know of. You can ask the shop clerk, I suppose."

Thorne expressed his thanks, and Duncan pressed a tin of lozenges into his hand.

"Please, take them in good health," the man implored.

"Exclusive patent," Thorne said as if reading the label for the first time. "And you discovered this by yourself?"

Duncan spread his arms, palms open and facing the heavens, as if to say, *Who else?*

While it would please Thorne greatly if he could prove this fool had indeed stolen Miss Peterson's salve, he could not base a man's guilt on his weakness of character. The agents of Tierney's were cautioned not to deliver justice if it could be sought through the common law. Their talents were used to help the helpless, not right petty grievances.

Tierney's had given Thorne a means to redress the wrongs he had committed in his former life, and he would follow the rules set out to him when he took employment with the firm seven years ago.

When Thorne took his leave of Rider, the young man again smiled broadly and waved as though they were friends parting forever. By the surprised fear in Rider's eyes as Thorne exited the shop, he assumed the scowl he wore matched Rider's smile in intensity, if not impact.

Good.

5

~-<<<◆>>>-~

"I CANNOT CONCENTRATE IN THESE CONDITIONS."

Lucy glanced over at Thorne and raised her brows in question.

"How do you expect me to contend with your accounts while a chicken stares at me?"

"Stop staring at Mr. Thorne," Lucy admonished the hen.

The chicken ignored her and kept her tiny little eyes on Thorne.

With a low huff, he bent his head back to his work for a moment, only to lean forward and put his pointer finger on the desk in front of him.

"Miss Peterson—"

"Lucy," she said.

Thorne hesitated until Lucy shifted the hen sitting on her lap so that it had a better view of him.

"Lucy," he said, clearly uncomfortable with the familiarity but even more uncomfortable with the chicken's fierce regard. "Can you not put the chicken outside where it belongs?"

"I cannot," Lucy said with false sympathy. "Mr. Gentry was quite clear that Andromeda has a delicate constitution and needs to be comforted while being left in strange places."

"Mr. Gentry takes advantage of you."

Lucy had taken an hour out of her day to sit with Thorne and go through a stack of scientific papers that he'd unearthed. While she'd insisted that none of them were her missing formula, he'd asked her to examine them all the same. As the hour of daylight she spent with him meant an extra hour of work that night, it had put her in a temper. Which was why, when Mr. Gentry came in with his pet hen, adither because he'd forgotten his newest list of symptoms at home, Lucy agreed to watch Andromeda so he could go back for it.

"Mr. Gentry is one of the few customers who pay on time," Lucy said. "I am perfectly content to pet his chicken if he continues that habit."

Thorne sighed. "Very well. I suppose I can tolerate—ugh. I'm certain it wants to peck me."

The novelty of such a large, confident man being unnerved by a tiny little chicken intrigued her, but Lucy took pity on him and left. When she came back without the chicken, Thorne did not bother to hide his relief.

"I gave her to Katie to watch while she waits for Juliet to come back," Lucy said. "We must be quick about it or that chicken will find its way into the Quinlavins' stew pot."

"Are they a particularly hungry family?" Thorne asked distractedly, sifting through piles.

"They are a spectacularly hungry family, and Katie is the main source of food for them all."

Thorne looked up at that. "I've seen the books. She's not paid enough to support a family."

Lucy sighed. "She wouldn't be paid at all if her father had

anything to do with it. Her mam fell sick after her fifth child—an ailment of the blood that leaves her spent. Her father, Joe, sent us Katie in exchange for the medicine they need."

He'd been in London long enough not to look shocked that a family would pay their bills with a child's labor. In most parts of London, children were sent to work as soon as they could follow directions, and many a girl was sold into circumstances much meaner than cleaning up after an apothecary.

"She's a bright girl," Lucy continued. "Bright enough that we decided to pay her a wage. In the best of all worlds, we'd send her to school as well, but her father won't spare her."

"Indeed," Thorne said. The sympathy in his eyes dimmed as he glanced down at the piles he'd made. "Speaking of best of all worlds—can you please explain these?"

Lucy came around the side of the desk and stood next to Thorne as he spread out a familiar set of papers.

"These are part of a failed experiment," she said as she traced the formulas with her pointer finger. "I tried to make a long-lasting scented soap, but it wouldn't come out right."

Thorne examined her from behind his spectacles. The light from the window shone behind him, casting his face in semi-darkness.

"Is it the same sort of ingredient list as you used with the salve? That might help me when I go to speak with your suppliers," he explained. "If they have a new request from Rider and Son Apothecary for an ingredient only found in your salve, this will prove your suspicions correct."

Lucy sighed. "I'm afraid not. I learned early on that it would take me time and money I don't have to make glycerin work that way. I simply don't have the time to experiment properly while I am running the apothecary. I will try to remember the original list and give it to you tomorrow."

"How long have you been developing formulas?" he asked.

Lucy gave up trying to read his face and glanced back down at her work. "As soon as I understood that what my father and grandfather did was chemistry and not some magical art."

Apprentices of the Worshipful Society of Apothecaries had to train for five years. Once the apprenticeship was over, they were not allowed to practice unless they'd completed courses in chemistry, medical botany, anatomy, and physiology. Many apprentices made the decision afterward to enter the Royal College of Surgeons.

While the Peterson sisters could not be denied admission to the society on the basis of their sex, they were not exactly welcomed by medical educators with open arms.

Guy's Hospital was the only voluntary hospital in London that allowed Juliet and Lucy to complete the education required for apothecaries, and even there they were not allowed to attend dissections. Lucy had been happy enough with this exclusion, while Juliet had disguised herself as a man and cut open as many corpses as could be obtained legally.

After her studies were completed, Lucy devised her own cures, marrying the knowledge passed down through her family alongside what she learned in modern chemistry.

"My father apprenticed my sister and me as apothecaries—for which he was considered eccentric and doomed to disappointment—but our pre-apprentice education was on par with any man's. He made sure we had lessons at a girls' school run by a remarkable woman, Madame Mensonge. Madame is a chemist, but she taught us physics, mathematics, and botany as well. Suddenly I had an entirely new language to describe my father's and grandfather's tonics and mixtures."

"I have been sending Sadie to a school. She can read and do sums," he said.

Lucy quirked a brow. What had this to do with anything?

"I never thought to educate her in science. I don't know that many fathers would."

"My father was . . ."

She tried to summon an image of her father, but it slipped away from her. Tiny glimpses of his face red with laughter or scrunched in concentration as he played a new piece on the spinet swam through her head like silverfish in sunlit waters.

"Madame still has her school," Lucy said instead of finishing her thought. "It's not far from here. Juliet passes by it on her way to the women's clinic."

"This clinic is in St. Giles," he said, a statement rather than a question. Lucy swallowed surprise and a sudden misapprehension when she realized Thorne would learn a great deal about her family in the course of the investigation. She watched his expression carefully as she explained what Juliet did at the clinic.

"It is a clinic for women who haven't the means to pay a physician, and who live in that area," Lucy said slowly.

Thorne's chin dipped slightly in acknowledgment of what Lucy had implied but hadn't said aloud. The clinic treated women who might very well be prostitutes.

"They cannot afford a doctor, so Juliet and her friend, Mrs. Sweet, provide the same care as a physician might as volunteers. This includes taking care of . . . women's private problems. The women pay what they can, and Juliet always manages to find sponsors when she needs them."

Lucy used the common euphemism for gynecological and abortion care, but Thorne understood this well enough.

"Freely you have received; freely you give." He quoted the Gospel of Matthew's observation on healing the sick in an approving tone.

Outside, the clouds had thickened. Lucy hadn't noticed how dark the room had gotten or how close they had been to each other, her hand nearly touching his where she leaned over the desk. He still wore gloves, contrasting with her own hand, stained yellow at the fingertips from mixing a tonic containing turmeric, nicked in a dozen places from the blades she used, glistening slightly from an earlier application of lanolin in a vain attempt to keep her skin from drying out.

"You could visit Madame's school with your daughter and see if she'd enjoy it."

"I shall consider it," he said.

Lucy imagined him examining the idea the same way he examined the chaos of her office: methodically, rationally, unconcerned that whatever he chose might not be the right choice or please everyone.

Perhaps it was not wickedness nor a weakness for lust that fueled Lucy's growing fascination with the man. Perhaps that confidence was what drew her toward him—a yearning to emulate such certainty.

If the alternative was true and the Guardians were correct that women such as her were powerless against base physical desire, she would remain forever alone. Desire was a form of blindness, smothering rational thought and self-preservation. Lucy had learned her lesson well and would never again believe that a kiss or a gentle touch meant anything other than a prelude to sex.

"What are you doing?" The voice came from behind her.

Nothing!

Still, Lucy jumped away from Thorne as if he were on fire, and turned to face her sister, Juliet, standing in the doorway.

It had been Juliet who found her and Duncan together and had known the truth of them in an instant. Juliet who was the most dependent on the income from the shop and most affected by Lucy's stupid decision to trust a man who said he cared.

"Juliet, please come in," Lucy said, forcing the words past her dry lips and tongue thick with embarrassment and nerves. "Allow me to introduce my sister, Miss Juliet Peterson. Juliet, this is Mr. Thorne, who will be keeping our books."

Dressed in a thick woolen cape with a high collar and a deep-brimmed poke bonnet, all Lucy could see of her sister was her slight frown, the tiny backward Cs at the corners of her mouth. When Juliet untied her bonnet strings, she revealed smudges of fatigue beneath her expressive gray-blue eyes.

Having arrived early when she was a babe, Juliet had always been smaller than her siblings. Her premature appearance in the world was a harbinger of her ferocious will, which gave her the presence of a much larger woman. Her hair, the same color as David's, fell in long waves when unbound. When she was little, she refused to have it cut, believing she would grow even less without it.

Juliet stared at Thorne without blinking, her eyes taking him in, from the scars on his face to the breadth of his shoulders, as well as the distance that now stood between him and Lucy. Thorne, for his part, observed her in return. Lucy tried not to draw their attention.

Rather like a mouse between two irritable owls.

"That you haven't run screaming in the opposite direction once you saw the state of this office is a testament to your fortitude, Mr. Thorne."

Releasing Thorne from her scrutiny, Juliet plopped her bonnet into the seat of a nearby chair and pulled off her gloves.

"I'm only home for a meal," she said, tossing her gloves next to her bonnet and speaking to Lucy. "There is a terrible influenza going round that's particularly bad in children. Mrs. Sweet and I are going to convert part of the clinic over to beds for the sickest babes."

"Be sure you don't get sick yourself," Lucy cautioned.

"Is David here? I'll need him to walk me back," Juliet told them as she riffled through a stack of papers on a side table. Thorne said nothing, but his shoulders tensed. Lucy admonished her sister not to make more of a mess.

"I'm looking for something," Juliet snapped, then sighed. "My apologies." Her gaze returned to the pile as she spoke. "Some of those Guardians were by the clinic earlier, shouting at the women as they came in. Mrs. Sweet's friend, Mr. Wintram, chased them off, but I don't want to go back alone."

Lucy glanced quickly at Thorne, but he showed no sign of recognition at the name of the fellow agent.

He must be practiced at such deceits.

Lucy, however, felt terrible for deceiving Juliet. She didn't want her sister to know how dire the situation had become. Her guilt was jumbled up alongside worry for Juliet and for David and . . . Lucy put a hand to her chest where she often felt pressure, like a fist slowly clenching.

"The Guardians?" Thorne asked. "Would that be those men who follow Victor Armitage?"

"Yes. Victor Armitage believes women should stay in the home and that foreigners are to blame for the high price of corn. He even sent his Guardians to picket in front of Athena's Retreat, and we are quite convinced they were behind the fire there last year." Juliet's eyes blazed, and her spine snapped straight. Papers forgotten, she set her hands on her hips, jaw jutting forward.

"They harass these women when they are at work, then follow them to the clinic and shout at them there. What is a woman with children and no man to do? Starve to death in order to placate them?"

She scoffed. "Now they are saying we shouldn't give women preventatives or correct their menses. So, they should have more children they cannot feed?"

"A group of them were here last week, shouting that a woman couldn't be an apothecary and we were duping our customers," Lucy added. They hadn't come inside and none of her patients had left, but the experience rattled her just the same. What more ill luck could rain down on her head?

Thorne frowned as his finger rubbed the edge of the desk. "Could the Guardians have anything to do with your missing formulas?" he asked Lucy.

Before she could answer, Juliet's eyes narrowed. "Why would you be interested in Lucy's missing formulas? I thought you were a bookkeeper."

"I merely confided to Mr. Thorne that my formula has gone missing," Lucy blurted.

Thorne did nothing to draw Juliet's attention away from Lucy. In fact, as her sister's fierce gray-blue eyes turned to examine what Lucy could only imagine was her very soul, he did something that turned him toward the shadow and nearly erased him from sight.

Amazing talent, that.

"In case he comes across any clues while he sorts through this mess," she continued, pretending her cheeks were not burning bright enough to light the room. "We need all the help we can get, Juliet."

Her sister's fire dimmed at those words. If Lucy asking for help was rare, Juliet asking for help was unthinkable. Two more prideful and recalcitrant women probably never existed in the British Isles.

They stared at each other for a long moment, the truth of their plight between them. Already Juliet bore too heavy a burden with her work at the clinic and work in the shop. Why tell her the truth about Thorne? It would do no good to get her hopes up if he could not help them.

"Are you ready, Sniffles?" David popped his head into the office. "Oh, Lucy. I sent Mrs. Parekh home with some rosehip oil, like you asked. Mrs. Lonegan was there when I gave it out and I sent her home with one as well. She was grateful, but it turns out that was the last bottle, so . . ."

Lucy would wager a pint of lager that David had not charged for the bottle he sent home with the recently widowed Mrs. Lonegan. David had the same soft heart as his sisters, he just hid it better. He might persuade a housekeeper to buy a few jars of liniment to have on hand for household injuries, but in the next moment a gaunt-cheeked urchin would be scuttling out the door with a wink from David and a paper twist of boiled sweets.

"Coming, Squeaky," Juliet said as she put her bonnet back on and tied the strings.

Lucy followed her siblings out to the shop as they squabbled between themselves. They were too intent on teasing each other to notice her standing in the doorway as they left, or at least, that is what Lucy told herself when she turned around and went back inside alone.

THE ONLY WOMAN THORNE HAD EVER LOVED HAD LIT-erally fallen into his lap seconds after he first saw her.

He'd won a massive purse at a fight somewhere outside of Bristol over ten years ago. After the obligatory post-fight cele-bration, he'd passed out and, when he woke, found himself in

Bath with a noisy contingent of third sons and hangers-on. While still drunk, they'd decided a night at the opera was the highest form of entertainment. It turned out not to be as fun as expected, as he sobered up and found himself in need of headache powder, water, and a piss all at the same time.

The banging in his head had drowned out the opera, and Thorne had leaned back in pain only to meet the eyes of the most beautiful woman he'd ever seen leaning over the balcony railing above him, flirting with the men below.

Geneviève Fournier, the brightest star in the firmament of the demimonde. A courtesan famous enough to be immortalized in song—though not the kind of song one sang in mixed company.

In the middle of the second act, Thorne had been so overcome with amazement at her appearance—and still quite drunk—he'd held out his arms and cried, "She's beautiful and therefore to be wooed; She is woman and therefore to be loved."

Geneviève had smiled and, in a gesture that encapsulated her entire life, jumped off the balcony without a single glance backward. Thank God he'd maintained enough reflexes to hurtle to his feet in time to catch her.

Thorne's visceral reaction to Genny's beauty never faded.

His selfish pursuit of Sadie's mother was a part of a past he'd spent years exorcising. That another beautiful woman had now entered his life, one in such obvious distress, gave him pause. If encouraged, would Thorne pursue this woman as well?

If he gave in to this vice, would he again take up his others?

His thoughts were still on Lucy as he sat down to dinner with Sadie that night.

"Science?" Sadie asked.

"Yes," he said as he cut his meat. "There is a school Miss

Peterson spoke of where girls learn science. We could visit if you'd like. It's much closer than Mistress Addison's school. I think you've outgrown your lessons there."

Sadie chewed her bread and swallowed, her eyes studying Thorne's face.

"I like glass eyeballs," she said.

About to fork a piece of ham, Thorne stilled, feeling much like a rabbit who'd been placidly nibbling grass when it caught sight of a fox. There was an intensity in Sadie's gaze that promised an inquisition was on the way.

"Do you like glass eyeballs, Papa? You seemed interested in them the other day. Your face got tight right around your nose like it does when you are interested. Or hungry. Were you hungry? Do you think Miss Peterson likes vegetables?"

Thorne returned his daughter's stare. He was the adult, and she was the child. Therefore, he would take control of the conversation.

"She likes science, and she attended this school. She uses chemistry to decide the ingredients in her cures. Would you like to learn about chemistry and how to make tonics and salves and such?"

Sadie put down the heel of bread she'd been eating and set her elbow on the table, chin in her hand.

"I like these rooms. They're much nicer than Mrs. Merkle's and it smells good here."

Slippery as an eel, this girl's brain. Still, he would wrest them back from the brink of where Sadie would like to push the conversation.

"You can learn about physics. Do you know why the sun hangs in the sky and never falls to earth?" he asked.

Aha. This flummoxed her. Thorne watched her tiny eyebrows

lift and drop as she debated which was more fascinating—the question of gravity or the question of whether he found Miss Peterson a marriageable prospect.

Sadie had been the one to precipitate his proposal to Mrs. Merkle, although not as enthusiastically as she'd advocated for him to marry Miss Highland, the milliner (she had a nice smile and Sadie would always have new bonnets), or their neighbor Mrs. Downwith (septuagenarian she might be, but she enjoyed baking biscuits and had a lapdog Sadie found charming).

"Why do you keep trying to get me shackled?" Thorne had complained on their walk home from church one Sunday, holding a basket of Mrs. Downwith's scones with one hand and Sadie's warm palm in his other.

"Because you missed your chance to marry Mama," she'd said, skipping every so often to keep pace with his strides. "I know you are sad she is dead, and so am I, but if you marry someone else, I can have brothers and sisters. Wouldn't that be fun?"

"You are all the children a man could want," he told her.

Vegetables and cleaning behind the ears might require made-up stories, but the question of Sadie's mama was not suited for outright lies. Sadie would grow up and, despite Thorne's best efforts, might hear some old gossip or rumors.

He'd told her that Geneviève died before they could be married.

This was true. What he didn't tell her was that even though his family had all but disowned him for prizefighting, Thorne had kept many of their highborn prejudices and would never have considered marrying Geneviève, a former courtesan. A gentleman simply didn't marry his mistress.

He'd been a selfish fool.

Since Genny's death, Thorne had learned that what makes

a woman worthy of being a wife or a man worthy of being a husband and father had nothing to do with birth or class and everything to do with the state of their soul.

Thorne fought every day to be worthy of his daughter.

He would take care of Sadie and never again confuse lust for love. As for his own life, it would remain free of temptation. Beautiful women, parties, song, and drink—they were part of the past and would stay there, buried.

As if to mock him, a song started in the rooms below their feet.

The strains of a reel rose between the floorboards, a fiddle and flute slightly off-key but charming enough. Sadie's eyes widened and she tapped her feet on the chair rail as he cleared away their dinner. Thorne said nothing about it when they settled into bed with *Oliver Twist*, and the music stopped after a while.

The long walks to and from school had exhausted her, and Sadie was asleep before he'd finished a chapter. With nothing to occupy him, the aches and pains from the cold and damp of the autumn night pushed themselves to be attended.

Thorne wanted a drink.

Instead, he left a note in case Sadie woke, and took a long walk. Temptation faded as an hour, two, three passed by in a blur until he found himself back outside the apothecary. A low light burned in the Petersons' window, and all seemed silent.

Thorne and Genny had been the most scandalous couple in Somerset. He'd bought a town house, and every musician and artist that made their living entertaining sedate crowds during the day would find their way to the Gentleman Fighter's abode at night. Many a time they'd had a piper and fiddler play reels with dancing until dawn.

"Let's have company tonight, Jonny," she'd say.

One night's revelry would bleed into two, two nights became two weeks, until he could barely remember when it began or why it should end.

Above the Petersons' home, his own window lay dark, his
daughter asleep in her bed, her world circumscribed to their set
of rooms, the schoolroom, and church on Sundays.

There was a way to live that sat somewhere in between the
two, but Thorne had no idea how to find it.

Checking the lock to see if anyone had disturbed it while he
was out, Thorne entered by the back door. He fell into a protective crouch at the sound of bone crunching bone before the
noise made sense to him. The slow grind of a pestle.

It had to be three o'clock, and Miss Peterson—Lucy—was
still at work.

"I'm hoping that is you, Mr. Thorne, and not anyone else, for
I have no more formulas to steal and no money for a common
thief," she called.

He stood in the doorway and sniffed.

"Fenugreek. It's for new mothers," she said, pausing in her
work. "It makes a lovely tea."

The chill that he'd managed to outwalk crept back into his
bones. The gloom of the darkened room covered them both,
but Thorne felt at peace knowing his daughter was warm and
safe in the rooms above.

When would Lucy reach her bed? After what Duncan Rider
had done to her, would she ever have another untroubled night
of sleep?

Her loneliness was a palpable thing, draped round her like
a shawl, weighted with the responsibilities she carried, the dis-
appointments she'd endured. As he watched her practiced

movements, some of his resentment at her beauty melted away. What use was holding her facial symmetry against her? It hadn't made her life any easier.

Not so far gone as to pity her, certainly Thorne felt some sympathy as he bid her good night.

6

LUCY HAD HER BACK TURNED TO THORNE WHEN HE said his good nights, grinding seeds into a fine powder.

"I hope we didn't disturb you and your daughter earlier," she said. Putting down the pestle, she took a step away from the counter and flexed her fingers, which often cramped after hours spent grinding dried herbs and seeds.

When Thorne did not answer right away, Lucy glanced over her shoulder at him. His large frame took up most of the doorway, letting in only a spear or two of light from the lamp in the corridor behind him. He'd brought the tang of a winter's night in with him, and it mixed with the homey scent of fenugreek and wool, tickling the back of her throat.

"No." When he spoke softly, his voice was the sound of shifting pebbles. There must have been some laryngeal damage earlier in his life. Coupled with his bent nose and scar, Lucy had a good idea of Mr. Thorne's occupation before becoming a "bookkeeper."

"Your hands are clenched."

She turned to face him.

Thorne lifted his arms slightly and stared at his hands as though just noticing them.

"It's the cold," he said.

"Would you like me to look?" she asked without thought.

Why?

He'd been about to leave, which would have been sensible. Lucy would have finished work and perhaps found a few hours of sleep, which also would have been sensible.

Instead, she stood here willing him to step into the room.

Not sensible at all.

Turning up the wick for more light, Lucy kept herself from moving toward Thorne as he tentatively made his way across the room, hesitation in his steps as though he feared the floor couldn't hold him.

The floors would hold, but crossing them meant stepping over the line into a certain familiarity. That knowledge crept up her spine with sharp claws of anticipation.

He came to a stop two feet from her, barely within the circle of light, and held out his hands.

Lucy understood well enough. The next step was hers. She was giddy with exhaustion, but her apothecary training demanded she see beneath his gloves.

For treatment, of course, not for seduction.

"I don't know as I can pull those gloves off you," she said in a brusque tone. "Do it yourself while I turn up the lights."

He made no sound while he complied, and Lucy lit another lamp while calculating how much lamp oil they had left with one part of her brain and running through a list of cures with another part.

"They are ugly," he said.

"They tell a story," she replied.

Now she was presented with them; Lucy took each of his hands in hers and turned them over and over beneath the bright light of her examination lamp.

They were a conundrum, was what they were.

The men who came to the shop had skin as hard as stone, calloused until yellowed and seemingly impenetrable. The tips of Thorne's fingers were rounded and his palms smooth, hinting at a life free of manual labor—other than the labor of boxing, of course.

Lucy held his left hand up and examined the side, the angle of his smallest finger unnatural where he'd fractured his metacarpal, perhaps more than once. Not only his knuckles, but the joints in his fingers between the middle and proximal phalanges were swollen, and he'd broken the right wrist at some point as well.

A nearly imperceptible shudder went through him when she ran her finger up the side of his hand. Lucy kept her eyes stuck on her own hands, not daring to peer up and see whatever expression he wore.

She didn't think he liked her much, but Lucy always knew when a man wanted her.

It kept her safe, that knowledge, because most men were not to be trusted.

"Hurts in the damp and the cold, does it?" she asked, knowing the answer already.

"Helpful when you want to know if it's going to rain," he said.

"Hmmm." She let go of his hands easily enough and went over to a cabinet, stepping on a low stool to reach the ingredients she needed.

Despite her back being turned to him, Lucy knew exactly where he stood in the room and that his gaze was trained between her shoulder blades.

Her heart beat double-time now, and a sweet sting of awareness rose beneath her skin, a flush of need blooming in her
chest. A low thrum of excitement pulsed between Lucy's thighs,
and for a moment she was dizzy. Here she was, blood afire with
the simple touch of his hands to hers.

Oh, but she was unnatural.

Duncan had been right.

Lucy didn't care so much right now. The hour was late, and
she was so cold. The warmth of touch, she craved it like some
men craved opium or some women craved gin. If Thorne saw
through her ruse of treatment and guessed at the need behind
it, she hoped he would only pity rather than despise her.

"I BELIEVE THAT TURMERIC WILL HELP EASE SOME OF THE
swelling about your joints. There's a powder you can put in
your food, but it is expensive. I will give you the root, instead.
Slice a thin piece every night, let it set in boiling water for ten
minutes, and drink."

As though he were any other customer, Lucy wrapped the
brown tuber in a scrap of paper.

"Now, in this jar is an ointment of capsaicin." She held up a
squat glass jar filled with a cloudy pinkish substance. "You
must be careful when you apply, for it stings the eyes and
mouth something terrible if you are clumsy."

Her right eyebrow was more pointed than her left.

Thorne cleared his throat of the tickle left by the dusty smell
of the turmeric while Lucy peered at his misshapen hand.

As she spoke, he concentrated on this second flaw in Lucy's
otherwise perfect face, unable to say why, exactly, it was so important to him. Perhaps because a second flaw allowed for the
existence of a third.

The more flaws, the less attractive he would find her. If Thorne could look at Lucy and see only her flaws, he could let down his guard. At the thought, his shoulders fell, and his head dropped an inch, which meant he caught the faintest hint of lavender water coming from her scalp.

"Are you ready?" she asked.

"Yes?"

Thorne had no idea what Lucy just said. It took all his concentration to keep from showing any sign of arousal at the sight of her forefinger dipping into the ointment and then gently circling his knuckles, one at a time. The hair on his forearms straightened along with his cock as she lightly traced a line of sensation up the back of one finger and down the next, rubbing ever so softly over and over in the space between his fingers.

Imagining his body as carved from stone kept him from trembling when she slowly twined her fingers with his and then pulled away. The ointment made their skin slippery, and everywhere she touched him it burned. The combination of pain and relief as Lucy rubbed her fingers against his made it hard to breathe.

The room around them—the long table filled with dried herbs and jars of oil and alcohol, the shelves stacked with books and piles of parchment, tins of supplies and chemical equipment, the whitewashed walls now yellowed—disappeared until nothing existed except the two of them in a circle of warm light.

Thorne could not take another moment of this torture—the eroticism of her tender touch and the beatific expression on her face, eyes cast down at their entwined hands, bottom lip tucked between her crooked front teeth as she mapped out the tendons and ligaments that held his aching bones together.

As Lucy strengthened her touch, Thorne took back some

control, stroking his thumb across the fleshy pad of her palm beneath her thumb. At her gasp, his cock jerked, and an answering buzz of desire woke at the base of his spine.

Her gaze snapped up to meet his, and Lucy's eyes were dilated, puddles of ink spilled into the blue sea of her irises. His own must be as well, and the ache of pleasure denied pooled in his belly.

She'd paused, her hands still clasping his, her face upturned so that all he had to do was lower his head an inch or two and their lips would meet. Thorne drew the spicy ointment and the smoky scent of lust deep into his lungs, letting his head drop slowly, slowly down toward hers.

Against his thumb, Lucy's pulse sped, an animal trapped beneath a blanket of satiny skin.

Her breath tasted of peppermint tea, and their lips hovered a mere fraction of an inch from the consummation of a kiss. Every muscle in his body had clenched, and his own blood pounded so hard he supposed it could be heard in the next room. When her lips opened slightly, he marveled at the perfect shape of her—

Damn it.

Thorne jerked his head up and stepped away.

"My thanks, Miss Peterson."

"My pleasure, Mr. Thorne."

Casting her eyes downward, Lucy took two steps back and, with trembling fingers, reached for a rag to clean the ointment from her skin. Thorne cleared his throat and executed a small bow, though he knew she wasn't looking.

For the rest of the night and well into the next morning, his hands burned until the cold no longer touched them and all he could feel was a relentless heat.

7

"MAYBE IT WERE FOR A MAGICAL SPELL. DIDN'T BELIEVE crocodiles existed till Mr. Peterson showed me a drawing of one," Katie said.

"I've never seen a drawing of one, but I've read about them," Sadie replied. The two of them stood side by side, peering down into the empty drawer that had once contained crocodile dung.

Although Katie was at least fifteen, she wasn't much taller than Sadie. Thorne watched the two girls speak and cataloged a variety of differences between the two. Alongside the most obvious difference in the color of their skin—Sadie's bronze skin glowed in the low light next to Katie's bluish-white pallor—Sadie was dressed as a young lady of her age, her teeth were straight and white, her diction of the upper classes. Katie, although years older, wore day dresses too short for her spindly legs, hair piled in a topknot like a young woman, but had the same interest in mysterious poo as a girl much younger than her.

Unless it was that all girls had a fascination with poo?

Thorne considered this question as he turned away from the girls and went into the office, staring at the desk.

Someone had gone through the papers last night or early this morning after he and Lucy had gone upstairs, he was sure of it. The lock showed no signs of scratches, so that someone had a key. When he'd opened the door this morning to look for his spectacles, he'd noticed a few papers askew from their neat piles.

"We want to make a good impression with Madame Mensonge," Sadie piped up from behind him. She and Katie must have abandoned the never-boring subject of crocodile scat. The wavering of her voice caught his attention.

Thorne set a hand on her head and tried to think of what to say to put her at ease, but another voice offered consolation.

"Madame Mensonge will be overjoyed to have such a delightful new pupil. And you can be sure that the girls will be nice." Juliet stood in the doorway of the office, regarding Sadie with pleasure.

"Lucy told me you were going to visit the school," she said. "I loved every minute of my time there, and I'm certain you will as well."

Some of the tightness around Sadie's eyes eased, and Thorne cupped her cheek.

"There now, you must listen to Miss Juliet. If any of the girls are not nice, they are not girls you want to be friends with."

"I should change my ribbons."

Thorne could not find voice to make a silly joke about ladies who forever changed their minds when Sadie rushed out of the room.

"I shouldn't have said that about other girls," he said, eyes on the door.

Juliet regarded him in silence until he glanced her way.

"Have girls not always been nice to her?" she asked.

A father always finds his daughters beautiful, or so Thorne assumed, so he allowed that Sadie might not be the prettiest girl in London, but it was close. She was also bright and kind and distressingly adept at guessing other people's feelings.

"It's not enough to counter the prejudice of some against her mixed race, or the fact that I never married her mother," Thorne explained as he finished his recitation of Sadie's attributes.

Tilting her head as though listening to a third voice, Juliet nodded.

"You have the right of it," she said. "Those girls who cannot befriend her are not the girls she needs as friends, but they may be the very girls she wants as friends."

"Girls are hard."

Without a shred of sympathy, Juliet agreed.

Thorne recentered a pile of papers at the corner of the desk and took a chance.

"Did you find the documents you were looking for last night?"

His voice could no longer reach a high enough range to make that sound like an innocent inquiry, and Thorne wasn't surprised when Juliet's eyes narrowed. Foolishly, he'd dropped the facade of bookkeeper and reverted to interrogator too early in their conversation.

"Why does a man who has the face of a brawler also have the diction of a peer?" She countered his question with one of her own.

Formidable. Girls were hard and formidable.

Juliet opened the door with one hand, staring at him over her shoulder. "I am off to the clinic, but when I get back—"

"Oh, Miss Peterson. That burning in my chest is your fault.

You set me aflame with your touch," a man crooned in the shop out front. "Won't you bring me back to your treatment room and . . . quench my fire?"

Thorne quickly followed Juliet out of the office.

A crowd of customers chuckled at the young man who stood before Lucy, holding one hand to his chest while squeezing Lucy's arm with the other.

"Your *flames* are not my fault, but yours," Lucy retorted, pulling at the man's grip.

Thorne started forward but Juliet put a hand to his chest to stop him.

"Let Lucy take care of herself," she said quietly.

Thorne paused at Juliet's order but kept his gaze fixed to where the man touched Lucy.

"I've told you, Mr. Johnson, to spend less time at the pub and more time learning your lines." Any irritation that had been present in Lucy's voice suddenly disappeared, and instead of fighting the young man, she leaned in toward him with a coquettish air.

"Did you not tell me your next role will make you a rival of William Macready? You cannot play Hamlet if you are forever belching and thumping at your chest," Lucy said.

Johnson loosened his grip as he turned to smile at the crowd around him. "Indeed, the opening night of *Hamlet* at the Covent Garden is just next week, and I promise you it will be talked about for years to come. I doubt even Macready could rival my performance as Guildenstern. Mr. Simon Titlinger from the *Times* will be there to review it."

A few of the older women clapped, and one of the younger girls fluttered her eyelashes at him.

"Now, wait your turn, Mr. Johnson, and I will mix you up a tonic. Mind, it won't work if you keep drinking your dinners."

Lucy detached herself from Johnson's hold and smiled benevolently at him.

A tonic. Perhaps that would ease the burning sensation Thorne felt in his own chest as he watched Lucy flirt her way across the crowded floor to help customers in much the same manner as Genny used to carve a path through a party on the few occasions they went out together before he realized that men weren't staring at him with envy, but with avarice—before Thorne understood that nothing he did would ever change Genny's need for attention from a crowd.

"I see Miss Peterson is more than skilled at taking care of herself," he muttered as he turned back to the office, stalking past Juliet and roughly pulling open the top desk drawer in search of his spectacles.

"What is that supposed to mean?" Juliet demanded.

Thorne regarded Juliet, who had followed him inside, hands fisted beneath her fraying cotton gloves.

"Simply that Miss Peterson does not seem to need help when it comes to pleasing her male cust—oof!"

A foot or more shorter than him, Juliet nevertheless had enough momentum to push Thorne back against his desk with her forefinger after bursting across the office.

"What is she supposed to do?" Her voice, low but intense, turned her words into snakes of derision. "What are any of us supposed to do when men become forward and belligerent? Toss them out of the shop?"

Thorne opened his mouth only to emit another *oof* when Juliet poked him a second time.

"Then we earn reputations as shrews, so men who come in are poorly disposed toward us, if they come in at all. We are apothecaries, Mr. Thorne. We must care for our customers— our paying customers—even if they're ill-mannered boors."

"Does no one speak up?" he asked, unable to believe no one would intervene should a man become too forward.

"Of course not. Whether we have earned it or not, women apothecaries are not considered gentlewomen who need protection from boisterous men. We are classed together with shopkeepers and barmaids. Where are you from, Mr. Thorne, that this must needs be explained to you?"

Juliet dropped her finger as Sadie hurried in.

"Do you like these ribbons?" Sadie asked.

Thorne knew that opinions regarding ribbons, no matter how positive, would be met with disbelief, but he still told Sadie they made all the difference in the world.

She sniffed and turned to Juliet.

"Are these the kind the girls at Madame's might wear?" she asked.

Juliet turned Sadie around by the shoulders and made a show of examining the strips of gold silk woven through her braids. One of the braids was crooked, and Thorne longed to fix it, but they were running later than he liked.

"I cannot speak to how the girls wear their hair at Madame's nowadays, but you look pretty. The color suits you."

Thorne nodded his thanks to Juliet as Sadie twirled twice and then pushed him toward the door.

"We must hurry," she reminded him. "Remember Mrs. Merkle always said you have only one chance to make a good first impression."

Indeed, Mrs. Merkle had many sensible sayings, most of which she'd cross-stitched and framed. Still, the humorless little widow had been kind to Sadie and took her influence over the girl seriously.

Outside, someone shouted something, and the crowd joked

in response. Lucy's laugh floated above them like a piece of silk caught in the wind.

Tonic aside, the burning sensation in his chest had subsided somewhat by the time Thorne and Sadie were nearly to the school. It had a name, that sensation, but Thorne would not use it. Nor would he meet Juliet's gaze when he returned to the apothecary, ignoring the censure in her eyes.

Instead, he shut the door to the office, pulled out the oldest of the accounting ledgers, and sank gratefully into the mesmerizing world of double-entry bookkeeping.

LUCY BREATHED IN THE STEAM OF HER TEA WHILE MASsaging her temples. David and Juliet were bickering quietly while doing the washing up, and the sound of their voices plucked at the headache.

She was behind again in the shop. A young mother with a sick child had appeared just as she was closing, her eyes round with fear. Lucy had dropped everything to examine the baby's yellowed eyes and sunken chest, and it didn't look good. The woman had taken the baby to a physician who'd diagnosed unbalanced humors and subjected the baby to a bleeding. Instead of getting better, the child's condition had grown worse.

While Lucy agreed with the diagnosis, she and Juliet were of the mind that children should never be bled. They did not have enough blood to make a difference, and the treatment caused more pain and suffering than it was worth. Lucy had spent precious hours soothing the mother and educating her on keeping the baby well fed and clean.

This was the most difficult part of her work, and the reason she often sent such women to see Juliet at the clinic. Juliet and

Mrs. Sweet were constantly educating themselves about the newest scientific discoveries. Lucy hadn't the time anymore to stay current, and besides that, she had too soft a heart to tell mothers the truth.

The truth was that most apothecaries could give relief from pain but could not cure the diseases that plagued the poor of London. Cholera, typhoid, consumption—while she had a theory as to how these diseases were spread, Lucy had no way to definitively cure them.

Her fellow male students may have had confidence in their skill, but Lucy knew that they were stumbling about in the dark. Women like those of Athena's Retreat were needed to break away from traditional practices and find new treatments.

"I am traveling to Bath tomorrow."

David's announcement dropped like a stone in the kitchen. Juliet made a noise of disbelief, and Lucy stared at her brother, waiting for him to tell her it was a joke.

"What do you mean?" Lucy asked when David continued drying dishes as though he'd said nothing of import. "You cannot go to Bath. Juliet just said at dinner she might well be staying over at the clinic for the rest of the week. How am I to run the shop?"

David flashed his smile that had lured countless men and women into his orbit, but his sisters were immune. Still, the way he tipped his head and hitched the smile up on the left to create an extra dimple was second nature to David, and he persisted, even knowing it wouldn't help.

"Lucy."

Lucy's teeth ached at the false sweetness in his tone. David leaned against the sink and threw the damp cloth over his shoulder.

"I've told you I have a business opportunity."

"Can you at least give us some details? Opportunity. What does that mean?" Juliet pulled the cloth from David's shoulder and dried her hands.

"It means nothing is final," David replied. The self-conscious smile fell away from his face as he straightened, genuine pleasure lighting his ocean-blue eyes. "I'm so close, though. Let me wait until I'm certain to show you, show everyone what I can do."

His voice broke on the last word, and a wave of resentment flooded through Lucy. Why had her father left the apothecary to her, the oldest, instead of to his son? If only he'd lived longer or written a letter with an explanation.

David believed Papa had found him a disappointment. He'd had no desire to apprentice at the apothecary, and instead loved socializing and thinking up ways to make money. Neither of their parents had been comfortable with David's fluid attraction to men and women and found his interest in money to be somewhat sinful. Whatever ideas David came up with to increase revenue, his father would immediately dismiss.

"We are not here to profit, we are here to serve," their father would say.

Easy to say when times were good and folks had coin. Since their parents' death, the poor of the East End were growing poorer. Families who could no longer make a living from crafting or farming had streamed into London. They lived six, seven, sometimes ten to a room in sickness-filled tenements, and when faced with spending a spare pence to quell a pain, were more likely to spend it on a cup of gin than an ounce or two of tonic.

In the beginning, David had been determined to help the apothecary grow, but unlike Juliet and Lucy, he had no affinity for medicine. While he could persuade a housewife to buy an impractical ointment for the wrinkles beneath her eyes, he did not have the stomach to listen to that same woman describe the fungus between her toes.

As his attention toward the apothecary had waned, he'd taken to hanging round the coffee shops near the London Exchange, listening to the plans of daring financiers and thrill-seeking adventurers.

Men who thought well of him. Unlike their father.

Lucy's guilt left her mute, and David accepted her silence as his due. Juliet, practically asleep on her feet, let the matter rest as well. What good would come of their circular arguments? David could leave tomorrow, and no one would fault him.

A man needed a purpose, their father had told them. Why he'd left his son without one was a mystery.

Once again, Lucy spent the haunch of the night in her workspace, stopping every so often when she heard a creak on the stairs or the floorboards above.

She was waiting, of course, like a fool.

Thorne had not spoken to her today.

After he returned from dropping Sadie at school, he'd burrowed himself in the dusty ledgers and didn't come out until it was time to fetch the girl back again. Lucy had greeted the duo on their return, and Sadie was happy enough to tell her about the amazements to be found in Madame's classrooms. While they did not have glass eyeballs, there were cages full of mice and jars filled with preserved pig organs.

As Sadie described the contents of the jars in depth, Lucy tried catching Thorne's eye, but he deliberately looked anywhere except at her.

He must be disgusted with her.

She'd practically thrown herself into his arms last night, driven by her need for comfort and spurred on even more by the dark magnetism that hovered over him.

The rest of her sleepless night and throughout the day, irritants like that blowhard Johnson bothered Lucy more than usual, and she'd started to second-guess her treatment of the jaundiced baby. Over dinner, Juliet had listened and agreed with the treatment, but what if Lucy had missed a clue in her examination? Had she balanced the mother's expectations with enough compassion and honesty?

"There is a crate in the hallway by the back door. Do you need it moved?"

So far gone into her worries, Lucy hadn't heard Thorne's approach.

She turned around, her hands clasped in front of her chest as though her body had already made the decision to plead with him to come closer.

No more than a second passed before her hands fell to her sides, the slight disdain on Thorne's face leaving her limp and cold.

"Please do not worry yourself over it. David said he would do it before he leaves on a journey tomorrow. You are not here to perform the tasks of a shop boy, Mr. Thorne."

Was her tone light enough? Her limp smile convincing?

Thorne remained standing. Unable to translate his silence, Lucy turned back around to the mess in front of her, pretending to be fascinated by it.

"Where is your brother going?"

A sigh escaped her. "Bath."

"Who will help you with the shop?"

This time she held her breath, keeping her shoulders from sagging even more.

"Katie Quinlavin will be here, of course. We will manage just fine together," she said to him. "She has a way with the rowdier customers. It helps that her father is well-known in the neighborhood as a hothead, so most folk won't push too far with her for fear of him. And she's a hard worker despite her aversion to certain bodily fluids."

The girl was smart as well as confident. Her weak stomach left her without any desire to apprentice as an apothecary, but she was quick with sums and understood the basics of chemistry and botany. Both Lucy and Juliet had tried to convince Katie's father to send her to an academy in Yorkshire for gifted girls, but he needed her help supporting the family. Lucy suspected that Katie didn't press him on it because she was being courted by a young man with a steady job at the docks.

Someday, Katie would learn that, unlike men, an education stayed with you forever.

Thorne leaned back as though pushed by an invisible wind, then lurched forward. His hands had been in his coat pockets, and now he drew them out for her to examine. Lucy's heart stuttered a confused rhythm of back and forth.

"The capsaicin," he said. "It helps."

She reached for his hands without removing her gaze from his face, desperate to see behind his rigid jaw and slight scowl.

Thorne scowled *a lot*.

Some stupid, girlish part of her brain found that attractive.

This was why Lucy had no time for biology. The whys of such primordial urges were lost on her. Chemistry was the only science that made sense. You bring two elements together and create a third. What you put in comes out in another form.

Fascinating.

Men?

Just plain confusing. For example, why might his scent of wool and paper, and a hint of the November winds he'd been walking through outside, make her head spin and bring a flush to her cheeks?

Embarrassed at the carnal direction of her thoughts once again, Lucy examined his hands. The swelling had gone down, revealing more of the bones beneath the skin.

"Did you perhaps punch rocks for a living before working at Tierney's?" she asked.

The scratchy rumbling coming from his chest must have been a chuckle, because a tiny smile flitted across his face.

"Men who choose to fight as a profession are stupid," he said. "It makes sense that our heads are hard as rocks, for that's what fills them."

The low light cast him in shadow, leaving only the tiniest glint in his eyes as a hint that he watched her. The wash of darkness softened his chin and made his cheeks appear gaunt, giving him a hungry look. A shiver rolled down her spine and curled itself between her thighs.

"Did you ever fight here in London?" she asked.

He flinched. "Once or twice."

Lucy squeezed his hands quickly, then stepped back. "I'm sorry. I shouldn't have pried."

Thorne stared at his hands, then at her. "Folks recognize me now and again. Not so much these days." He shrugged, the rustle of cloth against his back the only sound except their breath. "Up until now my assignments haven't put me in company with the sort who frequent prizefights. If I am to investigate Duncan Rider, I suppose I should be ready."

Two thoughts warred with each other as Lucy reflected on his words, so she allowed Thorne to choose which to answer or deflect depending on his mood.

"Duncan is the sort who goes to prizefights? Were you famous?"

He peered past her shoulder, then walked over to the counter and bent to smell the mixture she'd almost finished.

"I've been talking to the merchants on the same street as Rider and Son. Duncan has made good money from his lozenges and along the way acquired an introduction to a set of young aristocrats with more money than brains," Thorne said. "Would you say he was a gambler?"

"Oh, yes," Lucy answered. "There is nothing Duncan enjoys more than taking a risk."

For wasn't that the draw when he used his kisses to get her to agree to lie with him four months ago? The idea that someone could—and eventually did—walk in on them was exciting for him. So exciting he'd made promises to her that he'd no intention of keeping.

When she'd confronted him, Duncan repeated the sort of nonsense he'd heard from the Guardians. Lucy was not the sort of woman a man *married*. Not once she'd given her virtue away. Especially not since she'd *enjoyed* it.

"I was famous enough in my time." Thorne answered her second question. "That's in my past."

How she longed to pry him open and see inside his head to his secrets. Carrying himself with the surety of a man who had won and lost important fights and learned something each time, Thorne moved through space as though he wore an invisible extra layer of protection. A buffer between himself and the petty hurts of the world.

How many times must one fall to learn to stand so straight and uncompromising?

"David taught me to punch once," she confided. "My littlest finger was swollen for two weeks. You are lucky you still have the mobility in the joints that you do."

He stared at his hands with a hint of disbelief, turning them over and over as if searching for the lie in her words.

"I was tempted to try a punch today and risk a broken finger," she muttered.

Thorne's head snapped up, and one of his scowls graced his face.

Those scowls would be the death of her.

"Was it that actor this morning?" he asked.

"Oh, Johnson?" She waved the thought away. "His sort is simple to manage. You appeal to their ego and encourage them to talk about themselves."

The jaundiced baby and her undernourished mother were still taking up space in Lucy's head. The physician who bled the child should have given the mother a more honest estimation of the outcome; instead it was left to Lucy. She wanted to tell Thorne about it, confide her worries and see if his scowl might render them impotent.

"There was . . ." Lucy's voice thinned to nothing at Thorne's expression.

Cold.

Remote.

Uninterested.

Would she ever grow out of the childish notion that a man could want her mind before he wanted her body?

"I have wasted too much time," she said abruptly, then resumed her work. The camphor stung her eyes, and she inhaled the scent of wounding and healing. "Good night, Mr. Thorne."

His retreating voice rolled along the floorboards and crept up her ankles to her spine.

"Good night, Lucy."

8

—⟨⟨⟨◆⟩⟩⟩—

THE THIN BLOND CLERK AT THE PATENT OFFICE HAD AN underbite that gave him the look of a man unfulfilled and forever searching out something better.

That particular piece of fancy drifted through Thorne's head as he thanked the clerk for his time. The clerk could not be bothered with a response. He simply sniffed with disdain as if Thorne, too, had somehow disappointed him.

No new medicinal patents had been filed since the roaring success of Rider's Lozenges, a red-and-white tin of which sat on the clerk's desk beside a cup of tea gone scummy. After leaving the patent office, Thorne reviewed the list he'd made of apothecaries large enough to manufacture Lucy's croup salve in large doses.

For two days, he visited apothecaries across London. Beginning with Rider's, he spiraled out through the capital, inquiring at each establishment whether they had a cure for croup. He'd learned that there were as many opinions on how to cure croup as there were stars in the sky.

There were also entirely different means of measurements in these places.

When Lucy gave him a list of what she believed had constituted her croup salve ingredients, Thorne had been taken aback to find teacups, wineglasses, and even breakfast cups were universally accepted computations. In addition to these common-sense measurements, he learned about drachms and scruples, both fluid and solid, as well as minims.

Some apothecaries were little more than opium dens, continuing in the tradition of pharmaceutical "quackery" that plagued apothecaries in the last century.

Since the Society of Apothecaries was granted permission in 1815 to establish a professional system of education and registration, standards had become more rigorous in most instances.

None of the apothecaries he visited offered Thorne a salve with similar ingredients to those Lucy had told him were in hers. Whoever had taken the formula for Lucy's salve was keeping it to themselves for now.

Thorne had compiled a list of suspects, and while it made sense to continue investigating Rider and other rival apothecaries, he also needed to rule out David Peterson. Thorne didn't fully trust the handsome young man who swanned about the shop entertaining customers rather than applying himself to accounting—no matter that he was Lucy's brother. While there had been periods of fastidious recordkeeping and budgeting, everything had been neglected in the past three months, resulting in a tangled mass of debts and payments that led to more questions than answers.

What was this business opportunity David was willing to abandon Lucy for? Did it have anything to do with the three large payments he'd clandestinely made to a Mr. W. R. Wilcox that Thorne had uncovered yesterday with no corresponding invoice? Wilcox was not an uncommon name, but Thorne had sent word to Winthram to see if he might find something out.

He was now approaching their designated meeting location. ·

"*Dinoponera gigantea*?" Voices floated from behind the front door.

"Yes, sir."

"Gigantic . . . ?"

"Ants. Giant ants."

"Jesus, give me strength."

Thorne knocked on the half-opened door and stuck his head inside the library of Beacon House, the home of Arthur and Violet Kneland. The cozy chamber held a large polished wooden desk, and by a small fire sat two men, one much younger than the other.

"Mr. Thorne. Thank you for meeting me here." Winthram stood and ushered Thorne into the room, pulling a chair over so that Thorne could join them. Kneland rose as well and gave Thorne his hand.

A cart sat to the side, and Winthram poured tea and filled a plate with shortbread. Thorne accepted both and closed his eyes with pleasure—the shortbread at Beacon House tasted like lemons and contentment.

Behind the house, there once was a series of outbuildings and a small courtyard. Violet Kneland, the former Lady Greycliff, used her first husband's money to convert those outbuildings into workshops and corridors that led to the building directly behind them on the next street over.

Thorne had been to the public rooms of Athena's Retreat when he came to interview young Winthram about working for Tierney & Co. He had never been invited into the secret part of Athena's Retreat, the back laboratories and meeting rooms where the women scientists did their work.

From the stories Winthram told, Thorne did not feel envious. He hated explosions.

And chickens.

Explosions and chickens gave him heartburn.

"And Grey said yes to these giant ants living in the root cellar?" Kneland asked Winthram, continuing the conversation they'd begun before Thorne knocked.

Winthram nodded. "It was after Miss Fenley agreed to marry him. Lord Greycliff became . . .

Kneland harrumphed. "Lost his mind is what happened."

"More lenient with the members," Winthram finished.

"Are you saying there are giant ants in the root cellar of Beacon House right now?" Thorne asked.

Winthram smiled weakly while Kneland made another vague noise and frowned. Kneland had an intimidating visage, and Thorne did not forget that as a former protection officer and counter-assassin, the man had spent twenty years guarding some of the world's most unpleasant men in some of its most dangerous places.

"I'll take care of it," Kneland said. He shifted in his seat and examined Thorne. "You are working the Peterson case? Violet was upset when she heard the news about Duncan Rider stealing Miss Peterson's formula."

"He did steal it, didn't he?" Winthram asked. "Or was Miss Peterson mistaken?"

Thorne saw Rider once again in his mind's eye—the vapid smile and guileless blue eyes.

"I'm certain he stole her formula for the lozenges," Thorne

said. "As to whether he has also stolen the formula for the salve, I have my doubts. They are no longer intimate, and Rider does not have the same access to her work as he once had."

His voice remained steady as he relayed these facts.

Why wouldn't it?

It wasn't as though Thorne had any claim on Lucy. Not as if he would ever *act* on the growing attraction he had for the woman. It would be akin to allowing himself to drink a single beer again. One would turn into two, and if he had a beer, he might as well have a glass of wine. And if there was wine available, he may as well open a bottle of whiskey.

The same would happen with Lucy. One touch would become a night that would turn to two, and before you know it, Thorne would have chased the woman down the same path he'd chased Genny. For weren't they both the same, how they flattered the men around them to get what they wanted?

Even as that last thought formed, Thorne knew comparing the two women was unfair, but he was unable to stop.

For all the years he'd let himself get knocked down and beat bloody, he'd never known a pain like the heartache and betrayal he'd felt when he'd come home from a tour of Europe after eight months and found that Genny had left. A heart was the center of a body. Once it had been wounded, a man lived forever the slightest bit off-kilter. Like his other scars, the wound ached late at night in the cold and the dark. Unlike his other injuries, there was no cure for such pain.

"This croup salve," Kneland said. "Would it be as profitable as the lozenges?"

Thorne wrenched his attention back to the men in the library and breathed deep the comforting scents of sugar and bootblack.

"Yes," Thorne answered. "Miss Juliet Peterson told me that although putrid throat is more common than croup, parents are willing to pay almost anything to comfort a croupy baby."

A distant thud sounded in the background, and the ceiling above them shivered, setting the hanging oil lamps to swinging slightly back and forth. Thorne opened his mouth, then closed it again when neither Winthram nor Kneland reacted.

"I hope you don't mind I have inserted myself into your case," said Kneland. "Winthram and I were just going over how to narrow your search for your mysterious Mr. Wilcox."

Thorne did not mind at all. The affection between Kneland and the younger man was obvious, and he wouldn't say no to a third mind as sharp as Kneland's. Winthram and Kneland were enjoyable company, like-minded men who could talk without the temptation of a pint glass or the need to prove themselves to an ex-prizefighter.

Thorne helped himself to another shortbread, and they discussed checking the Worshipful Society of Apothecaries membership lists in case the thief was a fellow member.

When Thorne explained his suspicions around David's three mysterious payments, they agreed that Winthram would befriend a clerk at the Petersons' bank to see what he could find out about David's financial activities.

"Such a friendship will be useful in the future," Kneland said. "Remember, a true friendship is based on mutual need."

Thorne grunted. "Be careful, though. A close friend can easily become a close enemy."

"The two of you are curmudgeons," Winthram teased. "Did you go to the same school? The Academy of Taciturn Men? Took honors in scowls and black stares of impending doom, did you?"

Kneland's face remained frozen. "Who told you about the academy?"

Winthram's grin wobbled, and he swung his glance to Thorne, hoping for support.

"Feck." Thorne shook his head slowly. "Suppose we'll have to kill him now."

"No one is killing anyone today," a woman's voice announced. "I have just had the carpets cleaned. Hello, Winthram."

Violet Kneland, Arthur's wife, and the president of Athena's Retreat, entered with a beatific smile that lit the room more brightly than the fire and desk lamps combined.

"Cook wants to see you," she told Winthram. "Mind you, Alice is only home from the academy for a week, so go find her and say your goodbyes."

At the mention of Alice, pink streaks appeared on Winthram's cheeks. Awkwardly he took his leave but stopped in the doorway and turned to face them.

"The two of you were joking. Right?" he asked. "About the school?"

Kneland said nothing, but Thorne asked, "Who is Alice?"

Winthram disappeared.

"You tease him too much," Violet chastised Kneland as she poured herself a cup of tea and sat in the chair Winthram had just vacated.

"The lad can take it," Kneland told his wife. "He gives it right back."

"Hmmm." Instead of arguing, Violet Kneland turned her eyes toward Thorne.

"Winthram speaks highly of you, Mr. Thorne. I'm happy someone is helping Lucy Peterson get justice."

Thorne shook his head apologetically. "I am not charged

with delivering justice—that is a matter for a magistrate to consider. I have simply been tasked to find proof this latest formula has been stolen." Thorne shifted in his seat and regarded Violet Kneland. Before she'd married a second time, she had done some work for the government at the request of her former stepson, Lord William Greycliff. Despite her obvious affection for Lucy, her insight would be helpful in his search.

"In your opinion, Mrs. Kneland, is Miss Peterson's work worth the risk of theft? These lozenges, they cure putrid throats? This salve, would it be effective?"

Violet set down her teacup and smiled. "My guess is that any formula Lucy Peterson develops would be effective."

As she spoke, she laid her arm protectively over her abdomen. Kneland, noticing the gesture, leaned in toward his wife and put a hand on her shoulder.

"I'm fine, dear. Just indigestion." Violet waved Kneland away, but his gaze remained on the hand over her belly.

"Whether she is able to patent her salve or not, it is vital she keep the apothecary open," Violet continued. "Lucy, Juliet, and Mrs. Sweet are better healers than most of the physicians in London—even the ones who line Harley Street with their polished brass signs and their—"

Kneland cleared his throat and Violet stopped speaking. She glanced at her husband and laughed. "I beg your pardon, Mr. Thorne. I was about to subject you to a well-rehearsed rant about the willful ignorance of British physicians, their myopic refusal to allow women in their ranks, and how we suffer for it."

Thorne remembered what Lucy had said the first time he saw the state of her office. Peterson's was the only apothecary on the east side of London that did not offer quick cures of opium and gin.

Before he took his leave, Thorne asked both husband and

wife one more question. Were the Guardians a true threat to the Petersons' business?

"Very dangerous," Kneland answered. "If the Guardians are setting their sights on Peterson's Apothecary and the St. Giles clinic, you will have an entirely different problem on your hands."

He settled back in his chair, and Violet's smile faded as she nodded in agreement.

"A group of men who can't bear to see women in power is always a threat," Violet said. "Please, watch out for the Petersons, Mr. Thorne."

"MADAME SAYS THE HALLMARK OF A SMALL MIND IS THE unwillingness to admit a fault."

Lucy turned around on her stool as Juliet and Sadie walked into the back workroom, midconversation.

"Madame has plenty of opinions on small minds," Juliet said. She nodded hello to Lucy and set a hand on Sadie's shoulder. "I received word that Mr. Thorne will be back late, and he asked me to walk Miss Thorne home from school. Katie seems busy out there."

Lucy set down her half-eaten pasty and rose to leave, but Juliet gestured that she should stay.

"I have time to help out front. Besides, sister, if you do not eat, you will get sick and be of no use to anyone." Juliet smiled over at Sadie. "Miss Thorne can keep you company and tell you about what she's learned from Madame Mensonge."

Lucy swallowed her bite of pasty and opened her mouth to object, but Juliet had already left. Two pasties remained on the greased paper in front of her. If Thorne would not be home until later, who would feed the girl? Could she mind herself until her father returned? What did one talk about with a nine-year-old girl?

Ten minutes later, Lucy had yet to speak, as she learned that one did not have to talk to nine-year-olds, they did the talking for you. Sadie spoke as though the words poured directly from her brain out of her mouth while she stared at Lucy's pasties.

"Madame Mensonge says my arithmetic is good enough, but I must work extra hard to catch up in the mathematics necessary for physics and chemistry. She also said I could take home any book from her library so long as I ask first and return it in good condition. Did you know that frogs shed their skin and then eat it?"

Lucy said nothing for a moment until she understood that this question had not been rhetorical.

"Er, yes. I remember something about this from Madame's lessons in zoology."

Actually, Lucy had tried to block those memories out. Frogs disgusted her.

Sadie nodded. "Miss Peterson," she said thoughtfully. "How old were you by the time you learned everything you know about botany and chemistry and physics?"

Lucy pushed the last pasty in Sadie's direction.

"I cannot finish my meal and it would be a shame to waste it. Won't you share with me?"

Sadie clasped her hands in a graceful manner. "Thank you so much. I adore pasties."

Lucy scratched her chin as the girl bit into the greasy pastry pouch stuffed with potatoes, onion, and some sort of meat.

"Are you . . . ?" Did Thorne not feed his child? Why, she'd downed the pasty in three bites. "Are you often this hungry?" she asked.

Guilt crossed the girl's face as she reached into her reticule for a handkerchief to dab the corners of her mouth.

"Well, it's only that Papa does not think pasties a proper meal. He never lets me eat from pie shops because he cannot be certain of the quality of ingredients. Also, he says too much lard is bad for one's digestion."

Pasties were Lucy's favorite lunch. She'd never once questioned the quality of the ingredients, and searched out the pie shops that used a liberal hand with the lard.

"One time, he was a bookkeeper for the sister of a man who disappeared," Sadie said, pulling a stool over and setting herself beside Lucy at the worktable. "The man's wife owned a pie shop, and I don't know what she used, but Papa came home the first day with his face turned all white and gray and said no more pasties." She lowered her voice to a whisper. "No more pasties. *Ever.*"

Lucy cleaned up the crumbs and paper while Sadie spun around on the smooth seat of the stool and gazed at the shelves and cabinets that lined the room.

Lucy may have lost the ability to sleep through the night, but for once she wished to be awake in the comfort of her bed rather than bent over her worktable. She was too busy to entertain a child, and hadn't she resolved to have little to do with the girl?

She hadn't been in the Thornes' apartment since they moved in. Were there enough candles? Coals for the fire when the night grew cold? Only Thorne and his daughter lived in those rooms.

Lucy couldn't remember a time she'd been completely alone. If she wasn't in the shop, she was in her rooms or at the pub with her siblings. What would it be like to go home to emptiness?

No matter. Lucy had too much work, and children were a nuisance. The girl needed to leave.

"I have three more orders I must finish," she said to Sadie. "If you do not like to be alone, you may sit and do your studies back here."

"Thank you, Miss Peterson." Sadie swung her satchel onto the table and pulled out a frayed copy of Samuel Gross's *The Anatomy, Physiology, and Diseases of the Bones and Joints.*

Lucy said nothing and turned back to her worktable.

Why had she made the offer?

Why couldn't she stick to her resolve?

This same flaw was why she did not object to David's odd comings and goings with his "business venture." Why she did not insist Juliet stay and work at the shop more often instead of treating the women of St. Giles for free. This was what got her into trouble every time—why Duncan had been able to get his hands on her formula, and why Mr. Gentry spent hours in her office discussing the color and scent of his urine and whether it meant he was anemic.

"Lucy, Mr. Gentry is here and would like a word."

Oh, dear.

Juliet had popped her head in to deliver the message and raised her eyebrows at the sight of Sadie sitting at the far table reading her book. "Hullo, Sadie. Working back here with Lucy, are you?"

Sadie glanced up, a fine line appearing between her eyebrows. "If that's all right?"

Juliet waved her hand. "Of course, dear. Now, if you have any trouble with anatomy, do not ask Lucy. She is a proper idiot when it comes to memorization and is likely to tell you the tibia is found in the rib cage."

"Unfair." Lucy crossed her arms and huffed. "If you need

help with your physics, Sadie, be sure not to ask Juliet for help, or she'll . . . she's very . . ."

Lucy searched for a witty comeback, but it was too late. Juliet was already pulling her head out of the door.

"Don't worry, Mr. Gentry, Lucy will be out soon, and you are her first priority," Juliet said loudly.

"She really isn't good at physics," Lucy told the girl.

Sadie clasped her hands beneath her chin, a huge grin on her face. "You were teasing each other," she said.

"Well, that's what sisters do," Lucy said. The moment the words left her mouth, she wished she could take them back, for Sadie's smile dimmed.

"It must be wonderful to have both a brother and a sister," the girl said.

Hmmm. What to say? The truth?

"Like anything, there are good parts and not-so-good parts." Lucy thought about David and Juliet, what life would be like without them and added, "The good parts outweigh the not-so-good parts. Most of the time."

The girl fiddled with her book, aligning it with the side of the table, then turning it around and flipping it over while her eyebrows lowered and raised, as though she were having a conversation with herself.

Lucy admired that. Oneself was always a good source of wisdom.

"Mrs. Merkle says having many children is evidence of the Lord's blessing."

Lucy opened her mouth, then shut it. Having helped Juliet in the women's clinic many times, she'd seen exactly what having many children did to a woman who could not afford healthy food and had no husband. *Blessing* was not the word she would use. This wasn't something she could say to a child, however.

Instead, she asked, "Who is Mrs. Merkle? She sounds sure she knows what pleases God."

"Oh, she does," Sadie said a tad wistfully. "She was going to marry Papa, but someone gave her a house instead."

Marry Thorne? A woman who believed a large family to be a sign of God's approval? Questions clamored in her head, and though her cures sat unmixed, Lucy rose and joined Sadie at the table, burning with curiosity about the enigmatic man.

"Was your father sad to be thrown over for a house?" Lucy asked.

A rosebud of a smile appeared on the girl's face, and the worry about what lay on the workbench left Lucy as she watched the girl's expressive face change with each fact she imparted.

"I would have been more insulted on his behalf, but the house is by the seaside," Sadie confessed. "Houses by the sea are always in the novels Papa and I read. I would give up a husband for a house by the sea. Especially if it was haunted or a mad duke was locked in the attic."

Neither of those scenarios appealed to Lucy in the slightest. Then again, she'd never read a novel, considering them a waste of time.

"Did he love her very much?" Lucy asked, her voice low. She knew it was inappropriate to pry, but the question begged to be asked. The man was such a cipher. What kind of woman would seize his attentions? "Is she beautiful?"

Sadie shook her head and folded her fingers together, placing them atop the book. "Papa says outward beauty doesn't matter; what's in your heart is important. His favorite verse is from the first book of Samuel, 'The Lord seeth not as man seeth; for man looketh on the outward appearance, but the Lord looketh on the heart.'"

The girl sighed. "I was going to do a cross-stitch sampler of it, but Mrs. Merkle moved before we could start it together. Do you do cross-stitch, Miss Peterson?"

"I do not," she told the girl. "The only time I use a needle and thread is to stitch up a wound."

A curious gleam lit in Sadie's eyes. "Doesn't the needle make more blood? Do people scream when you do it?"

What Lucy should be doing was mixing her cures and helping Juliet out front. Or encouraging Sadie to read her textbook or pursue her cross-stitch plans. She should go see what ailed Mr. Gentry today before he came back here for her.

Instead, Lucy opened the anatomy book to the detailed etchings of the epidermal system and answered Sadie's every question about stitches and debridement.

Because sometimes women deserved to have fun.

9

―‹‹‹◆›››―

"YOUR FORMULAS ARE NOT IN THIS OFFICE."

Two days after Thorne sought aid from Arthur Kneland, he sat in the office, leaning back in his chair and appearing awfully proud of himself. He called her away from a customer and said he had something important to tell her, then ushered her into a chair in the office as if he'd solved the case. *This* was why he'd called Lucy just as she was going to sneak away for a bite to eat? It was half four and she hadn't had more than a piece of bread this morning.

"I *know* my formulas are not in the office, Mr. Thorne. That is why I am paying for your 'bookkeeping' services. I have hired you to find out who stole them."

Lucy wiped her hands down the front of her treatment coat. Today had been exhausting; she'd removed three cysts, reset a broken ankle, and conducted two tooth extractions.

In addition, the young woman with the jaundiced baby had returned, and while the baby seemed to be getting better, it was not as rapid a recovery as Lucy would have liked to see. She sent word to Juliet at the clinic that she should stop by the woman's house on her way home and double-check that Lucy had made the correct diagnosis.

Thorne's face remained expressionless, and Lucy wished there were some magic combination of words that would unlock him for her edification.

Lucy wanted to know his secrets.

She wanted to upend him the same way he roiled her peace and made her want what she shouldn't have. If Thorne kept taunting her with his scowls and rumbly voice and large, broad chest, Lucy wished to roil his peace right back.

So what if he didn't mean to make her a pudding-head with a simple glance? Lucy could not ignore his presence. The thought struck her that perhaps there was some chemical attraction happening, something on an invisible level she might explain away.

"I will tell you what I have found, however," Thorne said.

Gathering a deep breath, Lucy then let loose a sigh intended to communicate she had better things to do than stand here and stare at his compelling face.

"What *did* you find?" she asked.

"You are being cheated."

Lucy put a hand on the desk to steady herself, a cold tingling starting in the tips of her fingers. She must have misheard.

"I beg your pardon?"

Cheated?

"Do you know how much the apothecary has spent on calomel this month?" Thorne asked.

Lucy stared at the chair opposite the desk from him and took a seat.

Cheated.

"I . . ." Lucy cleared her throat. "Don't we order it from Denton Brothers? They were friends with my father. I can't believe Abel Denton would cheat us."

Proof, she supposed, of her family's gullibility and mismanagement.

Nothing to do with her formulas, however.

Thorne straightened the stack of papers in front of him. Tapping the top of the first page, he then pushed it over to her side of the desk so that she could read it.

"Hopper's?" she read aloud. "I don't know them."

"Sometime in the last year, David made the decision to switch to Hopper's. You pay the same amount each week, but Hopper's only delivers two-thirds of the calomel that Denton Brothers had."

"Well, David simply made a mistake. All we have to do is switch back to Denton's and—"

Thorne tapped his finger at the top of the next invoice. "Do you know where you get your turmeric and coriander seeds?"

"Patel's Trading Company. That hasn't changed, because Mr. Patel's aunt, Mrs. Parekh, was just in here the other day and she would have said something."

Thorne again slid the crumpled receipt toward her. "You still order from Patel's Trading Company, yes. The same amount of money is paid, but you now receive two-thirds the amount you once did. It is David's name on these receipts."

Lucy couldn't grasp hold of the thoughts flying through her head, and she tried to rationalize. "Prices have gone up in London, and—"

"There are four more like this. Do you know Mr. W. R. Wilcox?"

"Mr. who? What has this to do with the price of turmeric?"

In between his bookkeeping, Thorne had cleaned the office.

The ledgers sat in order on the newly dusted shelves. Mrs. Parekh's tiny neem sapling rested on the corner of the desk, waiting to be delivered to its new home. He'd even changed the oil in the lamp and replaced the wick so that it no longer sputtered and stank.

Tidying his physical surroundings while upending the people in his path.

Lucy hated him a little in that moment.

"If you—"

She left the office while he was still speaking, and closed the door quietly behind her. Katie was chatting with Mr. Gentry, and two matrons gossiped in the corner. Everything seemed so blessedly normal out here. If only Lucy would send Thorne away, everything would go back to before.

When one of the matrons opened the door to leave, the sounds of men shouting came into the shop.

"Whores!"

"Witches!"

"We know who you are. We know what you do!"

The ugliness of the words and the rage with which they were shouted jolted Lucy out of her stupor.

Katie came out from behind the counter to have a look.

"Come away from the door," Lucy said, pulling the shopgirl back from the exit.

Shocked, Katie stumbled back into her arms just as Juliet, David, and Sadie hurried inside. David turned to shut the door, and Lucy could see a group of a dozen or more men outside holding wooden signs with slogans painted on them.

WHEN MEN LOSE WAGES, WOMEN LOSE FAMILIES

STAY HOME AND STAY PURE

CLOSE YOUR LEGS AND CLIMB TO HEAVEN

ABORTIONISTS ARE MURDERERS

"What is— Sadie?" Thorne rushed out of the office to his daughter, running his hands over her cheeks and down her shoulders, eyes roving his child's body in search of any injury.

"Fecking Guardians," David hissed. He'd lost his topper, and his thick hair was windblown. Red smears of anger stained his cheeks. "I just returned from Bath, then fetched Juliet when they came to the clinic. Why did you speak to them, Sniffles?" he asked Juliet. "We could have gone right past and not—"

Juliet shook with anger or fear or a combination of both. Her skin was pale, and her large eyes glistened with unshed tears.

Definitely anger. Lucy had never seen her sister cry for any other reason.

"I will not be called names nor made to feel shame for what I do," Juliet said, her voice high and thin. "I won't be screamed at for having a brain or caring—"

All the dread Lucy had felt since Thorne's disclosure, the fear she'd known when she saw the men's angry faces outside, now burned away in a conflagration of rage.

Sadie stood in her father's embrace, her bonnet pushed back and forehead against his broad chest. David ran his fingers through his hair, breathing heavily and shaking his head.

These were her people. Lucy was responsible for them while they lived beneath her roof.

This could not stand.

Throwing open the door, Lucy stomped out onto the wooden walkway and shook her fist at the men who milled about, no longer shouting but still holding their signs aloft.

"What would your *mothers* say if they saw you screaming at defenseless women and children in the street?" Lucy shouted at them.

A few of the signs lowered, and the two men in front stared at each other.

One man with a gray patched beard came forward.

"She'd say those women ought to stay home and sin no more," he called out.

A few of the other men murmured their agreement, but one man put down his sign and dropped his head.

"I think she'd be ashamed of you," Lucy told him.

Gray Patch did not appear convinced but took a step backward when someone exited the shop behind her.

"Get out." Thorne's words were uttered without emotion, although Lucy could feel the heat emanating from Thorne's body as he stepped to her side and his hands clenched into fists.

A young man toward the front with close-set eyes scoffed. "Who is going to make us?" he called.

Thorne took two steps off the walkway and into the street. Once out of the shadow of the awning covering the front of the apothecary, his face became visible.

"Lads," Gray Patch said, voice shaking. "Lads, that's—"

"Get out," Thorne repeated at the same volume but with greater intensity. "I have memorized every one of your faces. If I see you again here, there will be trouble."

The young man at the front made a sound of derision, but someone behind him shoved him in the back. "Shut yer gob, Jemmy."

Gray Patch took off his felted cap and squinted up at Thorne. "Cor. 'Tis you for sure. I saw you fight Dunder Folkes in Clerkenwell. Never seen a man fight like that 'afore. Your fists were faster 'n lightning."

Thorne articulated his words so they sounded like bricks hitting the cobbles on the street. "Then you know to heed my warning."

Gray Patch nodded, but Jemmy wouldn't be dissuaded. "Who are you, old man? You've a face that not even a mother could love."

Jemmy was the only one who laughed. The crowd of men around him melted away and left him alone. His beady little eyes narrowed as he swung his head around, then back at Thorne.

"Ask your friend who I am," Thorne said. "Then ask him, did the man I fought that day die?"

Gray Patch didn't have to say anything; the pallor of his skin and shaking of his hands gave the answer for him.

Lucy watched in satisfaction as the men slunk away.

"Papa, you shouldn't make up stories."

David, Juliet, Katie, and Sadie had come outside during the exchange. While Sadie wore an expression of forbearance, the rest of them appeared almost as shocked as they had been when they'd entered.

"You're right, my dear." Thorne climbed up from the street onto the walkway and lifted Sadie's face with a finger beneath her chin.

"Mrs. Merkel always said the Lord detests lying lips," she admonished him.

"Indeed. Mrs. Merkle could always be counted on to proffer such nuggets of wisdom." Thorne regarded David and Juliet. "Was anyone hurt?"

David shook his head. "No. I can't say they would have done much more than shout their slogans."

"Daft buggers. They're not even from East London," Katie said. Then she spoke to Lucy. "It's my time to be off, miss. I'm goin' straight to the pub to find me da and be sure to tell him 'bout those bullies."

"Thank you, Katie," Lucy said. It galled her that Katie worked rather than go to school so she could finance her father's afternoons in the pub, but now was not the time to worry over that. While Katie fetched her wrap, the rest of them slowly walked back into the shop. Thorne matched his strides to his daughter's small legs, and David held Juliet's elbow solicitously as they crossed the threshold.

The shop was empty except for Mr. Gentry and the remaining matron, whom he'd backed into a corner while he regaled her in explicit detail about the time he was certain he had yellow fever.

"I know you will argue, but, Lucy, can we not close up shop early and have a meal?" David asked. "I'll ask Gentry to stop by Mann's butcher on his way home and have a hen delivered."

Before Lucy could object, Juliet clapped her hands. "Oh, yes. Let's have a little party. Mrs. Locksley brought us a plate of tarts in payment for that poultice. Apple."

"And you must join us," David said to Thorne and Sadie. "I was just thinking it was a proper shame that we haven't had you over for a meal yet." He smiled and raised his eyebrows at Sadie. "Mrs. Locksley is a dab hand at tarts, and she always brings too many for us to finish."

Sadie bit her bottom lip and gazed up at her father.

Thorne and Lucy stared at each other for a moment. His revelations earlier had made her sick with disappointment. How could she bear to sit across from him at dinner, knowing that he believed one of her siblings was a thief?

"Of course, you will join us," Juliet said.

The choice was taken away from them both.

THORNE GLANCED DOWN AT SADIE BEFORE KNOCKING at the Petersons' door. She'd dressed for the occasion and looked pretty. Nerves made his hands clammy; he resisted the urge to pick her up and carry her back to their rooms, covering them both with blankets and falling into the world of Oliver Twist and his hapless friends.

The door swung open. "My, aren't you splendid in your gown. We are so glad you could join us."

David Peterson bowed to them both, then took Sadie's arm to lead her in as though she were a lady. She stared up at him with wide eyes, her cheeks flushed with, well, perhaps the same nerves that left Thorne momentarily frozen in the doorway.

Would they dance?

Was there wine on the table?

The building owned by Mrs. Merkle was for teetotalers only. No drinking allowed. The tiny widow was pedantic when it came to her sayings, but Thorne had found her honest faith reassuring.

Thorne's faith had been born of desperation, a call out to the universe for someone to guide him from the life he lived to the life his daughter needed. He held on to God by his fingertips and always believed the ambivalence might be mutual.

"Mr. Thorne, you are most welcome."

Miss Juliet came and offered her arm, and there was nothing to do but bow correctly and promenade her the four feet to the Petersons' supper table, laid out with a cheerful red cloth and twinkling candles.

Lucy peered out from the kitchen and clapped her hands. "Ah, some new victims for my latest formula."

Sadie giggled and David grimaced. "Do not encourage her, Miss Thorne. Last week she decided to experiment with turmeric in our food as part of a new recipe, and we were subjected to strange, yellow-hued dishes."

Thorne's gaze went to Lucy, and her cheeks turned red. "Yes, I have procured recipes from Mrs. Parekh for dishes that include turmeric, and I tried them out on my unsuspecting siblings. Tonight, I have prepared their favorite."

Juliet's eyes narrowed, and she examined both Thorne and Lucy while David busied himself with setting Sadie at the table.

"I have no quarrel with the curry you have made for tonight," David said. "In fact, it is delicious. However, I am not as fond of the month you experimented with the properties of garlic."

His nose scrunched in a manner most folks would have found charming but Thorne found irritating. Had Lucy said anything about the fraud to him? Was this an act on his part?

When Thorne declined an aperitif, the party settled themselves at the table. No one said anything about his refusal, and he wiped his sweating palms surreptitiously on his trousers, feeling as though he'd passed an exam.

Lucy explained the origin of the dishes while she brought out a set of plain but elegant tureens that matched the delicate porcelain plates. The family must have been prosperous at one time to afford such a serving set.

Sadie's impeccable table manners impressed them all, David remarking that he didn't think they'd ever dined so amicably with a child. Thorne did not hold with too many compliments, but he kept silent while Juliet and Lucy agreed that Sadie was a perfect dinner guest, and they would invite her more often.

"You haven't touched your claret. Would you care for something else, Mr. Thorne?" Lucy asked.

"Papa does not partake of spirits," Sadie said matter-of-factly.

David's attention, focused on the savory curry, now shifted to Thorne, a canny look in his eyes.

"Why is that, Mr. Thorne?" the younger man asked.

Thorne could lie. He could say it was a matter of digestion, a matter of taste—he could come up with any number of reasons. He could spin a tale that would make his refusal look like a sacrifice and impress Lucy Peterson or make Sadie proud.

But he looked at Lucy then. She had been nothing but honest with him.

They will find out at some point, he reasoned. It was a small gesture that he presented Lucy with the truth.

"That is because I was once a drunkard, Mr. Peterson."

He observed their separate reactions—Juliet's eyes widened, and David had the grace to look embarrassed.

Why had he done this?

Thorne looked back to Lucy, but she simply tilted her head as though listening to the things he couldn't say with no sign of surprise or disgust.

He had done this for her.

Because no matter how much he tried to ignore it, Thorne wanted her.

"Mrs. Merkle always said wine leads to debauchery," said Sadie, seemingly oblivious to the discomfort of the adults around her. "I don't know what that is, but it sounds uncomfortable."

"Hmmm, it can be," Thorne told her.

Sadie was the reason he stopped drinking. She was the reason for everything he did or tried to do. He wondered if she knew that on some level.

"Alcohol is responsible for a multitude of physical ailments,"

Juliet said. "I believe it acts to unbalance our humors. Someone who drinks too much is often at the mercy of a bilious liver."

Therein followed a short but uncomfortably detailed discourse between the sisters on the efficacy of various treatments on bilious complaints, including bloodletting. Sadie followed the conversation with fascination while David gazed off into the distance.

When supper ended, Juliet and David were the ones who cleared the table, insisting that Sadie and Thorne sit and digest the meal. Juliet came back out with a plate of the fabled tarts, and all agreed they were indeed delicious.

"Shall we have a round of cards?" David asked.

"Papa does not play cards," said Sadie.

The Petersons looked at Thorne, who raised a shoulder. "Methodists generally look askance at games of chance."

David looked at Sadie. "Do you fancy dance, then? I'll roll up the carpet and we . . ."

"We do not dance."

David's mouth dropped open at Sadie's declaration, and he didn't bother to hide his shock.

Lucy spoke up, casting a worried glance in David's direction. "We shall play a word game, then. Do you know Grandmother's Trunk?"

Thorne unclenched his jaw as the siblings agreed enthusiastically.

"Rather than explain the rules, you can learn by paying attention," said Lucy. "Madame Mensonge always says it is better to show than tell."

"Now, I opened my grandmother's trunk and found an *apple*," Juliet said slowly.

David shuddered. "An apple in a trunk? How long had it sat there for?"

"Not the point, Squeaky," Lucy admonished. "I opened my grandmother's trunk and found an apple and a *bear*."

"Ha," said Juliet. "Much more disgusting to think of a bear lying in a trunk for months than an apple."

"Not the point," Lucy repeated.

"I opened my grandmother's trunk and found an apple, a bear, and a *coin*," said David.

Already having caught on, Sadie pumped her legs back and forth beneath her chair faster and faster as her turn approached.

"I opened my grandmother's trunk and found an apple, a bear, a coin . . ." Her toothy smile looked nothing like Genny's. Sadie's joyful expressions were her own, and never failed to pull Thorne's heart from its usual place in his chest and toss it about in the air. Sometimes so much so he couldn't breathe.

"And a dish!"

"Huzzah," David cheered, and the sisters clapped their hands.

"I opened my grandmother's trunk to find an apple, a bear, a coin, a dish, and an elephant." Thorne drew out the last word like the sound of a trumpet.

As they listed the contents of the grandmother's trunk, the candles burned low, and Juliet turned up the oil lamp on a side table. David glanced often to the spinet in the corner and the fiddle that rested atop, though he didn't say a word and seemed to enjoy the game as much as the rest of the party.

Well before Sadie was ready to leave, Thorne thanked the Petersons for a lovely time. When Sadie protested later in their rooms, he explained that a favored guest was like a fish—"Both can ruin an evening if they've been sitting around too long."

"Is that something Mrs. Merkle told you?" Sadie asked through a yawn.

Thorne tucked his daughter beneath the blankets and, after

a moment, pulled a quilt from out of the trunk at the foot of her bed and covered her with that as well. The wind was picking at the window casement, whining with displeasure at being kept outside.

"Mrs. Merkle is not the font of all wisdom," he said. "Your papa does know a few things himself."

"Mmmm," Sadie said. "You'll be looking for a new wife soon, I expect."

Thorne kissed his daughter on the nose and told her not to stick it in his business, but Sadie was half-asleep by then and the warning hung wasted in the air.

10

—‹‹‹‹◦›››—

"TWO WEEKS?"

Lucy swallowed against the tightness in her throat and forced a smile to her face as customers craned their necks to watch her and David. She'd just had to turn a customer away who had come looking for willow bark tea. Such a staple should have been out in one of the large glass jars, but Lucy had cut back on her orders that month to pay Katie, and the result was lost custom.

"I've got to go—" David flashed his special smile at a young woman hovering nearby, and she turned away to hide her blush. He pulled Lucy by the elbow into the office but left the door ajar so they could keep an eye on the crowded room.

"Lucy, you know this is important to me," he finished.

Juliet and Mrs. Sweet had met up at the shop earlier in the morning and taken a hack to the other side of London. Mrs. Sweet's employer, Mrs. Violet Kneland, the founder of Athena's Retreat, had arranged for Juliet and Mrs. Sweet to meet with a committee of men and women who were concerned about the health of children in the East End. The committee was considering fully funding the clinic's work with pregnant women. The latest science suggested that what women drank or ate—or did not eat—during pregnancy had an effect on their children. While Juliet was happy to provide a correction to the menses for women who wanted it, she and Mrs. Sweet wanted just as much to see women who wanted to become mothers be the best mothers they could be.

Juliet was near breathless with nerves, and it took all of Lucy's patience to persuade her not to fake an illness to get out of the public speaking. Between the meeting and giving the benefactors a tour, Juliet would be gone until late this afternoon.

Thus, when David approached her and told her he was leaving for two weeks—two weeks!—Lucy had little reserve of calm from which to draw.

"What is it that's so important to you?" she asked, her throat still tight with frustration. "If you would simply tell us—"

"If you would simply trust me," he snapped.

"Who is Mr. Wilcox?"

David jerked his head as though Lucy had slapped him, and she might as well have for the hot stream of guilt that weighted her stomach at his expression.

Why had she opened her mouth?

"Mr. Thorne found that name while 'organizing,' did he?" David asked. The lightness in his tone did not fool Lucy, and she braced herself for the sharpness of the words to follow. No one could wound her like the people she loved the most.

"Mr. Wilcox is my partner in the business enterprise. If you would just—"

Before she could hear his bootstep on the floorboards at the doorway, Lucy felt Thorne staring at the back of her neck.

David's mouth slipped into a sneer when he caught sight of the other man.

"If you want to know about mysteries, Lucy, ask Mr. Thorne here if that is truly his name. Ask him why the Gentleman Fighter is now working as a bookkeeper for an East End apothecary."

"Mr. Peterson." Thorne began to speak, but David pushed past Lucy and opened the door wider to slip past Thorne as well.

"Mr. Thorne. Be sure to continue your excellent work while I am gone," said David. Looking Thorne up and down as he passed, his sneer melted into a frown. "If you intend to remain with us, that is. You appear to be dressed for a much finer event than sifting through our dusty old ledgers."

Lucy took in Thorne's appearance for the first time. His hair was swept back and pomaded in the latest style, forelocks gleaming beneath an elegant topper. His blue woolen topcoat covered a deep aubergine pull-away waistcoat and his forest-green cravat glowed dully with the sheen of real silk. All the way down to his polished boots, he resembled a wealthy gentleman rather than a former prizefighter with a penchant for accounting. The only thing Thorne couldn't hide was the damage to his face, but dressed as he was, myriad explanations might be found for it that didn't include having been punched in the head for years on end.

Who was Mr. Thorne indeed?

David placed his own worn topper on his head and left without another word.

"That is a fine hat, Mr. Thorne," Lucy said.

Thorne's gaze searched her face, then shifted to examine the desk behind her. It was still perfectly organized, the pen wipes in a neat stack, the ink bottle and pen holders aligned at right angles; not a scrap of stray parchment marred its newly polished surface.

"You may ask me at any time about what I did before becoming an agent for Tierney and Company," he said.

The rumble of his voice contained no sympathy that she could discern, but the utter stillness of his body illustrated his sincerity. It was the same stillness that had accompanied his announcement last night. That he had been a drunkard.

"Miss Peterson, Billy Weston cast up his accounts in the treatment room." Katie poked her head around Thorne's shoulder, appearing sympathetic. Lucy knew her compassion most likely had not extended to having cleaned up Billy's mess. Katie's weak tolerance for any bodily fluid left her unsuitable as an apprentice apothecary, but she made up for her queasiness with plenty of good cheer, even when Lucy was at her most upset.

They waited until Katie left before speaking.

"I am going out this afternoon to follow a lead I've gotten about your formula and will not be home until perhaps tomorrow morning," he said. "Miss Juliet has been kind enough to agree to walk Sadie home after school today."

Lucy thought about the way Sadie had enjoyed herself the night before. "Will she come sit with us for supper, do you think? She's young to be home all night by herself."

Thorne nodded and sighed. "My landlady used to watch her when I had evening assignments. I'm afraid our move was rather precipitous, and I haven't had time yet to find a woman to stay with her at night."

"Was that the famous Mrs. Merkle?" Lucy asked.

Thorne closed his eyes and nodded. "She of the many cross-stitched proverbs," he acknowledged. "I do not mean to impose on you, but—"

"It is no hardship to have her sup with us." Lucy paused, the sting of David's disappointment still burning in her chest. "I won't—we won't play any music for her, if you are worried about our . . . our influence."

Thorne's head dropped and he took off his beautiful hat. She'd not noticed the matching silk band around its crown. This entire ensemble must have cost a fortune. Ten times the nominal sum she paid Tierney's for his time.

Who was this man?

"Your influence," he repeated, then raised his head. "Your influence is most welcome. Sadie is lucky to be surrounded by such hardworking and compassionate women as yourself and Miss Juliet."

Lucy waited for a moment for him to add a disclaimer. When he didn't, she set a hand to her throat where a lump formed.

"Until tomorrow, then," he said curtly, and left without another word.

Billy Weston had cast up his accounts with the same vigor that he brought to all his activities. While Katie dispensed medicines to waiting customers, Lucy reassured Billy and his mother that he wasn't suffering a wasting disease, as evidenced by his full cheeks and bright eyes, despite his current listlessness.

Billy was not the only patient to try Lucy's nerves. Her disappointment with David and Thorne's unexpected compliments had broken the last of her defenses, and three times that day she had to go back into the storeroom and give herself a stern talking-to so as not to succumb to tears. Katie tried hard to make up for earlier and surprised Lucy by washing the windows, but the impact was ruined somewhat when she knocked over the bucket of dirty wash water onto Lucy's shoes.

When Juliet arrived with Sadie that afternoon, she was elated. This committee seemed interested in the clinic, and she went upstairs to write letters of request to the benefactors she'd met that day. Sadie proved so exhausted by the day's lessons that she napped on the Petersons' couch instead of sitting and keeping Lucy company. Dinner was a subdued affair as they supped on the leftover curry and bread, all of them feeling the effects of the long day.

Lucy brought Sadie up to the Thornes' apartment and helped her ready for bed. She'd expected bare walls or biblical prints, but the rooms had been elegantly if sparsely furnished and smelled of lemon polish and bay rum. The candles in the holders were beeswax, and the carpets, while plain, were thick and clean.

Itching with curiosity, Lucy tried hard not to stare at the door to Thorne's room as she accompanied Sadie in her nighttime rituals.

"Thank you so much for including us in your prayers," she said to Sadie as the girl climbed beneath her covers. Lucy didn't think anyone had prayed for her since her mother died, and the tenderness this evoked tickled at her chest and scratched the back of her throat.

"I would invite you to read with me, but then Papa would miss that part, and he is much enjoying *Oliver Twist*."

Lucy had painted the room herself between tenants and knew the walls were covered with the cheapest ivory paint she could find, but the Thornes had put up lovely salmon-colored curtains and hung three charming watercolors across from Sadie's bed that, combined with the pastel scraps of her quilt, gave the girl's room a warm rose hue.

"I still have some work to do, but if you become frightened,

I will leave the door to our apartment unlocked and you may sleep on the sofa," Lucy said, surprising herself. "When I'm finished, I will come up and stay until your father returns."

Lucy had no pause to mull over why she'd made that offer. She didn't like children, did she?

The question fell to the side as she took in the sight of the darkened shop. Earlier, Katie had been rushed off her feet and had no time to tidy the shelves or clean the counters after having to rewash the floors. Loath to pressure Juliet after such a long day, Lucy worked for an hour to set the apothecary to rights before putting the lockbox in the bottom drawer of the office desk and lighting a small lamp that she carried to the storeroom. Time floated along without measure as Lucy inventoried and made notes on what was running low.

All she wanted was her bed, but the more Lucy worked, the more anxious she grew. After the inventory check, there was an endless list of medications to measure out and set aside. Katie had written a list of tinctures that must be restocked, and since David had now left for another two weeks, there were orders to place and bills to pay. More willow bark tea must be ordered, and a way to find enough coin for both Katie and food for the rest of the month was her most pressing issue.

On top of this were Thorne's revelations.

David's reaction to Wilcox's name had been difficult to read, but it was strong, nevertheless. Was all lost? Had David somehow managed to exacerbate the damage that Lucy had started by losing her heart—and her common sense—to Duncan Rider? What did Wilcox have to do with her missing croup formula, if he did at all? If only Thorne had found her formulas, Lucy would have gladly borne the humiliation of having been wrong about Duncan stealing them.

Her chest tightened with the thought of what would happen if they lost the business. There were, Lucy knew, thousands of women in London who had no control over their lives. They had no education, no loving family, no community that looked at them with respect. They were trapped and poor and helpless.

Lucy was not one of them.

She had an education. If the apothecary closed, she could apply for a position at one of the medical apothecaries attached to a hospital. She could work with Juliet and Mrs. Sweet at the clinic. She could marry a wealthy shop owner and never work again a day in her life.

Why, then, did their finances and the fate of the apothecary sit on her shoulders and push her down with a weight so great she could not breathe?

Lucy sank into the chair behind the desk. Her throat felt strangled by the fist of anxiety that squeezed and squeezed.

No matter how sternly she spoke to herself, her breaths continued to come short and shallow as though she sipped the air. The room began to spin, and Lucy clawed at the high collar of her dress, hearing the popping of buttons as if from far away.

Was she going to die?

The office door opened, and a dark figure slipped inside.

"I can't breathe," Lucy told Thorne as he walked around the desk.

"Tell me what you hear," he said, his lips close to her ear.

What did she hear?

"I hear me trying to breathe," she rasped in between gulps.

"What else?"

His voice was a rope flung through the thinning air around her head. His knees creaked as he knelt by her side, one of his palms against her back, the other holding her wrist lightly.

"Your knees," she said.

A small avalanche of pebbles fell when he laughed, and she raised her head so that her throat would be clear.

"Your laugh."

Thorne's fingers closed tighter around her wrist, and she stared at them as he unbuttoned the top back of her dress with his other hand, exposing part of her corset but freeing her lungs to inhale easier. Both she and Juliet wore the easy-to-remove day dresses of the lower classes, as they could not afford a maid.

"What can you smell?"

Lucy half turned in her seat to stare at him.

"What can you smell?" he asked again.

Pulling air in through her nose, Lucy gripped the chair's arm with her free hand, willing the room to stop moving.

"Brandy," she said, then narrowed her eyes at him.

"Indeed," he said. "An inebriated earl spilled a glass of it on my trousers tonight. What else?" he asked.

Clever man. Each time Lucy breathed through her nose, her lungs expanded. Her heart had been twisting about like a fly in a web, and it settled into an agitated but somewhat slower thump. Gradually, the haze around Lucy cleared and the lamp on the top of a cabinet came into focus. Thorne must have lit it when he came back to the apothecary.

"The cold from outside caught in the wool of your topcoat. Smoke."

The words now came without gasping, and Lucy counted the time it took her to breathe in and out, raising the count until Thorne let go of her wrist.

"What do you feel?" he asked.

Cold. The loss of his touch on the sensitive skin of her wrist. Hot. The heat of his body so close to hers they were almost touching.

"Foolish," she said aloud.

Gently, Thorne turned the chair toward him so that she didn't have to crane her neck to look at him. Whatever he'd been doing tonight, his pomade had long since given up the fight and his hair curled round his ears, released from the glossy prison.

"Better now?" he asked. His large hand remained pressed against her back, and she could feel the strength in his fingers through her corset to the thin lawn of her chemise.

Was it frayed? Lucy could not even remember if she'd pulled on a corset cover this morning. Her underclothes were service-able and clean but threadbare. But he wouldn't be looking at her corset, would he?

Thorne's thumb moved slowly up and down the top of her spine above the edge of the corset. He may as well have set that thumb at the pearl between her legs, considering her reaction. Lucy's nipples hardened and ached, and the thumping of her heart could now be felt at the juncture of her thighs.

One touch! One touch of a man and she was ready to roll onto her back for him.

Lucy squeezed her thighs against the trickle of pleasure that wet her there, and his breath hitched. She glanced over in time to see his mouth pull into a thin line, his pupils dilate.

One touch.

She was shaking now, an uncontrollable tremble he had to feel.

"Miss Juliet was not here most of the day," he stated softly.

Lucy told him the worry uppermost in her mind.

"Katie left the front a mess after she spilled dirty water on my shoes," she whispered. "Her da came in and brought her home early to care for the younger children—it's why he won't let her go away to school, so she can tend to them, and he can drink away her wages."

Why was she spewing such nonsense? He couldn't care. She should leave. Instead, she continued her list of worries.

"Juliet is anxious about the clinic funders," Lucy continued. "Mr. Gentry has found a book at the lending library about tropical diseases, and it is *illustrated*. Billy Weston's mother considers me a last resort to those useless toffs over on Harley Street. And I am behind on orders."

The words spilled out as though she'd lanced a boil; the petty complaints, the enormous terrors, all of it drenched in self-pity.

"I do not understand my brother. I am frustrated with my sister. I tried to read your ledgers and my eyes crossed and I am terrified that the baby I saw yesterday is going to die. No. I *know* he is going to die."

There. There was the worst of the poison come out now.

"Breathe," he commanded as the air in her lungs once again turned to stone.

I cannot. The words were stuck on repeat in her head as she lurched out of the chair. She had to get to the window, no matter that her dress now fell to her waist. Thorne must have loosened her corset strings as well, because the top of her corset fell away from her breasts as she struggled with the cracked and sticking windowpane, now nearly choking.

"Breathe," he said again as he came up behind her and lifted the casement with ease.

The sooty, damp autumn air hit Lucy like a smack, and she stumbled backward into his arms. He pulled her around so that they faced each other, and put his hand to her chin.

At first Lucy flailed when Thorne covered her mouth with his and pushed his breath into her lungs.

Though she welcomed the air, her relief was tangled with the shock of his actions and the reaction of her body to his embrace; her breasts exposed, they pressed against the slickness of his satin waistcoat and the chill of the brass buttons down the front of it.

He broke the kiss and stared down at her, no expression in his ruined face, barely out of breath, but Lucy knew their desire was mutual by the steely hardness of his cock pressed against her belly and the blackness of his eyes in the low light.

"Are you breathing?" he asked.

"I think so? Maybe you should help me once more to be cert—"

He kissed her again.

What could she hear?

The pounding of her blood through her veins as her heart sped in excitement, an altogether different pace than she'd felt before; the faint sounds of horses clopping through the street outside; and the whisper of skin against cloth where her breasts were pushed against the slickness of his satin waistcoat.

What could she smell?

The ubiquitous soot in the London air when it blew through the window and ran down her bare neck and shoulders above where Thorne's arms held her close, the scent of tobacco and alcohol, and the slightest hint of cologne.

And what did she feel?

He needed a shave.

Sometime between when he left this morning, clean-shaven and well-dressed, and the middle of the night, Thorne sported a shadow of stubble around his mouth. The friction provided a painful pleasure, and Lucy let herself relax into his embrace.

Thorne broke the kiss.

Lucy put her hand to her lips. The sensitive skin there

throbbed in time with the pulse between her legs and the beating of her heart.

Thorne said nothing, but the gentleness of his touch as he drew his fingers along her jaw, the way he stepped away from her as he pulled up her dress, the sympathy in his eyes—they spoke for themselves.

He'd divested himself of her.

"I must check on Sadie," he said, his voice so low it scattered. "Will you be all right?"

Lucy nodded once, then again.

With an answering nod, Thorne left.

For a long time afterward, Lucy sat and listened to her breath.

11

"YOU NEED NOT WORRY, PAPA. I HAVE MORE THAN enough books to keep me occupied. I won't even notice you aren't here except no one will be scolding me for not eating enough vegetables."

Thorne squeezed Sadie's hand as they rushed to school. They were late due to a stop at the dressmaker's to pick up her new winter coat, bonnet, and muff. November had turned the corner from autumn to winter, and Sadie had outgrown her coat from last year.

His daughter looked grown-up in her new winter clothing, but fortunately for him, she still allowed him to hold her hand when they crossed the busy streets, happy to give the street sweepers one of the pennies she kept in her pockets for that occasion.

Every time his child pressed a coin into the palm of another child her age, he shivered at the thought of the children in London working day and night for such pennies, the contrast between Katie's wan face and Sadie's eager eyes.

His stomach sank and Thorne didn't want to think. He wanted to clear his brain of everything but the feeling of Sadie's hand safe in his, the scrape of the wind's nails across his cheeks, and his gratitude that no one would be punching him in the head for sport tonight. Those were simple delights. Uncomplicated. Free of any obsession or entanglements.

"What about Miss Peterson's offer?" Sadie asked.

Thorne jerked his head around and stared at his daughter.

"What do you mean?" he asked.

She peered up at him, one brow slightly lower, a sign of her ever-present concern about the foibles of aging, then shook her head with a pitying scrunch of her nose.

"I worry about your memory," she said.

Before Thorne could contradict her by reciting the opening monologue from *Richard III*, she continued.

"Miss Peterson said if you were out all night tonight, that I am welcome to go downstairs to their apartment and spend the night. That she is happy to have me as a guest."

A sullen breeze swept down Shaftesbury Avenue and yanked at Sadie's bonnet strings, flipping up the hem of his greatcoat and sending loose refuse spinning down the street.

"Do you think she means it?" Sadie asked.

Once again, Thorne walked the precipice of parenthood, the dilemma of blanket reassurances versus the business of disentangling the worries and fears that lived in Sadie's head. Why would Sadie doubt the genuineness of Lucy's offer? What did he not see or understand?

Two years ago, Thorne took an assignment to hunt down a devious and immoral killer, a man who might slit your throat to spare himself the time wasted by arguing a point. Thorne found the experience of strategizing where a knife might strike a fatal blow in a fight analogous to figuring out which questions with his daughter might lead to information, and which led to tears.

Girls were hard.

"Yes. In my experience, Miss Peterson is to be trusted. I believe she meant her offer."

Sadie nodded to herself, and they arrived at her school without further conversation. After bidding their goodbyes, Thorne found himself a hack and made his way toward St. James's Street.

While no longer the center of the beau monde as it was during George's reign, the area remained popular with the aristocratic class, and the streets were full of well-dressed gentlemen and ladies promenading with their footmen trailing behind, laden with packages.

The pace of one's promenade told everyone they had no place to go, no fixed occupation, for the gentry did nothing so crass as work every day. This dividing line between themselves and the new middle class had faded somewhat during Thorne's lifetime.

Soon, living off interests, raising the rents on tenant estates, or accumulating piles of IOUs from deferential tradesmen— soon this would end. Thorne saw the signs better now that he had removed himself from his family's orbit. The great houses of London were being sold and split up into smaller dwellings. The anti–Corn Law movement was gaining strength as the price of grain stayed stubbornly high, but the harvests were poor. There were as many merchants as aristocrats standing elbow to elbow in the great banks.

Still, a well-dressed man commanded respect no matter how he'd paid for his togs.

Donnely and Sons was not the most famous tailor in London, but Thorne's father and his brothers used them, and if they were good enough for Thornwood men, they were good enough to create an outfit that showed—even from a distance—the quality only money could buy.

For the next twenty minutes Thorne stood for final fittings of two new jackets and another set of dress clothes. Last night before he'd arrived back at the apothecary to find Lucy in a breathless panic, he'd worn his only set of dress clothes out to the Earl of Westwood's gaming club, Grommots, where he'd been until the small hours gambling and pretending to drink with Westwood while plumping him for information about Duncan Rider.

Thorne's visits to other apothecaries were leading him nowhere. None of them were selling anything akin to Lucy's salve, and none of them had anything to say about Duncan Rider other than he was easy on the eyes and empty in the head.

Thorne agreed wholeheartedly with the latter.

He'd hoped Rider himself would be there, but Westwood explained that Rider wasn't moneyed enough to know how to comport himself at a place like Grommots. Thorne had peered around at the burgundy velvet–covered chairs and overstuffed settees, the cut of the crystal ashtrays that held an assortment of pipes and cigars, and the muted brilliance of dusty but ornate crystal chandeliers.

The familiar smell of smuggled brandy, sandalwood, and fresh playing cards filled his nose, but Thorne felt none of his past ease at finding himself in the company of men with deep pockets and expensive taste.

"Can't believe I ran into you. Thought you were dead," the earl said, not unkindly.

"Retired," Thorne said laconically, "not dead."

A few men looked twice at him as they walked past, wondering perhaps if they knew him from university or another club. Among this set, not many men found themselves watching prize matches unless they were well into their cups.

"Same thing," Westwood said, then laughed, a tinny bray that used to make Thorne's ears itch at school, and time had not improved on it. "The Gentleman Fighter. What a life you had back then. Did you lose it all?"

Luckily, Thorne had saved during his fighting years, and with his salary from Tierney's, this allowed for Sadie and him to live well enough.

Instead of answering, Thorne winked and set a finger to the side of his nose. The earl laughed again.

"Always the joker, Thornwood."

They sat side by side on tall, padded stools next to a roulette wheel. Once Westwood had gotten over his shock at seeing Thorne alive, he'd been delighted to have the chance to brag about his new title and old fortune.

"Never thought I'd come to it, but my cousin Hal had a dicky heart and Raphe ate some bad fish, so here I am."

Westwood had finished his third drink by then, and it didn't take much effort for Thorne to steer the conversation in the direction he was interested.

"Nice enough chap for all he's a mushroom," Westwood said when Thorne again brought the subject of Duncan Rider up. "Fellow has the brains to capitalize on an opportunity and should be encouraged. Not that I'd bring him home to meet my sister, mind you—"

This time he laughed so loud that Thorne grabbed the glass in front of him and clenched it tightly—for the first time that night, he was tempted to take a sip.

"But unlike you, I wasn't raised in a titled family, and sometimes it is a pleasure to simply . . . be my old self. Before I became an earl, I knew the men I drank and played cards with were my friends because they liked me. Now that I'm an earl . . ." Westwood stared at his brandy, his face a picture of wistfulness. If Westwood were a better person, Thorne might have had some sympathy for his circumstances, thrust without warning into a role that could break even the best of men. He, however, was not the best of men—

"Would you like to see a collection of cravats, sir?"

Thorne pulled himself from the memory of last night and stared at the tailor. The work had been finished and the sight in the mirror startled him, as always. He was thirty-five but looked ten years older. Despite his broken nose and scarred visage, in his finery one might mistake him for his father, Lord Blackstone.

The image wouldn't let him be as he left the tailor's and set out for more intelligence gathering. Sick to death of the smell of drink, Thorne nevertheless paid visits to various pubs in the vicinity of Rider's apothecary, standing rounds and, on the side, collecting information. More than one man had let slip secrets after a few pints, and there was a chance Duncan had done the same.

From the bland but well-kept Duck's Bottom to the King's Arms, cheerfully festooned with papier-mâché crowns, Thorne purchased round after round of ales. In some cases, he was recognized even after all these years, and in others, he made friends as well as any man who looked like him could. The denizens were happy enough to talk to someone new, especially someone new who was buying the drink, and gossip flowed as freely as the ale.

It appeared that Duncan Rider had been a cheerful if somewhat tedious companion until he'd come up with the formula for his lozenges. Since then, he might have been spending his days under the watchful eyes of his father at the apothecary, but his nights were now spent out with a new crowd, men who ran far faster and played far deeper than his old cronies at the local pub ever could.

Conventional wisdom held that the senior Mr. Rider reined Duncan in when the spending became too outrageous, but the elevated circles in which he now traveled had been a boon for their business. The Duck's Bottom especially missed Duncan's presence, as he'd been perennially available for a game of darts and so bad a player he made everyone else look good.

Thorne and his own father had never been close. He didn't know many men of his station who were close to their fathers, but he'd admired Blackstone and believed in his integrity and wisdom. Generally, Thorne's older brothers were the ones that took up his father's attention with spending habits similar to Duncan Rider's but no work ethic to accompany them.

Most likely Thorne would never have considered the nature of father-and-son relations or reflected on how important they were had he not asked his father for help and been denied.

That day Thorne had shown up at his ancestral home, Longlake Abbey, with his two-year-old daughter in tow.

It had turned out that his punching half-naked men until they bled was seen by his parents as an eccentricity Thorne would eventually outgrow.

Acknowledging a natural-born granddaughter of mixed race was different.

Blackstone never said this outright—in fact, he never said a word when Thorne arrived home with Sadie. It had been his mother who'd pointed out the unsuitability of Sadie's birth and strongly suggested Thorne find a loving couple to adopt her.

The suggestion made perfect sense to a man of his station.

Too bad it had been made after Thorne had fallen in love with his daughter.

The last time Thorne saw his father was when he left Longlake Abbey that same day with Sadie asleep over his shoulder.

Tonight, Thorne had arranged to meet Westwood at another club. This one, Freeley's, was not one Thorne knew well. When he entered a little after midnight, he understood why.

Unlike the club the night before, Freeley's was bare of such finery as red velvet settees and crystal ashtrays. Instead, the decor was similar to that of a fancy pub: mostly wooden stools and the occasional leather chair, functional clear glass lamps hanging from a plaster ceiling, and far more ale being dispensed than smuggled French brandy.

Here, the men walking by did not discreetly examine Thorne from the sides of their eyes. Instead, those who still recognized him greeted him with enthusiasm, slapping his back and proclaiming their pleasure that he hadn't died after all.

Eventually, Westwood waved at him, and Thorne made his way to where the earl sat together with Duncan Rider. Rider wore a forest-green coat and a bright golden waistcoat with a pink cravat—very au courant. He pumped Thorne's hand again and displayed a nice set of teeth, proclaiming his absolute pleasure in making Thorne's acquaintance once more. Westwood explained that Thorne was a gentleman who took up prize-fighting for a number of years. Duncan nodded, a blank look behind his eyes. Thorne figured Duncan was about the same age as Lucy and would have been too young to have heard of the Gentleman Fighter.

The thought made Thorne's bones throb.

They took up their cards, and he waited for the men around them to become absorbed in the game so that he could speak with Rider, but the night was an exercise in frustration. Word that Jonathan Thornwood, the errant nobleman formerly known as the Gentleman Fighter, was alive and well had spread throughout the club, and Thorne soon found himself being hailed by dozens of men to come settle bets or say hello.

"Not dead. Retired," Thorne explained for the thousandth time that night. He stood with the Earl Grantham, who peppered him with questions about his early fights. Like Westwood, Grantham had also acquired a title by surprise. Unlike Westwood, Grantham had more than filled his predecessor's shoes. The earl sat on two reform committees in Parliament and hid his political acumen behind a facade of harmless geniality, playing up his common roots. He was friends with Arthur and Violet Kneland but hadn't had occasion to run into Thorne in years.

"Well, congratulations on being not dead," Grantham said, slapping Thorne jovially on the back. Thorne was not a small man, but the earl topped him by two inches and had the shoulder span of a blacksmith. The slap nearly sent him flying.

"I'm quite pleased as well," Thorne said dryly as he kept his eye on Rider. Despite his newfound wealth and Westwood's patronage, the young man appeared uncomfortable in the rowdy company. Thorne had tried to coax him into casual conversation about the apothecary, but Rider avoided any discussion of his background. Instead, he engaged Westwood haltingly on horses and various bits of news from the scandal pages, sounding stilted and rehearsed.

Rider was out of his element, and Thorne had missed his opportunity to exploit it.

"And the lovely Geneviève?" Grantham asked. "Is she enjoying her retirement as well?"

The noise of the crowd had risen to thundering heights but wasn't loud enough to drown out the buzz of blood racing through Thorne's veins.

Grantham, for all he played the fool, was adept at reading others and immediately realized he'd said something wrong.

"Ah, feck, Thornwood, I've put my foot in it, haven't I?" the earl asked.

Thorne's left shoulder jerked up in a half-hearted shrug. "You couldn't know. She died of consumption seven years ago."

This time, the earl's enormous hand rested gently on Thorne's shoulder in a gesture of sympathy.

"My condolences. She was a sweet girl."

Thoughts of Genny led to thoughts of Sadie. Thorne wanted to go home. Though Grantham tried his best to cheer Thorne up with an impressively dirty joke or two, it was with relief he bid the earl good night when Westwood and Rider stood up from the table.

"Are we off somewhere else?" he asked as he joined the men at the coatroom to collect their belongings.

"'Fraid I must be going home," Rider said.

"He's a workingman, you know," Westwood said, his consonants thick from drink. "Not like us. Stands up at the cock's crow."

Thorne accepted the offer of a ride, asking to be let out around the corner from the apothecary. Nearing home, he saw a faint light in his windows. A sliver of worry woke in his spine. Before he could pick up the pace, Westwood's carriage returned.

Slipping into a recess between two buildings, Thorne watched as the carriage came to a halt in front of the apothecary and Duncan Rider jumped out of the vehicle before it had completely stopped moving.

The young man staggered toward the front door but froze

before he reached the wooden walkway. His head fell back as he stared up at the Petersons' set of rooms, and his topper fell to the dirt road behind him. After a moment, Westwood leaned out the carriage door and called softly to Rider to get back in the damned carriage.

Rider turned and picked up his hat, looked up at the Petersons' window one more time, and climbed shakily back in.

Thorne emerged from his hiding place, ruminating on Duncan's behavior.

Obviously, Rider felt conflicted about what he'd done to Lucy. This plus the information Thorne had gathered so far painted a picture of Duncan Rider as a not-too-bright opportunist. Lucy had trusted him and given him the formula for the lozenges, but Thorne was almost certain Duncan was neither clever nor devious enough to sneak back into the apothecary, sort through Lucy's papers, and steal yet another idea.

Who had taken it, then?

While contemplating that question, Thorne sneezed. The smell of cigar smoke and brandy had suffused his clothing. Other than to distract himself from Westwood's laugh, Thorne hadn't felt an urge to drink tonight. While the environs of the club—the low murmur of male voices, the scent of cheroots and brandy—were intimately familiar, they hadn't felt completely comfortable. Whereas before, time would cease to exist in a place with money, alcohol, and no windows, tonight the minutes had crept by.

The entire time Thorne was there, he'd been aware of someone waiting at home for him.

Letting himself into the side entrance, he took a swift look around the ground floor of the apothecary. Lucy must have finished her work for the night, for the workroom was empty. Out of habit, Thorne pulled at the drawers in the office desk to be sure they remained locked, then took himself up the two flights of stairs to his apartment. Upon opening the door, he spied Sadie, clad in her nightgown and thick flannel robe, standing in the hallway with a half-used candle in a brass candleholder.

"What are you doing up?" he asked. "I thought you were going to be sleeping in the Petersons' apartment."

Sadie shook her head. She'd seen to her own hair tonight, as evidenced by the puffy locks that had escaped from her two plaits.

"Miss Peterson came up here with me," she whispered. "By the time I got ready and came out, she'd fallen asleep on the settee. I left her there, thinking she must be tired to find our settee comfortable, and went to bed, but I woke up a little while ago."

Thorne pulled his daughter close, indulging in a rare embrace even though she was a big girl of nine years old. To his relief, Sadie did not remind her father she was a big girl and rested her tiny head against his stomach.

"Did you see the carriage that stopped outside?" she asked.

Thorne pulled back and examined Sadie's face. "I did. Could you hear it up here?"

Passing him the candlestick, Sadie tried to fix one of the unraveling braids. "I woke up because of Miss Peterson's snoring. That's when I looked out the window and happened to see a man looking up here. He seemed familiar."

Thorne was about to question Sadie further, when he cocked his head, listening intently.

"I can't hear any snoring," he said.

"Exactly." Finished with her hair, Sadie took the candlestick and started back toward her room. "It's so quiet it woke me. I'm used to having the floorboards shake through the night."

"Come now," he said. "I don't snore that loud."

Sadie stopped and raised one eyebrow, a neat trick that Thorne had never mastered. "You are louder than a herd of elephants."

Thorne did not bother arguing. He'd broken his nose so many times he could hear his breath whistle when it was cold. While *herd of elephants* might be hyperbole, he certainly did snore.

"I will make sure Miss Peterson gets downstairs to her rooms and be back right quick," he said as Sadie laid her robe on the chair next to her bed and climbed beneath the covers. "Did you say your prayers?"

Sadie nodded through a yawn so big she couldn't hide it behind her hands. Thorne bid her good night and took the candle with him as he closed the door to her room.

Sure enough, Lucy was asleep on his parlor settee. She hadn't even managed to lie down. Instead, she sat upright, fully clothed, her cap askew and topknot leaning to the left. Her hands were at her sides, unclenched, palms facing upward.

Thorne held the candle up and examined her, searching out her flaws. There was no hint of her worries on her face—he wondered suddenly how old she could be to not have any deep lines or wrinkles. Younger than him. Though even if they were the same age, he'd guess the same, having lived her life free of the influences Thorne had once surrounded himself with.

Like a puppet, Lucy snapped her eyes open, and he jerked in surprise, spilling wax on his polished dress shoes.

"I fell asleep," she said.

If Thorne had held completely still, she might have closed her eyes and fallen back asleep, but he uttered a curse when the wax dripped on his hand. Lucy leapt to her feet.

"I fell asleep," she repeated with a hint of surprise.

Thorne held the candlestick up so the light fell between them.

Lucy's eyes were wide, and a red crease ran down her cheek where she'd rested her face against the decorative stitching on the back of the settee. Fine locks of her hair had come loose from her topknot, and her cap had fallen to the side, so Thorne could see the naked skin of her part. It woke an unexpected protective urge within him.

"Are you well?" he asked.

"I am. Is Sadie . . . ?" Lucy covered her yawn with ungloved fingers, three of them wrapped with plasters.

How had she hurt herself? Thorne ignored the urge to ask, to hold her soft palm in his and fuss over her cuts.

"Sadie is in her room. Thank you for watching over her," he said.

Lucy smiled, and his protective instinct warred with the tapping of banked lust at the base of his spine. Grantham's mention of Genny and the nights spent in the company of alcohol and games of chance had worn away at Thorne's composure.

"Can you find your way downstairs by yourself?" he asked, stepping back. "I am just going to look in on her again and be certain she sleeps."

Any number of expressions could have passed across Lucy's face, but Thorne stepped back again so that Lucy stood alone in the dark. He held the candle up and pointed it toward the door.

"Of course, I can manage on my own," Lucy said.

After she left, Thorne pretended to himself that her voice held no hint of sadness.

"SO, IN SUMMATION, I'VE NAUSEA IN THE MORNINGS, ME ankles are swollen, I've fatigue and constipation, belly cramps . . ."

"It sounds as though you may be pregnant, Mr. Gentry." Thorne's voice boomed from the doorway.

Lucy looked up from her plants and scowled at both of them.

Early this morning, she'd received permission from the apothecary's guild to enter their botanical gardens.

The Worshipful Society of Apothecaries established the Physic Garden in the sixteen hundreds. Down the Royal Hospital Road almost to the Chelsea Embankment, behind tall brick walls that kept the public out and the heat in, four acres of land were given over to a garden that rivaled any in the known world. Only members of the Society of Apothecaries were allowed inside those walls.

Delighted, Lucy had carefully packed the plants gifted to her by Mrs. Parekh. They would make fine additions to the gardens and provide knowledge to apothecaries all over England. She'd planned on taking the plants during the afternoon lull but wouldn't have time if she couldn't escape Mr. Gentry.

Who was experiencing—

"Abdominal tumor, Mr. Thorne," said Gentry with a slight frown. "Canna be pregnant if I've no womb."

"Right," said Thorne. He turned to Lucy. "Miss Peterson, I have a question—"

"There's all sorts of ailments of the womb," Mr. Gentry continued as though Thorne had asked his opinion. "Some more serious than others. You can have tumors in the womb as well as the abdomen, of course. D'you know, one of the largest tumors ever recovered from a womb weighed twelve pounds and was in the shape of a horse?"

Thorne's mouth dropped open, a slightly green cast to his skin.

"Mr. Thorne," Lucy said quickly, interrupting Mr. Gentry. She knew quite well he could—and would—recite every known tumor ever recovered that he'd read about in his voluminous library of medical books, some of which dated from the last century. "Do you think you might spare an hour of your time to help me transport these plants to the Physic Garden?"

"Gladly," he replied, not bothering to disguise his relief. "Is there someone to watch the shop?"

"I am happy to stay and keep an eye on yon Katie," Gentry said pleasantly. "She's a good girl, but with those Guardians hanging about, you don't want to leave her alone too long."

Taking Gentry's hands in hers, Lucy squeezed them and smiled. "Mr. Gentry, what would we do without you?"

Gentry turned a lovely shade of pink, and Lucy deliberately ignored Thorne's rolled eyes. No doubt he had his own opinion on what they might do without Mr. Gentry, but she refused to let kindness go unacknowledged.

What carried her through the bad times were the memories of small kindnesses.

Gentry, delighted with being given his task, informed Katie of his duties and continued his ruminations on tumors, his own in particular. Meanwhile, Lucy showed Thorne how to wrap the remaining plants in damp burlap. With his help, Lucy split the plants between two boxes, which she covered in woolen blankets, and they left the shop by the back entrance.

Luckily, they managed to both find seats on a crowded omnibus heading to Chelsea. A comfortable silence fell between them as they inched through the London streets. Occasionally, Lucy would bite down on a smile when she caught Thorne's reaction to conversations nearby. Once, overhearing a young man speak disparagingly of his mother, Thorne cleared his throat loudly. The youth glanced in Thorne's direction with a sneer that disappeared when the boy caught sight of the disapproving stare leveled in his direction.

Within moments, the bell had been pulled and the young man exited the omnibus looking back once over his shoulder, his white skin having paled to the color of whey.

"You must be careful where you aim that scowl of yours," Lucy said, leaning toward him and speaking quietly. "Looks to be a powerful weapon."

Thorne glanced at her from the corner of his eye, but his mouth softened. "Don't know what you mean."

More people got on at the next stop, and Lucy found herself smooshed up against him, filling her nose with the smell of bay rum and wool. He stood after another minute and motioned for an older woman to take his seat, replacing his scent with that of camphor and peppermint. Finally, Thorne cleared the way for the two of them to disembark and they began their walk toward the Thames.

A callous breeze off the river assaulted them with the smell of soaking refuse and clawed at Lucy's scarf.

"It might have been preferable to listen to Mr. Gentry's tales in the warmth of the shop with this nasty wind," Lucy remarked.

Thorne looked at her askance. "I'd rather bathe in the Thames than listen to tales of forty-pound tumors."

Lucy sighed. "Mr. Gentry has been known to exaggerate his stories upon occasion. Although, I seem to remember mention of that tumor in one of my old medical journals."

Shifting the box in his hold, Thorne put out an arm across her chest to stop her as a wagon slipped on the cobbled streets and came perilously close to the side of the building where they stood. A rush of warmth gave Lucy some protection from the chill.

"Why do you let him stand around the shop so much?" Thorne asked before Lucy could thank him for his solicitousness.

"Most times he doesn't order any cures, just talks. I know he's put some folks off."

When he lowered his arm, they crossed the street.

"I suppose it's not a secret, but no one talks about it much anymore," Lucy said. "Gentry's wife and two daughters died in the same month as my parents."

A sudden and utterly unexpected longing for her mother squeezed Lucy's chest.

"What did they die from?" Thorne asked.

"Cholera."

As the wind bore down on them, Lucy ducked her chin deeper in her scarf.

"Mr. Gentry and his family had only lived in London for a few months before they died," she explained. "When we re-opened the apothecary after my father's death, we would see him sometimes, walking the neighborhood and talking to no one. Each day he grew thinner and sicklier until one day, he dropped to the ground and did not get up."

She and David had been arguing at the front of the shop that day when Lucy saw Mr. Gentry fall. She'd known a mo-ment of frightening envy at the sight. If there were no one rely-ing on her after losing her parents, she might have collapsed as well. What must it feel like to just let go of everything and leave it to fate?

"David and I brought him home and put him in our parents' bed. It took two weeks to get him back on his feet. After a few days, he was restless but not well enough to be on his own, so Juliet gave him a stack of periodicals to read."

Thorne's brows lowered. "*Medical* periodicals."

"If anyone is to blame, it's Juliet." Lucy slowed at a hole in the walkway, and together they picked their way through the half-frozen mud of the street until they could once again climb up on the wooden boards. "Once we realized what we'd done, David tried to rectify it. He brought home every conceivable novel from the lending library and a stack of literary magazines, but it was too late. Mr. Gentry had found an obsession that . . . filled a need."

"Filled a need?" Thorne repeated.

Was it right to share the Petersons' theory with Thorne? Although Lucy and Juliet had been trained alongside physicians, they'd never taken an oath of any kind to keep their customers' secrets. It simply never occurred to them not to.

"Because now he'll be prepared," Thorne said, nodding to himself.

Relief that he'd figured it out on his own washed through her. "Exactly. He'll see the symptoms coming and know what to do in case he or anyone else he loves becomes ill. I just wish . . ." The top of the greenhouse in the center of the Physic Garden appeared as they turned the corner.

"What do you wish?" Thorne asked.

She prepared to cross to the entrance of the garden and looked over at him.

Breathe, he'd demanded the other night. It had been an order, not a request, and Lucy had felt helpless to disobey. *Breathe.* She'd leaned into his command in the same way she leaned against his body, relishing the strength and surety that was so lacking in her life.

What did she wish?

I wish you'd touch me again, Lucy thought to herself. Caught in his stare, she let the chaos of the streets around them fade. *I wish you'd take me to bed and for once I would just feel and not think. I wish you would like me. I wish you would tease me and flirt the way Duncan once did, I wish . . .*

"Watch out!"

Lucy's foot hit the ground at an awkward angle as three boys ran past her in the street, two of them clad only in their shirts and the third in possession of a coat but no scarf or hat.

"Little monsters. They almost ran you over," Thorne growled.

"They have to run," she said, limping slightly as they crossed toward the garden's entrance. "They don't have enough clothes between them to keep even one boy warm."

Thorne looked up at the inscription over the gate, then down at her.

"Lucy Peterson," he said softly. "You are . . ."

"Good day, Jonathan."

The gates to the garden had swung open, and two men stood there, staring at Thorne. One of them Lucy knew well, Mr. Robert Fortune, who worked hand in glove with the *hortus praefectus*, John Lindsey.

The other was a tall man who towered over them with his high top hat. He wore polished boots, and his woolen great-coat had three capes, brass buttons shined to perfection, and fur lining the collar. The scent of privilege wafted from him like the most expensive of colognes.

"Sir," Thorne said in return with a slight bow.

What was this?

"Good day, Miss Peterson," said Mr. Fortune coolly. He eyed the boxes with an eagerness that contrasted with his faint air of disdain. "These are the plants you promised us? But let me relieve Mr. Thornwood of his burden. No doubt he and his father, Lord Blackstone, have much to discuss."

Mr. Fortune took the box of plants from Thorne's arms and chuckled nervously, glancing between Lucy and Thorne.

Thornwood.

Not Thorne.

Carts and horses rode past them, birds sung in the many

trees behind the garden walls, and the boys who'd run by them now came back in this direction shouting like brigands, but all she could hear was a sound like rushing water and the almost painful thud of her heart in her chest.

Ezekiel Thornwood, the Baron of Blackstone, for she recognized his picture from the broadsheets, bowed his head to her, and Lucy curtsied in return. Thorne stood to the side; his brows pulled back as if he'd asked a question, but no words emerged. Not even an introduction.

Of course. Why would there be an introduction? She was merely a lowly apothecary, and Thorne was the son of a baron.

Mr. Fortune bid good day to Lord Blackstone and gestured for Lucy to come with him. Without looking back at the two men, Lucy followed him blindly as the gate closed behind her. When asked a direct question, she stuttered out a yes or a no, offering nothing in return despite the curiosity rolling off her host.

Lord Blackstone.

His *father*.

This explained Thorne's fine gloves and cultured speech.

Disappointment burned from her stomach up to her throat no matter how much Lucy chastised herself that there was nothing to be disappointed about. Thorne did not owe her the history of his life, nor his real name, nor anything other than the promise that he would help her figure out where her formula had gone.

Whatever intimacy the two of them created in the dark of the office two nights ago, it was a cocoon of desire only. There had been no promises, no whispered words of false affection— just two bodies coming together for a short time.

Breathe.

The Physic Garden had been in existence since 1673, a home

to medicinal plants, the study of medical botany, and more recently an international seed exchange. Straight paths created a
geometric design and led along banks of teaching plants. Fortune pointed out one or two new additions since Lucy had last
visited as they picked their way past the pond rockery. When
the girls had been apprentices, they'd been awed by the lava
stones there, donated by the famed Joseph Banks.

Mr. Fortune and Lucy discussed the contents of her boxes.
He was especially thrilled with the neem sapling and had just
returned from China with new plants of his own. They left the
boxes at the end of an enormous greenhouse, then made their
way back to the estate, which once was a private residence and
now served as the central hub for the work of managing the
society's vast garden.

After entering Lucy's plants into a series of ledger books,
Mr. Fortune offered her a cup of tea, but she declined. Katie's
good nature would allow her to tolerate Mr. Gentry only to a
point.

"Shall I have a boy summon a hack?" he asked. "Or were you
planning on returning somewhere with Mr. Thornwood?"

Ah. Mr. Fortune's curiosity had won over his discretion, but
Lucy refused to give him any more information. Bad enough
he had always considered her and Juliet embarrassments to the
Worshipful Society of Apothecaries. Much to his chagrin,
there was no rule against women apothecaries because no one
anticipated a woman *wanting* to be an apothecary. Despite Mr.
Fortune's protests, Lucy's father had apprenticed his daughters
without hesitation.

There was also the ever-present assumption that because
they were young and attractive, Lucy and Juliet were in want of
a husband. Or, if not a husband, male attention of a certain sort.

Either way, Mr. Fortune would talk. She was an unmarried

woman walking the streets alone with a man to whom she was not related. Despite Lucy being an apothecary, she was still a part of society, and her unchaperoned status made her appearance with Thorne risqué. Mr. Fortune now held a juicy piece of gossip with no context and could be counted on to use it against her at some point.

Lucy accepted his offer of a hack and pushed the cab's curtain open as far as it would go despite the stench coming off the Thames and the biting cold. Perhaps Thorne would return to the shop as if nothing had happened. Maybe his father had come to bring Thorne back into the fold? An avalanche of questions ran through her brain. Was she in a position to demand the answers?

She pushed open the curtains even further, letting the wind blow away whatever nonsense had spun itself in her head like cobwebs, dulling her instincts and distracting her from larger concerns. The shop was what concerned her most, now and in the future. Anything else was a waste of her time.

12

─⋘◆⋙─

"YOU ARE WELL, JONATHAN?" LORD BLACKSTONE'S VOICE had been eerily familiar despite the years of separation. The winds whipping off the Thames had knocked Blackstone's hat askew and given him roses on his cheeks.

Even now, days after their chance meeting, Thorne wrestled with the words that had passed—and those left unsaid—between the two of them after all these years.

Lord Blackstone had always been a quiet man, relying on his wife, Lady Blackstone, to navigate society for them both. When in London to take his seat, Blackstone was rarely to be seen, believing his vote in Lords was a great responsibility and taking it seriously. When his father returned home from Parliament, it was as though he needed an equal amount of time away from people as he'd just spent with them. While Thorne was forever in a state of motion during childhood—running, swimming, climbing trees, and, when his temper grew too hot, fighting—his father spent his time reading, horse breeding, and going on extended rambles alone through the grounds of his estate.

Thorne hadn't replied right away, his attention split between his father and Lucy, who disappeared behind the garden walls. She'd told him the Physic Garden was open only to members of the Worshipful Society of Apothecaries and he would not be allowed to follow her inside. She was probably grateful for that rule right now.

"What are you doing here?" Thorne asked his father. The question came out too abruptly, but Blackstone didn't seem to care.

"I am considering a donation to the upkeep of the garden. I have great admiration for John Lindsey and his work. I was issued a special invitation to peek behind the walls that has only been extended to a handful of people. Who was that lady?"

"That lady is . . ." Thorne's voice thinned into silence.

What was he supposed to say?

"That lady is Lucinda Peterson, an apothecary and under my protection as an agent with Tierney and Company," he said finally.

Very straightforward, that. It sounded hollow in his ears.

"Tierney and Company, eh?" his father repeated, looking up at the gate to the Physic Garden, then back at Thorne. "This is what you do with your time now? You are finished fighting?"

A wave of sadness threatened to take Thorne out at his knees.

"Yes," he answered his father. "I suppose I am."

Blackstone had nodded, then adjusted his hat and glanced one last time at the gardens.

"I am in London to vote on the Bank Charter Act. Your mother and I are at home to callers on Wednesday and Thursday."

Before Thorne could collect himself enough to answer, his father had turned and walked away. Thorne made no move to follow him. His stomach lurched crazily, and he leaned against the high brick wall of the garden.

By the time he saw Lucy leave and enter a hack, Thorne hadn't recovered enough to approach her. Instead, he took himself off to catch the omnibus back to Tierney's, where he spent the rest of the afternoon in the communal library researching medical patents, listening to the wind, and readying himself for when this job would end.

The question of whether his father had known he would be there, if the reunion was planned, if the invitation was genuine, had sat like a menhir, silent and unmoving, at the back of Thorne's head for three days now. Three days with no words passed between himself and Lucy.

"Papa, are you ready yet?"

Not for the first time, Thorne contemplated a return to the boxing ring. With a few good purses, he could afford a town house. He and Sadie would have rooms on separate floors— perhaps even an indoor privy where he could sit and contemplate the larger existential questions that happened to pop into a man's head when he was taking his time.

"Papaaaaaaaaaaa." Sadie pulled his name into the thread of a whine, and Thorne finished his business, exited the privy, and accompanied her back to their rooms.

"All right, now this is what we will do."

Sadie was bouncing on her toes as she raced around the little table in their apartment, polishing forks and refolding napkins. Each plate held a piece of card stock, upon which Sadie had written the guest's name in her best handwriting.

Thorne followed his daughter's orders, lighting the candles and setting the pewter snuffer within reach, checking on the roast in the oven and assuring her there were more than enough drippings to season the boiled carrots and potatoes.

"I am so glad Miss Peterson warned us of Mr. Gentry's pet chicken," Sadie said, her whole body vibrating with excitement. "I would have felt terrible serving him a dead cousin of his dear Andromeda. She is a pretty hen. Have you seen her?"

When a knock came at the door, Sadie put a hand to her stomach, having made herself sick with excitement.

"I shall answer the door, I am the hostess. Someday when we have a proper house, our butler will answer, but tonight— *eeeek*—"

Sadie did a little hop when a second knock sounded, and scuttled out of the kitchen to let in their guests.

Thorne stood at attention next to the settee where Sadie had directed him earlier as she led Juliet, Lucy, and Mr. Gentry into the small parlor.

Mr. Gentry had bowed once they shook hands and presented Thorne with a bottle of claret. He'd dressed for the occasion, donning a black wool dinner jacket about ten years out of date and a handsome pair of breeches. Thorne regretted his own choice of less formal trousers when he saw the care the other man had taken to shine his shoe buckles.

Gentry then turned to Sadie and handed her a nosegay of hothouse violets. Sadie's eyes grew wide, and her lower lip trembled as she curtsied and thanked him with a quiet voice.

Tonight, Gentry might stand and recite the name and weight of every tumor known to man and Thorne would not bat an eyelid.

He'd never thought to get Sadie flowers.

Juliet and Lucy did a fine job of exclaiming over Sadie's dress and the color of her hair ribbons. Having no spirits in the house, Thorne offered their guests a glass of lemonade before supper, which they politely accepted. Sadie settled them each in a seat, then rushed to help Thorne with the drinks.

"Miss Thorne, you are an accomplished hostess for your tender age," said Mr. Gentry once he'd sipped and complimented the lemonade. "Do you and your father often entertain?"

Sadie set her lemonade on an end table and turned toward Mr. Gentry, hands clasped in earnestness.

"I have only become old enough to eat with adult company in the past two years. Before that, Papa would read to me from *The Girl's Own Book*, to ready me for grown-up dinners."

She set her hands in her lap, smoothing them down the lawn of her pretty rose skirts, and Thorne wished he could lean over and rub her cheek with the back of his hand. How Sadie would bristle at the gesture. She was, she had reminded him many times in the preparations for tonight, not a baby. She was almost a young woman.

"Our first guest ever was Mrs. Merkle," Sadie confided. "She told Papa he had done a good job of instructing me on my table manners."

"Did she have a particular Bible verse to laud such an achievement?" Lucy asked archly.

Thorne took the opportunity to speak to her directly.

"'Good God, good meat. Good prayer, let's eat' was her comment, I believe."

Sadie clapped her hand over her open mouth with an audible pop and, after a moment where they weighed Thorne's monotone against his small smile, the guests understood he'd made a joke and they burst into laughter.

She might be angry with him, but Lucy was never one not to join in when others were laughing.

He'd known that, somehow. Known he could de-thorn her if he let down his guard, just a little.

Letting down his guard to coax a smile from a beautiful woman.

What was next?

The bottle of claret sat on the dining room table.

"That's *not* what she said, Papa."

He turned to his daughter, who submerged her giggles with fluttering hands only to let them escape again when she looked at Juliet. It put him in mind of the bubbles in a glass of champagne, and he pressed two of his fingers against the pulse in his wrist.

Mr. Gentry told the story of a great-aunt who'd misplaced her false teeth but would not be deterred from saying grace at a family dinner, which had them laughing so hard the knot of worry tangling Thorne's guts slowly unwound.

The roast came in for a bevy of compliments, and Sadie accepted similar accolades for the delicacy of her rolls and the beauty of her table settings. Thorne opened the claret and poured a glass each for Mr. Gentry, Lucy, and Julia. Sadie had placed Lucy opposite him at the other end of the table. Not subtle, but it seemed to suit Lucy, who was able to engage in general conversation without seeming to ignore him.

"The Petersons were very kind to have us to dinner one night," Sadie explained to Mr. Gentry as he steadily cleared his plate. "Papa told me that in polite circles, one always reciprocates such invitations."

Thorne had said it in a throwaway manner, forgetting Sadie heard everything—she just didn't always listen. Especially when it came to the admonition that she shouldn't try to hide food under other food on her plate.

"Ah, well. Those of us who do *not* travel in polite circles invite our guests for the pleasure of their company, not because we feel beholden," said Lucy. She smiled so as to take the sting out of her words and stared directly at Thorne. "We might have you to dinner three and four times, Miss Thorne, but you don't have to put your papa through the time and expense of hosting us in return."

She tapped the side of her cheek with a finger. "Why, you might have to find other ways to hide your vegetables."

Sadie sucked in her lips to hide a grimace.

Gentry looked up from his plate. "D'ye not enjoy cooked carrots, Miss Thorne?"

She shook her head. "They look like little legs and arms."

A pause settled over the table as everyone craned their necks to better examine the carrots set before them.

"Never thought of that," said Gentry.

"Oh. Oh, I can see it. This one here has crooked knees," said Juliet.

Lucy locked eyes with Thorne.

She'd avoided him since their trip to the garden. Thorne had avoided her as well while he tried to organize his thoughts.

"More claret?" he asked Gentry, making sure to keep pouring until the bottle was empty. Thorne felt no desire to drink, but neither did he want the wine left in his home.

Meanwhile, Lucy's eyes followed his every move. It could have been Thorne's imagination that a shadow of distrust lay behind them.

Most likely, it wasn't.

"Shall we have a game?" Juliet asked.

Thorne cleared their places and set the water to boil while Sadie escorted the guests back into the parlor.

"We could play two truths and a lie," Lucy suggested. Thorne shuddered as he took down the tea from the top cupboard.

"Oh, can we please play Elephant's Foot Umbrella Stand? One of the girls at school told me the rules. Do you know it?" Sadie asked.

Neither Thorne nor Mr. Gentry had heard of the game. Gentry caught on much quicker than Thorne, much to Sadie's amusement. After twenty minutes of torture, Thorne decided to bring in the tea tray, and Sadie took great pleasure in being asked to pour. As she handed Juliet her cup, she startled herself and the party with an enormous yawn that she barely managed to hide with her hand.

"We have quite worn you out," said Juliet.

"But we are having such a lovely time," Sadie complained.

Gentry rose and gave Thorne a nod of his head, and to Sadie a deep bow. "Miss Thorne, I enjoyed myself at supper more than any entertainment I can remember. A good guest shows their appreciation by leaving early. The Spaniards always say the best-looking part of a guest is their back."

Juliet and Lucy thanked both Sadie and Thorne for a lovely night. Before she left, Lucy turned around suddenly and took Sadie's hands in hers.

"You take good care of your papa, Sadie. He is lucky to have you looking out for him."

Sadie's eyes widened, but she did not refute Lucy's assumption that he needed looking out for. The air in the room inexplicably thinned, and a bittersweet pressure squeezed Thorne's chest.

"However, you must let him take care of you in return. Old people need a purpose, you know." Lucy's smile gave Sadie permission to grin back at her as a silent understanding passed between them.

After their prayers, Sadie fell asleep before he'd even blown out the candle. The homey scent of gravy and tea filled the air, and Thorne collected the name cards to save for Sadie and listened to the small clock in the parlor as it clicked down the minutes, slow and sluggish.

He did not owe Lucy an explanation. She was his employer, not his keeper. Still, when he closed his eyes, he could feel her moving around the building, awake, angry perhaps. Alone.

She might not even care that Thorne was the son of a nobleman. She might be too busy worrying about the formula and what to do about her brother. Why, she might not have been thinking of him at *all* these past few days.

How dare she ignore him?

He'd better go confront her immediately.

Thorne left a note for Sadie in case she woke, and went downstairs.

"DID YOU FIND A HOME FOR YOUR PLANTS?"

"Did you have a nice chat with your father?"

Thorne leaned against the doorway of the apothecary office, his mouth partly open. It wasn't a fitting answer to his question about the plants, but it had been on Lucy's mind since they had parted ways at the Physic Garden three days ago.

"Thornwood," she said thoughtfully. "And that was your father, Ezekiel Thornwood, Lord Blackstone," she said.

A long breath escaped his pursed lips and Thorne rocked back on his heels, putting his ungloved hands in his jacket pockets.

Jonathan Thorne was not the only person capable of investigations. The day after she'd learned his real name, Lucy had stopped by the local pub and bought an ale for Katie's da, Joe Quinlavin. After she finished making her case, once again, that Katie be allowed to attend school and received, once again,

Quinlavin's refusal, Lucy asked what he'd known about prize-fighting and one Jonathan Thorne in particular.

Although Thorne had told her about the prizefighting, she'd no idea of how widespread his fame was as the "Gentleman Fighter." Quinlavin had been astonished that Lucy hadn't known of Thorne's boxing fame and his lofty beginnings, but how should she have found out?

Apothecary apprentices were not in the same social strata as barons' sons, nor had Lucy ever done anything as scandalous as go to a prizefight. Her family straddled the working and the middle classes carefully. There were parts of London she'd never set foot in, not because she would feel out of place—she would—but because there was no reason for her to leave her Newton Street shop unless it was on apothecary business. Even then, her travels had never taken her to places like Hyde Park or Fitzrovia.

For the past three days, she'd avoided him while mulling over the information she'd collected. All the while she chastised herself for listening to gossip. Thorne's past was not her business. Lucy had no claim on him and no belief in his permanence.

This man was not of her world.

She'd known that the day he pulled her arse-first out of a second-floor window, and it had only become clearer every day since then.

He liked *accounting*, for goodness' sake.

"Yes. I'm the third son," Thorne acknowledged. "The spare's spare."

"What does your father think of your current occupation as an agent masquerading as a bookkeeper?" she asked. "Does he view it as a step up or down from prizefighter?"

Thorne's mouth bowed into a frown of consideration. "I

didn't ask him. I believe the notion of *occupation* is what my father finds most confusing."

Lucy knew little to nothing about the members of the aristocratic class. She'd no time to follow the gossip columns and never would have met any of them in her lifetime had it not been for Athena's Retreat. She had attended various functions at the Retreat, both public and secret, and had overheard some of the ladies talking about the confines of the aristocratic life. If Thorne had remained in his family's fold, he would have been spending his time shooting birds in the countryside, making endless rounds of visits, and attending various balls. It sounded terribly dull.

Except for the pretty dresses one gets to wear at a ball.

Lord knows, Lucy would love a pretty dress or two.

"Does your family know that you have a daughter?" she asked.

"They know very well," Thorne said.

He came into the office, then shut and locked the door behind him.

Locked the door.

No shiver of apprehension pricked up and down Lucy's spine. No. That was a shiver of *anticipation*. She clenched her thighs together as he approached where she sat behind the desk.

"Do you have any other questions besides what my father thinks of my job or if I hide my child from society?" he asked.

Lucy tried to read his expression in the low light. The oil lamp on the desk had run dry, and all there was left to illuminate the room was a candle atop the credenza.

"Do you share the opinion of your brother Mr. James Thornwood that the women he calls 'unfortunates' should not be able to receive preventatives or the induction of menstruation but should instead be jailed and their babies given to the church?"

"James is an ass. When did he say that?" Thorne asked.

His brother was named James. He had another brother, Joseph, and a mother, Ruth.

Lucy had wondered now and again since they'd met at Tierney's offices where this man had come from and what had shaped him. That Thorne had a family and was third in line for a barony powerful enough to be mentioned in the broadsheets—well, that possibility had never entered her head.

"Mr. Thornwood was quoted in the Guardians' publication, *The Gentlemen's Monthly Magazine*." She pushed it toward him, but instead of picking it up and bringing it to the other side of the desk to read, like a gentleman might, he came to stand next to her and set his hands on the desk.

"James is absolutely wrong in his opinion and should reconsider whom he calls 'unfortunate,'" he said, squinting at the print.

"Do you need your glasses?" she asked curtly.

"You notice I wear glasses," he said, still staring at the magazine.

"I am observant," she said.

"You are beautiful."

Lucy had heard a version of the compliment hundreds of times, but not from this man.

"This makes you angry at me." Lucy hadn't known this for the truth until the words escaped her lips just now. He resented her beauty. While other women had done the same, this was the first time a man had acted so.

"I had a weakness for beautiful women in the past," he said.

"The past when you were a prizefighter? Or a drunkard?"

"Both."

As they spoke, Lucy stood and pushed the desk chair away with the backs of her legs. When sparring with this man, it behooved her to be standing.

"Why are you here?" she asked.

"You hired me."

Liar.

"Why are you here in this office in the middle of the night?" she asked.

"I want to kiss you again."

It took every bit of Lucy's self-possession not to swoon at the determination in his voice.

She groped for outrage but found only excitement.

"That's blunt, Mr. Thornwood. Do you speak to titled women like that?"

With a movement so fast and fluid it took her breath away, Thorne had her pressed up against the wall, narrowly avoiding knocking into the side table now clear of papers. He gently but firmly cupped her chin in his massive hand and held her gaze with his.

"My name is *Thorne*. I have no occasion to speak with titled women. You are the first woman I have touched in seven years."

A tiny gasp that melted into a groan left her lips when Thorne canted his hips into hers and set the bulge of his erection against the core of her.

"I don't just want to kiss you," he continued, his voice so low and gruff the words sounded like the hard scrape of boulder against boulder. "I want to touch and taste you, to make you come with my fingers and then my tongue, and if you consent, I want to make you come a third time with my cock. I want to be inside you when you make that noise."

With an ease that belied his strength, he picked Lucy up and hitched her higher against the wall so that she could wrap her legs around his hips.

"Just say the word, Lucy, because all I want to do is make you come."

13

⇝⇜◆⇝⇜

THORNE'S WORDS DRIPPED LIKE TREACLE FROM LUCY'S temple, where he'd set his mouth, down her neck and shoulders to the rest of her body. A fire burned beneath her skin, heightening her senses. The wall against her back, the insistent pressure of his cock between her thighs, the friction of her chemise against her nipples, all this conspired to leave her dizzy and unsure.

This was only lust, she told herself. What they did in the dark, away from the world, it held no meaning, no tenderness. She repeated these words to herself, not speaking until she was certain she believed them.

"*Thorne*," Lucy whispered. "Is that the word you want?"

He leaned in and set his mouth to the skin at her temple again. The slick heat of his tongue surprised her, and he tasted his way down her cheek, down her neck, and came to rest on her shoulder at the neckline of her dress.

Licking her once, hard, as though she were made of candy,

as though he would bite her if he could, Thorne then raised his head.

A dark hunger made him unfamiliar in the low light of the single candle behind them. Little about Thorne's face was handsome. What drew Lucy to him was not signs of past violence on his skin. She lusted after the grim certainty that accompanied him like an aura. The intensity of his stare, the honesty of his words, and the knowledge that he would never harm her.

"The word I want is *yes*," he said. "Yes, Thorne, touch me, and taste me, and make me come."

"What about me?" Lucy asked. "Will you tell me yes?"

Thorne leaned forward and pressed his body against hers as he slowly bit her lower lip. Excitement bloomed between her thighs, and she grew damp with anticipation.

Releasing her lip from his teeth, he spoke with his mouth slightly touching hers.

"Yes, Lucy. Yes, I want you to touch me, and taste me, and make me come," he said.

Lucy's fingers sank into Thorne's hair, and she gave in to her need, opening her mouth against his, tasting his tongue, his teeth, while she tightened her legs around his hips, grinding slowly against the solidity of his cock. She licked the roof of his mouth, and when he grunted in approval, she suckled his tongue.

He kissed her harder, deeper even than she'd imagined, as if he could enter her through her mouth, and when his bare hand slipped under her skirts, she nearly climaxed at the unbearable friction of his skin against hers. His touch lingered at the back of her knee, and a quiver of bliss shot straight to the center of her. Impatient, greedy, Lucy reached between them and began pulling up her skirts.

She'd dressed nicely, a plain mulberry-colored silk gown with a neckline only slightly lower than her usual dresses, her thinnest petticoat beneath. The material was slick beneath her palms, and Thorne reached down to help her without stopping his kisses. Lucy pulled him tighter, kissed him harder in return, pressing against him as though she could melt into his skin and quench the burning need beneath her own.

Thorne slipped his hand up between her thighs, keeping her aloft with one arm as he gently rubbed his thumb over her entrance. The pearl at the top of her quim throbbed in time with his movements, and he broke off the kiss to whisper in her ear.

"I'm going to make you come now, Lucy."

Lucy bent her head back against the wall and waited for the release he promised.

A cobweb waved at her from the top of the bookshelves.

Lucy squeezed her eyes shut. Now was not the time to worry about the cleanliness of the office. Not that there was ever time to worry when there were more cures to mix than she had hours in the day. So much work awaited her this week, the familiar choke hold of worry fought for supremacy against the pleasure of Thorne's touch.

"Lucy," Thorne said, his lips against her neck. "Where did you go?"

His warm hand had stilled at the juncture of her thighs. That sensation of melting, of falling, had left.

"I can't," she said. "I want to. I'm so sorry, but I can't."

"Did I hurt you?" he asked, concern pulling down the corners of his eyes.

"No, no. I just . . ." Her head dropped and she rested it on his shoulder while he continued to hold her up.

How was she to explain the way her mind worked against her body? Every time Lucy tried to let go, her muscles would clench and every thought she'd ever had would race through her brain like a herd of oxen, so noisy and distracting that she had no choice but to pull away from her pleasure.

"Were my kisses not compelling?" he asked. His question brushed against her mouth behind the rough tickle of his beard.

"They were," she said, her skin still afire with residual longing.

Thorne took his hand out from under her skirts and Lucy fought back tears. She'd ruined everything. He would think she was strange, would never want to . . .

"Were my touches not gentle enough?" he asked, trailing the back of his hand down her neck to her chest, then back around her to pull down her dress as far as it would go, freeing her breasts.

Once again, her clit throbbed, and Lucy nearly cried in frustration.

"I can't . . ." She lifted her head and rolled her bottom lip under her front teeth, trying to think of how to explain.

"I go too far and can't come back. My head won't stay quiet after that."

"Where are you going?" he asked.

Lucy knew he wasn't joking. His eyes held hers, and she could feel him listening to her with his whole body.

Where did she go?

"To work, always," she confessed. "To home sometimes. To where I am needed and where I am not."

"I can take you out of your head, Lucy, only if you give me permission."

Permission.

This would make them equal participants.

Lucy nodded slowly. Yes. Yes, she would do this.

"There are tins of prophylactics in the bottom drawer of the counter out front," she said. "Shall I go fetch them?"

Thorne embraced Lucy's torso, trapping her arms at her sides beneath his. He pushed his cock against her hips, and she wrapped her legs around his waist.

"Not yet. Not this time." Thorne's voice was so low and thick, she felt the words down her spine, beneath her skin.

"I give you permission, then," she said. "I want you to help me." Unsure of what help she needed, Lucy trusted that Thorne held the power somehow to quiet the thoughts and take her away.

"Let go," he said with no inflection.

Lucy didn't understand. She tried to move but he'd pinned her against the wall. There was no place she could go.

"Lucy. Let go," he said once more.

Lucy struggled against Thorne's hold, half-heartedly at first, and then when she realized he wasn't moving an inch, she twisted in his arms. As she did, the friction against her nipples woke the desire that hadn't completely disappeared.

Her petticoat had fallen back between them when Thorne had removed his hand, but her drawers were still untied. Thorne slowly thrust against her, his hips pulling the thin cotton against her bared center. Lucy was trapped.

Lucy. Let go.

So she did. Lucy let go of everything except what it felt like when she clamped her legs tighter around Thorne's waist and returned his slow thrusts. She let go of any embarrassment when she moaned, sucking his bottom lip while she pressed her breast into his palm. Any time her brain threatened to interrupt her pleasure, Lucy fought Thorne's hold, fighting him to let go when she couldn't force herself to do that.

Thorne ground his cock in a steady rhythm, hard enough to

tease her but not hard enough to hurt. He pushed her breast up with one hand and bent to take it in his mouth while he kept moving his hips. The pleasure from his mouth combined with the throbbing need at her center made Lucy see stars when she closed her eyes.

Tighter and tighter his hold, harder and harder they thrust, as though their friction could disappear the material between them until finally, the tension snapped, and Lucy truly did let go. Her head thrown back, she let loose a silent scream of completion, and Thorne lifted his head from her breast, grunted, and pushed his hips one last time against the softness of her center, his mouth exploring her temple and his hands coming up to frame Lucy's face. He made no sign of embarrassment at having come before removing his trousers.

"Lucy Peterson," he whispered, then ran the tip of his tongue along the curve of her jaw, painting a line of desire along her skin. "That was incredibly satisfying. Please, never tell me if you were thinking about Mr. Gentry's tumor while I came. I will never survive it."

Lucy giggled, then laughed outright.

"Jonathan Thorne," she said. "You can be assured that I followed your orders and let go, much to my satisfaction as well."

Their eyes met, then held.

A tickle of fear rose from Lucy's belly at what she saw in Thorne's gaze, but she squashed it with the reminder that a man's touch held no promises.

Sex did not mean love.

No matter how good it felt.

14

※≪≪◆≫≫※

"GOOD DAY TO YOU, SIR."

A short man shaped like a chestnut with legs doffed his hat in Thorne's direction and offered up a wide smile, only to yank the smile back when Thorne growled at him.

Thorne knew a moment of regret when the chestnut man scurried off, but it did not slow him in his march toward Madame Mensonge's academy.

That was the third time today a passerby had offered greetings.

Never had strangers smiled at Thorne in the street. He'd little control over the expression that rested on his face, due to the shoddy stitching and broken nose. On an ordinary day, his face was so grim that young children cried at the sight of him. This suited him fine. Thorne had no time for people who were indiscriminately friendly.

Friendly people made him itch.

Today, however, it seemed the whole world was smiling at him. This could only be because Thorne was smiling.

How humiliating.

It couldn't be helped. No matter how he filled his head with things that annoyed him—seagulls, naps, tight shoes, raisins in biscuits—the erotic encounter of the night before refused to leave his consciousness.

A shopgirl cleaning a display in a store window stopped what she was doing to wave at him.

Damn it.

Thorne wrapped his scarf over his mouth.

Tiny pellets of snow rattled on the cobblestones beneath his feet, and he stared at the street in front of him so as not to catch anyone else's eye.

For the first time in months, his first thought upon waking had not been to catalog the aches that riddled his bones, or how painful it would be to lever his body out of bed. Nor had his heart clenched with the fear that Sadie had not lived through the night.

Instead, his first thought upon waking had been that Lucy's slightly crooked front teeth biting down onto her lower lip was the most erotic sight he'd ever witnessed. This resulted in a cock stand that refused to settle down until he'd plunged his head into a basin of freezing wash water.

Later that morning, he stopped in at Tierney's, hoping to find Winthram, but the young agent had taken a trip to North Yorkshire of all places. In his stead, he'd left an envelope with information about the mysterious Mr. Wilcox.

Thorne read and then ruminated on this information, but it wasn't long before the lemony scent of another agent's half-eaten scone brought memories of Lucy back to the forefront of his brain.

This was worse than how it had been with Genny. More intense.

This was obsession.

And yet, the two women couldn't be more different. Genny had a hunger for attention that Thorne could never sate. Over time, he recognized this need was a substitute for something else, but he never persuaded her to reveal what that something else was.

Genny's life before Thorne was a mystery. He knew she was born in Jamaica to an unwed young mother who had traveled to England in search of a new life. Her mother died a short time after, and Geneviève found herself living with relatives.

She never told him which side of her family the relatives were, but considering slavery in Jamaica hadn't ended all that long ago, Thorne assumed she'd gone to live with her father's family. Had her father been a slaveholder? Genny had never said anything about her relatives.

He also suspected they were either unkind or, worse, indifferent. Genny eventually set out on her own and made a name for herself in the demimonde, that group of people who lived on the fringes of polite society either by choice or because society had pushed them there.

"Tell me a secret of yours," he'd croon into her ear after watching her drink champagne day and night.

"Secrets are currency," she admitted, her words slurred together. Thorne knew when she was drunk because the smallest lilt of her childhood accent would slip out. "I need enough currency to keep me in style once you leave me."

Thorne protested that he would never leave her. He'd spent scandalous amounts of money on beautiful furnishings, on gowns that complemented her features, on gardens, musicians, books, and paintings. Anything that would catch her fancy and keep her home with him at night.

Thorne had never believed Genny returned his love.

Now, there was another beautiful woman who took up his thoughts.

This time, he would not make the same mistake.

Later that afternoon, upon approaching the soot-stained building that housed Madame's school, Thorne spied three figures standing together. Right away he recognized Sadie and the waving feathers of her new goose down–trimmed winter bonnet. Next to her stood the small figure of Juliet Peterson. What brought him up short was the third in their party.

Duncan Rider.

Thorne crossed the street quickly, hiding his form behind a passing wagon, and secreted himself in the doorway of a shop. He pretended to peruse the wares in the shop's bow window, which hid him from the street.

Rider was gesturing in supplication while Juliet shook her head in the negative. Thorne debated whether to show himself now. If he did, Rider would know that Sadie was his daughter and might make the connection between Sadie, the Petersons, and all the questions Thorne had been asking him the other night at the club.

His decision was made when Rider turned away and hailed a hack. Sadie and Juliet walked in the opposite direction. By the time they reached Thorne's block, Rider had disappeared in the afternoon traffic. Thorne emerged from hiding, greeting the two of them.

"Did you know that a frog's poo can measure a quarter of its body size?" Sadie exclaimed after a rushed greeting. "Can you imagine if that were true for people?"

Thorne most likely could imagine but preferred not to. He and Juliet exchanged grimaces and Juliet kindly redirected the conversation from frog feces to their anatomy, which Sadie had begun to study this week.

Thorne waited for a pause in the discussion of scalpels and interjected.

"As I was coming along, I saw you talking to a gentleman. Was this anyone I would know, Sadie?"

"I don't think so," she said. "We weren't introduced."

Juliet slowed her steps so that she and Thorne fell back behind Sadie.

"I don't want you to think I wouldn't introduce Sadie to my friends," she said in a low voice. She needn't have worried that Sadie was eavesdropping, for the girl had spied a rider atop a pretty gray pony and had eyes only for the animal.

How long would it be before Sadie asked for a pony?

"I'm not certain you'd want her known to him," Juliet continued. "That was Duncan Rider. I know Lucy must have told you something about what happened with her formula for lozenges if she told you about her missing formula for the croup salve."

"Ah. There was some understanding of marriage, I believe," he said.

Juliet hummed in agreement. "Duncan was genuinely fond of Lucy. Anyone could see, but his father forbade the marriage. Duncan simply lacks the ability to say no to people."

"He said no to marrying Lucy."

A woman with a brain as sharp as hers could not fail to hear the edge to his words, but Juliet seemed not to notice. Her mouth thinned, and she stared down at her scuffed boots as they clacked against the cobblestones.

Juliet's shoulders slumped, and her pace slowed even more. "David was furious, of course, and Lucy deserved better, but I understand why he broke it off with Lucy. Defying expectations isn't easy. It's exhausting, actually."

Thorne knew a little bit about this. Unlike Juliet, he hadn't defied society to better the health and welfare of the poor. He'd defied it out of some dark adolescent urge to break things.

He'd no idea where the anger had come from or why it had retreated. A child with no patience, inexhaustible energy, and two fiercely competitive brothers, Thorne was most often to be found in the corner, where the tutor had likely sent him to await a strapping.

The more his brothers bullied him and the more the tutor punished him, the angrier Thorne became. It was by the grace of God that he discovered boxing. When Thorne fought, his frustrations and fears receded.

For a time.

When fighting didn't work, he had turned to the bottle.

"Duncan has asked for help getting back into Lucy's good graces," Juliet said.

"You can't be inclined to give it to him?" Thorne asked. Disbelief and something else, something stronger, turned his voice to a growl.

"Lucy needs a husband, Mr. Thorne," said Juliet matter-of-factly. "If she has help running the apothecary, David and I can be free to pursue our own paths and not worry about her."

It was a selfish reason to want a sister married.

Last night, Lucy had glowed with enjoyment from the unexpected orgasm, and a great ache had built in his chest alongside her increasing desire. He'd wanted to make her come, not for his own pleasure, though he had enjoyed it, but as a gift for her. A way to relieve the burdens she carried.

"Is it Lucy who wants a husband, or you who wants a husband for her?" Thorne asked. "You would shackle her to a man like Duncan Rider for the rest of her life so that you do not feel guilty when she is overwhelmed by her work?"

What were these words coming from his mouth? Why on earth should a bookkeeper care if his employer were to marry a vapid, selfish young man with excessive facial hair?

How had it come to this?

Thorne chastising Juliet Peterson was not going to solve Lucy's problems, nor help him finish his assignment. Lucky for Thorne, Juliet was distracted, whether by Duncan Rider or her own worries over the clinic and her patients, and she didn't take offense.

"Lucy needs someone to help her but will never admit to it," Juliet said, picking up the pace now that they'd rounded the corner. "It is a lonely life, being a pioneer, Mr. Thorne. She and I are the only women apothecaries in London, perhaps even all of England. We have no counterparts, and at the end of the day it is very difficult to come home and have no one there who understands your burdens or how to lift your spirits."

Thorne disagreed. Lucy did not need someone to help her at work, and she didn't necessarily need another apothecary. Lucy needed someone to support her so that she had the time and energy to work. She needed someone to hold her when the burdens she carried became too great. Did her own sister not see this?

His irritation at Juliet's ignorance faded as they rounded the corner and caught sight of the entrance to the shop. A claw of worry poked at his stomach.

Two women were knocking at the main doors to the apothecary, and one was peering into the front window. As Thorne, Sadie, and Juliet approached them, the women shrugged and left. The curtains were pulled tight, and a painted sign hung on the door's knob announcing the apothecary was closed.

"WHY HAVE YOU CLOSED THE SHOP? THERE WERE TWO customers walking away as I . . . Oh, my dearest. What happened?"

Juliet had come into the apartment calling Lucy's name, only to find her sister curled up in her bedroom.

Lucy pulled her bed quilt tight around her shoulders and gazed at Juliet, guilt warring with exhaustion. "I just couldn't go on today, and Katie's da needed her to watch the younger children while their ma is sick."

The same bedchamber in which Lucy had lived her whole life was like the comfort of a womb after this morning.

"It was me alone, which was fine, only . . ."

Lucy had received word that morning that the baby she had been treating had died.

Despite Lucy and Juliet's best efforts, the baby's humors could not be balanced. There was nothing Lucy dreaded more than the loss of a patient. She could never do what Juliet and Mrs. Sweet did, treat women who were destined to die young and often painfully.

"The baby's father was the one who came to tell me," Lucy said.

She'd been chatting with a customer while she wrapped up their purchases, and a young man had come into the shop. The sun was out for a change and the pale light, more watery than golden, was still blinding, showing off the dirty spots on the windows, allowing no comfort, only light.

A greeting sat at the front of her throat for a moment before she issued it, knowing from the hair standing on end on her arms and the back of her neck that something had knocked this man askew.

Tall, his shirt cuffs too short so that the white knobs of his wrists stood out, the man doffed a battered black felted hat. He was gaunt and unshaven, with black circles that made his eyes look sunken. His chapped lips were tightly drawn as he advanced toward Lucy at the counter, and she subtly stepped toward the back wall. On one of the shelves lay a hammer and a bell—the bell would have been more helpful if someone else had been in the shop. The hammer, Lucy had no idea if she could use to defend herself, but its presence reassured her.

Usually.

"Can I help you?" she asked, knowing the answer was most likely not.

"I'm James Hoekle," the man said.

Hoekle? The name hit her like a slap.

James Hoekle was also the name of the baby Lucy had been treating.

"Is it . . ." Lucy's mouth was too dry to finish the sentence, but she did not need to be told. Hoekle's distraught expression said it all.

"My son. My namesake. He's dead."

When he reached in the pocket of his coat, Lucy's skin went cold and clammy. Slipping one arm behind her, she searched for the handle of the hammer without being able to look.

Before she could feel her way to the weapon, Hoekle had tossed a linen pouch on the counter in front of her.

What was left of the tonic she'd given the baby's mother was in the bag, along with a handful of coins.

"My wife insisted we consult you," the man said. There was no specific inflection in his voice, but it made Lucy's heart start to race. Arm still behind her back, she closed her fingers round the hammer, finally, and readied herself.

"We went to a doctor, first. A man from Harley Street."

Hoekle paused, then nodded as if Lucy had asked a question. "That's right. A *man*."

"I am so sorry for your loss," she said, trying to buy time. "I will return your money—"

"My wife said apothecaries have the same education as doctors." The words shot from Hoekle's mouth like tiny pellets of hail. "She said a woman would better understand how to treat a baby, said you'd a womanly *intuition*."

Lucy did not bother to argue that her only intuition had been that the baby was certain to die as soon as she examined him.

This was the great dilemma of what she did here. There were no cures for so many of the childhood diseases Lucy encountered, but the palliatives she offered instead would sometimes prove to be helpful, enough to even save lives.

Sometimes.

"My uncle's been banging on at me to join the Guardians," Hoekle told her. Lucy's stomach sank and she briefly closed her eyes. This was not good.

"A woman shouldn't be allowed to dispense medicine like a real doctor."

Despite her certainty that this was a lost cause, Lucy tried to explain. "Mr. Hoekle, your baby had an imbalance in his humors that would not right itself. The only difference between the medicine I gave him and what a doctor would do is they would have bled the baby along with—"

Hoekle's hand flew up to deflect Lucy's calm explanation. "Aye. They would've bled him and let the poison out of him."

"That isn't—"

"You talked my wife out of listening to a doctor, and now my baby's dead." Hoekle's voice crackled with pent-up rage and sorrow. "You stupid cow. You just couldn't let a man have the last say."

Lucy slowly lowered the arm holding the hammer to her side and hid the weapon in the folds of her skirt. There was no point in telling Hoekle that her treatment and opinion would have been the same if the doctor were a man or a woman.

Holding a shaking arm up, Hoekle pointed to her with his first finger like an avenging angel pointing to a sinner.

"Don't ever come near me or my family again," he said. Lucy nodded quickly, unwilling to say anything that might antagonize him. "The Guardians will take care of women like you. They are watching."

As soon as Hoekle shut the outer door behind him, Lucy had rushed over and locked it. Slipping down to the floor with her back against the door, she'd sat there and concentrated on just breathing until she stopped shaking.

"Oh, darling. I am so sorry," Juliet said now, after Lucy recounted her day. "You and I both know the baby was too sick when the mother brought him to us for a cure to work."

Lucy shrugged. Did she know? Her fallibility ate away at her day and night. Nothing she did ever seemed to be enough.

Pulling open the curtains, Juliet let in the pearl-gray light of the winter's afternoon. "Do not stay in here and hide away. Come out with me. Imagine how much better you will feel someplace well lit and jolly."

Lucy barely listened as Juliet pleaded with her to come to a lecture at Athena's Retreat. Mrs. Sweet was giving a talk in the public rooms about the ideal diet for a pregnant woman. They hoped some of the women there could be counted on to help the clinic financially.

"No. Please. I am not fit for company," Lucy said. "I'll just have a lie-down and then I've masses of orders to fill. Just having you listen has helped so much."

Shaking her head, Juliet nevertheless did not argue. She'd

made her own blanket cocoons many times before when she'd
lost a patient.

"I can't leave you when there is no food in the larder," Juliet
said. "Shall I ask Mr. Thorne to order you some pies while you
sleep?"

"You will do no such thing," Lucy protested. "He has enough
to do with sorting our accounts and taking care of Sadie. I could
hear her chatting in the hallway about dissections. She will
have him out searching for frogs at the Serpentine, I reckon."

Juliet laughed and stood from the bed, saying something
about fathers and daughters and science, but Lucy had already
begun to doze by then.

Sometime later, a knock woke her.

Lucy stumbled to the door, wondering if Juliet's talk was
over and she'd forgotten her key, but the door had been left
unlocked. Standing on the other side was Thorne, mud at the
hem of his trousers and holding a parcel wrapped in newssheet
and smelling of hot lard.

Pasties.

Thorne.

The presence of both left her dizzy and weak in the knees.

She let him in.

15

⊰⊰⊰◆⊱⊱⊱

"MISS JULIET TOLD ME WHAT HAPPENED," THORNE SAID once Lucy invited him into the apartment.

Lucy smothered a yawn and nodded, staring hopefully at the bag. Had he chosen haste over concern and gone to the corner shop? They could be relied upon to mix oodles of lard in their crust.

"Is that for me?" she asked.

Thorne grinned.

What a gift, that smile. For a man whose talent was to keep any sign of emotion from his face, this was an offering as valuable as a hot, greasy pasty.

"Sadie told me about your favorite pie shop," he said.

"Bless that child." Lucy inhaled the blissful scent of roast meat and spices. "Did she tell you of my love for lard?"

Rather than answering, Thorne walked past Lucy and into her kitchen. Curious, Lucy followed.

"You've never been inside the kitchen of a pie shop, have

you?" he asked, opening cupboard doors, and taking out a plate and glass.

"No, and I don't want to. I don't want to know what makes these pies so—ahhhh." Lucy moaned with excitement as Thorne tore open the bag to reveal three plump, golden pasties. They might have been the prettiest she'd ever seen.

"Then you are unaware of where they get the fat they use to cook with?"

Lucy took the glass and filled it from a carafe of water, then grabbed the plate from his hands and set it on the kitchen table.

"Do you want to know why I prefer to remain ignorant about the process of pasty making?" she asked as she picked up the pie.

It was a shame about the stitching of the scar on Thorne's face. While she bit into the tongue-tingling combination of fat, flour, salt, and meat, Lucy imagined what he would look like without the scar.

Handsome, obviously. Even with the scar and slightly bent nose, Thorne was arresting and regal. Without it . . .

Lucy cast her eyes down to the table and studied her pasty.

Whatever was she thinking, outright ogling a man's face? What would he think of her?

"Why?" Thorne asked.

Lucy glanced at him and stopped chewing, raising her brows in question.

"Why do you prefer to remain ignorant?"

"Because if I learn the real story, it may put me off pasties forever," she said, wiping her lips with her napkin.

Thorne's eyes followed the movement and remained on her lips when she put the napkin down. Now that she'd eaten something, Lucy's mood lightened. Watching Thorne, she licked her lips.

Ah. His face didn't move, but he'd leaned forward—a fraction of an inch, to be certain, but enough to betray his interest. He had a presence so strong that if Lucy raised her fingers to his skin, she was certain she would feel him before she touched him. An aura of determination and intelligence. Closing her eyes, Lucy took a deep breath through her nose.

Tweed and paper. Ink and tea.

Sitting back in her chair, Lucy took the napkin and dried her fingers. Thorne watched this intently and set his elbow on the table, chin in hand.

Interesting.

"You see, if you put me off my pasties, then I won't be so grateful to you for bringing them in the first place."

His nostrils flared, and a furl of excitement woke between Lucy's thighs. The fear and pain from today's events drained from her body, only to be replaced with a heated anticipation. From the moment she opened the door to him, Lucy had been envisioning Thorne in her bed. The ghost of the climax he'd brought last night now set her to squirming in her seat, relishing the insistent drumming of the nerves at the center of her.

Let go, Lucy.

Let go of the fear from today, the pain of not knowing, the uncertainty that painted every corner of her life. Let go and feel good. That was what Lucy needed.

"And when I am grateful . . ." Lucy left him to imagine what might complete that sentence.

A spiral of lightness rose along her spine as Thorne leaned back and one corner of his mouth lifted in a sly smile.

"I would like to be the object of your gratitude."

Lucy did not let go of the sense of joy that buoyed her up and out of her chair, now leavened with the headier sense of being desired. More than anything in the world, Lucy wanted this man to see her—all of her.

She bent toward him, her voice trembling despite her eagerness.

"I was sleeping earlier, and it has left me with the need for a sponge bath. Juliet is not here. Do you think you can help me with my corset ties?"

A beat passed, but Lucy did not have any second guesses, because Thorne's cheeks were ruddy with lust and his fist closed onto nothing but air.

She beckoned him with a crooked finger and led the way from the kitchen to her bedroom. Slightly embarrassed at the sight of her unmade bed, she bent to straighten the cover, when Thorne ran a hand down her spine and over the rise of her bottom.

Lucy straightened and threw a saucy smile over her shoulder to him.

"I do worry that you will get your waistcoat wet," she said with patently false sympathy, turning around. "Shall I help you remove it?"

Thorne rubbed his thumb over her lips, then leaned in and kissed her, licked her lips, and straightened. It weakened Lucy's knees, the way he set his mouth to her skin as though he'd eat her, as though he were starving.

"If you please," he said, his crisp diction betrayed by the gravel in his voice.

Lucy glanced at the oil lamp on the side table and the closed curtains.

"It is seven o'clock. Your sister is not expected home until ten, and Sadie went to bed early."

"How did you know what I was thinking?" Lucy asked,

gently separating the lapels of his outer coat and pulling it down his arms.

Thorne shrugged and held his arms out to his sides so that she might take off his waistcoat. The forest-green silk was expertly tailored for all that it lacked embellishment.

When Lucy untied his cravat, Thorne put his hand over hers. "No. I will do this part."

He stared at Lucy's face with hungry eyes while he untied the strip of linen, ran it through his fingers, and then reached over and draped the cloth over her headboard.

She'd no idea why he had done this, but excitement swelled nevertheless, spurred by the heat in his gaze and the tension in his jaw. Lucy quite forgot she was supposed to be undressing him as Thorne pulled his shirttails from his trousers and then reached back and pulled his shirt over his head.

"Oh," she said. Or sighed. Or made some sort of incoherent sound of pleasure. The tiniest shadow of a smile curved beneath Thorne's lower lip, and he pulled off his undershirt as well. Because he somehow had the power to weaken Lucy's muscles simply by scowling, it came as no surprise to her when the steps she took toward him wobbled.

Thorne's body told a history. That he'd been raised with plenty to eat was apparent in his height, the breadth of his shoulders, and the strength and grace in his carriage. He stood tall and chiseled like the nude athletes etched on Grecian vases one saw in the British Museum.

As Thorne undid the tapes of his trousers, Lucy put her hand on his chest. Beneath his skin a powerful heartbeat thumped against her fingertips, and she petted the soft hair that ran from between his nipples down in a V to where his waistband started.

He wasn't perfect.

There was a bump beneath his left clavicle from a poorly healed break. A crescent moon–shaped scar ran, puckered and red, beneath his right nipple. Lucy did not look away from these clues, even as he pushed off his shoes and let his trousers hang down around his waist, exposing the cream-colored linen of his smallclothes.

Running her hand across his chest, Lucy stared up into his gaze.

"Why?" She whispered the question, not wanting to distract him from the important task of disrobing, but needing to know, nonetheless. Why go from being the son of a baron to a man who took money for pain?

He pushed his trousers down and they fell to the floor. They tangled their fingers trying to untie the tapes to his smallclothes at the same time, but Thorne took her hand and held it aloft in his closed fist and managed the tapes one-handed.

His smallclothes fell away from his lean hips, and Lucy bit down on her bottom lip. Sex with Duncan had been furtive and sometimes uncomfortable. She had never seen him fully naked, most times making love up against a wall or over a crate.

Not in her wildest imaginings had Duncan ever resembled this. Lucy sank to her knees and took Thorne's cock in hand. It was thick and hot, the foreskin softer than velvet. When she pulled it down and the head emerged, swollen and purple, she had to clench her thighs. The scent of earth and salt and something altogether heady filled her nose, and without being completely certain of what was correct, Lucy sucked the tip of his cock into her mouth.

"Ahhhh, Jesus, Lucy," Thorne groaned.

The vibrations from his exclamation rumbled down her

spine, and Lucy knew she was doing something right. Remembering a naughty song from a night at the pub, Lucy gathered him deeper into her mouth, gently sucked, and then pulled up.

"Ahhhh," Thorne repeated, his fingers now running down her scalp to where pins kept her hair in a topknot, knocking the tiny pieces of tin to the floor.

Lucy continued to taste him, wishing she had waited for his answer.

"Please," he said softly. Lucy released his cock from her mouth with a soft, wet sound and looked up at him.

"Please," he said. "Can I see you?"

She knew what he meant.

He meant see *her*. The whole her. The worries and the fears and the never-ending sympathy and love and willingness to sacrifice anything and everything for the people she loved.

Thorne wanted to see Lucy, naked.

Sex did not equate with love.

She fixed this thought in her mind as she rose from the floor and turned around, arms above her head, presenting him with the laces of her dress.

No reason Lucy could not enjoy it. If she remained sensib—*oohhh*, what in the world? As he pulled apart the laces to her corset, Thorne traced the line of Lucy's spine with his tongue. Every part of her skin tightened in pleasure. With a twist and a tug, he managed to divest Lucy of her clothing in a third of the time it had taken her to remove his.

Lucy turned around and tilted her head for a kiss when the thoughts started to pour into her head.

Where was Sadie now? What if she woke? Would she come looking for her father?

Thorne walked Lucy backward toward the bed, his knees prodding her thighs, his cock bobbing against her belly.

What if Juliet came home early?

Where was David?

Had Lucy remembered to fill the orders?

"Lucy," Thorne said. "I need to ask a serious question."

His tone jolted Lucy right out of her head. While the desire still hovered over her skin, a shiver of disappointment moved down her spine.

"Can you tell me to stop?" he asked.

Still standing at the side of her bed, Thorne's hands running up and down her arms, Lucy took a moment to consider his question.

"You want us to stop?"

"No," he whispered. Thorne put his hands on her shoulders, the ruddy skin of his fingers dark against the creamy white of her skin. He turned her around so that her back was to him, her knees to the mattress, and Lucy shuddered with pleasure as the length of his cock pressed between the cheeks of her bottom.

"I want to know that you feel safe enough to tell me to stop if I'm doing something you don't like," Thorne explained.

His hands dropped from her shoulders and smoothed down the slope of her breasts, then he cupped them in his palms and pinched her nipples.

"Oh, yes," she assured him. "I will tell you to stop, and I will also tell you when not to stop."

He laughed a dark brush of sensation onto the nape of her neck, then stepped away from her for a moment.

"Don't move." His order buzzed between her thighs even as Lucy frowned at the cold air on her back. In an instant, he was behind her again, scooping her hair back from her shoulders.

"I don't want you wandering away from me again before I can make you come," Thorne said. "So, I'm going to tie you up."

Lucy's head cocked as she tried to imagine what he meant. The breath left her lungs with a gasp when he reached around from behind and tied a strip of silk over her eyes.

"You have to do what I say, Lucy." A heady combination of apprehension and lust made her tremble. "Listen carefully."

Questions roiled in her head, but Lucy couldn't say them aloud, so distracted was she by the way Thorne's demands buzzed across her skin. Despite her confusion, she did not hesitate to follow Thorne's orders, leaning forward and feeling the mattress beneath her hands, then crawling onto the bed and bringing her hands together in front of her.

Thorne slipped his cravat loosely around one of her wrists and brought her arm up toward the bedpost.

"What . . ." Lucy crossed her legs, suddenly shy about the moisture that trickled down her thighs.

"Does it hurt?" he asked, pausing in the act of tying her other hand now to the opposite bedpost.

Lucy waited a moment to absorb the sensation of being tied down.

"No," she said in wonder. "No, I . . ." She pulled at the restraints. Thorne had tied her wrists tight enough so there was tension, but not too tight that she couldn't slip the bonds if she needed to.

"But anyone could be watching, and I wouldn't know," Lucy said. The vulnerability of her position struck her forcefully, and for the first time, she shivered from the cold.

"No."

Thorne lowered himself down onto her. Lucy drew in the scent of tea and paper while his body warmed hers. He rested on his elbows, his torso brushing hers, his muscular thighs parting hers so that his cock pulsed against her quim.

"No one will see you except for me. I will keep you safe," Thorne said.

Her mouth opened and a sigh escaped.

"Do you trust me?" He nuzzled her temple.

Lucy pulled again against the ties and opened her legs wider to accommodate his hips.

"You will remain here the entire time. Stay with me and take the pleasure I want so badly to give you."

Every random thought that tried to enter her head was met with the resistance of his mouth on her breasts and the soft grip of the ties on Lucy's wrists.

Every thought except one.

"I don't have any . . ."

Thorne pushed himself off her, the mattress sinking as he sat on the side of Lucy's bed. The scrape of a tin being opened set her heart to pounding.

"I took the liberty of bringing a tin of condoms with me tonight," Thorne said.

She couldn't see him, couldn't see anything except the black of her blindfold. The mattress creaked as he came back to the bed, coming between her thighs. She pictured him sitting between her legs as she lay there, bared to him. The rustle of the condom skated across her belly, and she tried to close her legs.

"No."

Lucy froze.

"I want to see you," he said. His hands settled on her knees, then smoothed down to the center of her.

"Trust me," he said.

Broken and imperfectly healed, his voice rumbled down her bones and along her muscles. An image of stones, heavy and immutable, settled in Lucy's head as Thorne parted her with his thumbs and lowered his head to the rise of her soft belly.

Small kisses ending with the promise of tiny bites peppered Lucy's skin.

"Can I move?" she asked, writhing beneath the hunger of his mouth.

"Yes. Please," he said, then slowly ran his tongue up and down the seam of her. Lucy made a noise, embarrassed for a moment, then enervated as Thorne gently parted her and brought his mouth to her quim.

Her physical excitement ratcheted up when she imagined Thorne's expression as he watched himself pleasure her. Tighter and tighter were the circles he made with his tongue, suckling her clitoris and pausing to praise her every so often; how soft her skin, how delicious the taste of her, how much he wanted to be in her.

The explosion came quickly, too quickly, after his praise. Her center still throbbing, Lucy raised her arms and pulled against the restraints. Without waiting for her to come down from the waves of pleasure, Thorne crawled up her body, tasting the hollows and the rises of her, whispering of how sweet and how pretty her belly and her breasts were.

She lifted her head in anticipation and, when he was close enough, bit him gently on the lips. Her arms pulled against the cravat, and she mewled in frustration when they prevented her from touching his skin, his face.

"I am here to take care of you," Thorne crooned as his cock nudged at her quim. "All day long, you are responsible for everyone around you. Life and death and . . ."

With a deliberate thrust, Thorne pushed himself into Lucy. There was a dull ache that only fueled her desire as his cock breached her entrance.

"Let go," he commanded. "Let go and let me take over."

Lucy grew dizzy with a combination of physical desire and a sensation of falling, truly falling without worrying what awaited her next. Clenching her inner muscles, she pushed back against him. A glorious friction rose as he moved inside her, inch by inch, stretching her to accommodate him.

All the time, Lucy played with her bonds, letting them go slack and allowing herself to feel Thorne's slow intrusion, then pulling them taut and fighting to prolong her pleasure.

When he'd pushed himself fully inside her, Thorne bent his forehead to hers. She flinched in surprise when a bead of sweat dropped from his temple to her cheek. They lay frozen for a moment, relishing the anticipation. Lucy, however, would not let this draw out any further.

Thorne had given her permission by denying her.

The ties that bound her wrists gave her a sense of calm that had been absent for so long as she carried out the never-ending duties of the apothecary. Lucy bent her knees, setting her feet on the mattress and tilting her hips so that Thorne sank even deeper within her. The discomfort of being filled so tight, the friction of the linen against her wrists, the knowledge that she could say anything, feel anything, inside this cocoon of darkness lit a spark within her. She wrapped one leg over his hips and pressed her heel into the base of Thorne's spine.

With a swift uptake of breath, he understood her need and began to move with slow, shallow thrusts. Lucy couldn't wrap her arms around him to urge him on, so she whispered her praise, surprising herself at the creativity and detail of her coaxing words. The inability to see Thorne's expression allowed for honesty because she couldn't imagine disapproval or judgment on his face.

Thorne's enjoyment of her stuttered pleas was made obvious

by the quickened pace with which he entered her, the feel of his mouth against the side of her neck moving back and forth, the occasional grunts of pleasure that vibrated in her ears.

"More," she gasped. He laughed, low and dark, then held himself still within her.

Lucy pulled against the ties and squeezed both legs around his hips.

"More," she begged.

When he didn't move, Lucy set her teeth to the meat of his shoulder.

"More," she demanded, then bit him there.

Minutes, hours, who knew how much time went by as Thorne moved his hips faster and faster. The darkness behind her eyelids lit with sparks as Lucy's pleasure overwhelmed her connection to her limbs and to her brain.

A blessed peace blanketed her as Lucy gave up control and let Thorne decide the rhythm of his thrusts, relishing the ache at the center of her and the slow buildup of pressure between her legs and throughout her body.

"Now." The order slipped out before Lucy could think to stop herself.

Thorne obeyed without pause, slipping his hand between them and setting his thumb on her clit just as he reentered her.

With a cry of surrender, Lucy came against him. Shuddering, she thrust herself up and reveled in the wetness of her release. Like thunder, the pounding of her heart deafened her, and she had no awareness outside of the throbbing of her womb. It felt like an eternity before the world came back to greet her.

Even as she relished the tiny waves of pleasure that followed her orgasm, Lucy became aware of the last long thrust of Thorne's cock and the low growl of pleasure at his completion.

Neither of them spoke for a moment, listening to each other breathe in stuttering gasps as though they'd run a race.

A red thread of sorrow pulled at Lucy's chest. She had never felt a pleasure so intense, never felt so free in her life. How sad it seemed to her, in the silence, that in order to feel good, she had to hide her view of the world around her.

With the utmost care, Thorne untied her blindfold. Despite the darkened room, there was enough light from the lamp that Lucy had to wait, blinking, while her sight adjusted. Thorne raised himself up, his massive chest moving over her as he untied her left arm. Softly, he kissed the red marks on her wrist where she'd tested the bonds, and did the same with her right arm.

Gathering both her hands in his, Thorne bowed his head over them, his lips grazing her skin as he spoke.

"Thank you for trusting me, Lucy. You are a brave and marvelous woman."

Brave and marvelous.

Of all the words he could use to describe her, Thorne picked the very ones she would use about him as well.

THORNE CAME AWAKE WHEN THE MATTRESS DIPPED. Lucy must have gone out to the privy, for she returned with the scent of winter mixed in the skirts of her nightgown.

When was the last time he'd slept like that?

Dreamless.

Spent.

"What is the time?" Thorne asked, his embarrassment at lying there, vulnerable, making his words harsher than he'd meant them.

"It is past nine," Lucy told him as she burrowed beneath her quilts and pushed her cold feet against his legs, laughing when he shivered.

"I have to go home to Sadie."

Rather than taking offense that he would leave so quickly, Lucy nodded in agreement.

"Of course, you wish to return to her. Tell me first, is she enjoying Madame's school?" Lucy asked.

"That school was such a gift," he said. "I never would have thought to introduce her to science. I barely understood geometry, and the only time I used my physics was to calculate the angle of a punch. Not that I was ever right."

Lucy reached over and took his hand, once again tracing the places where the bones had broken and rejoined. The elegance of her fingers and the curve of her arms prompted feelings of both lust and protectiveness. The combination felt strange, like a boiled sweet sprinkled with salt.

"Perhaps she got it from her mum?" Lucy asked.

Thorne considered this. "That might be so. Sadie's mother was interested in people the same way that Sadie is interested in animals."

Lucy pushed her palm against Thorne's, and they examined the difference in size and coloring of their hands, fingers to fingers.

"Tell me if it is none of my affair, but did she die?" Lucy asked.

Thorne inhaled this scent of warm cotton sheets and bare skin and braced for the old pain, but all he felt was the ghost of an ache in his chest. He broke contact with Lucy and rolled onto his back, examining the lumpy plaster of the ceiling above him.

"She did," he told the ceiling.

"She was the beautiful woman who made you swear off beautiful women?"

The ceiling waited for his answer.

"She was."

Lucy shifted herself so that she sank deeper into the mattress and pulled the covers up to her chin. "Does Sadie miss her?"

Thorne turned his head and regarded her. "You miss your mother, don't you?"

"Every minute of every day," Lucy said. She kept her eyes on the ceiling but pulled her arms out from beneath the covers and crossed them over the quilt. "I thought I would miss my father more, since we worked together so closely."

A lock of Lucy's hair fell across her forehead. Tiny strands of red glinted in the dim light of the table lamp.

"It is my mother's counsel I wish I could seek, though," Lucy continued. "I rarely have questions when it comes to my work. I always have questions when it comes to . . . everything else. Matters of the heart. Matters of the spirit."

She did not elaborate, and Thorne did not push.

"I can only imagine Genny—Geneviève's amusement at being consulted in such matters," Thorne said. "She tried hard never to consider any question weightier than what color feathers to wear with what color gown."

Lucy pulled away from him, lifting herself onto her elbows, disappointment clear on her face.

"I am not . . ." Thorne paused, while Lucy rolled on her side, keeping herself covered beneath the quilt, staring at him with her ocean-blue eyes narrowed in concentration.

"She wasn't silly. That's not what I meant. She was quite intelligent and well-read considering she hadn't much of a formal education. I think," he said slowly, "she had been damaged in a profound way that couldn't be seen from the outside. I think the damage was so great, she worked to be distracted so she wouldn't have to look at her wounds, nor remember what caused them."

Lucy's mouth opened into an O of sympathy, but she kept silent. When he finally spoke this next realization aloud, Thorne took Lucy's hand and once again pressed her palm against his.

"I was so young and self-centered. I never tried hard enough to find out what caused her so much pain. I simply believed that my love was enough to heal her. The more she suffered, the more I showered her with gifts and professed my love, and the more she sought further distraction."

Lucy pressed back against him, palm to palm.

"Sometimes I have patients who stay sick no matter what cure I offer up," she said softly, her eyes flickering between their hands and Thorne's face.

Thorne's gaze unfocused as he remembered times when Genny would dance like a dervish, spinning round for hours on end as if she could spin herself out of the trappings of her body and the noise in her head.

He sat up then, pulling the covers from his naked body, and swung his legs to the floor. The condom they'd used was wrapped in a square of linen resting on the tiny nightstand next to Lucy's bed.

A fierce need to beg forgiveness made him dizzy. It came upon Thorne whenever he thought back to when he left England for that extended prizefighting tour of the Continent. He'd joked to Genny that she wouldn't know he was gone because her admirers would keep her entertained. He'd promised to bring home a fortune when he returned. In truth, he left before he could do something stupid because he couldn't live with the jealousy that ate at him day after day, because it pained him never to be enough.

The house in Bath was empty when he returned almost a year later. Rumors around town had seen her leaving with this earl or that prince, setting off to Crescent Street, to Birmingham, to Albania.

Furious, Thorne hadn't looked for her. Fight after fight, Thorne leaned into the punches that reshaped his body and left him numb, then swung punches of his own, obliterating his intrusive thoughts with a blow to the chin, a jab to the gut.

He fought hard and dirty for another year until the bout in Chelsea when he never saw a left hook coming. Two days later, he woke up on the vermin-infested mattress in the back of a pub with a bell still ringing in his ears. When he could walk on his own without the world tilting left, he'd set out to find Genny and beg forgiveness.

By the time he found her in a tiny set of rooms in Birmingham, she was too ill to speak. A child, perhaps no older than two, played by her bedside while babbling a song of her own making.

Was it because he made a life from violence that Genny hadn't told him she was with child? Was he so repulsive that she didn't want her child associated with him? Had she been wanting to run the entire time they'd been together?

Those questions didn't plague him half so much as the one Genny never answered.

Was the little girl someone else's child? Would they come back for her?

Genny died the same day he found her, leaving Thorne and the child staring at each other, alone except for the doctor who had come too late yet still demanded to be paid.

"She never told me about Sadie," he said to Lucy now. "It was by the grace of God that I found out where Genny was staying in the days before she died. If I hadn't, Sadie would have been completely alone in the world."

"I'm certain you were not the reason Genny didn't tell you," Lucy said softly from behind him. "Sometimes women lose their center after having a child. The blue devils will torment them until the child is more grown. Midwives will treat it with cold baths and Saint-John's-wort. That must have been why."

"You don't know that," he said, running his hands through his hair. Wasn't he even now a selfish prick to sleep with a woman he wasn't going to marry?

Her hands settled on his shoulders, and the scent of eucalyptus and lavender enveloped him when Lucy bent her head and rested it against his bare back.

"I know you better than you think," she said. "I know about your soft heart from the way you touch me. I know about your bravery by the way you stand between the people you care for and the rest of the world. I know about your character by the way you have raised an incredible child."

It would be easy to reach around and pull her against him, to believe the words she spread down his spine.

The easy way was never the right way. Thorne knew that much.

Instead of falling back into the sheets with her, Thorne gave Lucy a handful of sweet words and a kiss on the forehead. She said nothing in return, watching silently as he dressed himself.

Thorne pulled his jacket straight and regarded the wrinkled strip of linen that hung over Lucy's headboard.

Still mute, Lucy handed him the cloth, which he rolled and tucked into a pocket. A dozen questions collided with unspoken answers in the silence of the room. Neither of them said a word for a while, their stares unbroken. Finally, Thorne reached into his pocket and pulled out the cravat, looked at it for a moment, then walked back to the bed and draped it around Lucy's neck.

"I am so grateful that you shared tonight with me," he said as gently as he could. With his ruined voice, the words sounded like the pestle and mortar Lucy used in her cures.

Lucy pulled the linen from her neck and wrapped it around her hands so that she was again bound, again free.

"Thank you," she said, lifting her hands. "Thank you for this."

Thorne nodded while he stepped backward, reaching out behind him for the doorknob, memorizing the way her eyes followed him, the slight redness spilling from the line of her lips, and the way her hair fell about her shoulders. Once satisfied that he would never forget this moment, Thorne turned around and left the room.

16

—‹‹‹◆›››—

THORNE LISTENED INTENTLY TO THE SERMON THAT Sunday, hoping for some insight into his addictions. He closed his eyes and sighed when the reverend quoted Corinthians. The Bible promised that God would not tempt Thorne more than he could manage.

The Bible also said he shouldn't eat oysters.

In the end, conquering an addiction came down to a faith larger than one that needed to be memorized or foisted on others. It came down to a faith in oneself, an acceptance that the right way was always going to be the hard way.

Thorne mulled this over as he left church. On the notice wall near the exit was a flyer for a Guardians of Domesticity rally that week. After quickly looking around, Thorne pulled it down and pocketed it.

If Duncan Rider hadn't a hand in the disappearance of Lucy's formula, Thorne might have to look harder at the Guardians. It would be a feather in their cap to close a woman-owned apothecary, and they certainly had it out for Juliet and her clinic.

"I believe we should bring Lester back to where you found him," Sadie confided as they walked home from church. For once, the sun had appeared, and the wind blew its sullen self away to torture folks in other counties.

"Lester," he repeated.

Thorne relished the sensation of his daughter's hand in his as they walked home leisurely. He'd started a roast that morning, and it would be simmering in gravy by the time they arrived. Inspired by the women around him, he'd been thinking like a scientist these days, grating the carrots finely before setting them in with the roast with the hypothesis that Sadie wouldn't notice them, or at least wouldn't mind eating them in a different state.

"Lester is the frog you borrowed from the park last night," Sadie reminded him. "Today, the sermon was about doing unto others, and I wondered if God meant animals when he said 'others.'"

This made sense to Thorne.

"I don't see why not. If God created the creatures on earth, he must have an interest in their welfare, too," he said.

Sadie sighed. "Yes. And if it were me living with my family happily by the pond and some giant took me home to be dissected, well, I shouldn't like it. Should you?"

"No, indeed."

As it was, they came home and set their dinner aside for later. They took a quick meal of bread and apples before heading back out with Lester to the Serpentine, having decided to return him to the bosom of his family.

Thorne was so intent on helping Sadie down to the edge of the water that he paid little heed when a man approached on horseback. It was Sadie who stood first, shielding her eyes against the sharp lemon light of the November sun and greeting the stranger.

"Have you come looking for frogs?" she asked.

"I believe it's too cold for frog hunting," said the man. The hairs on the back of Thorne's neck straightened with shock, and he turned to stare.

Seated firmly on an excitable young gelding was his father.

"Jonathan," his father said in greeting.

"Sir."

It took forever for Thorne to stand, his knees creaking loudly in the silence. The entire time, he met his father's gaze. With a little tug, Sadie slipped her muddied hand into his.

Thorne had been fond of horses as a boy and enjoyed spending summer afternoons in the lazy heat of the stables, lulled by the sound of nickering and the rustling of hay. His father's stables were well regarded in racing circles. Unlike some of his peers, Blackstone held on to his horses that didn't live up to their potential, letting them out to pasture for the rest of their lives.

"You don't punish an animal for not being what you want," his father would say. "God made all creatures for a reason." Thorne had forgotten until right now his father's interest and respect for animals.

"First, we meet at the Physic Garden and now by the shores of the Serpentine," his father said. "You always did have an affinity for the outdoors."

Sadie pressed her hand on Thorne's. She would be curious who the man on the horse was and why he used Thorne's first name, but he could likely get away with a nonanswer. Another lie.

Or he could tell the truth.

"It is my daughter who is the naturalist." Thorne glanced down, and his heart looked back at him from behind her eyes. "She is an avid student of the sciences and has been learning the anatomy of amphibians."

"Student of sciences?" his father asked. "I do not know many young ladies with that interest."

Rather than a sneer of disdain, his father's expression was one of open interest. All Thorne could think about was the last time he'd seen his father at home. He'd come with Sadie and asked his parents to care for her until he could win a few more prizes and buy a town house in London for them.

"Certainly not," his mother had said, eyebrows to her hairline in outrage. "You will put her in a home somewhere with a respectable family." She'd ignored Sadie as though the little girl were an uninvited pet. "That is what gentlemen do with their natural-born children. You pay the family a monthly stipend and help broker a match for her when she's grown."

When Thorne had insisted that he wanted to raise Sadie with his name, he might as well have slapped his mother.

"Your name? You don't even know if the child is yours, for God's sake."

His father had said nothing, silently deferring to his wife in this matter as in so many questions of a social nature. Thorne didn't know if the pained look of disappointment in his father's eyes was due to Sadie's presence, or the part Thorne played in her creation. Either way, Thorne made his decision. Leaving his family behind, he'd taken a name of his own to share with Sadie.

It was this name he offered when he introduced his daughter to her grandfather.

"Lord Blackstone, may I present my daughter, Miss Sadie Thorne. Sadie, this is my . . . this is Lord Blackstone."

Sadie curtsied as prettily as she could in the muck. "How do you do?"

"Tell me what you have learned about frogs," his father said.

Before Thorne could stop her, Sadie repeated her favored fact about the astounding size of a frog's feces.

Blackstone hid a smile behind his hand and pretended to cough as his mount stepped sideways.

"Did you know," Blackstone asked her, "that in the Dutch East Indies they drink coffee made from beans that are rescued from the civet cat's poo? It is called kopi luwak."

Sadie's eyes grew wide. "I've never heard of a civet cat. Is it enormous? Does it smell of coffee? Who rescues the beans?"

"These are good questions," his father said. "If you give me your direction, Miss Thorne, I shall send you a portfolio I found recently filled with pictures and information about exotic animals. Would that please you?"

"Oh, yes," Sadie replied.

"And you?" Blackstone asked him.

Was his father asking if it pleased him that Sadie be given a gift, or that his father had approached them in the first place?

"I suppose it does," he'd answered. To both questions.

Blackstone had opened his mouth but shut it again when nothing emerged. He'd touched his fingers to his hat in farewell and rode away into the purple light of an early dusk.

Thorne had no vocabulary for the feelings that swirled in his chest after his father left, but he tried to name them. Anger, certainly, that his father could speak so easily to the granddaughter he had refused to acknowledge. Sadness, that Sadie had to grow up without any grandparents or family other than Thorne.

Something else, too. Some strange lightness that he ignored until later that night, once the roast had been eaten and *Oliver Twist* read and discussed. Sadie fell asleep within seconds of the candle being snuffed, and Thorne sat in his room and stared out the window.

He had vowed never to speak with his parents again after they rejected his plea. A line he'd drawn in red, never to be crossed. Other lines followed as he remade his life.

No parties. No gambling.

Never again would a drink pass his lips.

Never again would he love a beautiful woman.

Red lines everywhere until he lived securely within his restrictions. His rules had saved his life, but had they also diminished it? For the past seven years, Thorne had spent his time and energy on protecting himself and Sadie from any trials.

Was it time to test himself?

Or was testing himself a prelude to indulging?

He did not lie to himself and deny that speaking to his father had prompted these reflections, but it was his attraction to Lucy that gave him the most pause. Even right now in the midst of his soul-searching, as if he were a scrap of iron and Lucy's presence a magnet, his body leaned toward the front door of his apartment, a visceral ache in his chest and a buzzing at the base of his spine.

The air was as clear as it could be in the middle of London. Buildings scored black lines against the purple night sky and slivers of the cold outside slipped in through the loose windowpanes. Thorne searched for some sign of the stars even though he knew it would be futile.

These second thoughts could be dangerous and self-serving. On the street below, people indulged in their weaknesses and suffered for it—more importantly, those around them suffered. Children went without food when their parents spent their pay at gin houses. Women were forced into workhouses while their husbands gambled their money on dice or cards.

Most people could be redeemed, but Thorne was unsure if the same was true for him.

As always, he returned to the question he'd asked of himself seven years ago. How do you live a good life without living a life of excess?

Thorne picked at that question through the long dark hours of the early morning while he rubbed some of Lucy's ointment onto his aching hands.

LAST NIGHT LUCY HAD LAIN AWAKE FOR HOURS STAR-ing at the ceiling. On the other side of the wood and plaster, Thorne was reading Sadie a story. They were a family of two, but their love made them seem bigger, somehow.

Love.

Lucy turned the word around in her head like a piece of marble. So much weight, so many sides to it . . . if cherished, it could build monuments that stood for thousands of years. But it could just as easily shatter into pieces that would cut you if you weren't careful.

This morning, Mr. Gentry had settled himself behind the counter while Lucy fetched cures for customers. "Did you hear about the one tumor they found in a man's brain that measured ten inches lengthwise and was said to have resembled the *Mona Lisa*?"

Every time she rested her feet, he would regale her with stories of objects found in human beings.

"Did you know they've worms in Africa that can live in your stomach and measure seven feet long?"

"Should I get married, do you think?"

Gentry's mouth fell open at Lucy's question. After a moment, he recovered himself and shook his head fast as though dislodging water from his ears.

"Should you *what* now, Miss Peterson?"

"I just thought—" Lucy paused when a customer approached, but Gentry stood up from the stool behind the counter and waved the man away.

"I know what you want, Albert Smith, and you're better off not drinking coffee if it's going to mess with your insides like it do. If you won't use the common sense God gave you, you'll be wanting a tin of Winter's Stomach Ease pastilles. Go ask Katie, they are right on that second shelf over there."

Mr. Smith wandered off sheepishly, and Gentry turned his attention back to Lucy.

"Marriage?" he asked.

"What if it isn't coffee?" Lucy asked, somewhat taken aback by Gentry's willingness to dispense medical advice. "What if it's a bleeding ulcer?"

Gentry shook his head at Lucy's question. "Albert visited his mother-in-law at the seaside two weeks ago and had no coffee for the entire time. Came back ten pounds heavier and looking ten years younger."

Holding up a hand, Gentry placated Lucy with a resigned air. "Don't worry, Miss Peterson, I would never advise one of your customers on a condition I know nothing about. I just know Albert and I know how many times he visits the necessary after a cup of coffee."

Satisfied that Gentry wasn't practicing medicine on her

customers without her knowledge, Lucy returned to the subject at hand.

"I could marry someone who would take over the books and day-to-day chores at the shop. This way, I would have more time to develop new cures and perfect the old ones. I could keep up with my chemistry journals and go to lectures now and again. Certainly, I wouldn't have to work so hard anymore," she explained.

Gentry squinted his eyes and tilted his head one way, then the other.

"You could apprentice another apothecarist. That would free up your time at the counter," Gentry suggested.

Here was an idea. Lucy tapped her chin in thought. Katie had a bright mind but little interest in treating patients. An apprentice would cost money, however. Every day their coffers grew lighter. No matter how clever Lucy had become at saving coin on household expenses, there was only so thin one could pinch a penny.

"Course an apprentice isn't going to warm your bed on a cold night or give you babies," he continued, startling Lucy from her worries.

"Warm my bed? Babies?" Lucy repeated the foreign words back to the man. "I'm talking about a business arrangement whereby I receive more help at work than—"

"Go on wi' you. Marriage isn't like hiring an assistant." Gentry's chuckle petered out as grief appeared, momentarily haunting his face. "Marriage is . . ." He swallowed once, then once more, as though feeding the pain back into himself. Lucy leaned over and put her hand on his.

"I'm sorry. I didn't mean to remind you—"

"No, no. You don't have to apologize." While his eyes

remained wet, his lips turned upward into a rueful smile. "My Betty and me, we'd only seen each other once, at a church fete it was, before her parents came up to visit with mine and set our match."

This was a story Lucy had never heard before. She leaned her elbows on the counter and stared out the front door at the mass of people moving back and forth. Two women passed by outside, one of them sporting a pink and blue silk poke bonnet.

"Did you think she was pretty?" Lucy asked.

"I thought she had a sharp nose and a sharper tongue," Gentry said. "There wasn't a day went by before the wedding that she said anything nice to me. My shoes were unpolished, my grammar was terrible, my teeth were too crooked, and I wasted my time reading when I could have been working to save money for our life together."

Lucy turned and regarded him. "She sounds awful."

Gentry's head tipped back as he laughed. "She was wonderful. She was simply scared. She'd never spent the night in any bed but the one she shared with her two sisters, and now she would marry a perfect stranger. For the rest of our lives together, whenever she complained about my dirty shoes or shoddy grammar, I knew to sit her down with a wee drop of brandy and find out what was scaring her."

Lucy faced front again and pulled his words apart in her head.

"Not that marriage wasn't business, too. Betty's da was a farmer, but his older brother owned a bookbindery, and I wanted to learn the trade."

This made sense. Lucy's father had been her maternal grandfather's apprentice. Her mother used to tease that it was easier to marry the boy already living in her home than to go out and find one on her own.

All it cost her parents was the money to paint over the name Stefanson's and change it to Peterson's.

Gentry spoke again. "Once Betty got past her fright, we found that marriage was lots of times an adventure. Sometimes it was a plod, sometimes it was grand, and sometimes . . ."

Lucy's throat closed in sympathetic sorrow.

"How long were you married?" she whispered.

"Twelve years," he said, his voice thick with pain. "I miss her and the girls every single day."

Lucy knew in her bones that if she'd gone ahead and married Duncan, she would never have forged a love like Gentry's for his wife.

She was better off without a love that powerful.

"Listen here, Miss Peterson," Gentry said, as though he'd heard Lucy's thoughts. "Was it Mary Wollstonecraft that said it was far better 'to be disappointed in love, than never to love'?"

"I don't know," said Lucy. "I haven't read her books."

"Well, you should." Gentry stood from his stool and absently patted Lucy on the shoulder. "You should read scandalous philosophies and dance with a few fellows and not marry anyone who you wouldn't trust with your darkest secret."

"I don't have any dark secrets," Lucy said, hopefully in a convincing manner.

Mr. Gentry smiled and tapped a finger to the side of his nose.

"What if . . ." Lucy fell silent as the sentence rearranged itself in her head. "What if the one meant for you is unavailable?"

Gentry's knowing smile melted on the sides as an expression of sympathy crossed his face. Lucy colored, the heat from her flush rushing from her throat to her ears. What did he know?

"Miss Peterson. Is something wrong?" asked Thorne.

Lucy tore her gaze from Mr. Gentry and settled it on Thorne, who must have come downstairs while she was distracted by the conversation. Her flush deepened and even her palms started to burn.

"No," she said. "It's just a little warm in here."

Thorne's expression was, as usual, unreadable. His torso bent toward her, and he thrust his hands into his coat pockets while his eyes touched her face—her lips, her cheeks, her chin.

"Miss Peterson is telling me about the man of her dreams," Mr. Gentry interjected.

What? Oh, how humiliating.

Lucy shot a nasty look at Mr. Gentry, but he pretended obliviousness. Meanwhile, Thorne's only response was to raise his brows a fraction of an inch.

For anyone else, this would be a sign of profound shock.

"Pray tell, Miss Peterson, what would this paragon look like?" Thorne asked.

"It wouldn't matter to me what he looked like," she said before she could reflect too deeply. "I judge a man by his character, not his face."

Thorne flushed, and Lucy's hands clenched beneath the counter.

"You're a mop," Gentry exclaimed genially. "You should be judging a man by the size of his purse and the quality of his compliments."

"Or the quality of his purse and the size of his compliments," Thorne added.

Now it was Lucy's turn to blush. "Mr. Gentry, don't you have somewhere to be?" she asked desperately.

"Aye," Gentry answered, turning to Thorne. "I'm headed to

the Lion's Den for a pint. Do you—" He cut himself off abruptly as he recalled Thorne's status as a teetotaler.

"No," said Thorne easily, "but I'll walk you there, as I have to stop by my bank." With a wicked smile, he winked at Lucy. "If you're interested in the size of my purse or my compliments, you can always ask."

"Go on with you both!" she cried.

The men left the shop chuckling like little boys, and Lucy wore a stupid smile for the rest of the day.

17

※⟪⟨⟨◆⟩⟩⟫※

ON A NARROW LANE LINED WITH SOOT-STAINED BUILD-
ings, their decorative lintels carved of Portland stone nearly
obscured by the layers of grime that clung to the structures like
a snake's scaly sheath, one building sat sandwiched between
the next, slightly bowed in over the cobbled street below.

Having been here before, Thorne barely registered the im-
posing set of bronze doors fronting the offices of Dawson and
Company, Banking and Lending Institution.

A uniformed clerk welcomed him at a small stand in the
center of the lobby, upon which lay a visitors' book and an ink-
stand. Thorne's hand hesitated as he took up the pen, but in the
end, he signed the book as Jonathan Thornwood. He made his
request to the clerk and walked across a cold marble floor, stopping to stare at a wall full of portraits while awaiting a reply.

Jacob Dawson, founder of the bank, stood out in the portraits, hung in the center of a long line of serious faces encased
in carved frames of gilt and oak. The personality of the man
inhabiting the canvas was so powerful it came through the

frame despite the mediocrity of whatever artist had painted it. An attempt had been made to present Dawson as a wise and steady man, dressed in black except for a white shirt and dark blue cravat, one of his spindly hands resting upon a Bible, and the other pointing toward a map of India.

Thorne suspected Dawson might have hired someone to stand in for him, as the man had been unable to remain stationary for any length of time. A famed explorer, he'd retired from the seas after losing a leg and made a second fortune as a shipping magnate. From there it had been a short step to opening a bank, funding the sorts of expeditions he once led.

When Thorne had been a boy, Dawson had come to stay for a fortnight at Longlake Abbey. Thorne's mother had retreated to her rooms with a megrim almost immediately after the first dinner with the old sailor, while Thorne and his brothers had spent every moment possible in Dawson's company.

Never had Thorne heard such language—colorful in every regard. Yes, he learned some mammoth curses, curses he pulled out only in the rarest of cases and that had never failed to impress, but that wasn't all.

For the first time, Thorne heard a white man speak approvingly of foreign cultures. Rather than project disdain for the natives of the countries he visited, Dawson spoke reverently, and with respect for the people he'd encountered and the sights and sounds of his journeys.

The rest of Thorne's family politely hid their disbelief behind hands of cards or linen napkins, but Thorne wanted to hear more. More about a world outside of the estate and the banality of the British schoolroom. More about life and how it could be lived differently in faraway places.

One might have expected that he'd sign up to serve on one of Dawson's ships, but Thorne didn't need to travel abroad to learn of different cultures or hear a cacophony of languages. He'd found those in his years of traveling the prizefighting circuit. In each corner of the British Isles, Thorne had encountered a panoply of ethnicities, religions, and beliefs as foreign to him as any he might have found in the Indies.

What Dawson did was to cement Thorne's fledgling ideas that there was more to life than the rigid confines of the aristocracy. The old sailor flung open a door to the idea that other ways of life might be just as good, or preferable even, to what Thorne had experienced so far.

Their contact ended when Thorne left his family to become a boxer. By that time, Dawson had begun to turn his back on society and even his own company.

"Mr. Thornwood? This way, please."

Thorne winked up at the painted Jacob and followed a middle-aged clerk with a small, humped back into the depths of the building. They passed row upon row of narrow desks occupied by silent men bent over their parchment.

"Mr. Dawson? I have Mr. Thornwood with me."

The clerk opened an office door and stood back so Thorne could enter first. Rising from his seat, a gaunt man around ten years older than Thorne leaned one hand on the desk and reached out with the other. Jacob Dawson had been a large man, large of voice, large of vision, and fond of excess whether in food, drink, or laughter. His son, Rudolph, was the opposite, for he was a man of moderation. In voice, appetite, and dress, Rudolph disdained excess.

Except for his own excess of wealth. Rudolph had no quarrel against that.

"Thornwood. How can I help you?"

Thorne had met with Rudolph a few times after his father, Jacob, died, once even performing an inquiry for the bank. As such, he knew the blunt words were not rudeness, but simply a manner of speech that was devoid of any small or frivolous talk.

However, Thorne had not lost the genial habits instilled in his youth.

"Good day, Dawson. I hope you and your family fare well."

Rudolph blushed and cleared his throat in a moment of chagrin. "They are quite well, thank you."

"I am here asking for a favor," Thorne said.

The slight twitch of Rudolph's eyebrows was the only hint of interest. "Hmmm. A favor for an agent of Tierney and Company. That might be worth something down the road."

"Indeed. I will owe you a favor in return," Thorne said.

Steepling his fingers together, Rudolph put Thorne in mind of a praying mantis. Intimidating insect, but it could always be stepped on.

"Tell me about Mr. W. R. Wilcox."

Before Winthram had left for up north, he'd discovered that the moneys paid to Mr. Wilcox by David had ended up in an account at Dawson's bank.

A tiny puff of disappointment escaped Rudolph as he sat back and folded his hands in his lap.

"Huh. If you are looking for skullduggery, you're looking in the wrong place. W. R. Wilcox is one of the Earl of Yarmouth's sons, Willem, the fourth in line, I believe. Do you know the family?"

Thorne shook his head.

"Rather lofty ideals, the lot of them. Mother and daughters are on dozens of committees to help the unfortunate, or find homes for foundlings, or what have you. Father is frail, fell ill from an apoplexy, but the sons seem devoted."

Rupert glanced down at his hands and Thorne wondered, did Rudolph miss Jacob, despite the differences between father and son?

"Wilcox is involved with a group of textile weavers in Rochdale who've formed some sort of cooperative credit union," Rudolph continued.

"A cooperative credit union?" Thorne was unfamiliar with such a union. "What is that?" Thorne asked.

The other man lifted his hand as though to brush the idea away into the ether where it belonged, distaste puckering his lips.

"Groups sell shares to members, then use the capital to buy goods at lower prices. They then sell on the goods at a profit and the savings go back to the members. Every member gets a vote in what they'll buy and an equal return on investment. Democratic nonsense, if you ask me. No way to make a true profit."

Rudolph's father, Jacob, had made huge profits first through his trade expeditions, then as a shipping magnate and banker. The more money he'd made, however, the more he despaired. Trade with England had changed the nature of the places and people he had so admired, and slowly their way of life disappeared. Eventually, Jacob was turned out as president of his own firm for railing against the British government's actions in India and his insistence on fair trade.

Thorne believed all men bore some imprint of the man who raised them. So had Rudolph resented his father's progressive beliefs and reacted against them out of spite, or was he simply greedy? Or was the truth something in between?

How much of his own father did Thorne carry with him? The memory of his father's eyes as Thorne left with Sadie so many years ago—Thorne had assumed the disappointment he'd seen there was with the way he had chosen to live his life. Could there have been some sympathy in that gaze as well?

For all that Blackstone stayed away, Thorne had never gone near home again.

"Right. Thank you for taking the time to meet with me," Thorne said now. He pushed his chair back and caught sight of a copy of the *Gentlemen's Monthly Magazine*, the mouthpiece for the Guardians of Domesticity.

Pointing to the magazine, Thorne asked, "Are you a follower of Victor Armitage and his group?"

A fierce snort of disagreement trumpeted from Rudolph's nose, and he drew a handkerchief from his pocket to wipe away the leavings. "Not a follower of anyone, but certainly not Armitage. Man has the subtlety of a night at Astley's theatre."

Refolding the square of linen, Rudolph motioned his chin toward the magazine. "He's an idiot, but he holds real power between his roving gangs and the propaganda he prints. The articles are almost unreadable, but it behooves me to know what he's saying."

Thorne reached over and pulled the magazine toward him, squinting at the cover. He couldn't read a thing without his glasses.

"Why is it important for you to know what these men say? They aren't involved in shipping or banking." He peered over the top page, watching Rudolph's reaction. "Seem more interested in hectoring women and maligning foreigners."

Rudolph hesitated, then answered slowly. "Times are changing, Thornwood. The aristocracy is losing its grip on power as everything in the countryside is upended by these new harvesting machines and failing crops."

A line appeared on Rudolph's forehead as he, too, gazed at

the magazine cover. "Uncertainty breeds chaos. Groups like those Guardians are appealing because they offer an alternative to uncertainty. Anger and prejudice are no good for my bank account, but they are preferred by the populace to insecurity and despair."

Thorne scratched his chin. "I cannot tell if you approve of them or not."

"Doesn't matter what I think. What matters is how a movement like this can affect the economy." Rudolph shook his head. "When people are scared, they make illogical choices and see conspiracies where there are none."

"What did Aristotle say?" Thorne asked. "'Wicked men obey from fear; good men, from love.'"

"Easier said than followed." Rudolph stood and held out his hand, a not-so-subtle message that their meeting was over. Thorne assumed Rudolph was less an adherent of Aristotle than he was of Benjamin Franklin, who admonished folks to "remember that time is money."

They took their leave of each other on good terms, but Rudolph's words rattled around in Thorne's head for the rest of the day.

When people are scared, they make illogical choices and see conspiracies where there are none.

Lucy Peterson was afraid. She was exhausted by her workload, and her sister was absent doing important work, her brother wanted to be anywhere but the apothecary, and she had the likes of the Guardians to worry about on top of it all.

Mr. Wilcox was the child of a wealthy and philanthropic family who cared for one another, not some villain who would have an interest in undermining the apothecary. Had Lucy concocted the scheme whereby Duncan Rider snuck into the apothecary and stole the formulas in order to keep herself from looking too close to home?

Thorne needed to speak with Lucy.

"I HAVE LEARNED MR. W. R. WILCOX'S IDENTITY."

Lucy frowned and kept her back to Thorne as she wiped the dust from a shelf. He'd come into the shop after lunch and said nothing to her, simply closed himself into the office for an hour or so. She'd had no peace since then, picturing him at the desk with his spectacles perched on his nose and his cravat loosened. She knew now what he looked like beneath the layers of respectability, beneath the gloves and the jacket and waistcoat, the way his body moved like a wave when he entered her.

"I see," she said to the dustrag in her hand. "You've spent your time investigating David when you were supposed to be finding out who took my formula."

On the one hand, Lucy did not believe her brother would do anything to hurt her. On the other, she trusted Thorne implicitly.

Why, though?

Why should she trust him? Because they had made love? The son of a baron, the drunken prizefighter, or the father whose life revolved around his work and his daughter—which Thorne was real? What if he were none of them?

Lucy got down from her step stool, then turned to look at him, crossing her arms like a barrier.

Ten feet apart. They could be twenty or even fifty feet apart, and the desire between them would still be as palpable.

Lovemaking with him had been a revelation. That he knew to tie her down was to hold her up still astounded her. Lucy didn't have any experience other than Duncan. What Thorne did with her, she'd never imagined that could be done, or done with such tenderness.

They *had* been tender with each other. What lay between them was more than simple desire.

Thorne must have seen something on her face that hinted as to the directions of her thoughts, because his eyes darkened, and his fingers clenched into fists. When she bit her bottom lip, he cleared his throat and she squeezed together her thighs.

"No one is home," she said.

Thorne did not pretend to look surprised. "Sadie told me she was invited to a tea by your sister. It will be at Athena's Retreat, where one of the members is giving a lecture on ornithology."

They wouldn't be back for hours.

The memory of his taste flooded her mouth, and Lucy swallowed. It was daylight. She would be able to see his body much clearer in the light. Running her fingers across her chest, she set down her cleaning rag and took a step toward him.

The front door burst open, and Katie rushed in.

"Miss Peterson, I . . ."

The young woman stumbled into the shop with uncharacteristic clumsiness, not even bothering to wipe her shoes, no coat or mittens despite the aching cold that had settled on London. Katie's hair had come down from her topknot, and her face was blotched with red spots, her eyes pink from crying.

Lucy hurried over to the girl and put her hands on her shoulders. Katie's teeth clattered and her whole body shivered, but somehow Lucy knew this reaction wasn't from just the cold.

Thorne quietly walked over to lock the front door and came to stand beside them.

"Did someone hurt you, Katie?" he asked.

Katie, who had buried her head in Lucy's shoulder, flinched at his words. A yawning despair tugged at Lucy.

"Oh, no," she whispered. "Katie . . ."

Katie still shook and pressed her head even more against Lucy, as though she would bury herself in the embrace.

"Mr. Thorne, if you would please close up the shop and put away the till?" Lucy stared into his eyes and willed him to understand. "I need to speak with Katie."

Lucy led Katie into the treatment room and helped her into the chair, then found a stool and stood on it to reach a blanket from the high shelf and wrapped it around Katie's shoulders.

For a long time, they remained that way, Lucy holding Katie's hand, Katie burrowed into a blanket, tears drying, eyes staring blankly ahead.

Eventually Katie let out a long sigh and dropped her chin to her chest.

"What do you do when you know a man loves you, but he hurts you anyway?" Katie lifted her head to ask, eyes blinking as though she were trying to focus on something far away.

What should Lucy say? Was this a time for comfort or for truth? She felt wholly unprepared as she gazed at the huddled figure before her.

"I think . . . we hurt people we love when we don't feel equal to them in some way," Lucy said. "Men, when they are unsure of women or do not feel equal to them, one way they tell themselves they are powerful is to overwhelm a woman."

The silence pushed at Lucy's lungs, and the brown clouds of damp and dirt crowded at the windows.

"Is that what happened, Katie?"

"Miss Peterson, I don't know what to do," Katie whispered.

Lucy didn't know what to do either in that moment other than hold the young woman close and promise her that she was safe, she was loved, and everything would somehow be all right.

Words that women have given to each other over the centuries in the aftermath of such trauma; offers of assurances, promises of healing. As well-meant as these sentiments were, both she and Katie knew the way Katie moved through the world would be forever changed.

18

AN HOUR LATER, THORNE WAS STILL WORKING IN THE small office, having closed the shop at Lucy's behest, when he heard the treatment door open and women's voices murmuring. He stood at the door of the office as Katie came out of the treatment room alone. She'd calmed some and gave him the ghost of a smile.

He remained still, not wanting to startle her, but nodded at her smile.

"Good night, Mr. Thorne," she said.

"Katie," he said softly.

She stopped, eyes wide, and once again Thorne regretted that when he spoke quietly, it sounded like grinding glass.

"When you are ready, if ever you should want me to . . ." He paused to swallow the surge of anger that clogged his throat. "When you are ready, I am here."

Katie nodded once, then again. "Thank you, Mr. Thorne." She fumbled with the lock, but Thorne kept himself from helping her, assuming she wouldn't want to be close to any man at that moment.

Lucy was sitting at her worktable when Thorne found her after locking back up. She gazed blankly at a row of glass bottles and tiny tins of dried herbs.

"Will she be all right?" he asked.

A useless question. Nearly as useless as he felt.

What was he to do when the worst had already happened?

Lucy touched the top of each of the jars, then lined them up and sighed.

"Katie has . . . had a sweetheart. A boy from the next parish over," she said.

Good. Thorne just had to get the lad's name and he could commence the beating.

"He forced her?" Thorne said, the old injury to his larynx turning his words into spikes.

"In a way . . ."

Lucy shifted her body away from her workbench and turned around on her stool to face him. Her eyes were slightly red, and the flesh around her lips was pink and puffy. The sight of her pain undid him. Thorne folded Lucy in an embrace. Not in the way he'd wanted to touch her earlier. Instead, he pulled her up from the stool, wrapped her tight in his arms, and dropped a kiss high on her forehead.

She held herself stiffly, so Thorne shifted back and forth on his feet like he used to do when Sadie was little and needed consoling.

After a moment, Lucy let herself be rocked in his arms.

A longing so profound it made Thorne dizzy swept through him.

This.

This need to touch without desire, to hold and comfort; this unnameable sensation took hold of him and set the room to spinning.

Taking a step back, Thorne stared down at Lucy's face and searched for neither flaws nor perfection. A whole person, both beautiful *and* flawed, stared back at him. He traced the line of her cheek with the back of his hand, unable to speak.

"His name is Timmy, and you are not to kill him."

Thorne grunted. That remained to be seen.

"What happened?" he finally asked.

Lucy pulled his hands into hers, rubbing her thumb up and down his ruined fingers.

"Katie knows how to use preventatives. She's asked about sex, and Juliet and I have told her how babies are made and how to protect herself against disease and pregnancy," Lucy said.

It took Thorne a moment to digest her words. In the upper classes where he was raised, women were assumed to be ignorant about such matters until they were married. He'd never thought about it, nor wondered why this would be so, simply accepted it as truth, right and moral.

Most likely because he'd never had to worry about it.

In the demimonde, the circles in which he'd met Geneviève, she and her friends had known about prophylactics. The assumption he'd made, that everyone made, was that women who had done this could not be considered as wives.

Katie was a member of the working class and not the demimonde. Her husband would expect her virginity. The idea of educating a young woman about sex and prophylactics before marriage struck Thorne as dangerous.

"Shouldn't you have also counseled her to wait until she married Timmy?" he asked.

Lucy's hands froze.

"She asked me to educate her about her body and its functions, not to deliver a sermon."

Thorne stared down at their hands, Lucy's stained and

scarred fingers entwined with his own, swollen and misshapen from violence.

"What I mean to say," he said, "is that if you tell young women how to protect against disease and pregnancy, they have less fear of it."

Even as Thorne spoke, he knew he'd said the wrong thing. How to describe the unease in his belly?

"Less fear of *it*?" Lucy stepped away from him, pulling her hands to her side. She laughed without humor and shook her head. "Do you believe it's for the best that women fear sexual relations?"

"Not fear them, but . . ." Thorne could not find the words he needed. "Women are at a disadvantage. They are the ones who die of childbirth, the ones who suffer if a man gives them a disease. I would think you wanted Katie protected."

"She and Timmy used condoms," Lucy interjected, speaking over him. "Today, she didn't have any. That didn't matter to Timmy."

Sympathy and anger warred with each other in Thorne's chest.

"I *shall* kill him."

Lucy shrugged, her emotions spent. "You cannot, or everyone will know what happened."

"Everyone will know what happened in nine months anyway," Thorne retorted. "I won't hurt him too badly; I shall simply ensure that he never fails to respect Katie's wishes ever again. They can be married in a civil ceremony and—"

"Are you joking?" Lucy's swollen lips twisted into a scowl. "There won't be a pregnancy, and Katie will not be forced into marriage. She convinced him to pull out before ejaculation, but either way, I've given her a tonic to induce her monthly courses."

Thorne's mouth opened and shut as he tried to make Lucy's comments make sense.

He wasn't certain he'd ever heard a woman say the word *ejaculation*. It quite took him aback.

And a tonic to induce her monthly courses . . .

Thorne rubbed his chin in thought, brows drawn as he contemplated what that meant.

"You cannot wish for Katie to do nothing?" Lucy asked, her voice rising along with her brows.

Could he not?

"I thought you believed in the work Juliet and Mrs. Sweet do at their clinic," she continued, taking a few more steps away from him.

"The women at Juliet's clinic are not Katie," he said.

"No, they did not have the benefit of a prior education about how babies are made and how to prevent them," Lucy said.

"Katie is different," he insisted, aware that he was unable to articulate himself better than this. "She is practically a child. She shouldn't be . . . her father should . . ."

Silence expanded between them like thick fingers pushing her away as he mulled over Lucy's words again.

"I . . . As you were speaking, I realized that I could not remember if Geneviève and I always used condoms. So many of my memories from back then are hazy," Thorne said slowly.

Lucy wrapped her arms around her middle in a gesture that could be interpreted as soothing or protective. Thorne knew he should comfort her, reassure her somehow, but terrible scenarios were presenting themselves to him, and the sick feeling wasn't going away.

"What if she did become pregnant one time when we did not use condoms?" he asked aloud. "What if she took a tonic, like Katie?"

Lucy tilted her head and examined him as though he were one of Sadie's frogs, laid out before her to be dissected.

"What if she did?" Lucy asked.

"Then . . ." What was the answer? Thorne looked around the room as though it might be written somewhere on the sepia walls. "There could have been a child before Sadie."

Now Lucy's hands came up and covered her face for a moment. A chill started in Thorne's fingers, and he rubbed his aching hands together.

Pulling her hands down over her face, Lucy breathed deeply, as though drawing from a store of patience, or perhaps anger.

"Before the quickening, there is only the biological possibility of a child," she said, her face expressionless. "Inducing menstruation is just that—bringing on a woman's natural flow."

"But the possibility—" he said, breaking off at the way Lucy's body clenched, her fists so tight that her knuckles turned white.

"The *possibility*," Lucy repeated. "Katie herself—her life, her body—is the *reality*. Katie did not have a choice. Timmy took that away from her."

The truth of that statement sat like a brick in Thorne's stomach.

Lucy's hands unclenched and she took a tentative step forward. "Do you think you would have been as good a father back then as you are now? Can you imagine the life that child would have experienced at that time in your life, and whether it would have been anything like Sadie's today?"

The churning wouldn't stop, and his mind raced.

"No," he admitted. "It's why I need to find a good woman. A godly woman who will guide and care for Sadie. Who won't fail her the same way I've failed."

"Ah," Lucy said, her smile so forced it bent to the side. "Someone like your Mrs. Merkle? A woman who would never do anything as immoral as take control over what happens to her body and her life. A woman who assumes a man will respect her wishes and provide for her."

This wasn't what he meant. Was it?

"What is it that Katie, and your Geneviève, and *me* for that matter—what is it we have in common that makes us less good than Mrs. Merkle?"

Thorne understood Lucy's point. What all three of the women had in common was that they had sex outside of the legitimacy of marriage.

By every known measure—the church, public opinion, the philosophers he'd studied at university—Lucy, Katie, and Genny were in the wrong. No one would question that it was his right to think less of women who demanded a say in what happened to their bodies.

Thorne had tried so hard to live a good life since he'd stopped drinking and become a father. If Lucy was correct, that meant that other assumptions he'd lived by could also be unfair or unfounded.

How much uncertainty could a man live with and still keep his moral compass?

"Lucy," he began, uncertain as to how he might repair this breach. How did you chart a course forward when the world kept spinning in unexpected directions?

"If you would please leave, Mr. Thorne. Your services are no longer needed today," she said softly.

His *services*.

The disappointment in her voice made him slightly ill.

"I shall retire, then, if you've no need of my . . . *services*." His ruined voice would never rise enough to attempt the icy inflection that Lucy had used, but his words had an impact, for she leaned back as though he'd pushed her away.

Which, Thorne reflected later, was for the best, as even after Lucy got up and put on her coat and bonnet and left the shop, he didn't know what he could say to make any of this better.

WITH NO IDEA OF A DESTINATION, LUCY WANDERED down the high street.

How dare he?

How *dare* he?

Admittedly, educating a young woman about preventatives before she was married was considered immoral, but Lucy had believed Thorne would see things differently than everyone else.

There were times when he looked at her, when he touched her, that Lucy thought he could see inside her mind, feel the very blood beneath her skin. It terrified and exhilarated her at the same time.

Now?

What terrified Lucy even more was if she were to come face-to-face with him now, he still would be able to read her, while she'd badly misjudged him.

Thorne had not condemned her outright, but he hadn't supported her, either. A godly woman was what he wanted.

Godly. What did that mean?

Lucy did not go to church services often anymore without her mother to prod her along. She remembered her psalms, though, as well as sermons that once moved her, and her favorite stories from the New Testament. She believed that God had created individuals in his own likeness. Whatever she did, Lucy tried to see that likeness of the divine, that expression of love, in every person she encountered.

What was more loving than protecting Katie from a fate she didn't want, or giving her control over the path of her life?

In her ire, Lucy had forgotten to take a warmer bonnet. The wind roaring down the street had amused itself by blowing up underneath her old bonnet's brim and pinching her cheeks while her eyes watered from the cold.

At first, Lucy thought she might go see Juliet to tell her of Katie and complain about the stupidity of the male race. The mud that seeped through the hole in her boots was cold, though, and the air smelled like rain, rather than snow.

The cold called up a twinge in her fingers that made her think of Thorne, and whether he was using her salve. His fingers, his hands, his scars—broken but eventually healed, like the man beneath them.

Not seeing the puddle in front of her, Lucy stomped into three inches of frozen, dirty water and felt it soak through her holey boots and into her stocking. The curse she let loose was not due to her cold, wet feet, however. Lucy cursed because the shock of the water was less intense than the realization that she'd gone and fallen in love with Jonathan Thorne.

Damn.

"I told you that I would buy you a bonnet to match the color of your eyes so you could leave off wearing that old coal scuttle."

Lucy stumbled over the cobbles on the street at the memories the voice behind her evoked. By the time she'd turned to face Duncan Rider, he'd come up close enough to take her hand and place a kiss on the back of it.

"Duncan," she said in greeting, filled with pride at the indifference in her voice. "You are looking well."

He preened; his chest puffed up, and a satisfied smile made the corners of his blue eyes crinkle in an attractive manner that once made her weak in the knees. Duncan touched the rim of his hat, drawing her attention to the fine quality of the felt and the expense of the black silk hatband. A lock of his blond hair peeked artfully out from beneath his brim, and Lucy wagered he'd spent a good half hour on this look. Lucy wished her mother had been alive to warn her about the contents of a gift that came in pretty wrapping.

"Good day to you," she said, then turned on her heel and resumed her rapid pace down the muddied streets.

"Is Miss Juliet minding the shop?" Duncan asked from behind her.

Undeterred by her about-face dismissal, he followed on Lucy's heels.

"Not your concern, is it?" she said.

Petty but satisfying to point that out.

"Lucy. Can you slow for a moment so I can speak with you?" Duncan asked, a slight whine pulling his vowels to the side and flattening them.

Turning the corner, Lucy spied the painted wooden sign for the Lion's Den. The pub took up the first two floors of a slanted stucco built during the Tudor times, and it had escaped not one but two of London's biggest fires. The exposed wooden beams were blackened and riddled with worm tracks, and the stucco had fallen off in patches, allowing for a bird to nest over the entrance. Regulars to the pub knew to look up when they opened the door and see if any of the nest's inhabitants were home before they passed below. More than one patron had been caught trying to lie about their whereabouts with a telltale lump of bird poo unnoticed in their hair.

Rather than answering Duncan, Lucy grabbed hold of the door's handle, looked up quickly to spare her old bonnet any indignities, and then made her way into the cheery confines of the Lion's Den.

A handful of customers were there, some having come from work, some getting ready, and the rest most likely having spent the day at the round oak tables, their surfaces polished by two hundred years' worth of elbows. Old women rested their feet by the fire, smoking clay pipes that spilled ash on their aprons, and a few of the men from a nearby warehouse sat in the far corner, playing a game of cards and insulting one another, sipping their pints as slowly as possible before they had to go back out in the cold.

"Miss Peterson, good day." A large, square-jawed man, Joe Quinlavin sat with his back against the wall on a wooden stool at the bar, surveying the room with a proprietary air. Although he wasn't the owner, Katie's da knew more about the lives of the people in this community than they knew about their own families; he was a magpie of gossip, collecting the tidbits strewn about by drunken patrons and hoarding them, partly for his own enjoyment and partly for future use if a favor was needed.

How long would it be before some hint of what Timmy had done reached Quinlavin's ears? Thorne wouldn't need to kill the boy; Katie's da would have already done it.

Sorrow for Katie outweighed Lucy's anger at Thorne, and she greeted Quinlavin more warmly than she might have otherwise. She smiled at the barkeep, who had already pulled a pint of her favorite lager when she stepped through the door, and took the beer to a small table in an empty part of the room.

"What are you doing drinking beer in the middle of the day?" Duncan hissed, looking around him in disdain. Lucy had never stepped out with Duncan during their affair, so she'd no idea what sort of establishment he took his pint at—most likely someplace cleaner and brighter than the Lion's Den. He picked up his foot and examined the bottom of his polished boot, frowning.

"I am a grown woman and answer to no one," Lucy said,

relishing the smooth licorice flavor of her first sip of beer. "I can drink a beer whatever time of day I like."

Duncan pulled out a chair opposite her, took a handkerchief from an inside coat pocket, and wiped the seat before flipping the skirt of his coat up and setting himself down.

At the other end of the bar, Quinlavin let out a quiet snort, and Lucy shook her head.

When had Duncan become such an ass?

Or had he always been this way, and Lucy ignored it because she was grateful for his attentions?

She took a bigger sip, more like a gulp, and licked the foam from the top of her lip.

Duncan grimaced. "You answer to your customers. What will they think if they find you've abandoned your shop for the pub?"

Another sip, and Lucy's shoulders fell. She removed her bonnet and set it on the table in front of her so there was no room for anything else other than her own pint glass.

"I suppose they'll think me feckless and take their money elsewhere. Perhaps to Rider and Son, where they can buy a tin of lozenges."

"Ahhh." Duncan's head dropped and he looked to the side as though the rest of what he should say might be written on the ancient wallpaper peeling into long strips that exposed the yellowed plaster beneath.

"You see, what happened was . . . what I mean is . . ."

Lucy contemplated the surface of her lager. The dark liquid held an image of her face, her mouth distorted and eyes overlarge. Small bubbles huddled at the side of the glass, and the scent of coffee and malt filled her nose, alongside the fug of the old women's pipes and wet wool drying by the fireside.

Did it matter what excuse Duncan came forward with? It wouldn't change a single consequence of his betrayal.

And what were the consequences?

Lucy immediately thought of lying in Thorne's arms, feeling a freedom she hadn't known existed. She thought of Sadie sitting in the workroom and asking about the anatomy of a toad, of the painstaking lettering on the name cards at dinner last week, of Mr. Gentry's expression as he presented Sadie with a posy of violets.

On the other hand, she saw David's growing frustration with the tedium of bookkeeping and the worry lines that creased Juliet's forehead when she dragged herself home from the clinic, exhausted and disheartened.

". . . and my father has agreed."

Lucy glanced up from her drink. "Your father has agreed to what, Duncan?"

A flush spread along his cheekbones as he gaped at her. "Have you not heard a word I've said?"

A sudden urge to take Duncan by the shoulders and shake him grew so strong, Lucy sat on her hands. If Thorne were here, he might once again accuse her of plotting murder.

"I work eighteen hours in the day, my brother has disappeared on me, and my sister is working herself sick. The Guardians have been protesting outside my shop and scaring patrons, and I've no money to hire an apprentice because my spurious lover *stole* my formula. Forgive me, Duncan, if I've so much on my mind I cannot concentrate on your complaints about the cleanliness of the floor or my irresponsibility in having a single pint after a difficult day."

There was no hint of a whine in her complaint, simply a recitation of facts.

Such as the fact that Duncan had lied and cheated her, and Lucy didn't owe him the courtesy of paying attention.

Slapping his top hat against his crossed thigh, Duncan then ran his gloved fingers through his perfectly pomaded hair.

"I said, I asked my father if we could be married, and my father agreed."

What?

Lucy set her glass down on the table and quickly glanced in Quinlavin's direction, but she'd chosen her seat well and he seemed not to have heard anything.

"What?"

A long-suffering sort of sigh issued from Duncan's lungs, and he rolled his eyes. "If you'd been listening to me—"

Lucy made a circling motion with her hand, and he huffed.

"I'm sorry about what happened with the lozenge formula. I feel terrible, Lucy."

Terrible? He should feel the tortures of the damned nipping at his toes.

"The time for apologies is long past," Lucy said. "You stole my work."

Examining the slick stains of pomade on his gloves meant Duncan avoided looking her in the eye.

"It wasn't like I stole it on purpose. You have to believe me. I took the formula back to the shop to experiment, like I said, and my father asked what I was working on." The flush grew until Duncan's face glowed red with chagrin. "I didn't want to tell him about us, so I told him . . ."

The handsome features that Lucy had dreamed about for so long crumpled and sagged. She caught a glimpse of what Duncan would look like twenty, thirty years from now when the patina of youth had worn away and his character had seeped into his features.

The picture wasn't pretty.

"You don't know what it's like, Lucy. Before this, I could never please him." Duncan's slightly fleshy lips sunk in a frown, his gaze unfocused. "I'm not like you. It takes me forever to mix a cure. My measurements are always wrong, and I am no good at diagnosing the imbalance of humors."

Lucy remembered Duncan's laments about his father and how difficult it was to gain the man's approval. The honesty about his failings was part of her attraction to Duncan. He never pretended to be smarter than her or became offended when she explained things to him.

Most men of Lucy's acquaintance were intimidated by a woman's success. Duncan, instead, had been admiring.

"When he thought I'd developed the lozenge, he was so proud, but . . ." Duncan's eyes squinted as though he were in pain. "It was terrible of me to let that happen, Lucy. I cheated you."

The bite of the lager and familiarity of his features—the sincerity in his voice—all conspired to loosen Lucy's muscles. Her hand unclenched around the glass, and she sank into her chair, studying Duncan's face.

"I cheated my father, too," he said. "Mostly, I cheated myself of the chance to earn his regard on my own merits."

Lucy's prediction of rain rather than snow had come true. A blanket of gray draped around the pub, and a steady tapping of the rain sang a melancholy tune against the buckled glass window behind them. The old women cackled in the corner as the occasional raindrop found its way down the chimney and was caught by the coals in a quiet hiss.

Strange how the world works, Lucy thought. The same day that Thorne disappointed her, Duncan showed up and tried to redeem himself.

Of course, there was still a world of difference between the

ce might

slay. Beneath their skin, too, the two men could not be less
alike. Thorne walked through the world with the confidence of
a king and the humility of a peasant.

Duncan, for all of his twenty-five years, was still a child.

A child who hadn't the intellectual wherewithal to break
into the apothecary, read through the piles of scientific papers
on her desk, and figure out which was a formula for a croup
salve.

Draining her pint, Lucy swallowed the bitter truth along
with tasteless foam and the knowledge that nothing could
change the course of her life. She'd gone and lost her chance at
a fortune and then, even worse, lost her heart. Nothing else
would matter until Lucy found a way to recover from that.

"Are you too high in the instep to join me in a pint?" Lucy
asked him, weary and thirsty. "This might go easier if you did."

Blowing out a long breath, Duncan nodded, and Lucy went
to the bar. As she waited for the barkeep to draw a pint of blond
ale, she smiled grimly at Quinlavin, whose eyes were wide with
curiosity.

"You don't have to marry me," she said when she returned,
setting the glass on the table in front of Duncan. "You can just
put my name on the lozenge patent."

Duncan frowned. "But I want to marry you."

At first, Lucy did not know whether to laugh or scream at
his self-absorption. Instead, she said nothing, her face frozen
in ambivalence.

More surprising was the question she asked herself in the
next second. Would that be so terrible?

Lucy would never love Duncan again the way she had before he'd broken her heart. The power he'd held was long gone.

Rather than being a detriment to marriage, though, this would be an asset.

There was no depth to Duncan that she would need to plumb, no secrets, no sordid history. Marriage with him would be simple and uncomplicated.

In fact, if Lucy suspected that she could ever fall back in love with him, she would never consider marriage.

Giving a man your heart meant giving him the power to hurt you.

The ache in Lucy's chest at Thorne's ambivalence this afternoon was still throbbing in her chest. Why carry such pain?

"I do not love you anymore," she told him without rancor.

Taking no umbrage, Duncan merely nodded. "I expect not after what I did."

"I am not, as you said," Lucy continued, "unnatural in my urges nor powerless to my desires."

Apple-shaped splotches of red appeared beneath Duncan's cheekbones. "It's not just my word. The Guardians say . . ."

Lucy finished the last of her lager and set the glass down on the table a little too hard. Quinlavin looked over from his hushed conversation with the barkeep, and Duncan's flush deepened.

"Never again quote the Guardians' assertions to me," Lucy said through gritted teeth.

His mouth opened, then closed. After a moment, Duncan took a sip of his beer, then shuddered at the taste.

"The leaders of the Guardians, they are men of high station. We do business with them," Duncan said. "That cannot change."

Lucy shrugged. "I will take their money. I am simply sick of their words. Do not repeat them to me and we shall get on famously."

Eyes narrowing, Duncan pushed his glass away, no longer pretending enjoyment. "Does that mean you will do it? You will marry me?"

Arms crossed, Lucy met Duncan's stare with a bold one of her own.

"That means you may fetch me another pint, please," she said.

"Excellent. I'll buy you as many pints as you wish, if you'll just hear me out. We have much to discuss," Duncan said, his smile suddenly bright.

Lucy just shook her head at his back as he made his way to the bar. She'd listen to Duncan for as long as he was buying, but doubted any argument he could concoct would convince her to trust him again.

A heart could only break so many times before it lost its original purpose.

19

"YOU ARE QUIET," THORNE SAID AS HE SET A CUP OF TEA at Sadie's elbow. She'd come home about an hour after Lucy left, arm in arm with Juliet, who had been surprised to find the shop closed. Thorne hadn't given her an explanation. He'd simply taken Sadie upstairs and plied her with scones and honey, but she'd had little to say about her day.

Sadie shrugged. "You are quiet as well."

"It's not polite to tell adults what they already know," he said.

She squinted as if hearing something other than his words. "Why not?"

Thorne blinked.

"Because . . ." he hedged, looking around for a distraction. "It makes you sound as though you know better than the adult."

"What if I do?" Sadie asked, a surprised hurt pulling down the corners of her mouth. "Am I supposed to pretend I don't? Isn't that lying?"

Thorne blinked again.

"There is a difference between not saying something so the other person won't feel bad," he said, "and not saying something to avoid telling the truth."

That sounded quite wise. Thorne gave himself an imaginary pat on the back.

Instead of continuing her line of inquiry or arguing a point that would make his eyes cross, Sadie picked her fork up and began mashing the scone on her plate into a pile of crumbs.

Hmmm.

"Is something amiss, Sadie?" he asked.

At his question, the girl's shoulders stiffened, and she bent her head to closer inspect the crumbs. Thorne waited, knowing Sadie could not stay silent for long, not if there were something on her conscience.

"If I don't tell you something I know about, am I lying to you?" she asked.

Thorne reached over and touched the back of her hand. Sadie dropped her fork and looked up at him.

So much for patting himself on the back. Something was worrying Sadie and he'd almost missed it.

"I haven't asked you directly about what you know, have I?"

Her eyes widened with relief. "No. So only if you ask me would I be lying?"

"Yes." Thorne nodded. "However, if you see someone in danger or doing something bad and you don't tell me? That isn't a lie, but it isn't honest, either."

"If I were to tell you, I would be tattling on Miss Juliet."

Ah. No one wanted to be a tattletale. Thorne remembered that vividly from his own childhood growing up with two brothers. Tattletales would find themselves sleeping on wet sheets or putting their feet into shoes filled with pudding.

"There is a difference between tattling to get someone in

trouble, or to hurt them, and telling a truth to keep someone *out* of trouble."

This seemed to appease her, because Sadie took another scone and drenched it in honey. In between mouthfuls, she told him what had happened on her walk after school the day before.

"D'you remember the man Miss Juliet was speaking to the day you came to walk us home?" Sadie asked. "I remembered that I'd seen him before. That night when the carriage stopped outside our window."

Duncan Rider.

"Sometimes he comes and talks to her and asks after Miss Peterson. Yesterday, Miss Juliet asked for something back that she'd given him, and he said no."

Thorne's stomach sank. "How did she act when he said no?" he asked.

"She seemed sad at first. Then she told me to go back into Madame's vestibule and wait for her." Sadie paused. "I didn't eavesdrop because I know that is wrong."

Damn.

"I did peek through the window at the side of the vestibule that faces the street," she said.

Excellent.

Eavesdropping was immoral, but spying was perfectly appropriate.

Thorne waited impatiently for Sadie to finish chewing.

"And then?" he asked.

"She talked to him some more and he laughed. That made her mad, and she shook her fist in his face like this."

Scowling, Sadie made a fist and shook it in the air.

"Did she say anything afterward on your walk home about the meeting?" he asked.

"Umm-humm," Sadie said around her last bite of pastry.

"Miss Juliet said that men were not to be trusted, that no good deed ever goes unpunished, *and* that you can make a frog's legs move after it's dead if you pull on the plantaris tendon."

Thorne ruminated on Sadie's revelation.

There were, of course, other options than Juliet having given the formula to Duncan Rider. She could have given him papers relating to her clinic, perhaps a request for funding. Or she could be in love with him herself and have given him a packet of love poems or an embarrassing gift.

Thorne wanted it to be the latter, but he didn't think this was the case.

Nothing in his investigations had pointed toward Duncan Rider having geared up to process a revolutionary croup salve. No patents had been requested, no excess of croup salve ingredients had been ordered by Rider and Son's regular suppliers, and he hadn't acted like a man about to reap a second fortune when Thorne encountered him at the cards table.

None of the other apothecaries Thorne visited had sold a croup salve containing ingredients that matched Lucy's list. There were no instances of theft in the neighborhood. A perusal of the last few issues of the Guardians' *Gentlemen's Monthly* had made no mention of medications or salves—other than the fact that courtesans should be put in workhouses to repent instead of receiving treatment for their most common diseases or the correction of their menses.

David's accounting system was a venal sin, but not particularly criminal. His payments to Mr. Wilcox might have something to do with that business of a cooperative up north, but in and of themselves were no evidence of his having done anything with the croup salve.

On the other hand, Sadie had witnessed the first piece of evidence pointing at someone having stolen Lucy's formula, and that someone was her sister. Juliet had told Thorne out-right that she thought Duncan should marry Lucy. What better way to force a proposal than offer a second fortune in return?

Even worse than giving Lucy the news that she had been cheated, now Thorne must tell her that he'd solved the case and witness her pain at the betrayal.

"YOU'VE BEEN DRINKING." THORNE'S WORDS, RIPE WITH disdain, smashed around her feet like rotting fruit.

Lucy stopped halfway through her workroom. Carefully, she turned around and met his darkened gaze.

"I've been drinking, yes," she said.

By the time she and Duncan left the Lion's Den, Lucy had finished two pints and was unsteady on her feet. Juliet had come home from Athena's Retreat by then and reopened the shop. When Lucy swayed through the door, Juliet was stand-ing behind the counter speaking with a pair of young women. Her sister said nothing, but Lucy knew from the pinch in Ju-liet's brow that an explanation would be requested later.

In addition to the drink, Lucy was experiencing regret now that she was in Thorne's presence. Not because she felt bad about having a drink, but because his mouth was set in a scowl. What *was* it about a man who scowled?

"Do you think that is wise, to come home drunk in the mid-dle of the afternoon?" he asked.

"No," she said, lifting her chin so she might stare beyond Thorne's face to the wall behind him. "I think it was *fun*."

Thorne's hands turned to fists, and he set them on his hips, disappointment streaming out of him so strongly, she fancied she could feel it pool around her ankles.

Lucy did not care.

She did *not* care.

"Do you know what else I've done that was fun? Danced all night at a masquerade. Played cards. Looked at naughty postcards."

Lucy refused to make the same mistake with Thorne that she had with Duncan—give her heart to a man who saw her as a woman unworthy of marriage.

She wasn't, though. She wasn't unworthy.

"You can do what you like," he said. "I'm not here to judge you."

Liar.

"Oh, but you already have," she said, trying hard not to slur her words.

His shoulders dropped, and Lucy turned her attention from the wall above his head to his face.

His beautiful, ruined face.

"I am not a lady, Thorne. I can never be what you want," she whispered. To him, to herself, to her stupid, stupid heart.

"How do you know what I want?" he asked.

"Duncan Rider asked me to marry him."

Thorne's head jerked as though Lucy had slapped him.

"Why . . . ?"

Thorne's question remained unanswered when a woman's head poked around the doorway behind him.

"Can I help you, mum?" Lucy asked in what hopefully passed for a professional tone.

"I beg your pardon for interrupting," the woman said. "The young lady out front told me I should come back here to speak with—"

Thorne spun around on his heel at the sound of the woman's voice.

"Why, hello, Mr. Thorne."

"Mrs. Merkle. What a lovely surprise."

Lucy's stomach hurt. Most likely from the drink, surely not from anything else. For a moment she watched Thorne tend to the skinny woman in a modest bonnet and a sour expression that turned her mouth into a warning.

A godly woman. That is what Thorne wanted. Someone who never would go drinking in a pub in the middle of the day or dance a reel on a whim.

Not like Lucy.

That's what Thorne meant to say earlier.

Someone not like Lucy.

Keeping her spine straight and her steps steady, Lucy Peterson walked away from Jonathan Thorne.

20

"A COW HAS FOUR STOMACHS AND EATS ITS OWN VOMIT. What do you think of that? It's the absolute truth, Papa."

Thorne listened to Sadie's chatter, but the words wouldn't stick.

Lucy was going to marry that weak-spined Duncan Rider.

This was not where she should lay her burdens—not onto a man who could barely help himself, let alone her.

"I told Mrs. Merkle, and she said I should save such information for the schoolroom. That ladies didn't speak of internal organs or vomit when amongst company."

"I have to think this is sound advice," Thorne said, gripping Sadie's hand a little tighter as they walked home from Sunday services.

The commotion amid the congregation this morning rivaled the time Mrs. Inglewood fell so fast asleep that she'd toppled off her pew and woke screaming that the devil had finally come to get her.

Today, the excitement was Mrs. Merkle's triumphant visit.

Both before and after service, she held court in the corner of the foyer, answering everyone's questions with an even voice and serene smile. Yes, Scotland was lovely. Yes, she liked her new neighbors, but, no, the services at her new church were not as inspirational as the services here.

She'd seemed pleased to see Sadie, squeezing the girl's hand and exclaiming about how much she'd grown and how pretty her new winter coat was. Thorne had pretended to read the announcement board, aware he was an object of scrutiny by many of the women who lingered to chat, a single man with a seemingly good income and a young daughter to raise. A goodly portion of the flock here had been expecting a match between himself and Mrs. Merkle for a while now.

One doughy old matron leaned over to gossip with her friend, and Thorne knew what she was asking. What had Mrs. Merkle found out about him that sent her to Scotland instead of the altar?

After twenty minutes of his feigning interest in knitting socks for the poor or contributing to the church upkeep fund, Sadie and Mrs. Merkle finally made their way toward him without any hangers-on.

Thorne had bowed over Mrs. Merkle's hand, and the three of them discussed the weather for the requisite two minutes.

"I hope we see more of you before you return to Scotland," Thorne had said.

Mrs. Merkle had blushed, and a load of rocks appeared in his stomach, weighing him down.

"I would be amenable to any invitation you might offer before I leave on Saturday," she said.

Well.

Mrs. Merkle was nothing if not plainspoken.

The blush, however, niggled at Thorne's conscience as he and

Sadie walked home from church and made their way up to their rooms, discomfited by Mrs. Merkle's expectation of an "invitation."

Passing by Lucy's door, Thorne could hear her and Juliet laughing. Bitterness filled his mouth with the taste of cold tea dregs, and Thorne decided it was resentment at Juliet and her deceit, not frustration that Lucy entertained an offer from Duncan Rider.

Surely not.

Thorne had been so distracted yesterday, he'd forgotten to go to the butcher's. Sunday lunch was leftover mutton, and Sadie wolfed it down in between her recounting of what Mrs. Merkle had said after services and more fascinating facts about a cow's anatomy.

"If I eat my peas, can I skip the washing up and look at my gift?"

It took Thorne twice the normal amount of time to wash and dry the dishes, not because Sadie wasn't helping—it took *more* time with Sadie's help than it did when he worked alone— but because every two minutes she would call for him to put down the dishes and come see the pictures in the folio Lord Blackstone had sent her.

When the kitchen was clean, Thorne insisted Sadie ready herself for bed first, then sat with her in the orange-gold light of the oil lamp as she exclaimed over the folio.

An impressively bound and embossed leather cover housed *A Picture Journey of the African and Asian Continents* published by Harvey and Darton. On one page was an illustration of an animal and, on the opposite, a description of the animal and where it could be found. Every three pages, the illustration had been colored.

It must have cost a pretty penny in 1825, when it was

published. Thorne didn't remember seeing it in his father's library, but he hadn't spent much time there before going off to school. He'd been a year younger than Sadie when he left his childhood home, only to return during holidays.

He and his father had never done this, lie side by side and read together. In fact, no one Thorne knew did such a thing.

Would Mrs. Merkle read with her children before prayers? Somehow Thorne couldn't conjure an image of her curling up in a nest of books and chatter.

By the time Sadie fell asleep, Thorne was lost to melancholy. On nights like this, he would set a chair against the front door as a reminder not to leave the apartment lest he be tempted by the company and cheer of the local pub.

There had been a note accompanying the book, but Thorne had neatly slipped it out from the brown paper wrapping and stuck it in his pocket, despite it being addressed to Sadie.

His father had sent his warmest regards to the delightful Miss Thorne with hope she found the folio edifying. Since its publication in 1825, more animals had been discovered. If Miss Thorne would care to come for tea at Lord Blackstone's home, he and his wife, Lady Blackstone, would be honored to host her and show her a more up-to-date collection of books about the natural world.

Lines and boundaries.

Which to cross and which to hold?

He read and reread the note, finally tucking it into the drawer where he kept his cravats, slipping it under the stacks of linen and silk. Stronger than his urge to leave the apartment for the warmth and conviviality of the pub was his urge to leave the apartment and see Lucy. Not simply because he desired her—which he did, very much—but also because he wanted to speak with her. What would she think of his father's overtures?

Would she suggest a rapprochement, or shake her fist in anger, like her sister?

Thorne worried about Katie as well. Juliet had told him that Katie was ill with a stomach flu and would stay home for the next few days, but he refrained from asking for more information, unsure of how much Lucy had confided in her. The puffy red skin beneath Katie's listless eyes, the hesitation before she set her foot outside the door, the memory of Katie's head bent so close to Sadie's—all these images ran through Thorne's head at various times during the day.

What Katie decided to do was of course not up to him. His concerns, his conceits, for that matter—they had no bearing on Katie's life or well-being. This Thorne understood. How should he then reconcile what the church and society had taught him about women's choices, and the very real gap between those expectations and reality?

What would he do if something similar happened to Sadie? To Lucy? Would Lucy understand his ambivalence and listen to his questions?

He went so far as to sit in the chair in front of the door to the hallway for a time, listing arguments in his head for and against going downstairs. In the end, he came to a decision.

It was time to leave.

Thorne couldn't bear to contemplate living above an apartment that Lucy would share with Duncan.

He would take his father up on the invitation for a visit. Sadie needed a proper last name and a family other than him, and this time Thorne would not back down without a fight.

They would leave by the end of the month. He'd buy a house for him and Sadie—he could ask Rudolph for a loan—and go back to being a Thornwood.

With the memory of Blackstone staring down at Sadie

lodged in his brain, Thorne finally fell asleep while the wind moaned long and low in the winter's night.

"DID YOU KNOW, A PERSON'S BRAIN WEIGHS THREE pounds, more or less?"

Lucy made a noise of agreement and carried on staring at the office door. Thorne had gone in there after dropping Sadie off at school and shut the door without saying a word of greeting to her. She hadn't greeted him, either, but of the two of them, Thorne was the one who should greet her first, not the other way around.

The person who had been the most wrong had to bend first. The Peterson siblings had always lived by this rule, and Lucy did not see why Thorne shouldn't, too. Never mind that she wasn't certain he knew the rule.

He should have, and that was that.

"D'you know what else? Over at London Hospital they cut a tumor out of a man, leaving him with two-thirds of his brain, and he woke from the surgery able to play the violin. Imagine that."

Frowning at the door as though she could make Thorne uncomfortable with the force of a stare he couldn't see, Lucy tapped her fingers on the counter.

"D'you know what else?"

"Mr. Gentry," Lucy interrupted, trying to mask her exasperation. "Do you think you can check in the back storeroom to see if there are any more bags of dried chamomile?"

"Yes, indeed," Gentry said, and gave her a little bow. "Anything else you'd like me to do back there? Alphabetize supplies? What do apprentices usually do?"

Lucy had done it.

She'd gotten herself an apprentice.

After one year probation, Gentry would be allowed to study at London Hospital as an apothecary just as she and Juliet had. Of course, he was decades older than most apprentices, but Lucy and Juliet had no doubt Mr. Gentry would be a model student and a huge help at the apothecary.

"Alphabetizing the supplies would be going above and beyond—"

"Say no more." Gentry left for the back, whistling a naughty song.

Decades older than most, certainly, but since Lucy and Juliet came to him with the offer, he'd looked twenty years younger.

He'd refused a salary but agreed to a bonus after the first year if Lucy and Juliet were pleased with his work.

If Duncan hadn't stolen the croup salve formula and Thorne's visits to London's other apothecaries had yielded no results, Lucy decided she would try to re-create her work. Even if she couldn't patent it exclusively, perhaps she could earn enough money from the sales to keep the shop open along with paying Katie's wage and putting some money aside for Mr. Gentry.

Meanwhile, Thorne had snuck out of the office while Mr. Gentry distracted Lucy. She cursed the agent under her breath.

In the interest of fairness and not for any other reason, certainly not because she missed his regard and craved his touch, Lucy stood in front of the office door. When Thorne returned a few minutes later, she pretended to be polishing the doorknob with a dusting rag.

"Miss Peterson," he said, in his low, stony voice, "if you will let me pass?"

Lucy crossed her arms and leaned against the office door.

Thorne blinked, then drew his brows together. "Miss Peterson?" he said again.

Lucy held her ground. She wasn't going to move a single muscle until he apologized for a list of faults that grew by the second. He not only had been unforgivably rude the other day but also must apologize for his terrible habit of making her feel safe and competent, and for smelling so lovely this morning.

Then he compounded his trespasses by scowling at her now. *What is a woman to do?* Lucy asked herself.

The scowl deepened, and Lucy's heartbeat sped as Thorne approached her, one slow step after the other, until they stood, toe to toe, in front of the door. One more inch and they would be touching, one more step and he would have her pressed up against the door.

Lucy's mouth watered as he reached out toward her, and she bit her bottom lip in anticipation.

"Good day, Miss Peterson," Thorne said, then reached toward her hip as she leaned back against the door, but instead of putting his hands on her, he put his hand on the doorknob and twisted. The boards beneath her feet disappeared.

"Of all the blasted—" Lucy looked up from the floor as Thorne stepped over her prone body.

She'd forgotten the door opened inward.

"What are you even doing in here?" Lucy asked, standing to close the door and brushing off her skirt as if she hadn't just toppled over onto her arse in front of the whole shop. "Shouldn't you be upstairs practicing your marriage proposal now that Mrs. Merkle is returned?"

Rather than answer, like a real gentleman, Thorne sighed and rubbed his eyes as though he'd gotten only a few hours' sleep last night. Too bad Lucy had no sympathy for the man.

"Sadie and I will be taking new rooms at the end of the month," he said.

The pain of his words was like the cuts from a reed. At first, she felt nothing, but then Lucy had to press a hand to her stomach to keep her insides from falling out.

Well. That made sense, didn't it? It wasn't as if Mrs. Merkle could live here. Not over so scandalous a place as a woman-owned apothecary.

Why, then, did Thorne saying the words aloud slice Lucy to the bone? More hurt pressed against her throat and chest. What else might he say that would wound her, and how bad would the scars be that those words left behind?

Fear of the pain caused Lucy to strike out, flailing like a fool against an end she should have seen coming.

"Unfortunate that you're leaving before finishing your assignment. I suppose Tierney and Company's reputation for delivering *full satisfaction* is unfounded."

Not the wittiest remark, but for some reason Lucy's throat felt tight and her eyes burned, keeping her from thinking up anything more cutting.

"I am leaving because I *have* finished my assignment."

"Ha," Lucy said, raising her chin and wishing she could look down her nose at Thorne, but he topped her by at least three inches. "You have shown me no proof that Duncan stole my croup formula. In fact, it doesn't matter, since he asked me to marry him—"

Thorne stepped forward and stopped a mere inch or two away from Lucy in front of the desk. The memories of their kisses here, the times he'd touched her, the times Thorne had told her to trust him, they floated in the air like ghosts.

"Don't," he whispered, his voice like an untanned piece of leather, rough against her skin. "Don't marry him, Lucy."

"Why not?" she snapped. "Why not marry a man who already benefits from my work? At least this way I'll finally be paid as well."

Through the grime of the windowpanes, the golden sunlight darkened to orange. The faint beams were reflected in Thorne's dark eyes like tiny flames. Lucy's heart thumped and she fisted her hands tight, pressing her arms against her waist so she wouldn't do anything completely stupid, like reach out and pull him toward her.

"You don't deserve—"

Laughter spewed from her mouth, and Lucy's desire to hold Thorne close now turned to a desire to push him away—or out the window.

"Do not," she said, each word honed so no matter where it landed, he would feel it. "Do not tell me what I do or don't deserve."

Lucy's foolish heart had thought she was meant for Thorne, but if he wouldn't help with the real burdens—the Guardians' hatred of women, the life-and-death decisions she made, the way doubt would never leave her—then he was not the man for her.

Her throat dried at Thorne's thunderous expression. Lucy almost stepped back as rage poured out of his skin and heated the air between them to an uncomfortable degree.

"Duncan has apologized, did you know that? Came to me and said—"

The office door flew open. "The two of you need to stop arguing this instant." Juliet poked her head in, hissing with displeasure. "Unless you want all of London knowing your business by the end of day."

"I don't care what London knows. I have nothing to be ashamed of, despite what Mr. Thorne believes." With a toss of her head, Lucy spun on her heel toward Juliet and gave Thorne her back. "Mr. Thorne is an agent of Tierney and Company. I hired him to find proof Duncan took my croup formula, but he hasn't found anything."

Juliet turned green.

This was not hyperbole; Lucy's sister turned the color of the bruised sky before a storm. Hurrying to her side, Lucy took hold of Juliet's wrist to feel her pulse while she put a hand to Juliet's forehead.

"Dearest, what is wrong. Are you ill?" Lucy asked, pulling Juliet toward the ladder-back chair in the corner of the office.

"No, I'm fine." Juliet stared at Thorne as though he were the devil himself. "Mr. Thorne is an agent for Tierney's? The same agency as employs Mr. Winthram?"

"Yes." Lucy pulled Juliet down into the chair, then opened the office window to let in the cold air despite the fog of soot that billowed in with it. There wasn't much else to breathe in East London.

"Miss Peterson is under the impression that I have not completed my mission and found her thief," Thorne said to Juliet, a quiet menace in his voice.

Lucy coughed, then returned to Juliet's side, frowning at the man standing like a great stone in the center of the tiny room.

"Well, you haven't, and thus you are dismissed."

"Lucy . . ." Juliet tugged at Lucy's sleeve.

"Dismissed, am I?" The menace vanished, and his words shot forward in an undercurrent of disbelief.

Lucy pulled her arm from Juliet's grasp and straightened her spine. "You are indeed. You have failed—"

"Lucy!" Juliet cried.

She and Thorne turned as one to regard Juliet, whose color had now faded to the whitish gray of cheese water.

"Whatever is the matter, dear?" Lucy asked her sister.

"I have something to tell you."

So small, her sister, Juliet. Most of the time, Juliet's tiny frame was barely noticeable, her personality taking up most of the space around her, fooling folks into thinking her a much larger woman.

Lucy carefully knelt on the floor next to the chair and held Juliet's trembling hand.

"I gave Duncan the first few pages of your formula," Juliet said.

"Oh. Oh, I see," Lucy said. This was a lie. She did not see anything, her vision blurring as Juliet's words sank in.

"Oh," she said again.

Lucy's head dropped into her sister's lap, the energy to keep upright drained away by Juliet's confession. Ever so gently, Juliet pulled a few pins and took off Lucy's cap, then started to stroke her hair.

"I knew you still loved Duncan. I thought if I gave him the first half of the croup salve formula, he would propose in order to get the second half."

"Rather mercenary of you," Lucy said quietly, letting Juliet pet her. A comforting numbness settled over her as Juliet spoke.

"When he didn't propose, I told him to give it back, and he refused. Said that he could figure out the rest on his own." Juliet sighed and looked over at Thorne. "Sadie must have said something to you."

"She told me only that he had upset you," Thorne said. "The rest was fairly easy to figure out."

"He must need help after all, for he proposed to me yesterday," Lucy said.

Juliet put her fingers under Lucy's chin and lifted her head up so they could meet each other's eyes.

"If you married Duncan, you would never have to work yourself to exhaustion the way you do now. You would have the time to work on your other formulas, or even stop work altogether. I hate to see you so burdened, my dear. I only wanted to find a way to help."

Lucy sat back on her heels and regarded her sister. "I do not need anyone to lift my burdens for me." A slight click of the tongue and Juliet's pursed mouth put Lucy in mind of her mother when one of her children told an obvious lie.

"You are so burdened, it is a wonder you are standing at the end of the day," Juliet said, shaking her head. "With the new funding for our clinic—"

Lucy gasped and clasped her hands. "The committee is giving you the money?"

"Yes." Juliet's radiant smile added inches to her height.

"They will pay you *and* Mrs. Sweet?" Lucy asked.

Juliet nodded, her bottom lip tucked between her teeth, eyes wide with hope for forgiveness.

Lucy would, of course, forgive her sister.

What did 1 Corinthians say?

Love is not irritable or resentful. *Love bears all things . . .*

The Guardians and their ilk might quote the Bible, but did they understand it? When her father first made Lucy an apprentice, he had her take a vow. Lucy promised her father, and her God, that she would endeavor to place herself in the shoes of anyone who came to her for treatment.

This didn't mean she wouldn't complain to Katie when Billy cast up his accounts on every conceivable surface of their treatment room rather than neatly into a bucket like everyone else.

It didn't mean she and her sister wouldn't make David laugh so hard he turned purple while telling stories of Mr. Gentry and how he'd mistakenly applied an onion poultice for his chest to his most private parts instead.

What it did mean was that along with every cure, Lucy doled out a modicum of grace. She allowed that fear and loneliness, that pain and isolation, that any of these circumstances can make even the kindest, wisest soul turn irritable or angry.

Forgiveness came easy if you allowed the people around you a bit of grace.

"I'm so sorry to make you worry. I just wanted to ease your mind," Juliet said now, setting her hand to Lucy's cheek. "I went about it wrong, and then I didn't know how to set things right. I just thought you deserved to be loved and cherished, and it wasn't enough for you to be loved and cherished just by me."

Lucy smiled at her sister and put her fingers to the corners of her eyes, where tears began to gather. Behind them, Thorne shut the door quietly, taking himself off to who knew where.

Lucy did not have the energy left to mourn his departure. Instead, she listened to her sister's excited chatter and waited for the pain to ease.

21

❦

TWO DAYS AND FOUR BAGS OF PASTIES LATER, LUCY HAD
forgiven Juliet.

"*That* is your new apprentice?"

Because she was so well-fed, Lucy was slow to reach Duncan and drag him toward the back of the shop before he could be overheard.

"Yes. Mr. Gentry is our new apprentice," she confirmed in a harsh whisper.

When Duncan rolled his eyes, Lucy gave in to her worst instincts and pinched him.

"Ow," he said. "Stop pinching me. What kind of apothecary apprentices a forty-year-old man? You'll be a laughingstock."

Praying for patience, Lucy leaned past Duncan to look at Mr. Gentry, who stood on a tall ladder, inspecting the contents of the tins on the highest of shelves. None of the Petersons had looked up there in ages, and Gentry's task was to see which of the contents were salvageable. Lucy did not need him distracted when he stood so high up. He was forty, after all. He didn't appear to have heard.

"I thought you were going to apprentice the shopgirl," Duncan continued. "You'd still be an oddity, but having a grown man is just ludicrous."

Lucy held a bouquet of hothouse lilies in one hand. Duncan had swept in a few minutes ago with the flowers while wearing a huge smile and an expensive beaver-fur-mantle greatcoat. For a moment Lucy had been speechless, not because the flowers were so beautiful—they were—but because her gaze had fixed on the gold buttons that glinted against the dark indigo wool of his coat.

Gold buttons.

Beaver-fur collar.

Paid for by her hard work.

All while Juliet had to walk to the clinic and listen to the sound of men screaming at her because she couldn't afford a hack. All while Lucy worked herself to exhaustion because she couldn't afford more help.

"Katie doesn't want to be an apothecary, and Mr. Gentry has not only memorized Lavoisier's catalog of known elements, but he's agreed to forgo his wages until after the probationary period," Lucy said. "Plus, he is my dear friend, so keep your voice down, please."

Duncan slapped his tall brown topper against his leg and examined the brim, no doubt concerned that some of the dust at Peterson's had snuck its way onto the hat.

"Your *dear friend*? How many male 'dear friends' do you have, exactly?" he asked.

She hadn't the energy to entertain such nonsense, so Lucy changed the subject.

"Have you spoken to your father yet? You promised to tell

him the truth about the lozenges twice now this week, and I've heard nothing since."

Throwing his hands in the air, Duncan huffed a sharp sigh as though he were dealing with a ninny. He took hold of the flowers and brought them to his nose, then set them down on the windowsill behind them. Golden pollen rose into a cloud like fairy dust, and Lucy opened her mouth to share the thought, then closed it again.

"Let's never mind that," Duncan said. "Why don't we take the omnibus over to Rider and Son? The building next door has rooms to let, and we can look at them together."

Lucy's attention was drawn to the patterns the pollen made as it settled back onto the dark wood beneath it. The yellow motes mixed with the layer of dust beneath them. Another detail left unattended by their inability to pay for a full-time shop assistant.

She made to wipe it away when a tendril of an idea tapped at the base of her brain.

Some folks had reactions to flowers, couldn't be in their presence long before they started sneezing and wheezing. Might it be the dust of the pollen rather than the flowers themselves? If so, how did the pollen reach their noses? Were there pieces of pollen that were smaller than the eye could see? How long would they sit in the air? What if there were other elements that were too small to see with the naked eye but also swirled about in the air?

". . . when we move. We'll need an extra room for the nursery."

The word *nursery* yanked Lucy from her thoughts with a sensation of dread.

Nursery. *Nursery?*

"You want to have a baby with me?" she asked, shocked.

"What else do you think we'll do once we're married?" Duncan retorted.

"Married?"

Both Duncan and Lucy started in surprise, neither of them having paid attention to who was coming in and out of the shop.

Standing next to them with a look of horror on his face was her brother, David.

"David," Lucy exclaimed. "Where have you been?"

"Never mind that," he said.

Wherever he'd been had agreed with him. Gone was his London pallor. Her brother's skin had sunned to a golden brown. Tiny white laugh lines had appeared next to his eyes, and his cheeks glowed with excitement. Although, right now, it looked more like anger.

"You cannot marry Duncan Rider of all people," David said, pulling his dove-gray topper from his head and running his fingers through his hair. When he shook his head to let the hair settle, a few sighs of appreciation rippled through the shop.

"You do not make decisions for me," Lucy retorted. "You leave without telling me where you're going, so you can't come back and be angry at what I've done. Also, your cravat is only half-done."

David huffed in annoyance. "I don't make decisions for you, but I am your brother. In some circles that would mean the head of the family, and in that role, I say, I'd rather you married Mr. Gentry than Duncan Rider."

Lucy did not bother to check on the loud thump to the left of them, assuming that was Gentry having fallen off the ladder in shock. If he needed a surgeon, certainly he'd shout.

"Furthermore, this is referred to as a tie," David continued, putting a hand to the knotted length of silk at his throat. "It is now de rigueur on the Continent to leave off with complicated knots when dressing for day."

"Tie, cravat, it makes no matter." Lucy's cheeks heated in anger. She eyed David's hat, thinking of all the things she wanted to do to it and wondering about its flammability. "You've gone and left me to mind the shop alone, *again*, you haven't touched the ledgers in weeks, you still haven't explained who Mr. Wilcox is, and you can't tell me whom to marry."

Like they were children again, David stamped his foot, and they faced each other, arms crossed in an identical manner, tempers high.

"I can tell you whom *not* to marry. That arse, Duncan Rider," David said.

"I'm standing right here," said Duncan with an air of disbelief.

Lucy and David ignored him.

"Tell me who Wilcox is and why Patel's is cheating us," Lucy demanded.

David's face fell, his glow nearly diminished. "This isn't how I wanted to tell you about Wilcox, or Patel's, or any of this." He took a step back and straightened his spine. "I gave part of our savings to Wilcox as a deposit for the East End Friendly Society."

Lucy's mouth opened but no words emerged. Of all the scenarios she'd envisioned her brother investing their money in, a friendly society was not one of them.

"The East End Friendly Society? What's that, then?" asked Mr. Gentry.

He, along with a dozen other customers, had clearly overheard everything. Granted, they'd done it by inching over to where Lucy and her brother stood, taking advantage of their distraction.

David pivoted toward the crowd, opening his arms and raising his voice.

"In two weeks, I and my partner, Mr. Willem Wilcox, son of the Earl of Yarmouth, will throw open the doors of the East End Friendly Society. We're modeling it on the friendly societies they've begun up north. Anyone can join, no matter their occupation or their sex. For a set amount of money each month saved with the society, you receive help with your apothecary balances or surgery bills if you are ill and a proper burial if the worst occurs. Like how building owners buy insurance with a fire brigade."

"What about those of us who are young and without medical debts?" a young woman asked, batting her lashes.

Another of the customers, an older matron with steel-gray curls that poked out in every direction from her bonnet, squinted her eyes at the woman and huffed.

"Mary Smith was one and twenty when her second birth killed her, and they had no money for anything but a wee wooden cross," she said.

The young woman paled at the reminder that childbirth could be fatal.

"Those of you who are young . . ." David winked at the woman. "And beautiful . . ." Then he winked at the matron as well. "Will be readying yourself for the future and paying for a good night's sleep."

Lucy had heard of the friendly societies up north, of course. They were popular in small towns and villages for providing mutual aid. Sometimes, as David suggested, for help with illness and burials; others saved toward a common goal, such as a school or service.

"Why would you not tell me about this?" Lucy asked.

"I didn't want to tell you until we'd gone through with the purchase of the building to house the society and its activities," David said. He turned his hat over in his hand, shaking his head at the memory. "The money Wilcox and I had collected wasn't enough, and we had difficulty convincing anyone to loan us money when they found out where we wanted to locate ourselves."

"Well, where are you going? The east end of Timbuktu?" Lucy asked.

"No, and here is the best part of the surprise," David said, his beautiful smile extending even more, his eyes finally shining like they used to before their parents' deaths. "We found a place next to Sniffles's clinic in St. Giles."

"Oh. You must have planned this for a while," Lucy said softly. Planned long before he'd left for Bath. Planned and told her nothing about it.

"I told you before, this wasn't how I wanted you to find out," her brother said.

"A friendly society for the people of St. Giles?" Duncan scoffed. "Open to anyone regardless of sex? You're going to have a barrelful of whores in your waiting room, Peterson. No wonder you couldn't get a loan."

Lucy wanted to do more than pinch Duncan. She wanted to wound David as well. But as soon as she had the thought, she felt small.

Like Juliet, David had accomplished something that would be of fantastic benefit to people who needed help the most.

Like Juliet, David's motives had been well-intentioned.

Like Juliet, David had broken Lucy's heart a little by keeping secrets.

"Mr. Peterson," Duncan said, stepping in between Lucy and

her brother, unwilling to be ignored. "If you would care to accompany me for a drink at my club, we can discuss—privately— my betrothal to your sister and the benefits it will bring. I'm certain we can see our way toward an arrangement that will please everyone."

"Mr. Rider, the only arrangement I wish to see with you is the arrangement of my fist in your face," David said, just as smoothly.

Duncan's smile thinned into a straight line and his cheeks flushed.

"I think you would do well to reconsider. Rider and Son is going to register a second exclusive medical patent for a croup salve," he said, all pretenses of bonhomie now vanished. "If you want your sister's name to be on the patent alongside mine, you'll change your tune."

Turning to Lucy, Duncan executed a proper, crisp bow. He shook his hair to the side and set his beautiful hat on his head so that only one buttery forelock peeked out.

David gritted his teeth, but Lucy set her hand on his chest and shook her head no before he could say anything inflammatory.

Duncan swanned through the shop as though he'd not been made a spectacle of, nodding greetings and shaking a few hands before he left through the front doors.

All at once a gush of excited conversation filled the apothecary. Lucy hadn't noticed how many customers were within hearing distance.

While David congratulated Mr. Gentry on his new position, Lucy made her way to the workroom. She'd left open a jar of liniment and the counter was littered with handwritten formulas, pamphlets advertising various cures, shop receipts, and a page of Sadie's homework.

The Thornes would be gone by the end of the month. With David and Juliet employed elsewhere, Lucy would be on her own. The ceiling wavered as Lucy's eyes filled with tears.

David, Juliet, and Thorne had proven without any ill intent that no matter how hard she tried, Lucy herself was not a good enough reason to remain.

SADIE SETTLED BACK INTO HER SEAT, SMILING WHILE looking between Thorne and Mrs. Merkle. "More tea, Mrs. Merkle?" she asked.

"No, thank you."

The three of them sat in the Thornes' parlor drinking tea. Rather, Sadie drank tea mixed with plenty of milk and sugar, while Thorne and Mrs. Merkle pretended to sip at theirs. Sadie had been the one to steep the leaves, and in her desire to impress Mrs. Merkle, had used three times the amount that she normally would.

Unwilling to spoil Sadie's pleasure, Thorne pretended he wasn't sipping bark juice and searched his brain for interesting topics of discussion. It came to him that the only thing he and Mrs. Merkle had ever spoken of was Sadie. Now that Sadie was present, he couldn't think of a single thing to say to the woman.

"Did you know a frog eats—"

"Might I have another scone, Sadie?" Thorne blurted.

Sadie and Mrs. Merkle both examined his plate, which held a half-eaten scone already.

"I meant when I am finished with this one. It is delicious," he said, picking up the scone and taking a mouthful. Luckily, it was quite tasty.

"They are indeed, Miss Thorne," Mrs. Merkle said, turning her attention now to Sadie, who sat by her side on the settee. While Mrs. Merkle wore a plain day dress of brown and cream stripes, she'd taken care to polish the gold clasp of her belt, and a shiny jet beaded hatpin sparkled in her fashionable brown felted poke bonnet, which sat on the sideboard next to her.

She'd dressed very nicely for a simple tea.

Thorne's throat closed on the crumbs of the scone, and he choked.

While Sadie rushed to the kitchen for a glass of water, Mrs. Merkle stared at him with a faint air of sympathy.

"Are you quite well, Mr. Thorne?" she asked politely.

If it were Lucy here, she'd probably have his arms over his head while thwacking away at his back.

If it were Lucy.

"Sadie has told me a great deal about her new school," Mrs. Merkle said. "There is a nice girls' school nearby my new house. They train in needlework, organization, and meal preparation." Mrs. Merkle's head tilted, and she peered at him from the side like a little brown sparrow.

"Mr. Thorne, we have known each other for a long time, so you will forgive me my plain speak," she said.

Oh God.

Was *she* going to propose to *him*?

The crumbs remained wedged in his throat, and Thorne wondered, could he somehow pass out from the discomfort? That might be preferable.

"I have had occasion to think back on your offer of marriage and have concluded that my declination may have been too hasty. After speaking with Sadie, my fears have been confirmed, and I believe she would be better off with us in Scotland after all." Mrs. Merkle settled her hands in her lap and leaned to see if Sadie were still in the kitchen. She lowered her voice. "It is one thing to indulge her uncommon interests in London, where you can remain anonymous."

Uncommon interests?

"In Durndee, she will have to be schooled as befitting her station in life. I think this is for the best. You don't want her aiming too high."

"I don't?" Thorne asked.

Mrs. Merkle's brow lifted at his tone. "Even if you had some greater social standing and had married her mother, well . . ." The widow shrugged as though explaining something to someone who should know better. "In a smaller town, Sadie's mother's *profession* won't remain a secret. Best get her trained up for service and give her a realistic idea of what type of man she might expect to marry sooner rather than later."

"Papa, here is your water."

Thorne did not know how long Sadie had been standing at his side nor what of Mrs. Merkle's words Sadie had heard. A low vibration of rage—or relief?—had deafened him while he fought to breathe.

If he'd asked anyone on the street, they would have agreed with Mrs. Merkle. There simply was no place in polite society for a child of unmarried parents. Thorne's mother had made that clear the day he left the Abbey for good.

Strict lines separated people based on birth, on religion or convention. Lines as immutable as those Thorne had drawn between himself and others.

All of society would agree with Mrs. Merkle and condemn Lucy.

All of society was wrong, however.

Sadie deserved a chance at any life she could imagine, no matter whether he'd married Genny, no matter that Genny had been born out of wedlock herself.

The room spun when Thorne pulled in a breath so deep it hurt.

If the lines drawn by society were too small and too rigid, what of the boundaries Thorne had erected?

What other assumptions had he made or ideals had he held that were untrue or unjust?

Somehow, Thorne got through the next twenty minutes without fainting or saying anything to Mrs. Merkle that might cause *her* to faint.

Although she hovered by the door, prolonging their good-byes, Thorne wordlessly escorted her outside the shop, then hailed and paid for a hack back to the hotel where she was staying.

He did not promise to call on her again, nor did he issue another invitation for her to call on him.

Instead, he watched the hack disappear into the London traffic, and only once it was lost from sight did he turn and make his way back to Sadie.

Back to home.

22

⋘◆⋙

THE NEXT DAY, THORNE WENT OUT WITH NOTICE OF A post. He returned with a package addressed to Sadie.

Inside, as he'd suspected, lay another beautiful folio of animals. These animals, however, were not exotic. This was a masterfully illustrated guide to the wildlife of the British Isles. For a long time, Thorne and Sadie sat together and marveled over the details of each drawing. They'd lived entirely in London. Animals Thorne thought of as common, such as badgers, were a source of wonder for Sadie.

Unlike last time, there was no note addressed to her. Thorne suspected this folio was message enough. His father was still interested in meeting Sadie. Thorne rubbed his finger along the edge of the vellum pages as Sadie readied herself for bed. During prayers, they could hear the Peterson siblings out on their landing, squabbling about something.

Yawning, Sadie plumped her pillows up behind her back.

"They are trying to convince Miss Peterson to come with

them to a concert," she confided, snuggling down and setting the folio open on her knees.

"Sadie. It is time for sleeping, not reading," Thorne admonished. He lowered the wick in her lamp and paused. "How do you know that? About the concert?"

Sadie flipped over a page. "I heard them arguing about it on my way back from the privy. Miss Peterson has been upset since Mr. Peterson came home yesterday, and Miss Juliet thinks a concert will cheer her."

A concert wouldn't do anything about Lucy's rash decision to marry Duncan Rider, that festering boil of a man. Thorne shuddered when he remembered exactly what constituted a festering boil. Working at an apothecary had been far too enlightening.

"Is part of why she is upset to do with your bookkeeping work?" Sadie asked while turning another page, trying to hide a yawn.

"Did she say it was to do with bookkeeping?" he asked his daughter.

Unconcerned with the flipping in Thorne's stomach, Sadie waited a long moment before she answered, enthralled by an etching of a blind worm.

"Sadie?" he prodded, horrified to hear a note of petulance in his voice.

"I think you should go down and visit with her to find out," Sadie said. Finally able to tear herself away from the pictures, she regarded Thorne with a serious gaze. "You don't want her to be angry with you."

A tiny bit of doubt at the innocence in Sadie's expression niggled in the back of Thorne's head, but this went unheeded beneath the larger concern that he'd hurt Lucy.

"I have been gone too many nights already—"

"I promise to go to sleep after five more pages," Sadie interrupted.

Oh, but his child was canny. Thorne frowned and weighed the desire to see Lucy against the desire to let Sadie know that he knew that she knew.

Girls were hard.

"Five pages. That's it," he said.

Two minutes later he stood before the Petersons' door. He raised his hand to knock but had second thoughts. Perhaps he should have brought her something? Pasties? Flowers?

"What are you doing?"

While he'd been debating himself, Lucy had opened her front door, dressed to go out. She wore a black velvet paletot and beneath it, the pretty mulberry silk gown she'd worn to Sadie's dinner party.

"I wanted . . . I heard you were upset," he stammered.

Her dress, like the ones she wore to work, came almost to her neck. Not as fashionable as most women. Even Mrs. Merkle's brown gowns dipped below her clavicles.

"You came to see if I was upset?" she asked.

When he jerked his head in a nod, her lower lip quivered, and it took a great deal of control not to take her in his arms.

Lucy pushed the door open wider. "I was going out. David and Juliet are celebrating, and they want me to join them."

Her hair was braided across the top, and her hairpins glinted in the light from the candle on the landing. Thorne rarely saw her bareheaded, since she usually wore her cap. Regret that he hadn't spent more time looking at Lucy with her hair down washed over him. What else had he missed out on?

"You do not sound in the mood to celebrate."

Lucy's head tilted one way, then the other, and she stepped back into her apartment.

"Would you like a cup of tea?" she asked.

Thorne followed her inside and she removed her paletot, laying it over the back of a chair when she led him into the kitchen. She didn't say anything as she set an iron pot on a flame and took down two clay mugs from a shelf.

Before the water could boil, Lucy faced him, one hand on the counter behind her.

"He wasn't cheating me. David."

Thorne took a seat at the tiny kitchen table and regarded her. The mulberry of her gown gave her skin a bluish cast in the orange light of the oil lamp. She looked tired.

"He split our orders from Patel's with Juliet's clinic, negotiating better prices for more product," Lucy explained.

Thorne had surmised as much, but only after he'd figured out what David's plans with Wilcox were.

"Is Wilcox going to help support Juliet's clinic as well?" he asked.

"David said as much, but we shall wait to see if Mr. Wilcox wants his family's name connected with the clinic. You know what he and David want to do?" she asked.

Thorne nodded just as the pot sang out that the water was ready.

"Of course you figured it out." Lucy turned off the flame. "David said that establishing the friendly society will be of help to me. He's come up with plans on how to draw custom to the shop from the society, how finally our patients will have a way to pay their bills rather than putting us off or paying us with tarts and the like."

This sounded good to Thorne, but he kept his mouth shut.

"Do you think . . . if I had just . . ." She paused.

"Are you disappointed that he didn't tell you, or disappointed that he will be leaving behind the apothecary for good?" Thorne asked.

Lucy's shoulders dropped and she sighed. After a pause in which Thorne feared she might tell him to leave, she pushed away from the counter and came to stand next to him. Uncertain, feeling his way for what he should do—could do—next, Thorne shifted his chair so that it faced away from the table, and held open his arms.

Without a word, Lucy sat in his lap and laid her head on his shoulder. Thorne put his arms around her and breathed through the pain in his chest.

"When we found out that my father left the apothecary to me, that's when David changed," she said. Lucy's temple rested on his shoulder, and she exhaled a puff of mint-scented air against Thorne's cheek.

"I felt guilty, and even though David told me it didn't bother him, I was certain it did. So, I resolved to make the shop a success—a place David could feel good about."

Thorne smoothed a hand down her arm. Her gown had short sleeves, and the cool silk gave way to warm flesh beneath his hand. The contrast excited him, but Thorne centered Lucy's words. This was a gift, he understood. He'd given Lucy a glimpse into what drove him; now she was doing the same.

"The harder I worked to keep this place open for them, the easier I made it for Juliet and David to go their own way." Lucy's sigh twined around his cheek. He must have made some response, for she sat straight, breaking her contact, though he didn't release her from his embrace just yet.

"You never told them you wanted their help," he said softly.

"No," she answered. "We are siblings for all that we are adults. I worried that if I asked David about his project, he would resent his younger sister interrogating him. I worried if I asked Juliet for help, she'd never tell me no, but silently resent her older sister telling her what to do."

Reluctantly, Thorne opened his arms to set her free, but Lucy stayed where she was.

"Juliet thought marriage would ease my work. She didn't think it through to where marriage would take my work away from me."

Don't marry him.

Thorne bit his bottom lip to keep his mouth from opening and those words from coming out.

"Juliet gave me back the second part of my formula, but I decided..."

As Lucy spoke, Thorne took one of her hands in his, rubbing a thumb over her reddened knuckles. Her soft bottom pressed against his cock, and he had to force his brain to concentrate on her words, not on the way her body called to his.

"I want love in my marriage. The same way my father loved my mother or Mr. Gentry loved his wife."

Love?

Thorne dropped her hand and stared at the thin S curve of Lucy's cheek while he picked through his words.

"Marriage is a merger," he said slowly. "It should be as carefully considered as a balance sheet. In one column you weigh attributes like a sense of humor or attractiveness. In the other you consider finances and shared morals."

Thorne knew how love upended such considerations, how it made men obsessive and women vulnerable.

Love had an unknowable power. It terrified him to think of being possessed by such power again.

"After what Duncan has done to you, I should think that you would find it difficult to love him," he said. "Are you seeing love where there is none so that you will feel better about your betrothal?"

What he wanted to know was, did she? Did Lucy love Duncan Rider?

Lucy stood up, and the ghost of her body against Thorne made him shiver with loss. Hands on her hips, she regarded him with a sneer.

"Why would you question my decisions when you yourself are about to marry a woman you do not love?" she asked.

The oceans in her eyes had darkened to storms, and Thorne stood as well.

"*I* never said I needed love for marriage. I need to marry a woman who can raise Sadie—"

"You have raised her just fine on your own. What Sadie needs is to live in a household filled with love," Lucy said, her words clipped and jagged.

"Love in marriage is chasing a foolish dream," he argued. "One person will always love the other less."

Feck.

Why had he said that?

Thorne abruptly walked out of the kitchen, away from Lucy, away from everything she made him want.

On his heels, Lucy continued to prod him with her words.

"You are blinded and bound by what you won't allow yourself to do."

Thorne spun around and advanced on Lucy. A dangerous combination of lust and anger and the sensation that he stood on the edge of an abyss heated his blood and clouded his brain.

"I am bound only by what is right—"

"You have trapped yourself," Lucy countered. "You are so afraid of going back to who you were that you cannot move forward."

"I am moving forward now," he said, crowding Lucy against the wall.

Her hands came up and rested on the velvet designs of his waistcoat. What did it say that he'd rushed out of his set of rooms clad only in a waistcoat and shirtsleeves?

The lack of control made him furious, and he set his mouth to the creamy skin of her neck, next to her ear.

"I want you, Lucy Peterson," he confessed, letting the words vibrate against her flesh. "I want to be in you one last time. Will you let me?"

STUPID MAN.

Of course Lucy would let Thorne back into her bed. She was weakened by desire and a desperate need to touch him one more time, just to be certain.

Their kisses were fierce and clumsy, off-center and desperate. Lucy tasted the smoky Darjeeling of his nightly tea from his lips and his tongue, while Thorne ran his battered fingers through her hair, dislodging pins and letting down her braids.

"Bed," he ordered, asked, pleaded? The grit beneath his voice made it difficult to distinguish, but Lucy knew it was all of those at once.

Bed.

A normal woman would break their kiss and lead him demurely by the hand into her boudoir, eyes lowered. Lucy wasn't a normal woman. This was why Thorne would marry that sour-faced widow and hie off to Scotland with Sadie. He wanted a woman who wouldn't question him or society or the powers that be.

That was not Lucy.

They stumbled into the bedroom, unable to keep from

kissing each other. Clumsy with either lust or frustration or a mix of both, they pushed at each other's clothes with a mindless abandon. As it was, Lucy did not have time to be relieved that she'd dressed in her prettiest corset cover because she gave Thorne no opportunity to admire it.

This was not a protracted seduction.

Her gown fell to the floor with his trousers and belt, her hairpins and stockings, a stew of linen and silk that tangled round their ankles and made them unsteady on their feet.

They fell into the bed, Thorne covering Lucy, warming her in the cool air with the heat from his body.

"I don't have a—" Thorne broke their kiss to speak, but Lucy put her finger to his lips.

"There is a tin of condoms in the bedside drawer."

In the pause that followed, Lucy prepared herself for his exit. A godly woman would not have prophylactics where her Bible should be.

Thorne stared at her, unblinking, then framed her face with his hands.

"Say they were there for me," he said. "Please. Even if it's a lie."

Oh, the pain of a broken heart. Even after it has healed, the scars can pull it off course. The most sensible of men turn into fools, and the most practical of women into cowards.

"I could never do this with anyone else," Lucy confessed.

She didn't mean sex.

Thorne gathered her hands in one of his and stretched her arms above her head, trailing his tongue down her neck to the dip in her throat, to the underside of her clavicle, to the tip of her nipple. Ever so lightly, he caught her nipple between his teeth and tugged once, twice, then pulled her into his mouth.

Lucy's back bowed in pleasure, and she littered words of

encouragement around them so Thorne would not, could not stop suckling her nipples and leaving a trail of tiny bites down her belly.

He reached over the side of the bed and came up with the cravat he'd just removed. Lucy bit her lip and contemplated what might happen next. She took the strip of linen from him and ran it over her eyes, her breasts, her throat. All the while he retrieved the tin from her bedside drawer and took out a condom.

"Are you ready?" he asked.

Thorne climbed back into bed, the condom tied at the base of his erection. He glanced at the cravat, his expression predatory like that of a wolf sighting a lamb.

Lucy was no lamb.

She raised herself up onto her knees and met his kisses with her own. While Thorne ran his hands down her spine to cup her bottom, Lucy made sure to touch every part of him that fascinated her. The last time, her hands had been tied and she'd let Thorne take control. The sensation of letting go was so foreign and delicious, Lucy hadn't minded that her touch had been limited.

Tonight, however. Tonight was to be the last time they would be connected, her tongue inside his mouth, his cock inside her quim, their skin pressing and rubbing and searching for ways to come closer together than physics allowed.

When Thorne reached for the cravat, Lucy rebelled. If this would be the last time, it would be on her terms.

"Lie down," she told him.

Thorne hesitated, his eyes moving from the cravat to her expression.

"If that is what you want," he said without a hint as to his feelings either way. Keeping his hands on her bottom, Thorne settled on his side, smoothing his palms against her skin so that by the time he lay on his back, he'd trailed his fingers in between her thighs.

Lucy bit her bottom lip, then pulled his hands away and brought his arms over his head.

He must have approved of her tying his wrists lightly together, for his cock lengthened and his breath came out in a hiss when she leaned over him to tie the bonds. He raised his head and caught one of her nipples in his mouth, gently sucking it and flicking his tongue against it in a wicked manner.

When she was finished tying him, Lucy climbed between his thighs and stroked his erection, taken aback by how hard the column of flesh felt beneath the condom.

"I don't know what to do now," she confessed. Although her desire had cooled somewhat since they first burst into the bedroom, Lucy hadn't pulled herself out of her body yet. Still, if she couldn't figure out what to do next, it would be difficult to remain engaged.

Let go.

Thorne had no judgment on his face, no charity in his gaze. Instead, he lifted his bound hands over her head and gently urged her forward so that she sat up against his erection.

Lucy frowned, trying to remember the naughty postcards she'd looked at so many years ago, the woman straddling the man's lap.

"I won't lose my balance and fall over?" she asked.

"No," he said. An unnameable expression changed the shape of his face as her body threw him into the shadows. "You will be in control, and I will hold you up."

I will hold you up.

Lucy dug her nails into the skin of her palms so she didn't cry. Over and over Thorne had urged her to let go. What he hadn't said, what Thorne could only *show* her, was that letting go during making love didn't have to be him tying her up and telling her what to do. She could tell him what to do—tell herself what to do.

Letting go meant trusting.

Lucy raised her hips and set herself over him, then slowly sank down onto his cock. He stretched and filled her even more in this position, and she had to close her eyes in order not to fly out of her body too soon.

Thorne, sensing her hesitance, brought his hand between them and gently circled her clitoris. A gush of pleasure eased Lucy's way until she had taken all of him.

When she opened her eyes, Thorne had his eyes closed, his face tense with desire. Tentatively, Lucy moved her hips, trying to find a way toward the friction she craved. A shudder of pure lust shook her spine when she raised her hips a fraction and pushed down. Without opening his eyes, he groaned, raising his bound hands over his head, then grasping the headboard.

Thorne had not granted Lucy this heady power to make him dependent on her for his pleasure.

She'd taken the power on her own.

Moving her hips faster, Lucy took note of every muscle that moved on Thorne's damaged face, adjusting her pace to provoke the clenching of his teeth or the tightening of his muscles as he gripped the headboard. The more focused Lucy became on Thorne, the less self-conscious she was about taking her pleasure. Leaning forward, Lucy kept the rhythm of her hips, but adjusted her angle so that every time their bodies came together, it pulled a spark of bliss from the center of her. She lowered herself, moving faster, searching for completion and unable to find it.

"Help me," Lucy told Thorne. "Help me come, I don't know how."

Thorne's eyes opened and Lucy sucked in a breath. His pupils had widened and the flush on his cheeks ran over the scar, making it pop. Something elemental and raw stared out from behind his eyes, and she'd never felt so present in her body, in her pleasure, as she did when Thorne gave her what she'd always wanted.

His vulnerability. His truth.

Bucking his hips, Thorne lifted them both off the bed, and Lucy's head fell back as he filled her almost more than she could bear. With a twist and a grunt, he pulled his wrists from the linen constraints and put his hands on her skin. They jerked and thrust, fighting to reach their climax, holding on to each other tightly though their grip slipped from the sweat created by a frantic coupling. Lucy fought for control. Of him. Of herself. Of her thoughts and her doubts.

I love you.

Lucy did not say the words aloud, but they shook her to the core as they echoed in her head, and instead of her mind directing her body, her heart took over.

She loved him.

It might be that he had no love for her. It might have been that this was a simple coupling, that the words he covered her with were lies as he urged her on.

It didn't matter.

Letting go means letting love take over.

Beginning in her toes, a sparking sensation lit her skin and rendered her immobile as the waves of her climax ran through her body. Over and over she shuddered, keeping her eyes open and fixed on his black stare as he bowed his back one last time and came, pulling her core against him and holding on so tightly there would be marks later.

The world around them, constructed of chemistry and physics, universal laws, and cold, hard realities disappeared for a split second, and all that existed was Lucy and Thorne, co-cooned in bliss, holding on to each other at the edge of a prec-ipice.

Just as Lucy decided to tell the truth, Thorne's eyes closed, and he turned his head away from her.

So.

No room for any more revelations tonight.

Thorne had his rules, and he might bend, but would never break.

Lucy was still, and might forever be, alone.

She didn't even know she was crying until a teardrop fell onto Thorne's temple.

"Are you hurt?" he asked. "Was I too rough?"

This time it was Lucy who looked away as she slipped off his body, keeping her eyes averted.

"No. No, I am fine."

Lie? Not a lie?

Lucy removed the condom for him, taking care not to spill it, and placed it on the handkerchief he'd left out.

If she were capable of great courage, Lucy would speak her truth to him, but what good would it do to know what they'd never have?

Instead, she got out of bed and covered herself with a pais-ley shawl, keeping her back to Thorne. Rather than dress him-self, he came to stand behind her.

"I . . ." he began, then stopped.

If he were to speak a declaration of love, Lucy would have

known. In her bones, she was certain she would have known and would have turned around to embrace him.

His silence hit her between the shoulder blades, and the room cooled.

"I'm not certain what time Juliet and David will be returning," she told the dresser against the opposite wall. "Perhaps we should . . ."

"Of course."

Lucy stared hard at the dresser, memorizing the curve of the drawer pulls, the joining of each corner, the width of each drawer. Again, he came to stand behind her, dressed now, ready to take his leave.

She did not believe it was pride that kept her from turning now to send him off with a goodbye.

No.

Lucy was scared that if she did turn, the truth would spill out of her and over his hands and onto their feet, and because Thorne would never break, he would deny her truth.

She didn't deserve denial.

Lucy deserved love in return.

So she kept staring at that dresser as he stumbled through a thicket of words that probably made no sense to either of them. She stared as he left her bedroom, walked down the hallway, out of her home, and out of her life.

23

---⟨⟨⟨◆⟩⟩⟩---

THORNE DRAGGED HIMSELF FROM BED THE NEXT MORNing, surprised that he'd slept at all. Though he'd washed when he returned home last night, he could still smell the faintest hint of eucalyptus and wool on his skin.

No. That was a passing fancy.

There was nothing left of Lucy on him.

She'd kept her back to him last night. All he could see as he got dressed was the line of her spine beneath the shawl, which made him long to scold her about not eating enough, even if what she ate was terrible. He hadn't, though. Scolded her. Thorne had no right. She was to marry another man.

A mountain range had been painted in frost on each of the windowpanes. A sharp wind promising bitter cold rattled the panes. Best to start early and get the day over with.

Thorne took himself off to the privy, then knocked on Sadie's door when he came back.

"You must up for school, Sadie," he said through the door.

There was no response. In the kitchen he sliced a day-old loaf of bread for toast. As he set the knife against the bread, something made him stop and listen.

The other night, Sadie said that Lucy's lack of snoring woke her. That the silence was louder than the noise of his snores.

"Sadie?" Thorne knocked on the door again, and when there was still no answer, he opened the door and regarded the neatly made bed.

"Sadie?" he whispered to the empty room.

No one answered.

Grabbing his boots, Thorne flew into the hall, trying to put them on at the same time he went down the staircase.

"Sadie!" he called, a terrible sinkhole of panic opening before him.

"Mr. Thorne, what—"

Juliet came out of the door to her set of rooms looking much the worse for wear. However she and David had celebrated last night had left her face swollen and eyes red and bleary.

"Sadie," he said, sitting on the stair above the landing and trying to force a boot on his left foot, only to realize it was the wrong foot. "She's not in her room. She's not at home. She's gone ..."

Lucy came and stood next to Juliet, and Thorne reached out to her, needing her to save him.

"Have you seen her?" he asked. Begged.

Lucy came to his side and took his hand, speaking in a calm, clear manner, as though he were a patient.

"We will get dressed and begin a search. When we find her, she will not be allowed to play with any of my jarred organs for the rest of the week, but *we will find her.*"

Thorne nodded, and the gray fog that had been obscuring

his vision cleared away. Ah. He'd forgotten to breathe. Lucy held his hand for three more deep breaths, then rose to her feet.

"I shall check with the omnibus drivers and ask if any of them picked her up this morning," David announced, coming out of his front door, fully dressed and well shod.

Shoes. Thorne leaned over and pulled his boots onto the correct feet. Omnibus, yes. Hacks. List of places she might go.

"Did she leave a note?" Juliet asked.

Note.

Thorne looked up at the three siblings, but no words came. How could he explain that the world was off-kilter, and he was drowning?

"What *I* want to know is how she opened the lock on the back door," Juliet said. "She's too short to reach it on her own, and it sticks."

With a glorious rush, the world returned to Thorne. Once more he could breathe, and he took the stairs two at a time. The front doors were shut, and when he tried them, they remained closed.

A split second later, Lucy poked her head out of the shop's back room, put a finger to her lips, and beckoned to him.

It isn't pleasant to live for any amount of time without your heart. Thorne's skin was cold and clammy, his hands shook, and his lungs stuttered when he entered the back room and saw Sadie, carpetbag at her side, slumped over the table where she normally did her schoolwork, arms pillowing her head.

Asleep.

Alive.

Thorne sank to the floor and put his head down. Imagine Sadie woke and found him fainted dead away? What would she think of her papa then?

Why had she done this?

Lucy crouched and put a hand on his shoulder. For a while they remained there, not moving, even when Juliet and David put their heads in, then left again.

"She has a pretty snore," Lucy whispered.

"Like her father," Thorne replied.

Lucy opened her mouth to speak, then seemed to think better of it and closed it again.

It took another minute or so for him to be certain he could stand and not make a cake of himself.

He rose, and Lucy slipped her hand from his shoulder to his elbow.

"Are you going to faint?" she asked quietly. "I can run to get some smelling salts."

"Might do," Thorne admitted. "Stay by my side, just in case?"

"I . . ." Lucy stared at him, open-mouthed. "Of . . . of course," she stammered.

They walked, side by side, to the sleeping child. On the table in front of Sadie was an ink bottle, a pen, and two dirty pen wipes as well as a sheet of paper with paragraph after paragraph of what looked like false starts of a letter, all headed "Dear Papa."

"Sadie," Thorne said softly. He touched a finger to her cheek. "You have a great deal of explaining to do, as well as drool to clean up."

Sleepy eyes blinked, then rolled up toward him. For the sweetest moment in Thorne's recent memory, a waking smile crept across Sadie's face, as if she were happy to see him. As if being here with him was preferable to wherever she went in the dreaming.

"Papa," she whispered.

The smile disappeared as she fully woke, and Sadie straightened. She wiped her sleeve across her mouth, then stared at the pool of ink where she'd drooled in her sleep.

Thorne sat next to her and drew the paper toward him.

"Is this a letter for me?" he asked gently.

Lucy put a hand on his shoulder and leaned in, pressing against him, giving him back the last of his composure.

"I shall just go put on a pot of tea and see what we have from Mrs. Locksley in the larder, shall I?" she asked.

Thorne nodded, then set his hand over hers and squeezed, like a survivor of a disaster bidding farewell to a fellow survivor.

When Lucy left, Sadie pulled the paper back toward herself and folded it in half.

"I think internal organs are exciting."

Thorne's brows went up as he digested Sadie's news.

"I have gathered this from your great interest in anatomy," he said, watching her mobile face for any clues as to where this conversation would go. Hopefully nowhere he couldn't stomach.

"I don't want to go into service," Sadie said so quickly that the words ran together. "I want to be a secret doctor like Miss Juliet and Mrs. Sweet."

Feck. Sadie must have overheard Mrs. Merkle the other day. Thorne took a deep breath and settled his nerves. Sadie bit her lip. "I was going to go live with Mrs. Downwith so you could marry Mrs. Merkle and have babies whose parents are married and who you wouldn't be embarrassed—"

"No, Sadie, God no." Thorne got out of his chair, knelt on the floor next to her, and took her soft, warm hand into his. "I have never been embarrassed by you."

Sadie's eyes filled with tears, but she was too proud to shed them. "Lord Blackstone invited me for tea, and you never told me."

Oh God.

"It's because I'm a bast—" she began.

"Don't." Thorne reached over and set his finger across Sadie's lips. "Don't you ever use that word about yourself or anyone else."

This conversation was long overdue because Thorne had never managed to come up with explanations that might make sense to a young girl. Or to anyone with a heart in them. He took a deep breath and did the best he could.

"The world gives people labels. They want everyone defined by a set of harsh rules."

"Rules like the Ten Commandments?" Sadie asked.

"No. Made-up rules, like who can go to school or be a doctor and who can't. Rules about what kind of person deserves respect and who doesn't. Rules that are meant to keep most people small and a few people powerful."

Thorne's knees complained so loudly he had to get back into his chair. Not wanting to lose contact, he pulled Sadie onto his lap while he spoke.

"Our hearts, though. Our hearts don't care about someone else's rules. Love happens where it will. Nothing Mrs. Merkle or anyone else who makes up the rules can do will change this. That word you said—that is a word soaked in cruelty and doesn't apply to you. If I were to describe you with words, they would be *kind* and *brilliant* and *wise* and . . ."

Thorne buried his nose in Sadie's hair and breathed deep, overwhelmed by what he should say and what he couldn't articulate, even now.

"You are a part of me," he said, "but also apart *from* me. You are braver and brighter than I ever was when I was a boy. You deserve the world, Sadie, even if the world doesn't deserve you."

Sadie set her hand to his cheek. "That is a lot of words just to say you love me."

Thorne's heart did some complicated calisthenics as he absorbed his daughter's observation.

"I suppose it is," he agreed. "I love you, Sadie. I'm not embarrassed by you. I'm embarrassed that I ever considered marrying Mrs. Merkle. I am embarrassed that I didn't tell you about Lord Blackstone's invitation. He's . . ."

Sadie's mouth drooped. "There was a note with the second book. It had been slipped between the pages. He is your papa, isn't he?"

Ah. That explained a great deal.

"I am . . . was . . . am angry with my papa. It has been many years since I've spoken with him," Thorne confessed.

"If he is your papa, that means he is my grandfather," Sadie said.

"Yes, well." Thorne steeled himself against the longing in Sadie's voice. He wasn't going to let anyone hurt Sadie the way Mrs. Merkel had, and would have a long talk with his parents first before bringing her anywhere near them.

"You and I have some talking to do," Thorne said. "I think you might have more questions than I'd guessed, and I owe you some answers."

Sadie leaned back against Thorne's chest, and he held her tight, listening to the sounds of London waking up outside while the rhythm of his pulse returned to normal.

"Are you certain you don't want to marry Mrs. Merkel?" Sadie asked.

"I will never marry anyone who doesn't love and care for you," Thorne replied.

"Hmmm."

Thorne's body tensed. Good Christ, what was Sadie going to say next? Would his heart take any more today?

"If you aren't marrying Mrs. Merkel, do we have to move to Scotland?"

Thorne's shoulders dropped in relief. "No, we will find a set of rooms somewhere else."

"Somewhere that smells as nice as here?" she asked.

"Umm . . ."

"With people as kind as the Petersons downstairs and Mr. Gentry and Katie?" she asked.

Er . . .

"Was Miss Peterson worried when you told her I was missing?"

"Oh, yes," Thorne assured her. "She was beside herself. You must go see her, and Miss Juliet and Mr. Peterson as well, and apologize to them for the worry you caused."

This did not propel Sadie from the safety of Thorne's lap. Instead, she shifted to examine Thorne's face as he spoke.

"If she was beside herself with worry, that means *she* cares for me." Sadie's eyebrows lifted like sinister little triangles.

"I'm sure she does," Thorne agreed. "However—"

Sadie slumped, her shoulders touching her earlobes. "How come good things have to be hard? Why can't being happy be easy?"

Well.

Thorne turned that question over in his head as he helped Sadie collect her bag. They held hands as they walked up the back stairs and came to a halt before the Petersons' front door. Sadie gazed up at him, resignation plain on her face, and something that had held Thorne together for a long time finally snapped.

"You are right," he told her.

"Right about what?" Her voice was low, a combination of hope and disbelief.

"Why *can't* being happy be easy?"

Sadie's frown melted as she examined his face.

"You go have a glass of lemonade and something to eat," Thorne said. "I will be right back."

A burst of joy made its way from his face to hers. Sadie's eyes lit, and a silly, wonderful, altogether ridiculous grin stretched her face wide.

"Don't stay away too long," she cautioned him.

"No. I don't want to be gone from you any longer than I have to be," Thorne promised. He could hear words of greeting on the landing above as he took the stairs two at a time and hustled out of the shop.

THE SCENT OF TURMERIC INFUSED THE APARTMENT AIR, and Lucy checked the boiled potatoes while, in the parlor, David played the spinet as Juliet and Sadie sang along. David hadn't practiced in forever, but he managed a song or two from memory, and Juliet had a beautiful voice. The surprise had been Sadie's skill with harmonies.

Not even Mrs. Merkle would have something bad to say about the rendition of "And Can It Be That I Should Gain" that filled the Petersons' rooms this evening. Unsurprisingly, this hymn beginning with a question about blood was Sadie's favorite.

Lucy sighed at the sound of paper crinkling as she smoothed down the note in her apron pocket. Katie had written to let her know that her menses had begun, and she would be absent from work for the next three days.

In return, Lucy had sent a boy to the Quinlavins' home with

a basket full of willow bark tea, clean rags, and a small jar filled with a tincture that helped soothe cramping.

What came next, Lucy had no idea, but she would take her cues from Katie. The last thing she wanted was to take away any more choices from the girl.

"I believe the potatoes are ready," Lucy informed the choir after they sang the last line.

She turned to Sadie. "I don't know where your papa might have gone, but I can hear your stomach grumbling even over the thumping and squeaking that my brother is making with that poor, tortured spinet."

David stuck out his tongue, but Lucy ignored him.

"I think we should sit down to supper, and if—"

A knock came from the front door. Sadie bit the corner of her bottom lip and jiggled in place. David frowned, and Juliet nodded once, as if confirming some unspoken question.

Thorne had not been in the hallway when they opened the door to Sadie a few hours earlier. She had prettily apologized for having worried them that morning and asked if she might come in for a visit while her papa carried out an errand.

"Whatever sort of errand must he see to right after such a scare?" Lucy had asked.

Sadie had held her hands over her mouth for a few seconds and composed herself poorly, then told them she wasn't exactly sure where he was going, only that it was very important and most likely a surprise, and were there tarts?

A second knock set Lucy to moving, untying her apron as she approached the front door. Like little ducklings, David, Juliet, and Sadie followed her. Thus, Thorne was greeted by a veritable receiving line when he entered.

"Good God, have you been hitting books with your face again?" David exclaimed.

Thorne tilted his head, confused, then hastily ran his ungloved hands through his hair. Lucy had never seen him in
such disarray. He'd neither top hat nor gloves, there was saw-
dust on the lapels of his navy wool greatcoat, and a tiny plaster
had been set over a cut near his ear, surrounded by bruising.

"I have not been hitting books with my face, no," Thorne
said, then lifted his nose in the air and sniffed. "Am I too late
for curry?"

"Never mind that," Lucy said. "Where have you been, and
why do you look as though you were dragged there and back?"

Thorne and Sadie exchanged a glance, and Sadie nodded
rapidly, her hands fisting her skirts.

What was this?

From an inside pocket, Thorne withdrew a crumpled and
dirtied envelope, then handed it to Lucy.

"This is the first part of your formula."

Lucy opened her mouth, but no sound emerged.

"Did you hit Duncan Rider?" David asked. He grinned and
slapped Thorne on the shoulder. "Good on you, Thorne—ow!"

Lucy had grabbed David by the sensitive skin of his under-
arm and pulled him back. "It is not good on anyone to resort to
violence," she admonished him. Tentatively, she took the envelope from his hand, noting the absence of bruises or cuts on
Thorne's knuckles.

"I didn't hit Duncan," Thorne said. He came to stand beside
Lucy and held out his arms to his daughter. Sadie walked into
his embrace, and a combination of pleasure and relief smudged
the hard line of wrinkles across his forehead.

"*I* would have hit Duncan," Juliet muttered beneath her breath.

Lucy crossed her arms over her chest, tapping the letter
against her side. "If you didn't hit Duncan, why do you look as
though you hit someone?"

Thorne put his hand on Sadie's head and smiled down at her. "I didn't hit someone, someone hit me."

He waved his hand to quiet the chorus of consternation that sprang up at his announcement. With a sheepish expression, Thorne explained that he'd gone to Rider and Son Apothecary to demand Lucy's croup salve formula be returned. Rather than fight about it, Duncan acquiesced easily. When Thorne inquired as to why, a pretty young woman with brilliant gold curls and wide blue eyes came out from the consultation room. Even if she and Duncan hadn't flushed when they met each other's eyes, Duncan's misbuttoned waistcoat and the woman's reddened mouth said it all.

Thorne looked down at Lucy, who stared at the envelope. "I am sorry, Miss Peterson. I know you loved him and—"

Lucy gasped in outrage. "Love Duncan Rider? Never."

"No?" he asked, confusion knitting his brows together.

"I never told Duncan I'd marry him. He simply assumed he could wear me down," she explained.

"But, Papa, who hit you?" Sadie asked, stepping from the circle of Thorne's arms, setting her hands on her hips, and tapping her foot. "And when do you get to the good part?"

The good part?

"On my way back to the shop, I happened to pass the Lion's Den," Thorne explained. A slight blush tinted his skin a soft pink beneath his cheekbones. "I stopped in and had a little chat with Katie's da."

"You hit Joe Quinlavin?" David exclaimed.

"Not exactly." Thorne loosened his cravat and cleared his throat. "You see, I have a reputation as a prizefighter. The Gentleman Fighter had only ever been knocked to the floor three times."

"Men," Juliet muttered with disgust.

Thorne nodded in agreement. "I had to let myself be knocked to the ground publicly in order to get Quinlavin's agreement."

"Agreement to what?" Lucy asked, staring at the man standing before her. Nothing about any of this made sense. Duncan and a golden-curled woman? Thorne letting himself be knocked to the ground?

"Agreement to let Katie go to the science academy for girls up in North Yorkshire when she's ready."

A thrum vibrated low in Lucy's belly as she put the pieces together. Behind her, Sadie bounced up and down on her toes.

Thorne cleared his throat, and Sadie hissed something that sounded suspiciously like "down on one knee."

Lucy turned and stared at Sadie, then back at Thorne, who was shaking his head like a dog with a flea and mouthing the word *no*.

Juliet and David stepped back, David covering his mouth so as not to laugh. Lucy couldn't move, frozen at Thorne's side like a great fool, the blood rushing to her head so fast she feared she might faint.

"Papaaaaaaa," Sadie whispered. "You must."

Thorne sighed a deep breath in the way one might sigh if one were tasked with pushing a giant rock up a hill. Now Juliet had started giggling, and she and David leaned on each other as their shoulders shook and eyes teared up.

With an audible snapping and creaking, Thorne dropped onto one knee and reached for Lucy's hand.

"You do not have to—no, please don't," Lucy babbled.

Thorne shook his head more slowly this time, seemingly resigned to this fate.

"You asked me to complete my mission, and I've done so," he said, the words rasping together like stones. "It gave me great pleasure to do it. Missions are like bookkeeping. There is a starting point, a list of facts, and a resolution."

Lucy nodded. "Very orderly."

Thorne turned Lucy's hand over in his. While his hands would never be pretty, they felt safe and secure.

"I like order and routine. Rules and schedules," he agreed. "When I make myself a promise, I stick to it."

Unable to bear it any longer, Lucy knelt on one knee as well. Their knees touched and Thorne took the opportunity to hold Lucy's hand close to his heart.

"Sometimes—and this will come as a surprise to you— sometimes I make mistakes."

Sadie let out a snort and Thorne scowled.

How perfectly romantic.

"I made rules for myself—I swore I would never fall in love with a beautiful woman," Thorne said. "I swore I'd never speak to my family again. That I'd never throw parties ever again."

"How sad, Mr. Thorne," said David quietly.

"Yes, well. I thought those rules would keep me away from the bottle and make me a better father to Sadie."

Lucy nodded. "I understand. Rules are there to keep us safe."

Thorne fixed his gaze on hers. "Yes, but Sadie and I had an interesting conversation just recently about how some rules are ready to be broken. The rules that keep us silent in the face of injustice. The rules that label us as good or bad, deserving or undeserving based solely on our sex or the class to which we were born."

A tingling started behind Lucy's eyelids, and she blinked away tears.

"Rules about how women are compelled to live by a separate code of morals than men, and the one-sided consequences women are made to endure when men take away their ability to choose," he said slowly.

A rush of happiness punched at Lucy's stomach, and she set her hands against her belly to hold herself in.

"You'd said I was trapped by my rules. You were right." Thorne lifted the back of Lucy's hand to his mouth and laid a kiss there, a burning kiss that served as a balm to Lucy's fears and worries.

"I wish to move forward," he whispered, his mouth hovering above her skin. "I wish to move forward together with you."

A lone tear traveled down Lucy's cheek.

"You *listened* to me," she said, fighting to force the words out past the lump in her throat.

"I did," he agreed. "All this time, no matter how frustrated or angry I might have been, I have always listened to you. It doesn't mean we will always agree, but if we listen to each other, we will come to a resolution."

Lucy gripped his hand and pulled it close, echoing his kiss.

"I love you, Jonathan Thorne," she said, another tear now free, rolling down the bridge of her nose. "Will you marry me?"

"Oh, no!" Sadie exclaimed. "You aren't supposed to ask. The man is supposed to ask."

Thorne shook his head, the corners of his mouth turning up, his wounded face alight with happiness.

"I think this is another one of those rules ready to be broken," he told his daughter. With a groan, Thorne got to his feet and pulled Lucy up next to him. "As is this bended knee nonsense."

He reached for Lucy and tilted her face up to his. "I love you, Lucy Peterson. And I am happy to marry you."

"Huzzah!"

Lucy chuckled at Sadie's cheer just as Thorne bent to kiss her. They swallowed the laugh and let the joy settle in their veins. While their family applauded, Lucy and Thorne sealed their proposal with a kiss, then another, and then one more before David began making retching noises and Sadie knocked over a pile of books while dancing with Juliet.

That night they sat over dinner for a long time. There was music and laughter, but no wine and just a little dancing.

Lucy knew, for all their differences, a way forward would come to them, not always easily found, but some things in life are not meant to be easy.

Except for love. It turned out that love was the easiest thing in the world.

AUTHOR'S NOTE

In 1865, the first woman doctor in the United Kingdom, Elizabeth Garrett Anderson, did what Lucy and Juliet had not thought to do. Once accepted into the Worshipful Society of Apothecaries, Elizabeth Anderson applied for the Royal College of Surgeons and passed the exams. The first woman doctor here in the United States, Elizabeth Blackwell, was sent an acceptance letter from the Geneva Medical College as a practical joke in 1847. Elizabeth showed up anyway.

Both of those pioneers had more rights to reproductive health care than women today in certain states of our union. Like Thorne, there are plenty of good people who are conflicted and ambivalent about abortion. In the end, however, abortion care is health care. There is nothing ambivalent about denial of care based on sex.

I like to think that Lucy and Thorne had many discussions about reproductive health care, especially as Sadie grew older.

I like to believe that Lucy continued to put herself in other people's shoes and search for the divinity in everyone.

I like to imagine that Thorne never stopped *listening*, even when, at first, he did not agree.

I hope in whatever alternate universe they inhabit, Thorne and Lucy continue to grant others a modicum of grace, the time and space to learn and understand, and the dignity that all human beings deserve.

We live in a world where such grace is rare, where complex discussions have been replaced with 280 characters, where listening is equated with capitulation. This is not a world in which science—or community—can flourish.

Nor is it a world that allows for romance. Real romance, true romance, is a state of wonder and peace that begins with a spark but is sustained by work. Hard work. Messy work. Work requiring grace.

ACKNOWLEDGMENTS

So many people have been supportive of my work, first and foremost my husband. When this book comes out, we will have been married for twenty-five years. Saying yes to him was the best decision I have ever made. Thank you to my children for all their encouragement and for their patience—I have amazing kids and I love them to the moon and back. Thanks to Mom and Doug for being such wonderful role models and for all the help and support. This book would not be nearly so good if I didn't have the editorial acumen of Sarah Blumenstock and the always positive Liz Sellers on my side. I am grateful for everyone at Berkley who helped put this book out, especially Jessica Mangicaro, whom I FINALLY got to meet in person (she is as delightful as you might expect) and the ever-resourceful Stephanie Felty. I will miss Jess immeasurably and am so grateful for all her hard work on the Secret Scientists series. Thank you to my production editor, Jessica McDonnell, copy editor Angelina Krahn, interior designer George Towne, and once again my amazing cover designer, Rita Frangie. Special thanks to my agent, Ann Leslie Tuttle. I am so grateful for her patience and enthusiasm and just general sensibility in the face of my madness. Big hugs and love to the 2021 #berkletes, to the Big Brained Broads (Ali, Mazey, and Libby), to the Park Ave. moms and the Highland Hotties. I am beyond blessed to have such amazing women in my life—your friendships keep me going, and I love and adore you all. In 2023 I was finally able to attend book conventions and meet readers in person. I am so profoundly grateful for everyone who has read my books, and it is now and forever the greatest thrill I can imagine to hear someone say they enjoyed reading my work. Thank you, thank you, thank you to everyone I've met in the past year at bookstore events, book conventions, and on bookstagram. Your kind words buoy me along on the hardest of days.

Keep reading for an excerpt from

THE LADY SPARKS A FLAME

the next Damsels of Discovery novel
by Elizabeth Everett

London, 1845

"HOW DO YOU MANAGE TO MAKE THE WORDS *'YOU* know best' sound like *'I* know best'?"

"Because . . . I know best?"

Oh, for feck's sake.

A large man sat opposite Sam Fenley at a cheap but polished wood desk. Sam considered the man a friend.

He also considered punching him.

That's how it was sometimes with men. Clap them on the shoulder one day, punch them the next—no hard feelings.

When Sam was younger, that was how it was with his sisters until they realized Sam couldn't stand it when they cried. Then all they had to do was wobble their lower lip and he'd wind up punching himself to keep them from sobbing.

Except for Letty. She was the oldest and never cried. Too bad Lucy, Laura, Laila, and Sadie didn't follow in her example.

"Listen to me, Fenley. I understand your crusade against the Corn Laws. You are in the right." The Earl of Grantham rubbed his face with a gloved hand. Dark smudges contrasted with his blue eyes to make him seem older than his two and thirty years. Sam had bought this very broadsheet from the earl last year and within six months made enough of a profit to buy a second.

The earl hadn't cared. He was recently married and occupied with walking around being an obnoxious mooncalf about it.

"However," Grantham continued, looking a little less mooncalf-y than he had a month ago, "the last article the *Capital* printed has overestimated the scarcity of Britain's wheat crop. I fear the *Capital* and other anti–Corn Law broadsheets will panic the population and more ill will come of this than good."

Sam knew that Grantham meant well, but this wasn't about how the earl felt. It was about money, about power, and most of all, it was about selling newspapers.

"If I back down now," Sam said, "it gives more fuel to the pro–Corn Law fires. The Corn Laws pour money into the landowners' coffers and beggar the majority of England's working folk."

Sam wasn't telling Grantham anything he didn't know, but he continued anyway, blood starting to boil as it always did when it came to the advantages the titled classes held over the rest of the populace. The Corn Laws taxed corn—including wheat, barley, and other cereals—from outside Britain. While on paper that might appear to help domestic agriculture, the effect had the consequence of making food more expensive for the bulk of the populace, a majority of them urban, while political power stayed in the hands of wealthy landowners who profited from the high price of domestic corn.

"In this great country of ours, if you don't own land, you don't get to vote." Simply saying the words out loud angered Sam. The landowners didn't only benefit from the artificial pricing, they also handpicked their members of Parliament and chose how they voted.

"How is that acceptable in our day and age?" Sam asked rhetorically. "Universal suffrage is the goal, and I'm not above embellishing when it comes to a worthy goal."

Grantham opened his mouth to speak but Sam beat him to it.

"Just like you are not above embellishing when it comes to stealing women away from other men."

Lord Grantham had, over the years, performed covert "favors" for Prince Albert and was built like a blacksmith—like two blacksmiths mushed together. If he'd wanted to kill Sam, all he would have to do was punch him with one of those anvil-like fists.

It said much about the earl that he took Sam's teasing about his new wife with equanimity. Sam had tried his hardest to court the engineer Margaret Gault, but she'd gone ahead and married the earl, her childhood sweetheart, instead.

Why she didn't choose Sam—a man who had made a fortune of his family's business, turned around a failing broadsheet, become its owner, and now set his sights on expanding his holdings even further—was a mystery.

Right next door lay the offices of the *Gentlemen's Monthly Magazine*, a mouthpiece for the political group the Guardians of Domesticity. Although Grantham and his wife, Margaret, had been successful in exposing the leader, Victor Armitage, and his accomplices as liars and investors in a fraudulent insurance scheme, the group and its propaganda machine, *Gentlemen's Monthly*, continued to operate, now under the direction of Victor's nephew, Lionel.

Gentlemen's Monthly was staunchly monarchist and took offense to self-made men, writing in its columns that the demise of the aristocracy was tied to the demise of the Empire. To the Guardians, men like Sam were upsetting the social order by wanting more than they'd been born to.

They'd printed a series of articles lately that, while they hadn't named Sam specifically, had railed against the rising influence of the merchant class on British society. As a result, some of the doors Sam had pushed open by dint of sheer charm and competency were slamming back shut.

"You are in a terrible mood. What ails you, Fenley?" Grantham asked, stretching out his legs and placing his hands behind his head, the picture of aristocratic indolence.

Sam knew very well Grantham was far from indolent, but the pose annoyed him, nonetheless.

Everything annoyed him these days.

"Nothing ails me, my lord."

Sam had meant the honorific as a tease, but the words came out hard and clipped. One long earlish eyebrow lifted on Grantham's face at the tone.

"If I were to guess, I'd say you were in want of one of life's great necessities," Grantham opined.

A fire sprung to life deep in Sam's belly, fueled by jealousy and kindled with myriad thwarted desires, the obstacles a man without title or a single drop of blue blood in his veins had to face every day in this godforsaken country.

"I can get sex any time or place I desire," Sam growled. "Simply because women used to fall at your lordship's feet at the thought of being a countess—"

A faint blush stained Grantham's cheeks as he dropped his arms and sat straight up in his chair. "I'm not talking about sex, Fenley."

What else might constitute one of life's necessities then?

"I'm not hungry," Sam said. "I've enough money to buy the crown right off Queen Victoria's head, I own two broadsheets now, plus running Fenley's Fantastic Fripperies, and I'm seldom bored, thanks to five sisters and the never-ending catastrophes those scientists over at Athena's Retreat come up with. I can't think of a *single* thing missing from my life."

With a patronizing sigh, Grantham ran his fingers through his hair, eyes rolling up to the heavens as though he communicated with God on a peer-to-peer level.

"I'm talking about love, Fenley."

What?

Sam nearly fell back out of his chair.

"What? You're talking about . . . You're talking about sex, you mean," Sam said.

Grantham shook his head slowly, an obnoxious half smile pasted across his face.

"I'm talking about marriage."

Oh, for feck's sake. Sam jumped up from his chair and paced around the desk that separated him and Grantham. He went to stand at the window that overlooked a small courtyard shared by the building next door.

Love.

What nonsense was this?

"You and the rest of those men at Athena's Retreat. You've all inhaled too many fumes over the years," Sam said.

Athena's Retreat, a secret haven for women scientists, created by Mrs. Violet Kneland and two friends. One of them was his older sister, Letty, a brilliant mathematician who'd gone and fallen for a man with a title herself.

The other was Lady Phoebe Hunt. Daughter of a marquess, no less. She and Grantham were almost engaged before Margaret Gault returned to England.

Yet another example of a beautiful genius who fell for Grantham's charms. He'd met her on occasion, and she'd provoked a terrifying mix of lust and intimidation in him.

Course Lady Phoebe had then shot Violet's husband and

was mixed up with treason and bombs and whatnot. Did she go to jail for any of this, however? No. She was shipped off to America and given a job because of her father's title.

Fecking titles.

What *ailed* Sam specifically was that his latest attempt to invest in a railway consortium had fallen flat. The consortium he'd approached had been full of second and third sons of barons and earls and that sort. Some secret code passed between them allowing them to recognize one another—a code excluding anyone who didn't bleed blue. An ill-timed reminder of the *Gentlemen's Monthly* article and suddenly they'd no more room for investors.

Grantham wanted to talk to him about love?

How about *influence*? That was what Sam needed.

"You remind me of myself before I married Margaret," Grantham said. The stupid half smile grew into a full-blown grin when the earl mentioned his wife's name.

"Carefree and ridiculously handsome?" Sam asked.

"At loose ends and needing to put your energy into something lasting, like a marriage."

"Marry." Sam scoffed. "Why would I want to do something so boring as that?"

The low, throaty chuckle and knowing look Grantham threw him nearly made Sam cast up his accounts.

"Marriage is anything but boring," said the earl, his smug tone grating in Sam's ears. "Weren't you lately seen with Flavia Smythe-Harrow? You could do worse than to marry a scientist. All this nonsense from the Guardians of Domesticity about how women should remain uneducated in anything beyond homemaking is sheer stupidity."

Sam had indeed taken the scientist Flavia Smythe-Harrow

out for a drive. Once her father heard of it, his further invitations were declined.

Flavia Smythe-Harrow was the granddaughter of a duke.

Sam was the grandson of an itinerant laborer.

"If marriage to a scientist is so wonderful, then why didn't you marry Lady Phoebe?"

Grantham's smile disappeared like quicksilver, and Sam turned back to gaze up at the bark-brown clouds of fog that crept over the buildings' roofs.

"She was one of the first secret scientists, has a title more famous than yours, and was a villainess of majestic proportions to boot," Sam pointed out.

"Sam—" Grantham began with a warning in his voice.

"That's what's missing in my life. A feckin' title. A man who works as hard as I do gets nothing, while she gets away with murder simply because her father's title is older than dirt," Sam continued, beginning to warm to the subject.

"Sam—" Grantham's voice rose an octave and satisfaction washed through Sam. About time Grantham heard a few truths.

"In fact, the only thing a woman with a title is good for—"

"Sam!"

The reflection in the window shifted and a dark figure stood in the doorway. A cold brick of embarrassment sent Sam's stomach plummeting to his ankles.

"She's standing behind me, isn't she?"

PHOEBE PULLED AIR IN THROUGH HER NOSE AND HELD it until her lungs hurt, then let it release. This was a trick she learned early on in her sojourn to America. Before then, words would spill from her mouth at the slightest provocation. Words with blades attached, meant to draw blood and flay skin.

Words that could get a woman in a great deal of trouble if she had no one protect her.

"Hello, Grantham. Mr. Fenley."

Grantham stood as the Fenley boy turned around, his fair skin scarlet with embarrassment. Phoebe remembered him as being much younger than he appeared now. Life amid the secret scientists of Athena's Retreat must prematurely age a man.

"Lady Phoebe." Grantham was as handsome as ever. More so. There was a subtle peace about him, his gestures slow and assured.

Marriage will do that, Phoebe supposed. Make one sluggish. She gave Grantham her hand, then turned to the Fenley boy. Man.

Man-boy.

"I understand you are the owner of this broadsheet?"

Sam nodded, the blush now turning the tips of his ears flaming pink. "I must beg your pardon, Lady Phoebe. I meant no . . . disrespect."

A laugh rattled at the bottom of Phoebe's throat, surprising her. She kept it trapped, however. No reason to let the man-boy off easily.

"I rather like the descriptor, 'villainess of majestic proportions.' Makes me sound intimidating," she said.

"Oh, you are that, indeed," Sam agreed.

"How can we help you, my lady?" Grantham asked.

Irritation at the solicitousness in Grantham's tone itched the back of Phoebe's neck. They had a history, she and Grantham.

Her last years in England had been like riding a whirlwind if the whirlwind was rage. Nothing would quench the anger that had built inside her for twenty-six years, and it had to come out somehow. At first, Phoebe turned the rage on herself, drinking, dancing, fucking, even cutting the soft skin on the inside of her thighs. None of it helped. So, she'd turned her rage outward.

Grantham had tried to save her.

As much as Phoebe resented him, Grantham had never played her false. He was a good man.

A bit simple, but kind.

Phoebe kept her gaze trained on Sam. "I need an advert placed."

Sam's brow quirked. "The clerk at the front desk couldn't help you?"

Just like his sister, this one. Had no idea what the daughter of a marquess did or did not do.

She did not speak with clerks, for one thing.

The daughter of a marquess didn't ride horses astride while wearing trousers, she didn't carry a gun with her, and she certainly didn't wash her own clothes or cook her own meals.

That, however, was what Phoebe had been doing these last three years in the western territories of America. Learning all sorts of new hobbies, such as how to braid her own hair and sew her own menstrual rags.

Seeing as how she was only back in England for a few months, Phoebe figured she could get away with playing a great lady for a bit. At least while she was out in public.

Grantham understood, the dear man. Phoebe had helped him, once upon a time, when he came into the earldom unexpectedly and didn't know his fish fork from his soup spoon. It had amused her to serve as a guide to the idiosyncrasies of the aristocracy.

"What would you like in your advert?" Grantham asked.

"I was under the impression Mr. Fenley here was in charge," Phoebe said, taking a few steps farther into the room, sizing Sam up with a glance.

The man-boy had filled out nicely. He was taller than Phoebe in her heeled boots, and his well-cut suit displayed his broad shoulders and strong legs to his advantage. He'd a handsome if unweathered face, white skin that had never seen a desert sun, thick blond hair, and eyes the color of a loch she'd once seen in the northernmost part of Scotland.

A bit like Grantham when he had been younger and oh so impressionable.

Comprehension deepened the blue of Sam's eyes. "Ah. My apologies, Lady Phoebe. I have been too long away from the pleasures of serving the ton and forgotten how uncouth it would be for you to converse with someone as lowly as a clerk."

Phoebe smiled in appreciation at the line Sam strode between obsequious and mocking. He smiled in return and an understanding passed between them.

"Well done, Mr. Fenley," she said. "As I was saying, I need an advert placed in your broadsheet."

Sam walked around behind a cheap oak desk and drew a pen from a pewter holder, then dipped it in ink. He stared over at Phoebe and raised one brow.

"Auction to be held for building and all furnishings at Hunt House, Number 2 Blexton Place, December first. The auctioneers are Singer and Sons and—"

Grantham ran his fingers through his hair. "But, that is . . . What are you saying, Phoebe? Your mother is selling Hunt House?"

"Mmm." Phoebe made a sound of agreement, certain there was no expression on her face other than boredom. They might be attacked by a swarm of locusts in the next second and her expression would remain fixed. She'd honed this skill in circumstances far more terrible than biblical catastrophes. "In addition, you may print a notice for sale of Prendiss Manor, North Cumbria."

"You cannot mean to sell the estate as well?"

Phoebe leveled a bored stare at Grantham. "I mean everything I say. You should know that."

Shaking his head as though he could dislodge her last words from his brain, Grantham continued to speak to her as though she were simple.

"I know your father died—my condolences—but isn't his estate entailed?"

"It is not," she replied.

"Is there . . . Can I help you at all?" he asked.

Phoebe again drew breath and held it deep within her. All the memories and shame that roiled her stomach when she'd caught sight of Grantham—memories of who she'd been and what she'd done the last time she was home—she pushed it all down into a tiny ball beneath her diaphragm.

Ever so slowly, the air trickled out of her nose and a delightful numbness spread through Phoebe.

That was how one dealt with a conscience. One strangled it.

"Why do you care, George?" she asked. Grantham's head jerked back when she spoke his given name. Phoebe took a step toward him, boring her eyes into his guileless stare.

"Do you regret having given up on marrying into one of the oldest families in England, and are you now second-guessing your match with a woman in trade? I hear your wife works very *closely* with her male customers."

If Phoebe hadn't numbed herself, she'd have felt the chill that entered the room with her words. Grantham's sympathetic expression melted into contempt and Phoebe felt nauseous. He stood and bowed to Sam, turned on his heel, and left the room without giving Phoebe a second glance. His abrupt exit was so cold there should have been frost on the doorknob when he left the room.

"His wife is a woman beyond reproach."

Sam's eyes had cooled to the color of a winter morning, and his hand gripped the pen, knuckles white.

"Yes, I know," Phoebe said. "I've met her on a few occasions. Brilliant woman."

Sam blinked. "Oh. I see. You wanted him out of your business, and instead of telling him politely, you insulted him."

"I am, after all, a villainess of majestic proportions." Phoebe smiled.

Sam dropped the pen, then sat, leaning back slightly in his chair, studying Phoebe in a blatant manner. "Didn't you try to kill Mrs. Kneland? Greycliff had you sent to the western territories instead of going to trial."

"I did *not* try to kill Violet," Phoebe corrected him. "I shot Arthur Kneland instead. By accident, if you must know."

This was true. Arthur had tripped over a pile of lemon drops and Phoebe's gun had gone off. If she'd actually been aiming it at him, he'd be dead.

While no formal action was ever taken against her, people knew Phoebe had done something wrong. The story her father put about was that she'd had some sort of conversion from science to religion and wanted to spend her life as a missionary.

As if *anyone* who'd met her believed that.

"If you please, Mr. Fenley. I'm quite busy."

Clever man, Sam left off his questions and took up his pen again.

"Of course, my lady. I am forever at your service. Disposing of the family pile, are we? How sad," he said without a trace of pity.

Phoebe rather liked what had become of Sam Fenley.

Pity never did anyone any good.